Moon in the Mirror

A Tess Noncoiré Adventure

P. R. FROST

DAW BOOKS, INC.

DONALD A. WOLLHEIM, FOUNDER

375 Hudson Street, New York, NY 10014

ELIZABETH R. WOLLHEIM
SHEILA E. GILBERT
PUBLISHERS

http://www.dawbooks.com

First Paperback Printing, September 2008

1 2 3 4 5 6 7 8 9

To Heather Alexander: friend, musician, collaborator, and bard; the only person I know who can filk herself and come up with a song that is as good or better than the original two. How many of you can catch a fly?

Acknowledgments

Lyrics for "Playmate" by Philip Wingate, 1894 as found http://ingeb.org/songs/idontwan.html

"March of Cambreadth" music and lyrics by Heather Alexander and "Courage Knows No Bounds" music by Heather Alexander, lyrics by Philip R. Obermarck used with permission from Sea Fire Productions. Copyright Sea Fire Productions, Inc. © 1997.

Both of Heather's songs can be heard on the CD "Midsummer" by Heather Alexander which is available at *www.heatherlands.com*. I have loved Heather's music for many years and am very happy to find a place for it in my work. I own the entire set of her albums and frequently buy extras as gifts, or to replace my own when children and nephews come to visit and abscond with them.

Sitting at a con and shouting the lyrics to "March of Cambreadth" with two hundred other audience members sends chills up my spine every time.

My amazing husband, Tim Karr, spent an evening educating me on the wonders of single malt scotch. This is one commodity where the price of a bottle is directly proportionate to the quality of the "water of life." I have thanked him privately.

Many thanks also to Deborah Dixon, Lea Day, Maya Bohnhoff, Carol McCleary, Sue Brown, and Bob Brown for their untiring help and thoughtful critique of this manuscript. You keep me going with encouragement and prudent kicks where I need it most.

Much appreciation has to go to Sheila Gilbert, editor extraordinaire at DAW, for guiding the vision of this series.

And I can't forget Carol McCleary of the Wilshire Literary Agency for believing in me when no one else did.

Chapter 1

In African folklore, trickster Hare was sent by Moon to first people with the message: "Just as the moon dies and rises so shall you." But hare confused the words and said: "Just as the moon dies and perishes so shall you." Thus trickster Hare cost humankind its immortality.

THE WIND CIRCLED and howled. It wailed with the pathos of an errant spirit trapped between heaven and earth with no hope. No end to its torment. It rattled the window latches and whistled down the chimney, seeking haven inside my old house.

My benign resident ghosts retreated, leaving me utterly alone.

That was all I needed. Another storm to knock the power out and trap me indoors with several feet of snow blocking the doors. I saved the latest draft of my novel to a flash drive and switched to my laptop.

Finished or not, I had to e-mail it to my publisher first thing in the morning. If I had power and phone lines. Maybe I should do it now before the storm robbed me of access to the world outside. I had a reputation for punctuality to maintain. I also had a reputation for meticulous editing before I allowed the name Tess Noncoiré to appear on the cover.

I sent the e-mail, with the promise to polish the last four chapters and resend them as soon as I was sure of power.

The wind increased its tortured moans.

I shivered in the preternatural cold. "Old houses are drafty," I reassured myself. If this kept up, I'd start believing my own prose.

Unconsciously, I edged my chair closer to the huge hearth opposite my antique rolltop desk. My eyes strayed to the book on the plank floor, propped open with two other books. A research text on the folklore, monsters, and demons of the New World.

Research.

"Windago," I read and shivered. I'd encountered a mated pair of real Windago last autumn. Once human, they became one with the frigid northern wind, reclusive until they needed to hunt. Then they turned cannibal. They craved the blood of other humans, ever seeking to replace the souls they'd lost.

The book went on to theorize that the myth developed as an explanation for people of the north woods having to resort to cannibalism to survive especially harsh winters. If a monster bit them and they lost their souls, then humans hadn't done the unthinkable. Replace internal demons with external monsters.

Yeah. Right. The author hadn't ever encountered a Windago. I had. And I didn't want to do it again.

Ever. I'd come *this* close to becoming freeze-dried coffee grounds. All from a single touch of a shadow.

What the research book didn't say, but I'd learned on my own, was that Windago always hunted in pairs. To propagate, they had to bite a victim and leave the person living. The victim in turn had to bite a lover from his or her former life to maintain a pair.

Last autumn I'd killed one Windago. His mate still hunted me.

Was she the ravening wind that sought entrance to my home?

Did she seek a new mate or stalk me until one or both of us died? I didn't know.

"Damn it, go away," I shouted into the big empty house.

Not even my resident ghosts replied. I think they decamped to warmer climes along with my mother. After the third month when the temperature on Cape Cod didn't break freezing, Mom suddenly found a third cousin twice removed she hadn't seen since childhood who just happened to live in Florida.

Stay inside, Tessie babe. Demons can't violate the sanctity of a home, Scrap, my otherworldly companion and weapon, whispered to me across the dimensions. From very far away. Too far away to come help me fight off a Windago.

Goddess only knew what Scrap was up to. Or where.

I'm stuck in the chat room. Big nasties trying to separate us permanently.

"Take care, buddy."

A pang of loneliness stabbed my heart.

Coffee. I needed more coffee. Well, maybe I should switch to decaf. My nerves were jittery enough with that wind preying on my sanity.

I wondered if the tension in my neck was the precursor to a migraine. Normally I didn't suffer from them like Mom did. The wind often triggered them in her. Something about changing air pressures.

This wind was more than changing air pressure.

I coaxed my shoulders into a more relaxed position. No way would I fall victim to my mother's ailments. I was just worried about finishing the book. And staying free of the Windago.

I applied myself to the keyboard once more. Just a couple more hours of work.

If the damn wind would shut up.

The window rattled again, sounding very much as if a human hand tried to open the latch.

"Stay inside. Keep the doors and windows latched. Wait for dawn. Windago can't survive daylight," I repeated to myself over and over.

I dashed to the window anyway and checked the aging latch. Still closed.

Who could I call for help? My Aunt MoonFeather, the Cape's resident witch, didn't answer her phones.

Gollum—Guilford Van der Hoyden-Smythe, Ph.D.—knew a lot about magic and demons and he'd helped me defeat the Sasquatch last autumn. Last I'd heard, he was still in Seattle teaching anthropology in some community college. Too far away to do anything but talk. He was good at talking and not much else.

Then there was Donovan Estevez. Handsome, sexy, a fantastic fencer, and knowledgeable about demons. Too knowledgeable, probably from firsthand experience. No. No way would I make myself vulnerable to him by asking for help.

Something crashed in the kitchen. I jumped. My heart lodged in my throat.

"Scrap?" Please, oh, please, let it be the mischievous brat returning from wherever.

No answer. I crept from my office through the long dining room and adjacent butler's pantry, keeping well away from the walls and any shadows that might lurk there. At the entrance to the modern kitchen and breakfast nook, I paused and peered out.

No pots and pans littered the floor. The curtains lay flat against the windows.

Bang!

I screamed and leaped back at least six feet. Freezing air whirled around me.

Bang.

"Scrap, where the hell are you? I need help."

Distant mumbling and grumbling in the back of my mind.

Creak, creak.

Was that someone twisting rubber soles on wet linoleum?

I grabbed a butcher knife from the utility drawer and inched forward again.

Creak, creak.

A quick glance through the narrow archway. The back doors, which opened into the mudroom, swung in and out, in and out in the freezing wind.

I wrapped my arms around my shivering body and cowered there in indecision for several moments.

Opening! I heard the wind wail.

Not daring to wait any longer, I ran with every bit of strength I could muster through the mudroom and slammed the outside door closed. I twisted the lock and the dead bolt for good measure, something I rarely bothered to do. Then I shoved the heavy boot box across it.

A wicked laugh. *Not enough to keep me out.* An almost face appeared through swirling snow and shadows in the glass top half of the door. Frigid air made the aging wood pull away from the fragile pane. Shadows cast from the streetlight across the yard played tricks on my senses.

I couldn't tell if the Windago pressed close or not. Didn't dare wait to figure it out.

I darted back into the kitchen and closed the inside door. A chair from the nook braced beneath the latch held it.

The laugh came again. This time singing a ditty from my childhood. A song my best friend Allie and I had cherished since kindergarten.

> *"Playmate, come out and play with me,*
> *And bring your dollies three*
> *Climb up my apple tree,*
> *Holler down my rain barrel*
> *Slide down my cellar door*
> *And we'll be jolly friends forever more."*

Cellar door! Oh, my God, were the slanted doors attached to the outside foundation latched? They'd been covered with snow for so long I hadn't checked the padlock on the outside, or the crossbar on the inside for months.

No way was I going down the dark, narrow cellar steps with only a single bare bulb down there to light my way. No way in hell.

I jammed another chair under that door handle. "No lock!" I screeched. Why wasn't there a lock on this door?

Because that would make it too easy to get locked in the cellar while doing laundry. Damn.

Three phone books on the seat of the chair anchored it better.

I sang the alternate version of the childhood ditty to bolster my courage.

> *"Enemy, come out and fight with me.*
> *And bring your bulldogs three,*
> *Climb up my sticker tree.*
> *Slide down my lightning*
> *Into my dungeon door*
> *And we'll be bitter enemies forever more!"*

It didn't work. I still trembled in fear.

Not enough! A really cold gust whooshed down the chimney. The flames died. Coals faded from glowing orange and red to black.

I whimpered and threw some kindling into the grate. A cascade of sparks shot up the chimney. I added a log of heavy maple. Bright flames leaped and licked at the new fuel.

An otherworldly screech of pain responded to the fire.

You murdered my mate, an almost feminine voice snarled into my mind. *I will have retribution. A little fire won't keep me away for long.*

"Scrap, get your sorry ass back here," I screamed into the night. If he'd just come back, he could transform into the Celestial Blade and I could defend myself.

Ordinary blades might slow down a Windago. All my mundane weapons were locked in a special closet in the cellar. Only the Celestial Blade could kill a monster.

The lights flickered, faded, then came back on. I bit my lip, waiting.

A crashing boom outside.

Dark silence. Not even the comforting hum of the refrigerator.

The wind kicked up three notches into a hysterical laugh.

I dashed from room to room replenishing every fireplace. In the parlor I used the very last piece of pine in the stack. Soft evergreen. It wouldn't burn long. I didn't dare close the damper or I'd smother in the smoke.

Ruefully I looked around, assessing the burnability of every bit of furniture in the house. The dining room table would last all night if I could break it up, along with the twelve chairs. Fortunately, I had a hatchet beside the big hearth in the office, to splinter kindling if I needed.

I double-checked every window and door. Prowling the house all night. Never once relaxing my vigil.

Neither did the Windago.

Chapter 2

AWN FOUND ME still wandering the house, testing window latches, keeping the fires roaring, starting at every noise and shadow. Somehow, I managed to stretch the last of the firewood in the house and didn't have to start on the dining table. I kept the hatchet or butcher knife in my hands at all times.

As a sullen gray light crept across the land, the wind faded. The temperatures plummeted. A new depth of cold descended upon Cape Cod.

My yard looked like a hurricane had hit. Broken tree limbs, roof shingles, and the neighbor's garbage lay strewn about.

A magnificent patriarchal oak tree leaned drunkenly against the power lines, pushing the supporting pole to a dangerous angle across my driveway. I could still get my car out if I had to. I didn't dare leave the house.

Windago weren't supposed to come out in daylight. The sky was so leaden it made the entire day one huge shadow. Lots of places for a Windago to hide.

Why hadn't I headed south with Mom?

"It's the friggin' vernal equinox," I moaned. "Where are the sunshine and spring temperatures?"

My cell phone chirped the theme from "Night On Bald Mountain." I jumped and trembled a moment before it registered. "I think I need to change that ring tone."

No power. No telephone. Cell phones only working communication.

"H . . . Hello," I answered, half expecting that whispery voice born of the north wind.

"Tess, you've got to come. Right now," Allie Engstrom pleaded desperately.

Not much fazed Allie. She stood nearly six feet tall, and had the breadth of shoulder of her Valkyrie ancestors. She was also our local cop and packed weapons comfortably.

"Calm down, Allie. What's wrong? And why can't you just call for backup? An entire squad of constables should be on duty."

"I can't call them. They wouldn't understand. You've got to come. And bring MoonFeather." Anxiety drove her voice up an octave.

"MoonFeather? What can my aunt do that you can't?"

"She's a witch. They're both witches. You've got to hurry. Before they attack!"

"Witches. Plural. Who's attacking?"

"Sh . . . she just came out of nowhere. Right in the middle of the street. I crashed my cruiser swerving to avoid her. And she's naked." Allie gulped air. I heard the boom of a fired gun. "My God. The bullets bounced off them!"

"Off of what?" Not who. What. They weren't human.

"Garden gnomes with teeth!"

I skid to an abrupt halt inside the chat room. This is the place that opens the doors to every universe. A big white room that stretches so far into infinity normal eyes can't perceive the dimensions and curves.

Each species calls the chat room something else. The Waiting

Room, Limbo, Purgatory, Avalon, Oblivion. A rose by any other name . . . You know what I mean. Call it what you will, it's the same place of transition.

Easy to get lost here. Any being can get into the chat room. Getting out again is a different matter indeed.

Late March and still two feet of snow on the ground with a subzero wind chill in Cape Cod. I may be the imp companion to the greatest Warrior of the Celestial Blade ever born, but I'm just a scrap of an imp. I don't like having my tootsies frozen to popsicles. My barbed tail is so frizzed it feels like it will fall off my cute little bum.

And I've got five beee-u-tee-ful warts adorning my backside. Another one dead center on my chestie. Hard-earned beauty marks they are. Can't afford to have them fall off.

Even my favorite perch on the cast iron spider hanging over the fire in the fireplace can't keep me warm. So, I make tracks for Imp Haven. To get there I have to cross the chat room.

My warrior companion, Tess Noncoiré, is just finishing a manuscript and is looking for some downtime. She won't need me for a few days. She can handle just about any crisis that isn't demon inspired if she keeps her head on straight.

But when she's deep in a book, I keep her inspired and on her toes. I clean up after her and make sure she eats. Without me, she'd be a total wreck instead of only half a wreck.

Her fashion sense is . . . well let's just call her challenged and be polite about it.

Our bond goes deeper than that. She is my warrior, I her blade. Neither of us can exist without the other now.

The Powers That Be dictated long ago that only demons should guard the chat room. They are nasty enough to keep everybody in their home dimensions unless they have a special pass from the all-powerful PTB. Hard to get a pass. Harder to slip through the chat room to someplace else, somewhen else.

Unless you are an imp. Even imps don't have *carte blanche.*

On this day Windago guard the chat room. The howling wind you hear in the middle of the night when storms rage is just their chatter. The misty black shadows swirling up to greet me feel familiar. I've fought these shadow demons before. I'd rather not have to do it again without Tess. Only when I'm with her and in the presence of a demon or tremendous evil can I transform into the Celestial Blade.

Damn, I wore my feather boa as a disguise, hoping to run into Bcartlin demons. Think a cerulean Michelin Man with a hot-pink ostrich draped around its neck. Such a passé color scheme. I mean bright blue and pink went out with . . . well I don't know for sure that they ever were in fashion.

Now if they'd go with the country blue with hints of gray and maybe a touch of yellow accent, I could do something with them.

I digress.

Two human larpers—that's live action role playing gamers to the uninitiated—in search of magical artifacts have wandered into the chat room, unaware of what they're doing or how they got there. These guys are trying to engage the Windago in conversation, asking directions to *The Comb*.

Give me a break. If you need to ask directions you have no business in the chat room. You have no business talking to a Windago, let alone six Windago, at all. The poor saps are doomed—I don't mean just their garish costumes—unless I do something.

But maybe I should let them meet the fate of the foolish.

Ever since I liberated a particular magical hair comb from freeze-dried storage—aka my home in Imp Haven—for my Tess, the Powers That Be have put a bounty on it. Word gets out, especially among wanna-be witches and sorcerers, and the search goes far and wide. One of these days Tess and I will have to fight off all kinds of nasties—some of them human—to retain possession of *The Comb*.

The Comb allows her to see through magical glamour when she wears it. But she can't wear it all the time because it turns her hair translucent and brittle. She'll go bald in a month if she wears it too often or too long. We can't allow her distinctive springy sandy-blonde curls to thin, straighten, and break off.

Six Windago—they always hunt in pairs—reach out with spectral shadow hands that can freeze-dry the larpers.

At least the humans have the sense to hunker down and cover their vulnerable heads and necks with their arms.

I whistle sharply between my two outer rows of teeth.

The bad guys hardly notice. They have a job to do, keeping beings in their home dimensions.

I wave my pink feather boa at them. Full-blooded demons—Midori as opposed to Kajiri half-breed—aren't real bright. It takes them a few moments to figure out I'm in their territory. These guys obviously don't have any human blood in their family shrubs to give them any smarts.

I'm on my own with six shadowy black whirlwinds, each the size of an industrial refrigerator. One of them turns away from the whimpering humans to see me full on. Most demons have no neck and have to turn their entire body to see beyond the end of their nose. This particular beastie has no shoulders either. Just an amorphous mass of black wind swirling ever faster into a tornado.

Demons may be dumb. But they are always hungry. Blood-thirsty. They'll eat anyone. Simply anyone. Even imps wearing perfectly wonderful pink feather boas.

The other shadowy masses spiral to their left and pin me with malevolent gazes. Glowing red coals burn through the dust storms.

The larpers make a judicious retreat through the nearest doorway. Fortunately for them, it's their home dimension. They never really got far enough away from it for it to close properly and seal their fates.

Meanwhile, I have six Windago to dupe into letting me back into my home dimension before they bite me and turn me into an antisocial cannibal. Mum would never forgive me.

Not that she approves of me much anyway.

"Get him. No imps allowed out of impland," screams one pair of the ravening horde.

"We must kill all imps on the loose," chimes in a second pair.

"Imps are dangerous to the dimensions," adds the third pair.

I flit above their heads. "I love my wings!" I crow to them. They'd grown enough to actually be useful—though still not up to snuff, just like the rest of my body. There's a reason Mum named me Scrap.

Blood-red talons at the end of a misty black fist reach higher than I guess possible.

"Yeow! That hurts." I yank my tail up and out of the way. But I now have gouge marks its full length to the arrowhead tip. And worse! They left red nail polish embedded in the furrows. Not quite the fashion statement I'd hoped for.

And then my stunted wings give out. I drop into the middle of the cold black crush.

Six churning storms of frigid air steal my breath and crumple my precious wings.

I gasp and nearly swallow half my weight in black dust and fur. It tastes of . . . you don't want to know how stale cigars sweetened with licorice and a touch of sulfur taste.

Black stars blossom before my eyes. "Oh, Tess, I'm sorry. I shouldn't have deserted you just because of a little frostbite on my tummy. Can you ever forgive me? For when I die, so will you."

Maybe Cape Cod isn't so bad after all. Tess does keep lovely fires in the hearths of her two-hundred-fifty-year-old home. And her mom might come home and burn some cookies for me.

Chapter 3

"PLEASE HURRY, TESS. I don't know what to do," Allie whispered. Two more shots sounding too loud across the airwaves.

A naked woman who stepped out of nowhere. The Windago in human form come to plague me?

What about garden gnomes with teeth? Where did they come in?

"Great, just great." I couldn't ignore Allie's call for help. She was my best friend. I knew her crushes and the color of her footed jammies. When we first met, at the age of five, she'd been too tall, and I too fat and bookish for either of us to be popular. So we'd bonded and found we had more in common with each other than we did with our families or anyone else at school.

She'd been an important part of my life for twenty-three of our twenty-eight years.

I pulled on heavy boots, sweaters, a coat, hat and gloves. Some things were more important than avoiding trouble. Then I dashed for the basement armory. I kept a key around my neck for emergencies like this. Without Scrap I needed a mundane weapon. A very sharp mundane weapon.

On my way, babe. This may take a few moments, Scrap reassured me.

But he wasn't here right this minute. No way to know if he'd make it back in time to help. I grabbed a broadsword off the rack though the replica of the Celestial Blade beckoned me. Made of imp wood, I knew it was sharp. Effective against monsters?

I stuck with the broadsword. The door closed on its own, and the padlock snicked shut. "Thanks, Godfrey," I called to the ghost who haunted the basement. He'd stashed runaway slaves in that closet and guarded it more zealously in death than in life. And that was as good a guard as I could get. No one knew he ran the local Underground Railroad until his memoir was published ten years after his death in 1893.

With fresh snow on the roads and no plows òut yet, I decided to drive my mom's black baby SUV rather than my cute, midnight-blue hybrid. Mom's car had a better niche for stashing the broadsword under the driver's seat.

In four-wheel drive, with studded tires, I inched the car beneath the listing oak tree. Low dragging branches grabbed at the car, scratching paint off the roof. Mom was going to kill me. Each scrape had me wincing and imagining the Windago opening the metal with her talons.

As I turned left onto the road, my rear tires slid on the icy surface. No new snow here. Just the arctic cold. Strange. I had almost a foot of white fluffy stuff around my house.

I steered into the skid until I had traction again, then crawled forward toward the Old King Highway. Reluctantly, I stopped at the intersection to check for traffic.

"Go ahead, gun it," my husband's ghost said from the passenger seat. He wore a western-cut plaid shirt, sleeves rolled up, blue jeans, hiking boots, and a white Stetson pulled low over his hazel eyes and sleek black hair. Like he always did. Before and after he died.

I sat back and closed my eyes. "Now what do you

want, Dill? Where were you last night when I could have used some company while monsters raged?" As much as I missed the man, he had a strange habit of showing up when I finally thought I could move on. Weird things happened when he was around. I wanted done with weird.

Maybe all I needed was a vacation in sunny Mexico.

"Take a chance, lovey. Why freeze our fucking asses off trying to stay safe. Your imp isn't around to tattle on you."

"You shouldn't use that kind of language, Dillwyn Bailey Cooper," I reprimanded him in death as I hadn't dared to in life.

After three years on my own, I wasn't sure I'd fall for him again. Wouldn't let myself become dependent on him.

But, oh, how I missed him. I longed for the mental intimacy we'd shared as well as the physical. He shared my love of science fiction/fantasy. His fascination with geology satisfied a lot of my curiosity. We even agreed politically. I'd never met another man I bonded with so quickly or so well.

Fighting demons with a Celestial Blade had given me confidence and self-assurance I didn't know I was missing when I married a handsome man who looked past the fifty extra pounds I carried then to the woman I was inside.

I'd lost the weight and kept it off for three years. Grief will do that to you. That and the rigorous martial arts training of the Sisterhood of the Celestial Blade Warriors.

For my newly fit and trim figure I really had to thank the otherworldly infection that had laid me low with delirium for weeks on end. The fever had opened new pathways in my brain that allowed me to bond with Scrap. I'd been with the imp nine times longer than I had been married to Dill.

"As much as I love you, Dill, you are dead. Isn't it time we both moved on?" Did I really want him gone?

"Can't do that, lovey. You and I were meant to be together. Forever. So you can't move on without me." His skin was smooth, nicely tanned, and free of the charring from the fatal fire.

The fact that his ghost showed no signs of his painful death always made me suspicious. Was this specter truly my husband or a demon wearing his face and form? Either way, he asked the impossible.

"Accept it, Dill, you are dead. I have."

"Have you, lovey?" He quirked an eyebrow at me just like he used to. "I've tried to pass over, Tess. Really tried. But the Powers That Be have decreed I can't completely die without your help. But I can come back to life if you just get rid of the imp."

"Not on your life! Or death. Or whatever. People don't come back to life, Dill. There are no 'get out of jail free' cards for dead people." I shuddered with more than just the cold. "Besides, if you were serious about replacing Scrap, you'd have come to my aid last night and we could have slain that Windago."

"How do you know people can't come back to life?"

He ignored my second statement. He'd had a bad habit of bypassing what he didn't like or didn't want to deal with when he was alive. I guess bad habits don't die.

Instead of replying I gunned the engine and shot onto the main road.

"It's the scar that keeps us apart, Tess. It's an interdimensional reminder of imp flu. If you hadn't gotten sick and had to have the infection cut out of your face, you couldn't see the imp. Go to a plastic surgeon and have it removed," Dill pleaded. He traced a ghostly finger from my temple to my jaw.

The scar burned beneath his ephemeral touch.

"A little hard when the scar isn't visible to mundane humans," I snapped.

Flashing blue-and-red lights atop Allie's monster white four by four with blue *Police* lettering came into view less than a block away. The front end teetered in a roadside ditch. A venerable maple as wide as the cruiser pressed deeply into the radiator. Steam hissed, froze, and fell back onto the hood as snow.

I slowed and skidded to a halt. I let loose a string of curses as the rear end fishtailed.

A dozen or more little beings in overbright clothing and mouths over-full of sharp teeth paced around and around the vehicle. A hideous replica of "ring around the rosie."

"Language, Tess. Watch your language," Dill chuckled, reminding me I had just reprimanded him for doing the same thing. "Your vocabulary has deteriorated drastically since I died. You'd think a writer would be more inventive."

"Shut the fuck up!"

You talking to me, babe? Scrap popped into view, his translucent gray-green body already turning vermilion and elongating into a solid shaft.

Dill popped out of view. "You don't need me for this fight, lovey." He sounded hurt and . . . and lonely.

"Glad to have you back, buddy. I was afraid you were trapped in the chat room."

Your call is stronger than the bad breath of six Windago.

I didn't like his metaphor.

No time to think. No time to mourn Dill. A gnome was gnawing away at the tailgate of Allie's cruiser. An industrial-strength can opener on the move.

"Scrap, now." I held out my palm for him while I released the seat belt and opened the door.

By the time my feet hit the ground, Scrap had thinned to a four-foot shaft with twin curved blades extruding from each end. Dozens of razor-sharp spikes flowed away from the outside curve of each blade.

I twirled him about like a baton around my knees. The swarm of bad guys backed off. Except for the one chewing through metal.

Nasty bastard, Scrap growled. His reflected eyes blinked in the right-hand blade.

An easy wipe separated the beastie from the cruiser.

Dark, dark blood, almost black, spurted from where his pointed nose should have been. It steamed when it hit the ice. The rear lock of the vehicle filled the gnome's mouth. Still he smiled around it, showing acres more teeth.

As he bounced across the road to the embankment where his cohorts huddled, the blood ceased spurting. His nose grew back, longer and pointier than before. It almost reached his long chin.

My scar throbbed. I only hoped it remained invisible. Allie was watching me too closely from the inside of her cruiser.

I stood guard over the SUV with my constantly moving blade. "Get over to my car now!" I yelled to Allie and the figure huddled in the back seat.

"Tess, what's going on here?" Allie asked, opening her door.

Her passenger remained inside.

"Shut the fuck up and get your girl over to my car. Now."

"I beg your pardon!" Allie said, blinking in startlement.

"You heard me. Do it. I can't hold them off much longer." Even as I spoke, the gnomes edged closer. Only one lane of blacktop separated them from me and my blade. Their jester-styled shoes with the upturned toes didn't slip on the ice.

My boots had problems with traction.

Allie's hands trembled inside her heavy leather gloves as she fumbled with the door. She wore a dark blue down uniform parka over her blue shirt, sweater, and Kevlar. I spotted the telltale ribbed neckline of silk long underwear at her throat. And she still looked long, slim, and feminine.

I could never carry off that look. Being vertically challenged and short of leg always made me look broader at the shoulder and hip than I really was.

Underneath the uniform, her height, her butch short hair, and her bravado, Allie was a shy little girl.

I made sure I stood between her and the bad guys. They grew braver and crossed the yellow line.

Allie grabbed at a lumpy figure huddled beneath a blanket in the backseat of her cruiser. They hesitated as two long, slim legs extended from the blanket. She stopped moving with just inches between bare feet and icy road.

"She'll be fine for ten steps," I reassured my friend.

They ran for my car. I sidestepped along with them. The gnomes respected my blade. But they followed our movements, staying just outside my reach.

Three gnomes took two steps closer.

I slashed right and left. Two tiny backbones severed. The top half of each gnome plopped sideways. Black blood shot up and out. The feet kept coming forward.

"Svargit! What does it take to kill these guys?" I cursed everything in sight, and a few things that weren't, in Sasquatch. That was the only word of Sasquatch I'd learned. It fit everything.

With one last vicious swipe, I leaped into my car and slapped the locks closed. Scrap shrank to normal size and disappeared in the blink of an eye.

I threw my jacket to Allie, adding it to the scant protection the blanket offered the shivering blonde woman. Woman? Girl? She couldn't be more than eighteen.

"Here. Use this if you need to. More effective than bullets against these guys." I hauled the broadsword free and handed it to her grip first. "This is the only blade you saw me use," I added, capturing her gaze with mine.

She nodded and gulped, standing the sword between her legs, point down.

"Where did she come from?" Allie asked after a long moment while I coaxed the engine to life. "I looked. No one was in the street. She just appeared out of nowhere. Out of *nowhere*. I looked. I swear I did," She shook her head as she peered over her shoulder at her precious wounded vehicle, guilt and pain shrouding her eyes.

"And then those gnomes walked out of the woods as if they owned the road." She kept blinking as if to clear her vision of the memory.

Then I realized she was looking at the center of the street, not her car or the troop following us. Was she hoping to see a doorway into Neverland?

"This isn't your fault," I reassured her as my heart raced and heat flooded my face. Bodies coming out of nowhere *shouldn't* surprise me. Garden gnomes with teeth *shouldn't* surprise me. I wrote weirder stuff every day. I considered an imp my soulmate. My husband's ghost haunted me for weeks on end. A bereaved Windago stalked me.

But it did surprise me.

"She came out of nowhere," Allie insisted.

Or another dimension.

Did she have to go through the chat room to get from one dimension to another? If she had, maybe Scrap knew something. No access to him for a while until he'd recovered from our battle. Nothing a full dose of mold wouldn't cure.

Rogue portals existed. Direct transport that bypassed the guarded chat room. They were rare. I'd closed one last autumn.

"Now you're in a dilly of a pickle!" Dill chortled from the backseat.

"Here we go again," I groaned.

The young woman crumpled in a faint. Bright blonde hair draped about her shoulders like a living curtain.

One look at her sweet face and I knew she wasn't Lilia David, the human persona of the widowed Windago.

(What a wonderful title. *The Widowed Windago*. I filed that away in the writer portion of my brain before the ideas could start tumbling around and blot out reality for me.)

"Where the hell did you come from?" I asked. "And why the fuck are those guys chasing you?"

"Tsk, tsk, language, lovey," Dill said, only half joking.

"Cold. So cold. Where did all the pretty flowers go?" the woman whispered.

"What?"

"I'll call ahead to the emergency room," Allie said. "I don't dare go through Dispatch. I'm going to have enough trouble explaining the car." She fumbled for her cell phone.

"Trippin' car," the stranger murmured, without opening her eyes. "Boss ghost."

"Haven't heard that word in a while," Dill said peering at our guest. "Oh, dear. She's an interdimensional refugee. I can't be here right now."

Dill vanished. Did he imply that he, too, was an interdimensional refugee? As good a description of a ghost as any.

Or was there more?

Chapter 4

*The March full moon is sometimes called the
Crow Moon because the cawing of crows signals
the end of winter. It is also called the Crust Moon
because the snow cover becomes crusted from
thawing by day and freezing at night.*

"WHAT ARE WE DEALING with, Tess?
Do you think MoonFeather will have any
answers?" Allie asked, her voice more gravelly than
usual. She shifted her utility belt, a habitual gesture of
domination, piercing me with her tough-broad glare.

"You tell me what you saw. Every last detail." I put
the car in gear and eased off the shoulder onto the
street, without bothering strapping the girl in. The emergency room was only a half mile up 6A, the official
name for Old King Highway. Nothing is very far away
on Cape Cod.

"The street was clear. I swear it. It was six AM. Rush
hour not started yet. Anyone who doesn't have to be
out in this cold isn't. Then she just appeared," Allie insisted.

"Just appeared? Any misting or morphing?" I knew
how I would write the scene. That didn't make my description correct.

I ransacked my memory for a clue, a hint of what she
might be. Besides human. Demons could assume human
shape in this dimension, but only if they had some
human blood in them. Kajiri, they called the mixed-

bloods. More dangerous than full-bloods because the human half gave them the ability to think and hold a grudge.

Like my Windago stalker.

"Maybe the light shifted. Like a halo. You'd call it an aura," Allie said. She tugged on her earlobe while she thought. "Sort of like a door opening from a dark room into a darker room. Not a change so much as a shift. And then she was there. Running, looking over her shoulder. Then she froze in place. A naked and unprotected living statue."

Scrap, if you are anywhere near, I need you! I called with my mind. Fat chance of that happening any time soon. I knew he needed downtime after transforming and fighting.

"Sounds like the lady dashed out of the chat room in fear for her life. Or her immortal soul," Dill said. He lounged in the backseat again. Had he dashed off to consult with his Powers That Be?

I was about to say the same thing, but Allie wouldn't understand what I meant. I'd never consciously been in the chat room, the empty space between dimensional portals, and couldn't say for sure what it looked like. My nightmare visits there while in the throes of a horrible fever didn't count.

"And the gnomes?"

"They showed up about a minute, maybe a minute and a half later. Just walked out of the woods."

"They didn't come from the same portal as the girl?"

"Maybe. I dunno. I was busy getting a blanket around her and hustling her into my vehicle. Warmer there even if the engine didn't run. My poor car. The chief's going to kill me for wrecking my car."

Did I say that Allie loved her cruiser like a pet dog?

"Tess, this is like something out of one of your books. What's going on?" Allie looked worried.

"I want to go back to the faeries and the flowers. It's warm there. And pretty," little-miss-drowsy-and-half-naked mumbled. Her head nodded forward. She threatened to tilt into the space between the front seats.

Shit. I knew I should have taken the half second to strap her in.

"We'll talk later, Allie," I stalled, negotiating the ruts and snow drifts as rapidly as I dared.

"Promise?"

"Promise." I hid my crossed fingers inside my clenched fist on the steering wheel.

Allie grabbed my hand and opened my fingers. "Promise?" She knew me too well.

"Promise," I sighed. Then I turned to our mystery woman. "What's your name, honey?"

"Names are like dandelion fluff. They scatter in the wind and only take root in places that give them meaning." She drifted off again.

"Sheesh, she sounds just like MoonFeather," Allie sighed.

A flicker of movement in my peripheral vision froze my thoughts.

Off to the left a flash of impossibly bright green against the dirty snowbank. The fine hairs at the base of my spine stood on end. Alarm spread across my back.

You anywhere close, Scrap? I called into the ether.

No answer.

"Of course you aren't around. I need some answers, so you take off," I muttered low enough Allie couldn't hear me. She was busy trying to keep our nodding guest in her own seat while holding on tight to the sword. As if her life depended upon it.

It might.

Motion on my right. I got the impression of vivid red.

"Wrong time of year for Christmas colors, guys. If only you were garden gnomes blowing around in the wind," I said out loud. Some of their black blood had landed on my parka and was eating away at it like acid. Hopefully, the blood wouldn't manage to work its way through both the parka and the blanket the girl was wrapped in.

Mom's garden club had sold lawn monuments to bad taste as a fund-raiser a year ago. Because of the political prominence of a number of the club members, everyone on tasteful Cape Cod had a dozen of the tacky things on display.

"At least Dill's disappeared," I subvocalized, hoping Scrap would hear my mutterings better than my mental voice. I didn't need my husband's acerbic comments at the moment.

But, Goddess, I missed him.

"Not so lucky, lovey. I'm right behind you."

"Well, stay there. Out of the way." Again with the barely audible grunts.

"Your ghost isn't warm. He's colder than cold," the girl said. For a brief moment her eyes cleared, and she looked almost alert.

How come she could see Dill? Allie couldn't. Or, if she did, she didn't acknowledge that she could see a ghost.

"Don't move about so much. You don't have a seat belt on," I replied.

"Seat belts aren't groovy. They restrict our freedoms."

Both Allie and I rolled our eyes at that one.

"She has a point," Dill added. "People should have the choice to die or not."

"Why don't you go back to whatever ever after you came from?" I muttered, louder than I'd intended.

"Don't be rude," Allie admonished me. She must think I spoke to the girl.

"Love to move on to the ever after, lovey, but I'm stuck in limbo until you and I are truly united forever," Dill said.

"Not in this lifetime," I mouthed.

"That's what I mean." I didn't have to see his grin in the rearview mirror—couldn't see him at all in the mirror—but I knew it was there.

"I didn't come from the ever after, I came from Paradise," the girl whispered. "I want to go back."

"Looks like you got kicked out of Paradise, kid. If I

remember my folklore right . . ." And I did. "Wrong time of year for easy passage between dimensions for humans. You need the solstice and a massive ritual for that," I told her, trying to figure out what was going on.

Something, an old story, tickled my mind then vanished.

"Kicked out of Paradise?" Allie repeated. She pulled on her earlobe again, thinking hard.

I grabbed her hand. "You'll end up like Carol Burnett with a long and drooping lobe," I chided her.

We grinned at each other.

I proceeded forward at a crawl that seemed breakneck on the snow and frozen ruts.

Try All Hallows Eve for dimension moving, Scrap chimed in. He popped into view leaning on the dashboard, feet braced against the center console, one wing folded neatly around his shoulders. The other wing canted at a strange angle. It looked like it hurt. He looked more faded and washed out than usual. The aftermath of a fight without a full dose of mold or, lacking that, beer and orange juice to restore him. If he started to glow pink, I needed to be wary. When he got full red, we'd both need him to transform into the Celestial Blade.

Not likely to happen for a while, until he recovered. *Not to worry, babe. I found a stash of mold along the upstairs bathroom floor trim.*

About time you got back from kissing the ass of that golden weasel you worship, imp. There's more trouble brewing. I had no idea if that was where he'd been. But he was always on me to believe in something, anything. Lots of Gods and Goddesses out there.

Yeah. Right.

I caught a flash of a little being pacing me on the left. Green cap and tunic. Yellow leggings and pointy shoes. The cheap plastic statues that littered the Cape were just that—cheap. Their colors had faded in the long harsh winter. This guy was impossibly bright.

Same for the red one on the other side.

Greenie grinned at me with a mouth full of far too many dagger-shaped teeth. Three rows of them up and down. The flare of warning along my spine became full fledged ripples of alarm.

"You see that, Allie?"

"See what?" All her attention was on the girl in the back.

On it, dahling, Scrap said. *By the way, that bulky sweater over jeans is so not you. Black may be classic, like this car, but it drains the color from your face. You need the teal cashmere sweater Dad gave you for Christmas and a lavender turtleneck—silk, I think—in this weather. Such a nice insulator silk is.* He disappeared with only a little whoosh of displaced air.

"I'll worry about my fashion sense later. Tell me about the garden gnomes, one right, one left."

Allie turned pale.

That told me a lot.

"Pretty little imp," the girl crooned. She reached a bare arm out of my parka to grasp a handful of air where Scrap had been.

"What's she talking about?" Allie asked.

"She's hallucinating." No one but me, or another Warrior of the Celestial Blade should be able to see him. And most of the warriors were locked up tight in their Citadels. I was the only reject on the loose that I knew about.

They'd have taken Scrap from me if they could when they kicked me out. But our bond was too deep. Metaphysical ties knotted and tangled us together for life.

I took my eyes off the road for half a second to stare at the girl. An icy rut grabbed my tire and swerved me toward the curb and a parked car.

Cautiously, I corrected before my tires skidded and I totally lost control.

The two escapees from the trailer park say they came for the girl, Scrap said, popping back into view and chomping on a black cherry cheroot. Out of respect for Mom, he never smoked in her car. *They say they'll take down*

*anyone who stands in their way. We're on the hit list now,
babe.*

I tensed my shoulders and clenched my hands tighter
on the steering wheel.

"Don't let them take me back," whispered the girl.
"They're mean and they hurt me."

"No one's going to hurt you, honey," Allie reassured
her. "We'll take care of you."

"What's this *we* business?" I raised my eyebrows at
Allie. "I'm going to Mexico, just as soon as I e-mail the
rest of my book to my editor."

I didn't think the Windago could find me on a sunny
beach south of the border.

Ahead I saw the blaring red neon arrows pointing to
the ER. Two more blocks. Get the girl safely inside, then
I could get on with my *normal* life. In my head I made
vacation plans.

I slid into the covered entry of the ER. Allie stashed
the broadsword beneath her seat and hopped out before I came to a complete halt. Using the authority of
her uniform, as well as her intimidating size, she
grabbed two orderlies and a gurney.

Gratefully, I let them ease my passenger into the welcome warmth of the ER. I retrieved my jacket the second they covered the girl with another blanket. Then I
followed, keeping my eyes and other senses open and
wary. Scrap hovered above my head and off to my right,
stubby wings and wide ears flapping. (The left wing was
still drooping unnaturally. Where had he been playing?
Or rather who had he been playing with?) His pug nose
worked overtime seeking hints of demon blood. Shades
of pink outlined his edges. He'd lost the cigar, ready to
work his magic.

The moment the automatic doors whooshed shut behind me the warning flares across my back soothed.

Hospitals are sacred. We're safe here. Scrap paled and
dropped back to his normal pudgy grayish-green form.
He flapped his wings once and landed on my shoulder,
as substantial as dandelion fluff.

The kid had mentioned dandelion fluff when I asked her for a name. Now the admissions people were asking her the same question.

"Names have meaning only to the person owning them," she said on a breathy sigh.

Allie looked at me and tsked in disgust. "Want to get your aunt down here? Maybe she can make sense of this.

"Not yet," I replied. "Stow the New Age crap and give it to me straight, lady. What's your name?" I ordered the girl. I'd learned long ago, when I made my living as a substitute teacher, that sometimes kids will only respond to direct commands snapped in an authoritative voice.

"WindScribe." Her eyes rolled up into her head and she lost consciousness.

Allie choked.

"What?"

"Weirdest story ever to come out of the cold case files. We pass it around the station about once a year." She swallowed heavily. "Twenty-eight years ago, about the time you and I were born, twelve women from the same Wiccan coven disappeared. All on the same night. No trace of them ever found. We presume they ran away to California where witchcraft is more acceptable. But the case file is still open."

There went that flare of warning up my spine again.

Chapter 5

It was once believed that the Moon was a gem worn by the Goddess, and that the stars were decorations upon Her Gown.

"TWELVE WICCA WOMEN?" I thought I knew where this story was going. No one on Cape Cod talked about it much, but kids whispered it around the campfire when they wanted to scare the youngest members of the scout troop.

"A Wiccan coven celebrating the sabbat of summer solstice," Allie added.

I caught a glimpse of the red-and-green gnomes peering in through the glass doors.

"A coven has thirteen members. MoonFeather says the rituals always need thirteen," I insisted, ignoring Dill. Maybe he'd go away.

Part of me hoped he wouldn't.

"But that night MoonFeather didn't attend. It was her coven," Allie said. "Her father—your grandfather—locked her in her room and tried to get the family priest to perform an exorcism on her, to cure her of her devilish ways. She missed the sabbat, so only twelve were there. Only twelve went missing."

"And WindScribe here was one of those women." Hard to believe, she looked so vulnerable, innocent, and young. Way too young to have gone missing thirty years ago.

Time is just another dimension, babe, Scrap mumbled around his black cherry cheroot. *Those who know how to manipulate it can flit hither, thither, and yon in a single night while decades pass in their home dimension.*

"Rip Van Winkle in drag. Times twelve," I said. "I think my vacation in Mexico just vanished into Neverland when it dumped this broad in my lap."

The sounds of coughing, hacking, retching, moaning, and crying filled the ER lobby. The cold weather took its toll on the health of the community. With disease and accidents.

The place was full to overflowing.

"I'm going home," I told Allie. If I was on anyone's hit list, I wanted to fight on my own turf. Without an audience or endangering bystanders.

"Not yet you don't." Allie grabbed my arm and steered me toward the desk. "I want your statement, in writing. Before my boss gets here."

"But I wasn't there. I didn't see her appear."

Allie bit her lip. "But you heard her talk about paradise and flowers. You saw that she was naked. You heard her say her name. You made those garish apparitions bleed. Who's going to explain the blood?"

"Um . . . Allie, is this a good idea? Can't we just put the whole thing in the X-files or the UFO folder or whatever you call it?"

"No. I was there. I saw something really strange, and I want explanations." She stood between me and the door.

The gnomes continued making faces at me from the other side of the glass. They also shook their tiny fists and bared their rows and rows of teeth.

"Come on, Allie, what am I going to put into that report? That you told me you saw a beautiful blonde step out of nothing directly into the path of your car and that she claims to be a witch who disappeared thirty years

ago but hasn't aged a day? That the garden gnomes that
litter the Cape came to life and tried to chew through
your bright and shiny new cruiser to get to that girl. If I
wrote that anywhere but as fiction, we'd both be
laughed off the Cape. Or into the loony bin."

"I've got to have something to tell my boss."

Anything resembling the truth was suspect.

"Coffee. I need caffeine before I can think this
through." I jerked away from her in search of the cafeteria, or (shudder) a vending machine. "The Pacific
Northwest has great coffee on every corner, and I bet
the weather behaves itself, too," I grumbled. Dill's folks
lived in Oregon. Maybe I could take refuge there from
the Windago and garden gnomes with teeth.

Not a great idea. My in-laws were weirder and more
suspect than Dill's ghost.

Allie followed me to the cafeteria where they had an
espresso machine. Over hazelnut lattes we tried to find
a way out of the dilemma.

"They call hazelnuts filberts in Oregon," I said, still
daydreaming of a refuge elsewhere.

Then Joe Halohan, Chief Constable for our township,
wandered in. "Thought I'd find you two in here." He
pulled a chair up to our miniscule table and straddled it.
He draped his portly frame over the back, chewing on a
toothpick. "Care to give me a saner explanation than
the doctor and the naked woman did?" He raised bushy
gray eyebrows at us both.

"Can't find anything saner, sir," Allie reported.

"Then until you do, I suggest our novelist here takes
the fictional character in hand." He heaved himself off
the chair, the matter concluded.

"What does that mean?" I snapped at him.

"Very simple. The hospital doesn't have any spare
beds. The jail is full, too, with all the bums we've pulled
off the streets to keep them from freezing to death.
There is nothing visibly wrong with the woman who
calls herself WindScribe. Someone has to take her in.
Until the FBI gets here. I elect you, Tess."

"FBI?" I gulped.

"A cold case of kidnapping warming up. It's their jurisdiction."

"But ..."

"No buts about it. Either take her in, or find a logical explanation for where she came from, who she is, and why she's totally naked in subfreezing weather." This time he escaped me.

"Shit."

"You don't *have* to do this, Tess." Allie didn't look convinced.

"He's right. Who better than me? I've got that big rambling house that used to be a bed and breakfast. I just finished a book, so I'm not on deadline. I only have to e-mail the last four chapters as soon as I get power and phone lines back. And I've got MoonFeather to help us untangle this. Come on. Let's take WindScribe home. The sooner we get answers, the sooner I can take off for vacation in warmer weather." I needed at least a couple of days to make reservations and pack. And do laundry, check my stacks of unopened mail, take out the garbage, and wash four days of accumulated dishes before I could leave.

Then I was outta here.

If the gnomes let me.

An hour later, I zipped up my parka and huddled into it a moment. A bewildered WindScribe sat beside me in the car clutching a little white paper bag with two vials of tranquilizers. She huddled into a hospital blanket draped around her hospital gown and robe.

The garden gnomes were nowhere in sight. Scrap remained a peaceful gray, and the hairs on my spine lay flat. We were safe.

For a while.

"You can't imprison me with that," she protested the seat belt, swatting at my hands.

"It's the law, kid. Strap in or walk." I glared at her.

She stared out the window a moment at the frigid weather. The wind had picked up again, bringing the wind chill even lower. The lowering skies threatened to dump more snow.

Born of nature or the Windago?

"If you insist. But I want it on record that I protest this infringement upon my rights."

"At the moment you don't officially exist, so you don't have any rights," I said sweetly, putting the car into gear.

Allie had gone back to the station armed with fingerprints and dental X rays to try to match WindScribe to any *recent* missing persons reports. A DNA swab would take three days to process. Too long for me to wait. Allie also promised to notify any relatives the original WindScribe had left in the area.

Scarcely noon. Would MoonFeather be up yet? I needed to call her. She'd want to know about her Wiccan sister from thirty years ago. A woman who hadn't aged a day while the ravages of time had worked on my aunt. Though if the phrase aging gracefully applied to anyone, it did to MoonFeather.

Damn, I wanted a vacation. Two weeks alone on a warm beach sipping *piña coladas*. Maybe find a luscious man who had no connection to demons and monsters and witches who fell out of another dimension. Someone more satisfying than the vibrator I'd considered buying. Almost any man would prove more interesting.

Silently, I drove home. The short distance seemed to take forever with the scowling presence beside me. Even Dill was cheerier than this unexpected and unwanted passenger.

"It's all so different," WindScribe murmured. "So different and yet so much the same."

"Not much changes on Cape Cod. Just the latest tech toys."

Power company crews packed up their chain saws, having cut up the fallen oak and repaired the lines. My twisting driveway was clear and lights blazed from my kitchen. I pulled into the gravel parking area outside my kitchen door with a sigh of relief. Heat. Hot coffee. Internet!

Not everything was bad.

"I think I know this house. A lawyer owns it." WindScribe peered through the windshield, leaning forward as far as the seat belt would let her. She released it and twisted around, surveying my entire property.

"I own it now." All two and one half acres. No mortgage, thanks to Dill's life insurance.

"Houses are sacred. No bad guys allowed," I reminded myself. "We'll be safe here. Or should be."

Braced for the blast of frigid wind born over arctic snows, I opened the car door and moved around to help WindScribe into the house. "Tomorrow's the first day of spring, for Goddess' sake!" I protested to the charcoal-gray sky.

Something rattled in the shrubbery. Hopefully, just the wind.

The wind came in gusts that shook everything in its path.

Only a single bush rattled.

I didn't want to battle demons outside in this weather. Even demons should have the sense to stay home today.

Maybe it was an animal. Stupid people let their dogs and cats wander in this weather.

Not with my luck.

I caught a flicker of movement out of the corner of my eye. I paused for just a moment, waiting to see if the base of my spine flared in warning again.

Only a tingle of watchful waiting.

Good. I could outwait the best of them.

The storm door to the mudroom stuck. Cursing in Sasquatch again, I kicked the metal door. My big toe threatened to fall off inside my boot and wool sock from the blow. But the door unstuck.

I hustled WindScribe through the kitchen to the butler's pantry into the dining room. Then up the new staircase (added on in 1850 as opposed to the old staircase from the original building in 1743 between my office and the parlor) to the long attic room. My nose wiggled. The house smelled different. Clean and fresh rather than musty and moldy. Maybe Scrap had done a hasty cleanup.

Normally, I used the attic over the dining room as book storage. It still had a double bed with a brass frame tucked into the corner, left over from the previous owners.

WindScribe wilted with every step. I'd planned to put her in the guest room on the other side of my bedroom above the office. She wouldn't make it that far. So I tucked her into the bed. Got her a glass of water from my bathroom and left her sleeping peacefully with one tranquilizer in her. The bottle said she could take two every four hours. One seemed more than enough. She was confused and stressed, not suffering panic attacks.

"Woo wee, it is colder than a titch's wit out there," I said to no one as I headed for the coffeepot in the kitchen. I rubbed my hands together.

The smell of burning sage stopped me in my tracks. The strains of Heather Alexander singing a Celtic lay about a stag hunt played on the stereo.

"MoonFeather," I greeted my father's sister. She must have been in my office or parlor, so I didn't notice her when I hastened upstairs with WindScribe.

I like my aunt. She's the closest thing to normal in my life, less than twenty years older than me and ten younger than Dad, we're closer in age and philosophy to each other than to most everyone else on either side of the clan.

My aunt is *only* MoonFeather. She'd never taken the names of any of her four husbands when she dropped the family name of Noncoiré. That was thirty years ago when she embraced her true calling as a witch, just before her coven disappeared on the night of the summer solstice.

I needed to talk to her about that.

"Is it family game night already?" My odd assortment of relatives on Cape Cod gathered every Sunday night to play Trivial Pursuit®. We didn't have to pretend we liked each other the rest of the week because we had spent four hours of quality time together.

Their presence might make talking about WindScribe difficult.

"It's only Thursday, Tess. I decided to clear your house of evil spirits now that you have finished that manuscript. You need to invite good spirits back into your home. You drive them away with your foul moods when you are on deadline."

"Foul moods on deadline are part of the job description."

"Yes, I know, but this is something ... different. More intense." She scowled and added lavender to the burning sage wand.

A waft of smoke brushed my nose. I jammed my finger under it to keep from sneezing. This smoke smelled more like Scrap's black cherry cheroot than Moon-Feather's herbs. First time I could remember welcoming his bad habits. I wanted the imp close right now.

"How did you know I finished the manuscript?" Despite myself, I found my foot tapping the rhythm of the next tune on the CD.

MoonFeather gave me *that* look that said I was stupid for asking how she knew.

She knew things. I had a lot of trouble keeping Scrap a secret from her. She was the one person who might believe my tale of spending a year in a hidden Citadel learning to be a Warrior of the Celestial Blade.

I'd fallen to pieces after Dill died and the Sisterhood welcomed me, nursed me through a near-lethal fever, gave me a reason to live beyond my grief. Our purpose was to keep demons from crossing into this dimension. Good thing they kicked me out of the Citadel for questioning too many rules and asking why ten times too often. If I'd still been stuck there guarding a single doorway to another dimension, I'd never have been available last autumn to close a rogue demon portal they missed.

I wouldn't have been under WindScribe when she fell out of Paradise.

Maybe it was time to use the ultra secret, in life or death, emergencies only phone number Sister Serena had given me.

Probably no one would answer the damn thing.

Chapter 6

"**Y**OU READ A completion or closure for me
in the tarot, MoonFeather." I was sure I
hadn't said anything about my progress or my deadlines
last Sunday at game night. Uncle George, my sister Cecilia, and Grandmother Maria never paid any attention
to my career anyway. The money I earned just made it
more convenient for them to gather in my big house.

Dill and I had bought it right after our marriage. He'd
liquidated his trust fund for the down payment. Then
we'd returned to central Washington to collect his stuff
and gather a few more rock samples before he began
teaching at the local community college. He'd died before we could get back here. His death was another con-
venience for the family, if not for me. He had a Ph.D in
geology and usually beat the pants off the entire family
combined against him on game night. They wouldn't
allow me to team up with him; the two of us together
made an even more formidable team.

I really needed the last cup of coffee in the pot.

But not garden gnomes with ten extra sets of teeth.

Or a Windago with a grudge.

"I saw the end of a segment in your life and the be-

ginning of a new one in the cards. So of course I knew
that you finished a book and I knew you'd need help
cleaning house." MoonFeather waved the glowing sage
wand at a dark corner where a cobweb had taken up
residence and threatened to engulf the refrigerator.

I knew it was there and meant to clean it out when I
finished the book, when I had a few spare minutes,
when I couldn't find anything better to do.

Or when Mom came home and cleaned it out for me.

"You made a new pot of coffee," I sighed in relief.

"I also scrubbed the pot," MoonFeather said emphat-
ically.

I cringed. I hoped she hadn't collected all my dis-
carded, half empty mugs with a thick patina of mold
growing in them. I was saving those for Scrap when he
got back from wherever. Beer and orange juice might
revive him after a battle, but he craved mold like I crave
chocolate and coffee. Only mold was more essential to
his metabolism than chocolate and coffee were to mine.

Maybe not.

"You washed the dishes." So much for the mold farm
for Scrap.

A chuckle in the back of my mind told me that Scrap
had gotten to a couple of them before MoonFeather
did. I relaxed with a sigh.

Now how to ask her about WindScribe.

"I also took a bunch of messages for you," Moon-
Feather continued. "Two of them from men I don't
know." My aunt raised her eyebrows in speculation. She
might be nearing fifty, but she still had a fine figure and
great legs. She'd divorced three husbands, buried a
fourth, and now lived with a man fifteen years younger
than herself. She'd raised two daughters, mostly on her
own, who were now off at college. She knew every eligi-
ble man on Cape Cod and a good many more throughout New England. With way too much info on each one.

And she didn't like sharing.

I poured coffee, thick cream—the real thing—and
three sugars into my favorite cup; heavy natural-colored

pottery with a bulbous center and a blue dragon circling it. Then I reached for the notepad hanging on a string beside the telephone.

"Donovan Estevez?" My heart went pitter-patter. I'd met Donovan last autumn and slept with him. Once. He was the sexiest man alive and he had the hots for me. He'd make a good diversion on that beach in Mexico. . . .

At the same time my spine bristled with anxiety. I couldn't trust the man. No, I'd never invite Donovan to meet me anywhere. Well, maybe on vacation if no demons threatened.

"Mr. Estevez is a very spiritual man. Is he part Native American?" MoonFeather gazed into the ether as she drew information into herself.

I nodded. Part Sanpoil Indian, Russian, Dutch, and a few other ancestors, as well as possibly Damiri demon. I didn't know about the spiritual part. I'd leave that assessment to MoonFeather. I don't do spiritual or religious.

"He says he will be on the Cape tomorrow on business and hopes to meet you at the *salle d'armes* for a fencing bout in the evening." MoonFeather read her scrawled handwriting over my shoulder.

"And Guilford Van der Hoyden-Smythe." I looked at the next message. Gollum to his friends.

"Quite a nice and scholarly gentleman. Isn't he the one who called to reassure your mother when you were kidnapped by terrorists last autumn?"

I nodded again. Those terrorists had been Sasquatch demons. I didn't like talking about that episode. That's where I learned to curse in Sasquatch.

"Mr. Van der Hoyden-Smythe says that he is lecturing to the National Folkloric Society in Boston tomorrow night and requests that you attend."

"Can't," I said. I didn't want to explain about the two men who were almost in my life. For various reasons, neither one of them was always welcome.

Should I invite Gollum to join me in Mexico? He might be a comfortable companion, but a sexy one . . . ?

Tall, lanky, with glasses that slipped down his nose, he always looked crisp and pressed. He also had a tendency to drone on and on and on about obscure topics of interest only to himself. A true nerd—um—scholar.

Gollum's expertise might be valuable in figuring out what happened to WindScribe and where the garden gnomes with teeth came from.

MoonFeather added her sage wand to the fire in the breakfast nook. "Do you want me to exorcise your ghosts?" she asked.

I needed a moment and several sips of coffee to jump thoughts with her.

"Why would I do that? I'm comfortable with them and they with me." Except for Dill. I wasn't sure if I wanted his ghost in or out of my life. Pretty soon there wouldn't be room for me in the house with all of the ghosts.

"They bother your mother."

Since Dad moved in with his much younger tennis coach, Bill Ikito, the rest of the family tried to take care of Mom. They failed, and most of the responsibility fell to me.

"Mom isn't here."

"But she is coming back. When the weather breaks. Soon, I think."

"It's my house. She lives in the guest cottage, which is not haunted."

"That's what you think."

"Have I acquired a new one?" Half jokingly—but only half. The previous owner had included the ghosts in the earnest money agreement along with the monster dining room table and twelve chairs as part of the sale.

If I did burn the table and chairs, I could turn the dining room into more library space and not have room for family game night. Hmmm. Something to think about.

"I'm not certain. There is a new presence hovering nearby. It could be a ghost returned to a place of comfort or something else. The air tastes of . . . I don't know what. Something odd."

"Uh, MoonFeather, we need to talk about something odd that happened today. Or, rather, thirty years ago . . ."

Her eyes narrowed in speculation and . . . did I detect worry behind her scrutiny?

A flicker of bright red and green flashed before my memory.

That's right, babe. We're about to have a close encounter of the weird kind, Scrap laughed in my ear as he settled into my hand, flashing neon red, ready to transform into a weapon.

Why couldn't these guys wait until I was safely snoozing on a sunny beach somewhere?

Chapter 7

It was once believed that the Moon was a spinning wheel, upon which the Goddess spun the lives of Men and Women.

"TESS, WHAT IS happening?" MoonFeather stared at the elongating staff that suddenly materialized in my hands. Then her eyes shifted to my face. "When did you get that scar?"

"Later," I snapped at my aunt. Damn, the scar pulsed and burned as if it were a newly opened wound. Maybe something about Scrap transforming and the presence of an enemy brought it into the real world.

I twirled the shaft, giving Scrap centrifugal force to continue his transformation. Between one eye blink and the next, mirror-image, half-moon blades extruded from the ends. Metal spikes grew out of the outside curves. They mimicked a special configuration in the sky when the Milky Way touched the top of a waxing quarter moon and revealed the face of the Goddess Kynthia.

The music on the stereo kicked up a notch. Throbbing drums, rousing pipes, a husky alto singing/snarling:

"Axes flash, broadsword swing
Shining armor's piercing ring
Horses run with polished shield
Fight those bastards till they yield

Midnight mare and blood-red roan,
Fight to keep this land your own
Sound the horn and call the cry,
How Many Of Them Can We Make Die!"

"Stand back, MoonFeather."

The mudroom door burst open. A gush of frigid air blew at me along with a ravening horde of tiny beings, all gnashing their nasty sharp teeth.

The first wave lunged for my bare ankles.

I swept the blade down and sideways. Three were caught up in the curve, swinging from the blade. They clung with their gnarly fists, using my weapon as a swing. One of them laughed at me.

I hadn't cut a single one of them.

Then I backhanded and impaled two more on the spikes. They died instantly, spewing black blood and a ghastly smell.

Holding back my gag reflex, I flipped the blade and attacked again with the spines.

Caught another one! Scrap chortled.

"Bloodthirsty imp," I growled. A little bit of relief washed through the tension in my shoulders and in my gut. These guys could hurt and die. I had a chance.

"Follow orders as you're told,
Make their yellow blood run cold
Fight until you die or drop
A force like ours is hard to stop
Close your mind to stress and pain
Fight till you're no longer sane
Let not one damn cur pass by
How Many Of Them Can We Make Die!"

The second wave of invading gnomes backed off. They stared at their fallen comrades, then up at me. Clearly, they were reconsidering their attack—or their strategy. I had surprised them. They didn't know who they faced.

A screech of pain came from behind me.

I whirled, flashing the blade right and left.

MoonFeather stood atop the round table in the nook. She fended off a gnome with my dagger-length dragon-grip letter opener.

As I watched, a gnome grabbed the blade in his fist and grinned. No blood oozed from his grip. With a laugh that welled up from the depths of hell and reverberated around my kitchen, he yanked the dagger away from MoonFeather.

Damn, these guys were hard to kill.

MoonFeather retaliated with a frying pan, flattening the little guy with quiet efficiency. But another one clung to her calf with its teeth. As I watched, it tore a chunk of flesh out of one of my aunt's gorgeous legs and spat it out. Blood gushed everywhere.

She cried out in shock and pain as her leg crumpled beneath her weight.

> *"Guard your women and children well,*
> *Send these bastards back to hell*
> *We'll teach them the ways of war.*
> *They won't come here anymore*
> *Use your shield and use your head,*
> *Fight till every one is dead*
> *Raise the flag up to the sky,*
> *How Many Of Them Can We Make Die!"*

I stomped my feet in rhythm with the drums and bagpipe and swung my blade in time with the lyrics. Then I dispatched the offending tiny monster attacking Moon-Feather with a clean sweep and spun again to make sure no others slipped by my guard.

"Perhaps we should talk." A little man held up his hand, palm out. He had a nose that met an elongated chin Jay Leno might envy, and a few scraggly whiskers. His equally ugly fellows cowered behind him.

"Talk about what? Maiming my aunt—my favorite person in the world?" I swept the blade back and forth between us.

MoonFeather whimpered something behind me.

I gave her half a glance, not daring to take my eyes off the enemy.

> *"Dawn has broke, the time has come,*
> *Move your feet to a marching drum*
> *We'll win the war and pay the toll,*
> *We'll fight as one in heart and soul*
> *Midnight mare and blood-red roan*
> *Fight to keep this land your own*
> *Sound the horn and call the cry,*
> *How Many Of Them Can We Make Die!"*

The flattened one, now looking more like a two-dimensional cartoon than the menace I knew him to be, slid off the table and sidled along the wall until he could meld into the pack of miniscule invaders.

With a popping sound he puffed out and filled normal space again.

What would it take to off these guys?

"You have felled several of Our subjects. We do not forgive easily," the leader said.

Was that the royal "We"? The little fellow did sport a tiny bit of gold around the rim of his peaked cap and a golden feather stuck jauntily into the folds of red fabric.

"You're the king of garden gnomes, so what?" I sneered. "You invaded my home without provocation. Aren't there rules against that?"

"You attacked us first."

"Because you were menacing my friend. A police-woman doing her job!"

"We sympathize with the one you call Allie. We respect her duty. But we have a mission. You stand in our way."

"You're in the wrong dimension to be dictating anything."

"You harbor an escaped prisoner."

I raised my eyebrows at that. "You look like something an escapee from a lunatic asylum might dream up."

"You know better than that, Teresa Louise Noncoiré, Warrior of the Celestial Blade."

The Blade vibrated in my hands. Scrap had something to say but was having trouble communicating in this form.

"So you know my name. What's yours, and why are you crossing my threshold without an invitation?" I dredged up a fragment of a folk memory. "Homes are sacred. Invitations and hospitality a requirement." Out of doors was where the battles took place.

Only outside today was a frozen hell for both of us.

I kept the blade moving, not daring to give these guys an opening.

"Names are a source of power. Not to be given lightly." WindScribe had wandered all around that subject.

MoonFeather moaned again. I hoped she'd managed to find a dish towel or a place mat to staunch the flow of blood.

"You forfeited your right to secrecy the moment you crossed my threshold, you little piece of trailer trash." I increased the arc of the blade, coming within a hair's breadth of the gnome king's chest.

"Yeep!" He jumped back, plowing into the crowd of his minions like a ball and ninepins. Among much jostling and staggering and muttering of curses in an oddly fluid language, the king righted himself and faced me once more.

"Give us the dangerous prisoner and we will depart your presence, never to bother you again," he offered. But his eyes wouldn't meet mine. I also suspected he crossed his fingers behind his back.

Tricky little bastard.

"I don't know what you are talking about," I lied.

"Windscribe," he said, slowly.

"WindScribe? Dangerous? She's a ditzy hippy." She was also human, one of my tribe. I wasn't about to give her up without a fight.

The king advanced one step. "You do not know the dangers you court. We will have the prisoner."

I gave him a taste of my blade.

The entire horde popped out with a whoosh.

The vacuum resulting from their departure brought a ringing to my ears and a new rush of arctic air into my kitchen.

The music faded to a poignant ballad.

My bloodlust died with the music.

"Oh, my," MoonFeather groaned. "I think I need more than a poultice on this wound."

No amazement. No protestations of the unreal. No questions about Scrap becoming the Celestial Blade.

That's my Aunt MoonFeather.

Nasty little beasties. Nasty. Nasty. They taste worse than their blood smells.

My babe needs answers. Like little Mr.-more-important-than-Ghod's name, rank, and serial number.

We need help. Help Tess won't ask for until she's desperate. Just once I wish she'd put aside her stubborn independence and ask. Gollum is nearby. But will she call him?

No.

Will she even think about it?

No.

Instead, she'll moon over that stinky Donovan. That man does not smell right. Old dust and sage and copper. Not fully human, but not a demon either. What is he?

Old. He's old. I can smell that much. But how old is old when one hops dimensions? Time is just another dimension.

I don't think my babe wants to know what he is. Then she'll have to feel even more guilty for sleeping with him.

Now if she'd just use a little common sense and hook up with Gollum . . .

I need a bath.

I need some mold and a nap.

Chapter 8

"YOU AGAIN?" a tired orderly in the ER asked. "What have you got this time, Snow White and the Seven Dwarfs?"

I grabbed the wheelchair from him and dashed back to the still running SUV. "My aunt is ensanguining while you malign my veracity!" I deliberately used words I didn't think he knew.

WindScribe dozed in the backseat, tranked to the gills. And hadn't I had a lovely time getting her back into the car. But I didn't dare leave her alone in a strange house.

MoonFeather was so absorbed in her own pain and staunching the torrents of blood from her wound she barely noticed the extra person in the car.

"Hey, how many of those pills did she take?" the orderly asked, checking WindScribe's neck for a pulse and shaking his head at her pale skin.

"I gave her one." I hadn't bothered to check the bottle in my hurry to get my aunt to the hospital. I could move faster with four-wheel drive than the local ambulance.

"Looks like she took half the bottle."

"She's not the patient! My aunt is bleeding to death."

We'd managed a crude pressure bandage on her leg. Blood saturated it and seeped down her leg.

A nurse appeared, took one look at the blood that spattered both MoonFeather and myself, and started barking orders. Life sped up to fast forward. Medical professionals whisked MoonFeather off to surgery, leaving me with the paperwork and a dreaming Wind-Scribe.

I'd managed to call Josh, MoonFeather's current significant other, and begun to fill in name and basic information when Allie returned.

"Now what?" she asked.

I shrugged and dredged a few more pieces of vital information out of my tired brain. Date of birth. Current residence. Contact phone number. Had to check the call list on my cell phone for that.

"Hospital said violent wound. I've got to investigate," Allie persisted.

"A raccoon got into the kitchen seeking warmth. It bit MoonFeather before we could evict it." That sounded more believable than the truth.

"That the truth, Tess?"

I looked her square in the eye. "You want the truth or what sounds logical?"

"Is this day going to get weird again?" She sat down beside me with a sigh. Her long legs stretched into the aisle between chairs, blocking my exit.

The place had mostly cleared out since this morning.

"Probably get weirder yet." Especially if both Donovan and Gollum came to town. "Weird describes my life."

"Shit. Do I need to find a new best friend?"

"I'd rather you stuck by this one."

We grinned at each other and touched fists, knuckle to knuckle, thumbs extended and entwined.

"You want to know how weird this day is?" Allie asked.

I groaned.

"They gave me a rookie for a partner."

"You don't usually partner."

"Didn't think I needed one. Boss Joe says no one goes out alone anymore." She shook her head, then jerked it sideways.

I noticed the uniformed man leaning on the reception counter. He didn't look much bigger than me.

"Rookie, indeed. Still wet behind the ears," I said. "What is he, twelve?"

As if he heard me, the young man swaggered over, thumbs hooked into his belt. A classic stance of a scared little boy trying to make himself look bigger and older. He'd be almost handsome if he didn't try so hard.

"Tess, meet Mike Gionelli." Allie gave no further explanation.

"Pleased to meet you, Mike." I politely held my hand out to shake.

He grabbed it eagerly and firmly with dry palms. His smile spread from ear to ear and lit his eyes. "I've read your books. I'm really looking forward to the next one."

"Flattery will get you everywhere, young man."

An hour later I got MoonFeather ensconced in a private room—amazing what good insurance will get you. The hospital wasn't as full as they pretended.

WindScribe, who had no insurance that we knew of and therefore no hospital bed, dozed in a chair in the corner.

"A garden gnome came to life and bit me with dagger-sharp teeth," MoonFeather told the intern, keeping a straight face and her eyes wide open in innocence.

"Why that's . . . that's . . ." the young man spluttered. He looked cast from the same mold as Mike Gionelli, far too young for the responsibility he wielded. "Must be the pain meds." He shook his head and left us.

"Did you see his face?" MoonFeather giggled through her intravenous drugs.

I sat on an uncomfortable stool, holding her hand. I told her the raccoon story.

"They're afraid of rabies. If we don't come up with a better explanation in the next few hours, the doctor's going to require shots. They aren't pleasant." I tried to keep my voice calm and low. Too many people ran about eavesdropping in this small but well-appointed hospital.

Cape Cod may be small, but we have some of the priciest real estate in the country. Our local billionaires demand state of the art medical care whenever they need it. So the rest of us peons benefit from the facility.

"I can't lie, Tess." MoonFeather's eyes cleared of the drug haze a moment. "Everything we do—good or bad—comes back to us threefold. I won't lie."

"Then let me do it for you." I should have built up a fair amount of good karma to make up for a little white lie when I dispatched a couple dozen Sasquatch. Besides, a lie couldn't be *too* bad if I told it to protect the innocent from information they wouldn't believe and couldn't process.

"Something will turn up." She dismissed it all with an expansive gesture that nearly dislodged her IV. Her eyes glazed over and drifted closed.

"MoonFeather, before you drift off into the land of nod, we need to talk."

"Hmm?" She cast me a beatific smile.

"MoonFeather." I jostled her arm a little to get her attention. "Your friend WindScribe has come back." I pointed to the witless lump in the corner. She'd roused enough to hum something I didn't recognize.

"WindScribe. Such a beautiful girl. Blonde hair as light as a feather in the moonlight." She paused long enough that I thought she'd gone to sleep.

Odd that she would describe another witch with the attributes of her own craft name. When people join Wicca, they often take a name that describes themselves better than the name their parents gave them. I'd seen MoonFeather dance nude in the moonlight. She moved as gracefully as a feather drifting in the wind.

Would she ever dance again? I hoped so.

Those gnomes had a lot to answer for.

She mumbled something I couldn't catch. Then she swallowed deeply and stopped slurring. "I always thought you'd take the name WindScribe if you ever embraced your true calling. Your spirit is as free as the wind and you are a scribe." Something more unintelligible. Then, "Society didn't grant as much religious freedom in those days as they claimed. We had trouble keeping a sacred thirteen."

MoonFeather opened her eyes and sat up abruptly. "Have you called Josh?"

"Yes. He's in court and will be here as soon as he can. He has to clear his schedule so he can stay home and take care of you. But I think you should plan on coming to my house. So he can work." Josh's law practice was just starting to take off. He needed to be in the office, or the courtroom, as much as possible. He also needed to make money to keep up his health insurance premiums to cover MoonFeather and this hospital visit. Hospital administrators do not look kindly upon people without insurance.

Like WindScribe.

Besides, those little beasties had tasted MoonFeather's blood. They'd be able to find her anywhere, in any dimension. I needed to stay close to protect her.

"Your mother is coming home."

I groaned. "But the weather hasn't turned yet."

"She's still coming home. You need to think about protecting her. Until I can devise a ritual to banish the bad guys. You'll need help. You need an apotropaic."

I knew that archaic word. It meant something designed to avert evil, like a gargoyle protecting a cathedral. How did she know it?

Yeah, I needed a gargoyle. A live one with a sharp and pointy weapon.

"I always need help with Mom," I said instead. But I didn't like the idea of my naïve and defenseless mother all the way across the yard in the guest cottage. Alone.

So much for two weeks in Mexico, or Southern California, or San Antonio . . .

With a weary sigh, I dug out my cell phone. Gollum wasn't the first on my speed dial, but close. (That spot was reserved for Dill's extinct cell phone. I'd never allowed myself to delete the number. Too final an admission that he was truly gone forever.) Gollum was the closest thing to a gargoyle I could think of.

I'd never seen him fight, but he knew things about demons no mortal should. He had access to more information from arcane sources he never talked about.

Come to think about it, he didn't talk much about himself. Just myth and legends and demons. About those, he talked endlessly. And he hid behind his scholarly tinted glasses so that I couldn't read his eyes.

Maybe he was busy, and I could just leave a voice mail.

No such luck. He answered on the first ring. "Tess, good to hear from you. Are you coming to my lecture tomorrow?" His clipped upstate New York accent sounded all too comfortable and familiar, even though I hadn't heard from him since I left him in Seattle last November, other than a generic holiday card with a scrawled signature I could barely read.

I easily imagined him stretching his long legs and lanky frame, then folding himself into the nearest armchair and setting up camp with his laptop, his cat, and *my* beer.

"I don't think I can make it." I glared accusingly at WindScribe. If I took her with me maybe. "Um, Gollum, what's your schedule like while you're in New England?"

"Actually, I've taken a teaching gig at your community college. Seems like your anthro prof has complications in her pregnancy and has to take to her bed for four months or so. I'm filling in."

"Oh." He'd be on my back step for months. He and his cat. Scrap hates cats. He's also allergic and can't smell evil when the cat is around. "Um, do you have an apartment yet?"

"Got a line on two but haven't committed to either yet. I'd planned to do that this weekend and move in next week during spring break."

"Would you like to stay in my guest cottage?" I had to grit my teeth to make the offer. But I needed his expertise in dealing with flesh-eating garden gnomes.

"What about your mom?"

"I'm moving her into the mother-in-law apartment attached to the house." No way would I leave her alone out in the cottage, easy prey to my latest supernatural enemy.

Dill had set up an office in the house extension. I'd locked the connecting door after his death and never looked inside since. But it had three good-sized rooms, a private bath, and a kitchenette.

"I'll meet you at the house in an hour," he said on a chuckle.

"Where are you now?"

"Halfway between Boston and Cape Cod."

"Like you knew I'd make the offer?"

"Like I hoped you would when you saw my smiling face."

"House rules. You sleep in the cottage, not the armchair in my living room. You drink your own beer, eat your own food, and keep your cat out of my house and Scrap's way. And you never, ever, under penalty of death, speak French to my mother."

Chapter 9

*In old Alchemical prints, the lion and the unicorn
are frequently used to describe the opposing
forces of sun and moon.*

I LEFT MOONFEATHER in Josh's loving arms a
few minutes later and returned home by way of
the liquor store—for empty boxes to move Mom's
things. And a bottle of single malt scotch. I had a feeling
I was going to need it if Gollum was moving into the
guest cottage. The scotch was for me.

WindScribe brightened enough to notice the booze. I
think she wanted to start in on it the moment I set the
bag in the backseat of the car.

"Not yet, kid. You're still drugged. Can't mix booze
and pills."

"Why not?"

I rolled my eyes at that.

"Makes for a boss trip." She started humming something catchy about a white rabbit.

Oh, boy. I was going to have my hands full with this one.

I knew that tune. Where? The only lyrics that came to
mind were filk, parodies of the original with a science
fiction or fantasy twist. I spent a lot of my time at the
SF/F conventions, or cons, filking. We'd sit up half the
night singing the parodies, or Celtic lays, and punning
ourselves to sleep.

Dill's death had closed my throat, seemingly forever. I couldn't even sing at the funeral of my best friend, Bob Brown, though he'd asked me to with his dying breath. Then, last autumn, I'd finally let the songs within me bubble up and out.

I could use a rousing round of filk about now.

By the time we got back to the house, WindScribe was swaying on her feet.

The moment I got her back into bed, she reached for the vial of tranquilizers. I grabbed it away from her. "Well, I guess you can have one. It's been over four hours since I gave you a dose." I shook a few tablets into my hand.

The bottle seemed fuller than before. I counted. The label said thirty tablets, should be twenty-nine now. I counted thirty-three. And some of them looked suspiciously like aspirin.

"How many did you take before?" I demanded, not at all happy with my unwelcome guest or the way my life had slid downhill since . . . since last night when a Windago tried to gain entrance to my home—against the rules of hospitality.

WindScribe answered me with a snore. No wonder she was so spacey and incoherent.

Then she twitched and thrashed. "Don't lock me under the stairs, Mama. Please don't. I'm afraid of the dark."

I thought about waking her from her nightmare. Then she settled down and smiled. "Pretty flowers. No darkness in Faery."

Shaking my head, I took the pills with me and stashed them in the downstairs bathroom on my way to clean the kitchen.

I downed one small shot of the scotch while staring at the bloody mess and scrunching my nose against the stench of dead gnome and drying blood. In the movies no one had to clean up the mess. There's no *smell* in the movies.

Three, no, four miniature bodies lay scattered about

the breakfast nook along with blood spatters and gore. On the walls. On the table. All over the muted blue-and-brown calico café curtains and chair pads Mom and I had lovingly made when Dill and I first bought the house. I wanted eight chairs so that we could seat an entire family here to start each day.

Together.

Ruined. Both the furniture and my dreams.

I'd have to get a new table and kitchen chairs along with some new dreams. No way would I ever be able to eat at this table again.

Those garden gnomes had a lot to answer for.

"It's just a table, lovey. Don't cry." Dill enfolded me with almost tangible arms. Instead of warmth and comfort, I felt cold.

An ache opened in my gut.

"If you trade in the imp and come to me, we can still have all those children together and get a new table."

"Don't start on me, Dill. I'm not messing with fate and death. That's too weird, even for me. I won't write it. I won't write vampires either, so I certainly don't want to live with it."

Maybe a shot of scotch would numb my gag reflex, my anger, and my grief long enough to fill a basin with bleach water.

I was still stalling when I heard a car pull into the driveway, idling roughly before it backfired and cut off. Then a brisk knock sounded on my kitchen door.

That could only be Gollum. His rattletrap van always sounded as if it was on its last legs, held together with rubber bands and chewing gum. But it kept going, and going, and going.

Dill faded into the woodwork. Not totally gone, not totally here.

I dashed to the door. Gollum would know what to do. Despite my grumblings about him and the way he tended to invade my life, I did like the man. I trusted him.

More than I could say for Donovan Estevez, the other man almost in my life.

The grin froze on my face as I looked through the glass half of the back door. A cold knot of suspicion formed in my stomach. Followed instantly by warm relief and a need to give all my troubles to the man smiling at me on my back stoop.

"What can I do to help, L'akita?" Donovan Estevez asked the moment I opened the door. He traced the worry lines away from my eyes and mouth. His hand felt warm and inviting even without gloves on this frigid day.

More real than Dill. More alive. And sexy as hell.

"You're a day early," I hedged.

"Yet obviously you have need of me. Now what brings a frown to your face and makes your shoulders reach for your ears in tension, hm?" He edged closer.

I had to back up or fall into his arms.

"Donovan Estevez, why are you driving *that?*" I pointed over his shoulder at a mud-and-salt encrusted yellow Subaru station wagon.

I didn't want to look at his handsome face with the high cheekbones and chiseled jaw, at his sleek black braid that hung down between his shoulder blades, at his long legs and broad shoulders. I didn't want to feel the warmth and strength of his embrace.

Yeah, right.

His black leather jacket and tight black jeans only emphasized his fit physique, making it harder for me to hold my distance.

"Economizing," he growled. "Had to sell the Beemer when the casino and my economic empire imploded down a demon portal."

That about explained what happened last November.

"You're a day early." I closed my eyes to override the magnetic pull of his smile. My head cleared the moment I shut out the vision of his face.

I couldn't bring myself to move aside and invite him in. Unlike Gollum, I didn't dare trust this man. I had evidence that he had demon ancestry as well as sympathies.

I also had evidence to the contrary. Until I knew

more about this enigma of a man—a mysterious and wildly handsome man—I had to keep my heart intact.

I'd lost my heart and my will to Dill. When he betrayed me by dying, I'd fallen apart. My extreme grief had left me vulnerable to the imp flu. I wasn't sure I could survive that kind of loss again. Having his ghost around reminded me to keep my resolve to resist Donovan firm.

I dared open my eyes.

"Mind if I come in anyway?" He flashed me one of his famous grins, and my knees forgot to hold me upright. "It's a bit brisk out here."

"Yeah. Oh. Sorry." I stammered something and stepped aside with a sweeping gesture.

"Help yourself to coffee." I couldn't help but stare at the horribleness just to the left of the door beneath the broad bay window. "I'm kind of busy at the moment."

He muttered something in a strange language filled with clicks, pops, and hisses. "No wonder you look worried. What happened here?" he finally asked jerking his gaze away from the bloody mess to me.

He pulled me against his chest, letting me bury my head in his shoulder. At five feet two, against his nearly six feet, I didn't reach any higher.

Faced with the task of cleaning up the gore, I chose to embrace a demon instead.

I told him, the last part of my day's adventures, not the part about WindScribe stepping out of Neverland.

"Well, you can't bury the bodies," he said. "And you don't want to burn them in your fireplace, they'll stink up the place something horrible."

"I figured I should leave them where they are until Gollum gets here."

Donovan snarled something else in his demon language.

He had nothing to be jealous about, but until I knew enough to trust him implicitly, I figured I'd let the emotion simmer between the two men.

"He'll know what to do."

"*I* know what to do. We build an equinox bonfire in the backyard and burn the critters. Where's your woodpile?" He eyed the vastly diminished stack of split firewood beside the kitchen hearth.

"Around the corner of the house, toward the woods." Half of which I owned. I stepped away from him. "Wait a minute. Why can't we just wrap them in plastic bags and dump them down a deep hole?" That sounded more sanitary to me than burning the carcasses.

The scotch I'd drunk for lunch threatened to come up. I had to turn my back on the nook.

"You have to burn any corpse from another dimension to make certain it's really and truly dead. Besides, the ground is too frozen to dig." He touched my shoulder with reassurance and affection.

I wanted to lean in to him again, let his arms enfold me and make all this horror go away. My body and my instincts craved a deeper intimacy with him.

Not until he comes clean about who and what he is, my logical brain kicked in just in time.

"But I speared them with the tines of the Celestial Blade. They are well and truly dead," I protested, making my way toward the coffeepot on the other side of the kitchen island, a full ten feet away from the nook and the stench that had begun to rise.

"Then they probably are dead. But we have to make sure." He followed me across the kitchen, staying far too close. I could feel the heat of his body along my back.

All too easy to lean back, just a little, and snuggle into his arms . . .

Stop that! I admonished myself even as my nipples puckered in anticipation of feeling his touch on them.

"Fine," I snapped. "You and Gollum take care of it when he gets here. I have to clean an apartment and move Mom's things." I walked stiffly to the right, away from him. Away from my own stupid desires.

"I'll call the firehouse and get a burning permit for a bonfire. Equinox. Religious purposes. They should grant it," I continued.

"Tess . . ." He reached out to me with a fine-boned hand and his very long fingers.

I remembered seeing him at a con in California last September. He'd worn a bat costume.

I hated bats. I feared bats to the point of phobia. Illogical and unlikely, but I couldn't overcome my panic at the merest thought of a bat touching me.

When Dill had learned of my fears, he'd made me read up on bats, learn just how harmless they were. It hadn't helped. But I did learn that the bone structure supporting a bat's wings were actually super elongated fingers. Donovan's fingers weren't *that* long, but they were long enough to remind me of one of the reasons I couldn't trust him.

"Just take care of the bodies. And . . . and the table and chairs. I'll clean up the mess later." I stalked off toward the opposite end of the house and the attached apartment. It would be cold back there with only minimal heat all winter. I'd have to turn up the thermostat, mentally calculating the increased heating bill. Those rooms had their own furnace, a much more modern and efficient one than I had in the cellar for the rest of the house.

If Donovan followed me, and I half hoped he wouldn't, he'd have to stay close on my heels to keep from getting lost in the maze of rooms.

My home had started as a standard New England saltbox. Three rooms down and two up, all clustered about a central chimney. I kept those rooms as my office, library, and parlor, with my bedroom and a spare upstairs.

Succeeding generations had added on to the house starting with the dining room and the attic over it that was now WindScribe's room. The huge kitchen and breakfast nook at the opposite end of the house and the mother-in-law apartment off the dining room were the latest additions. Bathrooms were odd shapes cobbled out of old nooks or closets or attachments on the outside walls.

Donovan didn't even trip on the odd changes in floor level. Each addition changed up or down an inch or three depending on the lay of the land.

If I didn't look at Donovan, I could almost resist him. Damn it, I needed help fighting my own lust.

Where was Scrap? He couldn't get close to Donovan for some mysterious reason. Still, he should be able to communicate from a distance.

"Scrap?" I whispered into the ether.

No answer.

▶▶▶

El Stinko is here. He doesn't smell right. I know he's not human, but he doesn't smell like anything I've ever encountered before. As long as he is near my babe, his smell and an invisible barrier keeps me at bay.

How can I protect and comfort my babe when she insists on keeping him around?

She knows this, but when he smiles at her, she falls victim to his magic. A demon glamour. It has to be that. But he doesn't smell like a demon.

I wish she'd kick his butt back to Half Moon Lake in Washington where he belongs.

I don't think he belongs there either.

What in the six hundred sixty-six dimensions is he? The air around him tastes almost familiar, yet totally alien at the same time.

I think I should go diving in Mum's dump for another talisman to protect my babe, though I shudder to face the cold of Imp Haven. Freeze-dried body parts are not comfortable at all. But is Cape Cod any warmer?

Then, too, I'd have to traverse the chat room again. I wonder who's on duty today? Maybe the faeries have posted the j'appel dragons there. Pocket-sized flying mites that they are, I can flit past them with no trouble. They are actually smaller than me. Unless someone calls them by name. Then they jump to full size in two heartbeats. Can't get more than one full-sized dragon in the chat room at a time.

Trouble is, you never know what name a dragon is using today. It could be Hello. Or Jackknife. Or even Because. And just because he didn't use that name yesterday doesn't mean he's not using it today. Gotta keep my mouth shut around these guys.

I can't stay close to Tess while El Stinko is around, so I might as well try something useful at Imp Haven.

Chapter 10

It was once believed that the shadowed areas of the Moon were forests where the Goddess Diana hunted, and the bright areas were plains.

*L*OUD VOICES OUTSIDE drew me from the apartment back to the kitchen. I watched through the window of the back door as Donovan and Gollum stood on opposite sides of an unlit bonfire in the middle of the gravel drive with my round maple breakfast table upside down on top of the pile. The eight chairs and their bloodstained pads stood around the fire in a circle, inviting people to sit and toast marshmallows.

"What the hell do you think you are doing, Estevez, burning up Tess' furniture and half her woodpile?" Gollum screamed at Donovan. He flung his long arms about wildly, his fist almost connecting with Donovan's jaw. His silver-gilt bangs flopped into his eyes as his glasses slid down his nose. At six-feet three-and-a-half inches, he towered over Donovan's more modest five-eleven. But I was willing to bet they weighed about the same. Gollum stood with his big feet braced and fists clenched. Not a good sign from the most nonviolent person I knew.

"Go back to your books, Smythe, and leave the real work to those who were invited," Donovan sneered. He kicked a loose log toward the pile.

"Invited? When were you invited. I live here!"

"Where, in the root cellar?"

"No, in the guest cottage, where I can watch her back."

"Fat chance she'd let you back into her life, let alone live here."

They both looked toward the house. By the light dawning in their eyes, I knew they could see me standing in the window. They both puffed out their chests in high dudgeon. (I love that phrase and use it in my books whenever I can.)

The schoolteacher in me knew I should break it up. I needed both these men at the moment. Having them at each other's throats wouldn't help.

But a perverse imp of mischief deep inside me made me step back and watch the fireworks. The bonfire wasn't even lit yet.

Donovan took one aggressive step closer to Gollum. "Get off this property, van Der Hoyden-Smythe, before I throw you off."

"I'd like to see you try." Gollum unzipped his down parka and eased his shoulders. He shifted his feet to a balanced stance, not quite an *en garde,* nor did it look like a standard martial arts stance. Something more esoteric. Probably just as effective.

Uh-oh. Time to intervene.

"We can't light the fire until Allie gets here with the burn permit," I called, descending the two steps from the mudroom to the yard. "In the meantime, I could use some help taking down the soiled curtains so we can burn them, too."

I turned back toward the kitchen, hoping the circling dogs would declare a truce before they engaged in an all out territorial battle. The alpha bitch had spoken.

I hoped.

"What's going on, Tess?" Gollum asked the moment we all stepped into the warmth of the kitchen.

I avoided looking at the bare nook. "Grab some coffee and meet me in the parlor. It's the warmest room in the house."

They followed me, still keeping a substantial distance between them while trying to stay closest to me. A little hard in the narrow confines of the butler's pantry between the kitchen and the dining room. Dill danced around all three of us, fading in and out of the woodwork to keep from having to share space with our bodies. He frowned during the entire trek.

Gollum tripped on the two-inch step down into the dining room. He flopped around but strangely did not spill a single drop of coffee from his cup.

Donovan grinned and didn't offer to steady his balance. They stared at each other suspiciously as we passed the entrance to the apartment.

We twisted past the chaos of my office, the long room of the original saltbox. The front door of the house that faced the street stood between the office and library, but I'd sealed it for the winter. No one used it anyway since the driveway and gravel parking were closer to the kitchen door. The very steep old stairs opposite the entry led to my bedroom. I led the men to the other side of the office and into my parlor.

I checked for a sign of Scrap swinging on the spider over the fire, his favorite spot. He was still AWOL.

Finally we came to a halt in the sitting room that shared a chimney with the office and the library.

"Now isn't this cozy. Your own private harem, Tess. Oh, do they call men a harem? If I'd known you were into polyandry, I'd have killed you before I died. Isn't that what they call divorce Italian style?" Dill sat stiffly in a corner of the sleeper sofa. No humor lightened his quips. His eyes glowed red with anger.

Donovan peered around as if mapping an escape route. Gollum settled easily into the wingback chair closest to the fireplace and plunked his feet onto the matching ottoman. Just like I knew he would. I took the matching chair. That left Donovan with the sofa beneath the window that overlooked the side yard and a screening copse between the house and Old King Highway. He'd have to share it with Dill. Did he sense the ghost's presence? Why else would he press himself into the arm, occupying as small a space as possible.

"Want to talk about it?" Gollum asked casually, as if he were a psychologist and I his patient.

For all I knew, he might have a psychology degree among the long list of academic letters after his name.

I took a deep breath, closed my eyes, and told them everything from the moment WindScribe ran out of nowhere into the freezing street, stark naked. They didn't need to know about Dill. If they stayed long enough, I was sure they'd see his ghost eventually.

And the Windago? Not now. Later. I wasn't alone and vulnerable with these two around.

Donovan whistled through his teeth and shrank back as far as he could into the stiff cushions of the country style blue-and-cream sofa.

"What do you know?" Gollum pinned him with an accusing glare.

"That we don't want to wait for that burn permit." Donovan jumped to his feet and stalked back toward the kitchen. Dill followed close on his heels, as if tied to him in some way.

"Why?" I inserted myself in front of his broad frame. Too close. The heat of his emotions—anger, worry, and something else I couldn't identify—nearly swamped my senses. I gritted my teeth and held my ground.

"Because those garden gnomes are Orculli trolls. If we don't burn the bodies quickly, they'll reanimate and with twice as many teeth and less sense. You've also got to get some bleach into the spilled blood fast to keep it from reanimating on its own."

"And if we burn them?" Gollum had also regained his feet. He pushed his glasses back up his nose and focused his eyes on something beyond my shoulder.

A quick glance where he looked confirmed that he really gazed into another world, or deep inside himself, not on me or Donovan.

"If we do it right now, then the bodies and the spilled blood will remain dead." Donovan pushed me aside, grabbed his leather jacket from where he'd dropped it on my desk chair and a box of matches from the mantel and stalked back the way we'd come.

The phone on my big rolltop desk chirped. I cursed and thought about ignoring it.

"Better grab that. With all that's going on, you never know who it might be," Gollum advised quietly.

"Yeah?" I barked into the receiver.

"Teresa Louise, I'll forgive your rudeness this time, but only because I'm soooooo happy," my mother crooned in her light Québécois accent. She sounded excited. Soon she'd devolve into the bastard French she had made up out of childhood memories and called a pure language but wasn't much more than baby talk.

She didn't need much provocation.

"Mom?" This didn't sound like my mother, the control freak harpy who hadn't been happy a single day since Dad left her and their three children for Bill, the love of his life.

"Yes, Teresa, your mother. Your wonderfully ecstatic mother." She said something else in French that I couldn't catch. I speak, read, and understand Parisian French. Mom's dialect had little in common with it.

"Mom, what's going on?" I crossed my eyes and tried to picture my mother ecstatic, or anything but disapproving.

"I'm getting married!"

My knees gave out. I fumbled for the rolling office chair.

Gollum guided me. "Breathe, Tess," he whispered. "In on my count, one, two, three. Out, one, two, three. That's good. Again. Keep breathing."

"Who?" was all I could manage to ask. I waved Gollum off.

"The most beautiful man in the world, Tess. He's tall. He's dark. He's handsome. And he loves me!"

"When did this all happen, Mom?" She'd only been in Florida three weeks. I had visions of a Latino Lothario out to marry Mom for my money. I might not have a lot of cash on hand, but my royalty checks twice a year had started looking very pleasing. And I owned the house and land, which was worth a whole lot more than it was when Dill and I bought it.

"Time means nothing when you're in love, Teresa. You taught me that when you ran off and married Dillwyn."

That was a first. She usually refused to acknowledge that Dill and I had even legally married. Just because we ran off to Reno for a quick and private ceremony, the same weekend we met at High Desert Con, didn't make the union any less legal.

"Um, Mom, this doesn't sound like you."

"I've never been more me in my life!"

Now I really was worried. "When am I going to meet this man, Mom. You haven't even told me his name."

"Darren. His name is Darren Estevez. And we'll be there in an hour. Your sister Cecilia is driving us home from the airport in Providence now."

I gulped and jerked my head toward the kitchen, wishing I had a window through three rooms to the drive where *Donovan* Estevez lit a cleansing bonfire. *Donovan* Estevez who might be half demon.

"And I think you know Darren's son, Teresa. His son is Donovan Estevez. That casino owner you met back in Washington."

So what did that make his father? He couldn't be a full demon and take human shape in this dimension. He'd need to be in the chat room or his home dimension to do that. Maybe Donovan inherited his demonic tendencies from his mother. A mother very much out of the picture for Darren, Mom's fiancé.

Now I was totally confused.

Chapter 11

FRANTIC DOESN'T BEGIN to describe the next hour.

"New plan," I announced to the two men in front of the bonfire. "Donovan, you and your father get the guesthouse. Gollum, take the apartment. MoonFeather gets the sleeper sofa in the sitting room, Mom goes upstairs in the guest room next to me." I wanted my mother as far away from the demon contingent as possible.

If Darren had even a fraction of Donovan's charismatic charm, she was easy bait.

I already had WindScribe in the attic. I doubted the house was this full when it was a fully functional bed and breakfast.

Maybe if I charged them all rent . . .

"Won't your mom want to sleep with her fiancé?" Gollum asked, seemingly innocently. His glasses, firmly on the bridge of his nose for once, hid his true emotions. Then he flashed a goading grin toward Donovan.

"My mother is a French-Canadian-Catholic-June-Cleaver. She sleeps upstairs. Alone," I snarled. I seemed to be doing a lot of that lately.

Then Allie showed up with the burn permit. Sans the infant Mike in tow. She stepped out of her squad car and surveyed the landscape and the two men with the keen interest of both a woman and a good cop. Her beloved monster SUV was in the shop. She had to settle for a sedan with studded tires.

"Did you get the permit for me?" I asked anxiously. "And where's Mike?"

She pulled a folded piece of paper out of her inside jacket pocket as she approached, long legs eating up the distance at about twice my speed though she looked casual and unhurried. When she got within three feet of me, she carefully returned the permit to her pocket.

"Allie?"

"You promised to tell me what is going on, Tess. I left Mike doing paperwork, so feel free to tell me anything. *Anything.* Now would be a good time." She raised her eyebrows at the sight of the table and chairs, the curtains, and my parka on and around the bonfire. "That's good furniture to waste on a pagan religious rite. And I happen to know you are pretty agnostic if not downright atheist."

She gulped and her eyes went wide, fixed upon the splotches of blood on the chair cushions.

"Do I need to get a crime scene team out here and arrest somebody?" Her hands hovered over her radio and her weapon.

"Um . . . No more than you did this morning." I tried to signal with my eyes and my chin that I'd faced down alone the same unexplainable bad guys she'd seen before.

"And just what did happen this morning?"

"Um . . ."

Donovan fixed her with a feral grin. "This is what happened." He reached into the guts of the bonfire and delicately withdrew one of the Orculli trolls. He held it gingerly by the coat between his thumb and index finger, careful not to let any of the blood touch him.

"That's not a run-of-the-mill plastic garden gnome, is

it?" Allie gulped. She looked a little pale, as if she could no longer dismiss this morning as a nightmare that didn't really happen.

"Let's go inside and talk about this. . . ." I grabbed Allie by the elbow and tugged.

She planted her feet and hitched her utility belt.

"I've got to call someone with more authority. We have to alert the feds. There is a paranormal unit in the FBI even though they don't advertise it. They should already be on their way to investigate this WindScribe person." She grabbed her radio.

"Allison Marie Engstrom," Donovan said quietly. How the hell did he know her full name? "Look at me." He smiled that wicked grin of his.

Allie's face went slack, and her eyes glazed over.

"If word of this gets out," Donovan chanted, "people will panic. The roads are a mess. How will you safely evacuate the Cape if people can't drive? How will you explain this to normal God-fearing people? Think about the chaos and the danger if you tell anyone."

"I can't tell anyone," Allie agreed in a monotone. Her eyes glazed over. Her lips moved, but her voice seemed to come from Donovan.

"Now come inside and help me clean up while Donovan lights the fire." I tugged on Allie's arm, and she docilely followed me into the kitchen.

The moment we cleared the threshold and got out of range of Donovan's smile, Allie's face cleared. Panic filled the blankness. "Oh, my God! We have to stop him. We can't let him burn the evidence." She turned to dash out the door again.

A whoosh of rapidly heated air pressed against the windows. Flames exploded into life and hungrily ate at the bonfire.

Not a natural fire. More of Donovan's demon magic?

"Too late, Allie. He's already started the fire. The bodies are at the heart of that conflagration." Sure enough, an awful stench filled the air. I slammed the door closed once more.

Goddess, my heating bill was going to eat up most of the money the publisher owed me for turning in the book if people didn't stop coming and going, leaving the door open. And Donovan had pilfered most of my remaining woodpile. Could I get another cord of wood this late in the season?

"But . . . but . . ."

"No buts about it, Allie. We can't let this information past the door. Even to the FBI. I have to have your promise that you won't breathe a word of this to anyone." I stood solidly in front of the door, feet braced, hands on hips. I automatically shifted my weight, ready to launch myself into a wrestler's lunge to stop her if I had to.

Allie seemed to shrink in on herself. "This isn't right, Tess."

"You don't have any evidence anymore."

"I'd call the blood painting your kitchen evidence."

As she spoke, one of the splotches began to move, slithering into the rough outline of a gnome, complete with hat, coat, striped stockings and pointy shoes. And teeth. Lots and lots of teeth. They took shape before the rest of the face.

From one heartbeat to the next it took on three dimensions.

Heart in my mouth, I threw an entire basin of bleach at the thing. "Please, oh please, let this be enough. I don't have the energy to fight them again," I murmured.

The blood dissolved into a pink puddle. Was that a screech of a death rattle humming behind my ears?

I sank to the floor with a sigh of relief.

Allie stood there for a long moment, mouth agape, eyes wide and horrified. Then she swallowed heavily and regained a bit of composure. "So what do we do next? You know you can't exclude me. I'm part of this."

"The next step is to clean up this mess and con Zeb Falwell into letting me have that antique pine table in his showroom for a decent price, and deliver it within the hour. It's been sitting there for two years. He should be anxious to get rid of it. He's only three blocks away. Maybe Gollum can fetch it in his van."

As I filled the basin with fresh bleach water, I related the latest development with my mother. I didn't tell her that I assumed Darren Estevez was part Damiri demon.

"I can't believe Genevieve is really going to put the past behind her and marry again." Allie shook her head as she shed her jacket and donned rubber gloves.

"It will seem kind of strange for Mom not to have a reason to complain about Dad deserting her, leaving her dependent on her ungrateful children." Financially, she didn't have to be dependent. Dad paid gobs of alimony every month. He and I handled her bills. Emotionally, she had reverted to the age of thirteen.

Come to think about it, on the phone she sounded like a giddy adolescent with her first crush.

I handed Allie the basin and then dialed the local antiques emporium.

Somehow in the next hour we managed to get enough of the bonfire burned to disguise the fact that I'd trashed my own furniture, I conned the local antique dealer into delivering a plank table with six chairs for two thirds the asking price, stuffed Mom's clothes into the guest bedroom next to mine and installed Gollum in the apartment. Donovan unloaded his own gear into the cottage, grumbling all the while. I didn't catch his exact words but got the impression he wasn't happy about sharing digs with his dad. I also made up the sleeper sofa for MoonFeather even though she wasn't due to be discharged from the hospital until the next day.

WindScribe drifted downstairs three times, trailing her fingers along the wainscoting or pieces of furniture as if checking for dust.

I figured she was too wobbly to stand on her own two feet and was keeping something close at hand to catch herself. She continued to hum that white rabbit thing. A promise of more pills—that I never delivered—got her back into bed and out of the way.

"WindScribe—if she truly is the woman who disappeared twenty-eight years ago—her real name is Joyce Milner," Allie said after the first appearance of the girl. She poured lemon oil onto the faded and worn tabletop, rubbing it in with an aggressive stroke.

I sensed a lot of frustration in her work.

"Can we send her home to her parents?" I asked hopefully. "If you haven't noticed, my house is full to overflowing." I scrubbed the walls around the table, trying desperately to get out every trace of the dried blood. I'd have to run to the new discount store on the highway to find something resembling curtains, chair pads, and coordinating place mats and napkins. Nothing less would please my mother. Or me. I like a coordinated and well ordered kitchen when I'm not ignoring reality while on a tight deadline.

Speaking of which, I still had four chapters to finish editing.

"Presuming she really is Joyce Milner/WindScribe—we don't have any fingerprints or DNA samples in the cold case file, and we didn't get any hits on her prints on any of the networks. I've ordered a DNA test to match her against Milner's father. But that's going to take to the middle of next week, with the weekend coming up and the backlog. Dental records came up blank. Seems Milner's mother didn't believe in dentists." Allie shook her head and applied more of her considerable elbow grease to the table.

"Milner Dad is in a nursing home with Alzheimer's," she continued with grunted punctuation. "Milner Mom hasn't been heard from since she locked up her husband two years ago. Local opinion is that he's better off in the nursing home without her."

"That good a marriage?" I quipped. The particularly stubborn stain beneath the table must be Orculli troll blood rather than MoonFeather's. It was as big as my fist and *would not* come out. I could barely keep enough bleach on it to keep it from reanimating.

"We do have a medical record of WindScribe having

a broken arm at age ten. Possibly caused by the mom. They took a couple X rays this morning to rule out injury under her bruises. Our WindScribe has an old break in the same place. Little enough evidence to claim she is who she is, though."

"My wireless card isn't talking to your router," Gollum said from the doorway. He pushed up his glasses and peered appreciatively at Allie—who was still in uniform and officially supposed to be supervising the burn.

Something bitter twisted in my midsection.

"If it can't wait, then boot up my computer and get the protocols off it. It's not password protected," I snapped rather than deal with strange and unwanted emotions. "Is your cat locked in the apartment?"

"Of course. Gandalf is very well behaved."

"Like hell he is," I muttered.

He wandered off.

"So that's the new anthro prof at the community college," Allie breathed through her teeth. "Where did you find him? And why didn't you tell me about him?" She preened a bit, smoothing her uniform over her lush figure.

"He found me. And if you can drag his attention away from his books and the Internet, go for it, Allie." I redoubled my efforts with the scrub brush on the stain, not certain if I felt relief or anxiety at my last comment.

"He's so . . . tall," she said with a sigh and dumped more lemon oil into the pine. Tall was definitely a priority for Allie in her search for her soul mate. She had a hard enough time finding any men she liked and she could trust, who were not criminals or fellow cops. Allie did not mix her personal and professional life. Ever.

She'd told me once that she got to know her workmates too well and often saw the ugly and brutish side of them when handling lawbreakers. Dealing with scumbag criminals brought that side of her out too often, and she didn't want to have to live with it or be reminded of it during her precious free time.

"So, you want to tell me now what's going on?"

"My mom is returning home suddenly with a surprise fiancé."

"That's not what I mean. Like where WindScribe came from? Like why you are burning garden gnomes that came to life? Really ugly garden gnomes, not those cute things the garden club sells. And why your kitchen was smeared with enough blood to overload the blood bank?"

The blood that was still left must be MoonFeather's since it stayed in place.

"You don't want to know, Allie." I couldn't meet her gaze.

"But I do want to know. I have a right to know." Allie abandoned her polishing and hunkered down beside me. "I'm more than the local cop. I'm your best friend, Tess. There's a lot of strange in your life, I've seen some of it, and you need to talk about it."

"Trust me, Allison Engstrom, you do not want to be dragged into the strangeness that is my life now." This time I pierced her with a firm glare worthy of Miss Wilcox, our third-grade teacher.

"In case you haven't noticed, I am involved. I got you the emergency burn permit so you can destroy the evidence of weird bodies. I'm helping you scrub blood off the floor and walls. I *saw* WindScribe step through a doorway from . . . elsewhere. A woman who should be as old as your aunt but looks ten years younger than you or me. I watched you attack those gnomes with a really weird weapon that appeared and disappeared in an eye blink. So what's going on, Tess? Or do I have to take you down to the station?"

"This isn't a Saturday night brawl at McT's Bar and Grill."

"I'm a cop, Tess. Not much in this world scares me."

"This should. It isn't part of this world."

She sat back on her heels a moment, thumbs in her gun belt, thinking. "Okay. Shoot. I'll believe weird. Couldn't be much weirder than skinny little you tossing McT's bouncer over your shoulder last January when he got a little too fresh."

"That was balance and training, not supernatural."

"And the other stuff?"

"Read my books."

"I did."

"They're real."

"Not the post-apocalyptic world part, I'm guessing."

I kept my silence.

"The Sisterhood with the imps and enchanted blade weapons?"

Again I let silence speak for me.

"You one of them?"

I nodded.

"Of course you are. That's where you were during the year you went missing after Dill died. Okay. So how come you've got *two* luscious men drooling after you, and I don't have one?" She cocked me a grin and returned to her lemon oil and rags. But she was really looking out the window at Donovan and Gollum at the bonfire.

"I don't have two. And I'm not sure I want the one. He doesn't always tell the truth, and when I do get a few words out of him, it's only half what I asked." That could apply to either Gollum or Donovan.

"Look again, Tess. They're both in love with you. Let me know which one you really want and I'll take the other."

Before I could issue a sharp retort, gravel in the drive crunched under the heavy tires of my sister Cecilia's double cab pickup.

Chapter 12

The term "Honeymoon" comes from the custom of providing the bride and groom a moon's worth of mead, a honey wine, to ensure fertility.

EL STINKO DONOVAN doesn't smell like anything normal on this plane, if you can smell anything beyond his cloying cologne—too much is not better than nothing, dahling. So how can he and Darren be related, if they don't smell alike? Mom and Tess have smells of kinship. Cecilia belongs in the same circle. Tess and Cecilia have a similar bond with Moon-Feather. All born of common factors in their blood.

Darren, the dad, is part demon. I know it. I feel it in my bones and in my nose. My internal combustion engine pumps overtime and flashes me bright red. I want to witch myself into the Celestial Blade the moment he steps out of Cecilia's truck.

Cecilia likes the big tires and heavy engine truck so she can blow lesser vehicles off the road. It makes her feel like she is in control. Now, if she'd just gain control over her figure and her clothes, she wouldn't need to drive that phallic symbol. You'd think if she needed to make such a bold statement, she could pick a pretty color for the truck, like pink or basic black. That dirty mustard yellow makes her skin look so sallow she can't do anything with it.

She should have paid more attention to her mom.

Mom does classic so well, you'd think her daughters would have inherited *some* fashion sense.

Back to D & D. D the dad has the classic silver wings of hair at his temples, and the portly figure of a Damiri demon. His name begins with a D and ends with and N. He even has that extra flap of skin under his arms where he hides his batwings when he's in human form. The whiff of ultra dough I get from his titanium credit cards and the gold chain about his neck also tell me he has Damiri connections. They are all as rich as Bill Gates. They just don't advertise it.

At least he dresses well. I love that microfiber jacket. Looks like brushed silk, or maybe very fine suede in a lovely buff color. I'd forgotten how beautiful men can be. (purr) But his khaki slacks and pink-and-green-flowered shirt won't cut it in Cape Cod. Especially in this weather.

Donovan has decent fashion sense if you go for that brooding all black look. He's got the hair of a Damiri. He's got the name. But he's lean and fit and he doesn't have a trace of wings beneath his arms.

And he lost all his money last year when the casino imploded down a rogue demon portal.

▶▶▶

"What is that!" Mom exploded the moment her feet touched the gravel. She pointed over the kitchen door. She didn't even notice that the melting snow soaked her casual shoes, or that the wind must be cutting through her light sweater like a broadsword through leather armor.

I spun to see what strangeness had offended her. At least she hadn't pinned her attention on the bonfire.

A bleached white bone skull, bigger than a dead steer's in the desert, with spikes that would put a Texas longhorn to shame protruding from its head. Eight horseshoes ringed the skull, all with their open end pointing up so the luck wouldn't drain out.

It's your new gargoyle, Scrap whispered in my ear from the top of the chimney. The closest he could get to Donovan.

"Why, Mom, it's nice to see you, too." I gave her a hug and ushered her toward the door. "You must be freezing.

Come inside and get warm. We'll do introductions there. Your friend can unload the luggage. I've put him and his son in the guest cottage. You're bunking with me."

Good move, dahling. He can rest in his natural form out there. Keep him happier and less mean during the day. Scrap yawned, exposing three rows of teeth that rivaled those of the dead gnomes for sharpness and plentitude.

"Really, Genevieve, I knew your daughter was rebellious, but that pagan idol is too much." Darren shuddered and looked at the sky rather than the house. "I cannot enter such an ungodly house."

The gargoyle! Scrap chortled. *He can't enter the house. Scrap, what is it and where did it come from?*

I grabbed it from Mum's home in Imp Haven. You can find anything in the freeze-dry garbage dump of the universe.

He wiggled all over in delight.

"So they're demons," I muttered sotto voce.

"Did you say demons?" Mom asked. Her eyes narrowed and I could almost see her running calculations in her head. "I'd say that skull is demonic." She dug in her heels and refused to budge.

"It's just a resin sculpture, Mom. I picked it up at a con. And I said lemons, not demons. We need lemons for the fish sauce I'm planning for tomorrow night."

"Speaking of food, what are you planning on feeding this crew *tonight*?" Cecilia asked. A malicious gleam in her eyes told me she knew the state of my refrigerator. Empty.

"We can have pizza or Chinese delivered. That is unless you plan on cooking," I replied sweetly. I met my sister's gaze.

Pure malice poured from her. She was older than me and our brother Stephen, shorter than me by almost one half inch, and heavier by fifty pounds. She resented every breath I took, and had ever since I was born. Especially since I lost my extra poundage when I had the imp flu three years ago. Now I ate everything I wanted and didn't gain an ounce.

Staying thin was part of my revenge for the horrible

trick she played on me with a bat costume when I was three. She was the source of my phobia.

"Genevieve," Darren pointed to the dragon skull over the door.

"Tess, be a dear and take that horrible thing down."

I jerked my head and Donovan leaped to obey. Donovan? How could he touch the damn thing if his father couldn't even get close to it?

A memory of something back in the Citadel ...

Sister Gert had just said prayers for the newly repaired refectory roof. She'd invoked the powers of the dozens of copper gargoyles to keep out all those who harbored evil in their hearts.

Before I could remember what had happened next, Donovan climbed onto an overturned half barrel that had once held potting soil and tulips. His long arms reached the skull easily. "I'll just put this somewhere safe," he muttered after he had lifted it free of its supporting hook.

"Like over the old staircase?" I quipped. That ought to keep Darren out of my mother's bedroom. So how did I keep her out of his?

"You really should consider your obligations as hostess, Tess," Cecilia admonished me as we trooped inside. She already had her head in the refrigerator and half the cupboards open. They really were empty.

"Actually, I'd planned to take Tess out to dinner tonight," Donovan jumped into the conversation. "Since you didn't give us any warning, I'm sure you can fend for yourselves."

"I'm sure I told you I was coming when I called you last night, D," Darren said. He clapped his son on the back hard enough to make Donovan stumble.

"No, you didn't," Donovan growled. "I thought I had Cape Cod to myself."

"Why don't Allie and Gollum come with us?" I returned Donovan's smile, trying to hide my grimace and my questions at his last comment.

Scrap said that Donovan's father reeked of demon

scent. Therefore, Donovan must also be a demon. I couldn't trust him alone. I'd seen what demons—even half-blood demons—did when their natures overcame the thin gloss of civilization a human form gave them. So why did my insides still turn to liquid and my skin tingle in anticipation of his touch?

I needed a buffer between us. I also needed a breather from my mother. Why not do a little match-making between Allie and Gollum on the side?

But that would leave Mom alone with Darren. Presumably, she'd been alone with him down in Florida.

I gnashed my teeth in indecision.

He won't hurt Mom yet, Scrap whispered from the far reaches of the house. *He wants something, so he can't dispose of her until he gets it.*

I really didn't like the idea of any of us being disposable.

"But if you all aren't here, it will spoil our surprise," Mom whined. "I want the whole family together tonight."

The crowd had stalled in the kitchen. Like they always did. It was usually the most inviting room in the house. But I couldn't get beyond the stench of bleach and blood; the image of an Orculli troll taking a hunk out of MoonFeather; the crunch of breaking bones as I impaled one of the beasts with my Celestial Blade.

"Dinner sounds good to me. Pick me up at six-thirty," Allie called as she hastily exited. She'd disposed of the evidence of our speedy cleanup. "Much as I'd love to stay and watch the fireworks, I've got to file some reports and clock out at the station." She waved jauntily and closed the door firmly behind her. Leaving me alone with my family and assorted extras.

"Surprise isn't always good, Mom. Tomorrow we'll invite Dad and Bill and Cecilia and Jim and their kids to come, too, make a big celebration of it. MoonFeather will be here, too. She's been hurt. I offered to take care of her before I knew you were coming home."

We settled around the new table with coffee and

some stale cookies I found in the freezer and hastily nuked. Mom and Darren scooted their chairs so close together they might have been made from the same boards. They held hands atop the table and rubbed thighs beneath it.

"We met at a dance in Cousin Clothilde's condo on the beach," Mom gushed.

"She was the prettiest woman in the room. I couldn't look at anyone else," Darren picked up the story. He spoke with a faint accent that I couldn't place. It might have been Spanish, from Spain with the Hapsburg lisp not generic Mexican, but I couldn't place it exactly.

I watched Gollum mouth the words, a puzzled look on his face as he, too, tried to place the accent. Professor Guilford Van der Hoyden-Smythe spoke four or five living languages and read a couple of dead ones. He claimed he could learn an American Indian dialect in six weeks. He also claimed that his family had studied and archived demons for generations. Surely he'd find the origins of that accent if anyone could. Any human, that is.

"It was love at first sight," Mom sighed.

"True love, everlasting love," Darren echoed.

I'd known that kind of love. With Dill. How could I fault Mom for falling head over heels for such a charming man?

A demon. I had to remind myself. Darren was a demon. And he was using my mother.

Donovan smiled at me, and I grew hot all over. That was his magic. He could calm a riot with that smile. I'd seen him do it. He'd lulled Allie's cop instincts and suspicions. He could also make a woman fall in love with him.

The only time I could resist him was when I wore a magical hair comb Scrap had given me. It allowed me to see through demon glamour to the man beneath. Except with Donovan I saw only a man, no demon hiding beneath the surface. I'd never figured out his strange aura though: an inviting golden glow laced with a tight black chain. Darkness and light. Good and evil.

Most people had both elements in their souls.

"Mom, I have an engagement present for you. I want you to wear it on your wedding day." I kissed the top of her head as I retreated to my bedroom where I'd stashed the comb. Right now, Mom needed it more than me.

The best offense was a good defense. Mom needed all the help she could get defending herself from that man . . . demon.

A quick check on WindScribe showed her dreaming happily in her bed. With the vial of tranquilizers beside her.

Damn. I knew I should have flushed them. But right now, having this extra guest sound asleep seemed advantageous. I pocketed the tranquilizers.

When I returned to the kitchen, I paused a moment in the narrow entry from the butler's pantry. Curious, I gathered up my mop of sandy-blonde curls and jammed the comb into them.

Instantly colors shifted and intensified. My balance tilted as well. When the moment of disorientation cleared, I peered closely at Darren and Donovan. As I expected, Darren assumed an aura with a bat's sharp features and furred face overlaying his handsome human countenance.

Now that I knew for sure, I had to stop this marriage. One way or another, even if I had to kill Darren. In open battle or by stealth.

Donovan remained enigmatic. I could see layers of energy radiating out from him, red and orange swirling together in an angry mix above the gold and black I'd seen before. At no point did his aura touch Darren's. Indeed, they seemed to repulse each other.

On the other hand, Mom and Cecilia seemed joined. Their energies reached out to each other in a blood bond. They also included me. No matter our likes and dislikes, the baggage of sibling rivalries and parent child differences, we were family.

Darren and Donovan were not related.

But I still couldn't figure out who or what drove Donovan.

>>>

"How sweet of you, Teresa Louise," Mom gushed as I fitted the comb into her French roll. Her hair was thinning and quite straight, as was Cecilia's, but she insisted a lady always kept her hair long and wore it up. My mop of tight curls tended to tangle and frizz if I let it get too long. Mom'd look ten years younger if she cut hers properly and let it frame her face.

I tried to be gentle with the metal tines, but still Mom grimaced as the comb took hold. I'd experienced the same thing the first few times I wore it. The comb grabbed hold of more than just hair.

Darren clenched his fists tight. He looked as if he was about to launch himself over the table to strangle me.

Come and get me, big boy. I've taken out more hideous critters than you.

Donovan just grinned.

"There now, that looks lovely, Mom," I said as I settled in my chair with my cold cup of coffee.

"It's going to take some getting used to," Mom said. She tugged the magical artifact free of her hair, keeping her eyes closed.

Damn!

"But it will look nice supporting a veil. I do so want a traditional wedding gown and veil." She sighed and placed both her hands on Darren's. "Will you mind terribly, *cheri,* if we wait a few weeks to book the church and send invitations?"

"Not too long, *querida,*" Darren murmured. "My love burns with impatience." He leaned over to kiss her. Their lips met in an explosion of passion. Arms around each other, they lingered and tongued, and explored.

I had to look away in embarrassment. Even Cecilia had the grace to blush. An unnatural silence descended upon the table as that kiss went on and on. Well beyond the bounds of propriety.

Anyone else and I'd have told them to get a room.

The comb sat on the table in front of Mom. The gold filigree sparkled in the reflected light from the hanging milk glass lamp. I stared at it mesmerized, even after Mom and Darren broke their teenage-style clinch.

The conversation resumed and flowed around me, I continued to study the tiny gold flowers interlaced with Celtic knotwork on the comb. I picked out stylized symbols from an assortment of cultures: Russian, Irish, French, Italian, Jewish, Arabian, and even an Aztec feathered something. In my perusal, I noticed a blank spot with a few rough edges. An important piece had broken off.

What? Possibly whatever was missing kept me from identifying Donovan.

Scrap and I needed to talk. But Scrap wouldn't, or couldn't, come near me when Donovan was in the room.

If Darren's demonhood ever overrode Donovan's barriers, I wanted to save it for a real fight.

Tonight I'd leave Scrap to keep an eye on Mom and Darren, WindScribe, too, while I went to dinner with Donovan, Gollum, and Allie.

Chapter 13

"THE SUMMER I GRADUATED from high school, Dad and Bill took me and my brother Steph to England. I loved the gargoyles on the cathedrals. Much to my dismay, no one would let me climb onto the roofs to examine them more closely," I explained to Gollum.

I held the dragon skull. He measured the support beam across the old stairs. The steps rose so steeply that even I had to duck beneath the upper story where it cut across them. Gollum had no problem reaching the beam with tape measure and marking pencil.

"Have you ever heard gargoyles gargle?" he asked in all seriousness.

"Actually, I have heard gargoyles gargle," I replied, handing him a hammer and the hook to hang my new treasure.

A blur of white movement behind and below me. Gollum's cat, Gandalf, had got loose. As long as Scrap didn't complain, I'd leave the beast free for a while. At the moment Scrap was busy playing voyeur on Mom and Darren while they ordered pizza in the kitchen. Donovan had retreated to the cottage across the yard with a scowl on his face and his fists clenched like sledgehammers.

"The term gargoyle comes from the Medieval French *gargouiller,* to gargle." He pronounced the long word melodiously.

I'd read it but never heard it before. "Because of the sound they make when rainwater funnels through them, as they drain it from roofs and spit it out in arcs to the ground below," I completed the lecture for him. "Their primary purpose is a kind of decorative gutter and downspout. The idea of using grotesqueries to repel evil came later."

He looked at me strangely. Then a big grin spread across his face. "A woman after my own heart," he sighed. "I heard them during an autumnal thunderstorm in Notre Dame de Paris. I have friends. Next time you go to Europe, I'll see about getting you a pass to explore the gargoyles more thoroughly."

"I heard them at the Citadel. The refectory roof had copper gargoyles. But one of them was broken. I noticed the tracery of a wing left behind when I helped repair the roof. It might have been a bat."

"Bats are a quite common form of gargoyle. Your phobia against bats has roots in ancient times." Gollum actually stopped speaking for a few moments while he hammered the hook in place. "Did you know that the Native American totem pole can be considered a form of gargoyle?"

"Actually the totemic animals are more clan symbols than wards against evil."

I handed him the dragon skull. Then a bit of mischief lightened my mind. "The gargoyles at the Citadel did have apotropaic qualities. Sister Gert invoked them to repel all those who held evil in their hearts and darkness in their souls."

That was it. That was the memory that had eluded me. When I tried to enter the refectory after the prayers of dedication, Scrap disappeared for a time. I remembered thinking I'd heard something splash in the puddle directly behind me. But it could have been anyone. In the middle of the prayers a thunderstorm had hit and the gargoyles did their job of channeling the runoff out and away from those of us huddled under the eaves. Except where the broken bat had been. Water cascaded straight down on top of Sister Gert's head.

"If you know that word, I'll have to challenge you to a game of Scrabble later," Gollum said. He kept his eyes focused on getting the dragon straight and keeping it from drooping any lower than the already low support beam.

"If you know that word, you'll have to join us for family game night. We play cut-throat Trivial Pursuit every Sunday."

"It's a date. Um . . . I mean . . ." he blushed.

"Don't worry. I know what you mean."

We'd decided to put the dragon head in the corner where it was shadowed. Mom wouldn't be as likely to notice it there.

"Do you think this gargoyle will really keep Darren from sneaking up the stairs?" I asked, admiring the stately proportions of the thing.

"It should. Given its position, on the main support beam of the original 1753 house, it might also keep him from doing harm to any human inside the entire house."

"Let's hope so."

"Interesting that Donovan had no trouble holding it," Gollum mused. He stepped down six steps to admire his handiwork. That put him two steps below me and close to my eye level.

"What is Donovan? Scrap says he's not a demon, but Darren is."

"Not one of the usual suspects. I'll put some feelers out into the community, see if my colleagues have any ideas."

"There's more than one of you? I thought the archivists who follow a rogue Celestial Warrior were rare."

"We are. As rare as you. But that number is increas-

ing, or so I'm told. More and more rogue portals have
cropped up in the last fifty years. The Warriors of the
Celestial Blade have to spread out to cover them. Iso-
lated Citadels aren't enough." He covered the intensity
in his gaze by pushing up his glasses. "That aside, there
are always scholars interested in obscure tales and legends though. I know most of them. My grandfather
knows more. We'll find out what Donovan is whether he
wants us to or not."

"Darren is not my father," Donovan growled. We sat in
the front seats of Mom's car while Gollum escorted
Allie from her apartment.

"I know," I replied, keeping my eyes straight ahead.

"How?"

I turned an enigmatic smile on him. Let him wonder
about the powers of a Warrior of the Celestial Blade. At
least I'd managed to change into tailored slacks and the
new teal V-neck sweater Dad had given me for Christmas. Paired with the lavender silk turtleneck that Scrap
recommended I presented a less scruffy image of a true
warrior than usual.

Of course, a down parka over it all kind of marred the
image.

But then we were all bundled up to combat the
weather. So far it was all natural weather. The Windago
hadn't shown up. Maybe she wanted me alone. Or whatever kept Scrap away from Donovan, also kept the
Windago at bay.

"So if you aren't Darren's son, what are you?"

"I . . . was orphaned. As a teen. Darren took me in."

Too many pauses in there. Maybe the truth. But not
all of it.

"So who was your father?"

"Don't know."

"Your mother?"

He rattled off a long string of liquid syllables. I didn't
recognize the language.

"And that translates as . . ."

"No translation available. Her tribe has been absorbed by the Okanogan peoples. Just a few words of the original language exist."

"I thought you had Sanpoil Indian in you. They're part of the Colville Confederation, not Okanogan."

He didn't answer.

Gollum and Allie emerged from the apartment building's exterior stairwell onto the parking lot. They were laughing. He took her arm to steady her on the ice. The temperature had actually reached thirty-six this afternoon, melting a little snow, but quickly refreezing and becoming treacherous as soon as the sun went down.

Allie and Gollum laughed at something. She leaned closer to him, almost resting her head on his shoulder. He didn't react to her attempted affection. But he didn't push her away either.

Something inside me twisted at the easy way my two friends seemed to fit together.

"The Orculli trolls won't give up, Tess. Everyone in your house is in danger. What are you going to do about your mother?" Donovan changed the subject.

"What are *you* going to do about your father?"

"Actually, the garden gnomes are after WindScibe, not Genevieve," Gollum said, handing Allie into the backseat. He gave my mother's name the proper French pronunciation, *Jahn-vee-ev* with the soft G. "Between the new gargoyle and the wards I set, I don't think they'll hit the house tonight."

Maybe they'd keep the Windago away. Forever.

"What makes you think that?" Donovan asked, immediately defensive.

"Because there is a strange sort of twisted honor among demons on a mission. And these guys sound like they are on a mission. Tess is the vowed protector. The Orculli will honor that and wait until Tess is there to defend the girl before taking her. We have until tomorrow." Gollum climbed into the car and closed the door on the weather and the subject.

A fat waxing moon three days off of full broke through the cloud cover, promising an even colder night.

Well past the waxing quarter moon when the Goddess Kynthia was wont to show her face in the sky in warning. I'd seen it twice. Special moments when I felt connected to the entire universe. A demon attack had followed immediately after. Both times.

Somehow, I didn't think the Orculli were limited to moon phases for their entry and exit from this realm. They might not even need the chat room.

"When they come, they won't be frightened off by a few whacks from your blade, Tess," Donovan warned. "We need a plan."

"We need fire," Gollum added.

"We need barricades and AK47s," Allie grumbled.

"Not enough," I mused. "We need the most elusive defense of all. Information and logic. We have to know why they want WindScribe and what we can do to counter their motives."

►►►

So Darren the demon and Mom take over the sitting room, smooching and cuddling in front of the fire.

I assume my usual perch on the spider, swinging in time to the lilting waltz playing on the stereo. Show tunes. Stories and good music all rolled into one. What more can you ask for? I love them. So does Mom. That's one reason we get along so well, though she doesn't know I'm here.

Tess' taste runs to filk, New Age, and Celtic. Not bad. But nothing beats a show tune.

"I don't want to wait to make you mine, *ma petite chou chou,*" Darren whispers as he nuzzles Mom's neck.

I'll never figure out why the French think it's romantic to call each other little cabbages. Mom eats it up as if it was candy, practically purring like that wicked cat Gollum keeps in his rooms.

"I didn't get a church wedding the first time around," Mom pouts.

Liar, liar, pants on fire. Oops, that's my tail on fire. I jump down to the hearth and beat my poor mangled appendage against the hearth. A few embers fly free and die on the bricks.

Tess says Mom burned all her wedding photos when Dad walked out with Bill. Tess remembers seeing photos of a lavish wedding with lots of heavy white satin and banks of red-and-white flowers. They got married on Valentine's Day.

I'm pushing for April Fool's Day for this wedding.

"I will wait, if that is what makes you happy," Darren sighs as if he's making a huge sacrifice.

Mom soothes him by running a delicate finger along his cheek. Is that a hint of red in the glaze that comes over her eyes? She blinks and it's gone.

"Being married in the church with a priest officiating is very important to me. It makes the entire thing more real, a sacred bond."

Is that a shudder I detect running through Darren? Oh, my, I think he's afraid to step foot inside a church, sacred ground and all. Doesn't bother me. But then I'm not a demon, though my past isn't lily white. Just ask my one hundred two siblings. Darren is part demon, and I sense his past is darker than mine. That takes some doing.

"We could drive to Maine and get married tonight. I know a city clerk who can do the paperwork after hours and a lawyer who can perform the marriage. Any officer of the court can do that in Maine. Then we can have the priest bless the marriage later. Perhaps here in this beautiful old house," Darren said. A smile lit his face like he'd just thought up this brilliant idea.

Yeah, right. The conniving bastard's worse than a Barrister demon.

"But . . .?" Mom has to think about that one.

From the flush on her face and the way her hands keep wandering down his torso, she doesn't want to wait for the wedding night either.

I've got to stop this. Right now. Before Mom actually brings a demon into the family. If only I could force him to transform in front of her. But he's an old demon, well in control of his urges and his form.

What to do? What to do?

I know, I can let the cat loose. Gandalf will hiss and snarl at Darren. He doesn't like demons any more than I do.

Chapter 14

The oldest ring of holes at Stonehenge may have been used to mark the nineteen year cycle of lunar eclipses.

"AS WORRIED AS I AM about the Orculli returning and taking a hunk out of our flesh," Gollum said, resting his elbows on the round table in the corner of Guiseppe's Restaurant, "we also have to do something to prevent the impending marriage." He pushed his glasses up onto the bridge of his nose and blinked rapidly.

I knew that gesture. The eye blinks were his way of recalling something he'd read. I think he sort of replayed a videotape in his brain.

"Waiting for the church and the priest will delay it until we deal with the garden gnomes," I replied.

"But aren't your parents divorced? Will the priest even allow your mother to remarry in the church?" Donovan jumped into the conversation. He and Gollum sat on opposite sides, as far away from each other as they could get and maintain this temporary truce.

"Mom had the marriage annulled in Rome. Seems that since Dad turned out to be gay, his marriage to Mom wasn't a real marriage after all," I replied studying the menu rather than look too closely at Donovan and be lost in his eyes and his smile. Without the comb to strip away some of the glamour of humanity, I could fall into his arms and his bed all too easily.

From the look on Allie's face, she wanted to fall into Gollum's bed. She just needed to find some way to let him know. But he was concentrating on the problem at hand. None of us mattered while he did that.

"Speaking of gay men," Allie whispered and jerked her head to the left toward the entrance.

Sure enough, Dad and Bill waited for the hostess to seat them. I waved to them.

Dad wandered over, leaving Bill to deal with the hostess. Bill was better with people than Dad. Dad prefers things he can reduce to a column of numbers with debits and credits. People outside his circle of family and a few close friends have too many variables for his taste. Even so, he manages to put on a polite and friendly, if baffled, face in front of strangers.

He gave me a hug, and I introduced him. He shook hands like a polite little puppet. Then he surprised me beyond measure. "Aren't you the friends who helped rescue my little girl from those terrorist kidnappers last fall?" He pulled up a chair from the adjoining table and sat between me and Donovan.

"Uh, yes," Gollum replied, trying to be truthful.

Actually I'd rescued myself and a Native American girl from tribal mythology come to life. But if we told the truth, we'd have to explain the unexplainable in Dad's black-and-white world of numbers that have to add up.

"Well, I want to thank you both for bringing my baby back safe and sound." Dad reached across the table and shook first Gollum's hand, then Donovan's.

We sat and made polite chitchat, wondering if the weather would break in time for an upcoming tennis tournament. Then Dad stood up and planted a kiss on top of my head. "Have a good dinner and try to stay out of trouble."

"Oh, uh, Dad, some family matters have cropped up that require your attention," I mumbled.

"You mean about your mother remarrying?"

"Cecilia called you," I replied flatly.

"Yes. She wanted to upset me. I refused to play her game. If your mother can find happiness with another man, more power to her. I certainly did." He turned a fond gaze upon Bill, a wiry Asian man who kept fit as the tennis pro at the country club. His boundless energy pushed Dad to stay on his toes and active, even after sixteen years together. "Maybe the wedding will give Steph a chance to come home."

"Maybe," I hedged. My brother had split to Illinois the day after he graduated from college and only came home once a year if he had to. I talked to him on the phone every week and I saw him every time I was in the area. He talked to Mom and Dad less often. A lot less often.

"If Genevieve remarries, I don't have to fork out alimony every month," Dad half laughed. "Might think about retiring."

From what I understood of their relationship, Dad didn't mind supporting Mom. He did love Mom and us. He just couldn't live the straight life with the narrow world view dictated by Mom's church.

We exchanged a few more pleasantries before he rejoined Bill at a table on the opposite side of the dim restaurant.

"One major hurdle behind us." I breathed a sigh of relief.

"Might be easier to postpone the wedding if he did object," Donovan growled.

"Why do we have to stop the marriage?" Allie asked. "If Genevieve is happy . . ."

"Darren is half Damiri demon," I hissed at her.

Her eyes widened in wonder. Then she turned a frightened gaze upon Donovan. "What does that mean?"

"It means that he sleeps hanging by his feet with his wings wrapped around him," Donovan replied. "He drinks pig and cow blood instead of milk."

I sensed the anger rising in him before his face flushed and his fists clenched.

"And I'm not one of them," he insisted.

But you are something. Something strange and wonderful and ever so scary, I thought.

"Darren Estevez gave me his name and an education after he manipulated ... made a patsy of me. But that is all he gave me."

"Is he like a vampire bat?" Allie persisted in her questioning.

"Bats aren't truly vampires," I said, as much to convince myself as her.

"The Damiri were among the first of the demon tribes to infiltrate humanity," Gollum jumped in. He put on his professor face.

I prepared to sit back and let him ramble on.

"Besides their need for blood for sustenance—they prefer human but will resort to animals if they can't get it—they are extremely long lived. I remember reading that they can adapt to daylight, but they are normally nocturnal."

"Could these Damiri demons be the origins of the vampire legends?" Allie asked, clearly fascinated by the topic. Or by Gollum.

A primal response deep inside me wanted to growl at her.

I took a sip of wine instead. "Allie has read every vampire book printed," I said quietly.

"Pity there is no such thing as vampires," Gollum took off his glasses and polished them on his napkin. "No one comes back from the dead."

Tell that to Dill, I thought.

"One thing the legends are consistent on is the vampire's ability to mesmerize its prey. And there is frequently a sexual aspect to the exchange of blood." Allie settled back to discuss her favorite topic in depth. She couldn't understand why I wouldn't write about vampires.

I found nothing sexy about bleeding or giving over total control of my mind and body to another. Like I almost had with Dill.

Did I really love him? More and more I resented him.

Resented his haunting me, resented him dying. Resented . . . too much.

Still the gaping hole of loneliness in my gut that he'd created by dying gnawed at me. I couldn't move on while he haunted me. Maybe that's why I held Donovan at arm's length.

I still didn't trust him.

"Damiri have that hypnotic ability," Donovan said quietly. "It would explain the love-at-first-sight aspect of Genevieve and Darren's romance."

"Is Genevieve in danger from your . . . er . . . foster father?" Gollum asked.

"I don't know.

"Of course she's in danger!" I insisted. "The question is: how is he going to use her before he disposes of her?" I borrowed the phrase from Scrap.

"I don't even know why he's here." Donovan shrugged his shoulders.

"He's after me." I began to shake. "He's the latest in a pack of demons that are hunting me. I'm a rogue, outside the protection of my Sisterhood or a Citadel. I'm vulnerable. But, I'm also outside the hidebound rules of the Citadel, and therefore unpredictable, a serious danger to them all."

"And you are a danger to the demons who are living among us. A lot of them are just trying to get by, settle in to a human lifestyle."

"Until their craving for blood overcomes their human gloss and they kill," I reminded him.

"You're the only one around who can defeat them in open battle." Donovan moved closer, as if to put his arm around me.

I told them about the Windago.

Gollum whistled through his teeth.

Donovan sat up straighter, worry creasing his brow and around his eyes.

I held myself stiff and aloof, distracted by a flurry of activity near the entrance. Flashes of vivid red and bright green darted around people's ankles.

Chapter 15

The Masons who laid the cornerstone of the Washington Monument in Washington, D.C., chose the date July 4, 1848 because the moon went into Virgo at noon of that day.

"**D**ONOVAN, I WANT you to finish your dinner and then take Allie home in a taxi. Quickly."

By the pricking of my thumbs, something wicked this way comes. Actually it was a tingle at the base of my spine.

"Tess . . ." Allie and Donovan protested at the same time.

"I'll take her home," Gollum said.

"Don't argue with me. I know what's best." I fixed them all with a glare that had been known to quell a classroom full of rowdy seventh graders.

"Scrap can't come near me with Donovan around. I'm going to need Scrap very soon."

"What?" Gollum asked. He stretched casually, using the gesture to look around the crowded restaurant. Tall plants and a scattered seating arrangement gave the illusion of privacy. It also blocked a clear view of the enemy.

From my place in the corner, with my back to the wall, I had a better line of sight to the hostess podium at the entrance.

"From ghosties and ghoulies and long legged beasties, and things that go bump in the night, good Lord deliver us," I quoted an old Scottish prayer attributed to Robert Burns but really much, much older. I must be nervous if I started spouting literary citations. "Ankle biters hiding in the shrubbery at your seven o'clock."

"Those are just statues," Allie protested. But there was a note of question in her voice.

"Not statues. Just very good at holding still as stone when someone is looking. Now get out of here."

"You'll need help." Allie set her shoulders stubbornly. She reached for her capacious purse. Allison Engstrom always carried a weapon, on and off duty.

"Allie, I need to know that my best friend is safe." I grabbed her hand and pleaded with her through my eyes. "Please let Donovan take you out of danger. Conventional weapons and tactics won't faze these guys. Leave them to me. Please. I know what I'm doing."

"I'm armed." She patted her purse. No room for a shoulder holster beneath her good tweed blazer.

"Won't do any good. You know that bullets bounce off them. You tried that already."

"Are the bullets silver?" Gollum asked. His raised eyebrows almost hiked his glasses up onto the bridge of his nose.

"Plain old lead."

"Won't do any good," I repeated. "I've seen a man shoot a dozen demons with a military automatic weapon." That man was Donovan, and he might have been aiming over their heads to make them take dives. Then, again, maybe he had been aiming for their hearts knowing the bullets wouldn't penetrate demon skin, even in human form.

Donovan had the grace to blanch.

"The bullets just bounced off demon hides," I continued. "I tried slicing these garden gnomes with the Celestial Blade, which is sharper than any mortal-made razor. They used the curved blades as a swing. I had to pierce them with the tines."

Gollum whipped out his PDA and started taking notes.

"Donovan, take Allie home and keep her safe. I'll call if we need reinforcements back home."

Donovan reached for his wallet. I stayed his hand. "I'll take care of it. Just get Allie out of here and keep her safe. I trust you to do that." I fixed him with a look that brooked no defiance.

"You can trust me, Tess."

I kept my mouth shut.

"At least let me leave the tip." He tucked a ten under his water glass, flowed to his feet, and held Allie's chair for her.

While he was occupied helping my friend into her parka, I slipped a twenty into his pocket for the taxi. I didn't know just how strained his finances were and I could afford to help a little.

He reached into his pocket and took out the bill. Without really looking at it, he pressed it back into my hand. "I may not be wealthy anymore, but I'm not broke." He bristled with affronted pride.

They left without looking back.

I didn't take the time to breathe a sigh of relief.

"Scrap, you around?" I whispered into the air.

I am now, babe. Now that you've ditched El Stinko lover boy. My imp settled onto my shoulder. His skin took on a pink cast as he surveyed the remains of our dinners. *You could have left me something,* he wailed. *I'm wasting away to nothing and you didn't even order me a beer.*

"Can the crap, Scrap. Keep an eye on the Orculli hiding in the shrubs."

"So what's the plan?" Gollum asked, all business. He hadn't even looked twice at Allie when she left with another man.

Part of me sighed in relief.

"Plan? You don't have a plan?"

"I'm just the archivist. I research. You fight. That's the plan."

I snorted something disgusting and waved the waiter

over for the check. Gollum paid out of a thick wad of bills he always seemed to have hidden somewhere on his person without obvious sign of a bulge.

"More of the archivist's trust fund?" I asked. Gollum's family had a history of working with rogue Warriors of the Celestial Blade, male and female. When they were on duty, they had access to a seemingly limitless bank account.

"Moving money and apartment deposit that I won't need now. I'll reopen the trust tomorrow after I check in at the college."

"Provided we survive the trip across the parking lot." As we moved toward the exit, with studied good-byes to Dad and Bill and a few patrons and staff, I caught flashes of bright colors around the edges of my vision.

"I really don't want to fight these guys on ice with an arctic wind blowing."

You don't? I'm the one with a bare tushie hanging out. I could lose a wart to frostbite.

"Nice to have you back, Scrap." I suddenly felt more complete, more confident, ready to tackle this world and several others. "Stay behind me, Gollum."

We made our way across the parking lot with an escort that kept a six-foot circle around us. One cute little guy in blue and yellow—almost surreal colors in their brightness—strayed inside that perimeter. Scrap growled and bared his teeth. He had almost as many as the bad guys. The gnome jumped back to his place, eyes wide and frightened.

Okay, so they respected the Celestial Blade. What else could I fight them with? Flattening them with a frying pan barely set them back. But if I spilled their blood and didn't burn the bodies, they'd reanimate. What would work?

Fire.

"Scrap, can you light a little fire?"

Sure, babe. What's up? A tiny flamelette appeared at the end of his finger.

"Point it at the bad guys."

The gnomes scuttled backward, giving me a wider circle to work in.

Mom's car sat beneath a light—no shadows for the Windago to hide in.

The little king of the Orculli trolls perched on the hood of the vehicle, the gilded braid perfectly straight on his sagging pointed cap. Bright gold buttons also gleamed on his red-and-green tunic. He held a miniature white flag on a chopstick.

An honor guard of three in green stood behind him, arms crossed and elongated chins jutting aggressively.

I stopped at the rear door, finger poised on the unlock button on the key chain. "You mind getting off my car?" I glared at the pushy troll.

"I request parley," he said, as arrogant as ever.

"Talk to him," Gollum whispered in my ear. I hadn't realized how close he had come to me. The warmth of his long body against my back reassured me.

"What do you want?" I extended my left hand, palm up. Scrap jumped onto it, skin turning redder than the fire that bounced from pudgy fingertip to palm and back again. He stretched and thinned, halfway into a transformation.

The king jumped to his feet and scrambled to the center of the car hood.

"Call off your imp," he demanded.

"Answer my question first."

"The girl. The one you call WindScribe." The king's voice sounded a little squeaky to my ears, without the resonant tones of the otherworlds.

"Not an option. She's under my protection."

"Then we are at war."

"Sorry, I've already got a war with a Windago Widow." There was that title again that demanded attention. A scrap of an idea whistled around my brain louder than a Windago generated wind.

"My mission takes priority over Windago revenge. You will deal with me first and if you survive, then you are at the mercy of Lilia David. Choose the time and place for our battle."

I raised an eyebrow at that.

"Noon, three days hence," Gollum hissed.

"Why?"

"Just do it. I'll explain later."

"Okay. Noon."

The king winced.

"Three days hence." On the day of the full moon.

He nearly gagged. "So be it." The entire troop disappeared in a poof of displaced air.

Now what have we got ourselves into, dahling? I sure hope Gollum pulls some magic out of his computer and lets me know. I can stab these guys and kill them, but there are so many of them, Tess and I just might wilt in the middle of the fight. I can hold a tiny bit of flame in my hand, enough to light a cigar. Not enough to wipe out this herd.

We need help.

But not from Donovan.

I'm sure if I just knew what he was, then I could overcome the barrier that keeps me away from my babe when he is near. He's like imp's bane, but I don't get tiddly from him. He's more like a lock on a dimensional portal.

But locks are just puzzles if you know the key.

Hmm . . . this will take some thought.

And I don't have enough time to do any research!

But time is just another dimension and can be manipulated by those who know how.

When I got home, I tiptoed up the stairs so as not to disturb Mom and Darren in the parlor. They were curled up like two puppies, arms and legs tangled, almost indistinguishable from each other.

I knew my mom. She wouldn't do anything stupid, like sleep with the guy. He might be half demon with a talent for mesmerizing his prey, but my mother was an old school French-Canadian Catholic. I'd bet her church upbringing against his seduction any day.

WindScribe sat cross-legged on her bed, playing cat's cradle with a piece of decorative braid from my sewing bin. I cursed. That bit of brocaded ribbon had cost several bucks a yard!

"Good night," she called to me cheerily. Her eyes still looked glassy, her expression dreamy.

I dashed downstairs to check on the vials of tranquilizers. Damn. One vial was all aspirin, the other still sealed. I flushed the lot.

As an afterthought I locked the now empty vials inside my rolltop desk and pocketed the key. I'd be interested if my guest managed to find them.

Mom and Darren didn't even acknowledge me standing in the doorway.

Fuming at life in general and the host of predatory guests that had landed in my lap, I slammed back into the kitchen. I needed a snack to make up for the skimpy dinner I'd barely eaten. Not even any desert.

Empty fridge. Empty jar of coffee beans. Not even any peanut butter.

"Gollum, I'm going to the grocery store," I called down the hallway to the apartment. "Do you need anything?"

I heard a series of grunts and nothing more. Nothing from the lovebirds in the sitting room.

"Keep an eye on WindScribe," I called to Gollum.

Another series of grunts.

So I trundled to the discount store down the Six A. I still wanted Scrap watching Mom and Darren. He'd pop over to me if I ran into trouble of the demon kind.

The wind remained calm, the sky clear. The waxing moon kept a lot of shadows at bay. I'd be safe if I hurried and stayed near crowds.

Eggs, milk, bread, the cod (I do live on Cape Cod after all) the lemons I'd promised for dinner tomorrow night, and a bottle of white wine for the sauce. The pile in my cart kept growing and growing. I could see the balance in my checking account dropping rapidly. While I was there, I checked on table linens for my kitchen.

Nothing I'd spend money on. Just cheap and tacky prints with pigs and kitties in ugly light orange or uglier dark orange.

I was not a happy camper.

I may not have the fashion sense of Scrap or my mother, but I know what I do and don't like in décor. And I don't like orange.

When I stepped outside the store with a cart full of bagged groceries, the wind bit through my gloves and slacks. Litter whipped about the parking lot in sudden frenzy.

"Scrap, I may need some help," I whispered into the night.

On it, babe. My imp flew three circles, deosil or clockwise, around my head, then lighted on the handle of the cart.

I couldn't discern his color in the weird blue-white fluorescent light circles around the poles. First time I noticed how many dark spots lay between those lifesaving circles. Did they grow darker and denser as I watched?

"Are there any Windago lurking about?" I kept looking over my shoulder and peering into the distance. Anxiety crawled up and down my spine. No way to tell if that was the flare of warning of demons present or just my own nerves.

I had been on edge pretty much all day and the night before.

Scrap wiggled his pug nose and slipped his forked tongue in and out, like a snake tasting the air. *Naw, you're safe from demons for the moment. But I'm not too sure about those three thugs hugging the shadows behind that black van next to your car.*

"Probably just teens out after curfew sneaking smokes or drinks." This parking lot had a reputation as a cool place for boys with aggressive tendencies to hang out.

As I stowed the multifarious bags in the hatch of the SUV, the light directly above me spat, fizzled, and winked out, plunging me into shadow.

I swallowed my curses and slammed the door down. I kept the key in my hand, letting the long, sharp prong of it extend through my clenched fingers.

"Nice purse, lady. Got anything in there for me? Like your wallet?" A male voice oozed menace from the area around the driver's side door. A glowing cigarette butt in the region of his mouth provided the only indication of where he stood.

No way was I going to press the unlock button on my key set with him standing between me and the dubious safety of the interior.

"Nice car, lady. We think you need to share your wealth with us downtrodden poor folk," another male voice said from behind my right shoulder. Stale alcohol on his breath.

"Need a little Dutch courage to harass a defenseless female?" I asked mildly. Judging by the price of their athletic shoes, these kids weren't poor by a long shot. I could buy two weeks' worth of groceries for the cost of one pair of their shoes.

Oh, this is going to be good. Scrap dissolved into laughter. He found a new perch on the luggage rack, swinging his bandy legs.

"What's that supposed to mean, lady?" Cigarette Guy snarled. He moved three steps closer, blasting me with his bad breath. "We ain't Dutch."

I sensed a third presence on the other side of the car. They hemmed me in, my back against the hatch. My butt resting on the bumper.

Right where I wanted them.

Chapter 16

*In the late nineteenth ccentury, Sir John Herschel
supposedly discovered a winged batman Vesper-
tilio Homo on the moon. In 1874, Richard A.
Proctor wrote a book that treated the story as science rather than science fiction.*

"**Y**OU REALLY DON'T want to do this, guys,"
I warned them. "I'm not in the mood to take
your crap."

"Oh, yeah? What's a little bit of a thing like you
gonna do to us?" Cigarette Guy puffed out his chest and
pressed closer to me.

"This!" I yelled.

Before I could think about what I was doing, I balanced against the bumper and lashed out with both feet.
I connected with a very satisfying thunk. Cigarette Guy
and Beer Breath grunted and staggered backward,
clutching their bellies.

Adrenaline flowed through me and lit my senses like
fine single malt scotch.

Unseen Guy launched at me, fingers extended toward
my eyes. I barely registered long nails and a hint of feminine curves beneath her baggy jacket.

Instantly, I was back in the Citadel with Sister Paige
screaming at me. She wanted no mercy.

I gave none to this wanna-be bad girl. She got a sweep
of my leg behind her knees and my key raking her
cheek.

It came away dripping blood. "Oooh, you're gonna have a scar just like mine!" Speaking of which, the scar pulsed hot and angry. I wondered if it was visible.

The first two were up and coming at me again. Backward kick to the balls of one. Then I kept turning and jabbed my fingers in the throat of the other.

A siren erupted at the far end of the parking lot. Blue-and-red lights strobed the kids.

The girl took off. The other two curled into fetal balls, choking and gasping.

"You didn't have to hurt them!" Allie yelled from the safety of her cruiser.

"You want a piece of me, too?" I snarled at her.

"Easy, girl," she said holding both hands up, palms out in a universal gesture of surrender. "What'd they do to you?" She wandered over.

I told her.

Mike crept forward in her shadow. He knelt down and examined the two youths. "This one may never contribute to the gene pool and the other might not talk again," he said with more humor than I gave him credit for.

"There was a third one. A girl. She's bleeding on the cheek," I advised them, holding up the stained key.

"I've been wanting to nail these kids for weeks. Had six complaints from women shopping alone at night, but the kids always disappear with purses, groceries, and cars before we get here. Then they abandon the cars a few blocks away, taking the food and the cash and not much else. Not smart enough to figure out how to do identity theft, I guess."

"How come I haven't heard about this, Allie?"

"Because you've had your nose in a book on deadline for the last month and haven't even turned on the TV."

"Oh."

Mike radioed for an ambulance. Then he leaned over the kid I'd struck in the throat. "Oh, my God! You broke his trachea. Allie, get that ambulance here fast. The kid's not breathing."

He was choking and gasping, clawing at his throat. Panic turned his face white. Lack of air had turned his lips blue.

"CPR?" I knelt beside the kid, prepared to go into action. Damn. Damn. Damn. I hadn't needed to hurt these guys, I just needed to work off some frustrations. And now I'd killed one of them.

"CPR won't work. He can't get air through his throat. I'm going to have to open him up." Mike pulled a jack-knife and a ballpoint pen out of his pocket.

"Aren't you going to sterilize that or something?" Allie asked. She'd already added an ASAP to the ambulance call and closed her radio.

"With what? You got any matches?" Mike asked.

"I do." I made a show of fishing in the pocket of my slacks. *Scrap, I need a little flame,* I begged. With a little sleight of hand ...

I grabbed Mike's open knife and cupped my hand around the blade, shielding it from the wind. Then I spun around on my knees, turning my back to the two cops.

Scrap landed on my shoulder and touched the blade with a blue-white light. He ran it back and forth, both sides, until my hand felt as scorched as the blade.

"Hurry up, Tess. He's beyond panic, gone into stillness," Allie warned. She blew ink out of the pen cartridge.

Calmly, I returned the knife to Mike. "If you know how to do this, go for it."

Mike breathed deeply, closed his eyes a moment, then slashed the kid across the throat.

Blood flowed along the line of the cut. Quickly, Mike separated the folds of flesh with the fingers of one hand. He probed a few seconds, found something white and gristly. Another quick cut with the knife, then he plunged the ink tube in.

Instantly, air whistled through. The kid's chest moved. We all sat back and breathed a little deeper ourselves.

Sirens penetrated the sound of the wind, still blocks away.

"You saved the kid's life, Mike. Thank you." Energy left me in a flood. I hadn't murdered the boy.

"Cool thinking." Allie slapped him on the back. "We might make a good cop of you yet."

"Three years on the Miami force didn't do that?" He raised his eyebrows and quirked a smile.

So he wasn't a raw rookie after all.

"Can I go home now?" I didn't think I had the umpf to deal with the rest of this emergency.

"No. I need to file paperwork on this. You don't go home until I go home."

"Allie, I'm done in. How about tomorrow? I can come down to the station and give an official statement."

"Nope."

My shoulders sagged in defeat. I was very, very tired. "How come you're back on duty? I sent you home from dinner over an hour ago."

"Somebody called in sick. I was wound up after our . . . um . . . meeting." She looked pointedly at Mike, acknowledging her need for . . . er . . . discretion. "So I volunteered to come in."

"So why are you here?" I gestured around to the sparsely occupied parking lot.

"Customer heard an altercation and called 911 as they peeled out," Mike said. "We were cruising close by and answered the call."

The kid with his hands wrapped protectively around his balls moaned and opened an eye. His gaze lit on me. He slammed his eyelids closed again and groaned even louder.

"Remember that, Beer Breath. Maybe you've learned a lesson that mugging ladies in the parking lot doesn't pay," I snapped at him.

"Julie's idea," he rasped around his aching groin.

"Julie? Typical. The kid with the ideas is the first one to hotfoot it the minute the action gets tough," Allie said. "Shouldn't be hard to pinpoint her at school tomorrow. Only kid with a bloody cheek."

The ambulance arrived and carted the kids off. They glad-handed Mike and offered to write up a commendation. Allie rolled her eyes. "No living with him now. First day on the job, and he saves a kid's life." She presented me with a clipboard filled with official looking forms.

"You know all this information," I whined. "I just want to go home."

Not yet, dahling. Scrap took possession of my right hand. He pulsed a bright vermilion as he stretched longer and longer.

While I'd been occupied with Allie and the muggers, I'd ignored the way the wind had jacked up the pitch of its wail and how the bottom had fallen out of the temperature.

The Windago scented blood.

No wonder my scar pulsed and the nerves along my spine tingled.

"Windago," I breathed. I had no adrenaline left. "I really don't want to do this now."

"Windago?" Allie mouthed, eyes wide with wonder and a touch of fear. She reached for her holster.

You've got me, babe, Scrap sang.

At least the parking lot had been scraped clear of ice and heavily sanded. I had traction.

I took a deep breath as I began twirling Scrap like a baton. He solidified and extruded sharp, half-moon blades.

I stepped out into the clear space between parking aisles.

"What do we need to do?" Allie asked. A note of panic and awe squeaked out of her.

Mike's mouth hung agape. "I never thought it was true," he whispered, pointing to my now visible Celestial Blade. Then he clamped his jaw shut and drew his weapon.

Allie already had hers out.

Mine. You are mine, the wind howled.

"Wanna take a bet on that?" I called back. I swung my weapon in a full circle over my head, around my knees, and back and forth at waist level.

Vengeance is mine! the Windago screamed. *The Orculli don't order me around.*

The real wind swallowed her words.

A shadow coalesced between the puddles of light. Tall, bulky, vaguely humanoid. At least it had arms and legs. And lots and lots of unkempt, smelly fur.

No wonder these critters became antisocial. No one would come near them until they bathed.

Mike emptied his weapon into the shadow. The bullets passed right through it.

Silly human. You can't hurt me. But you can become my new mate. The shadow advanced on Mike.

He shook so badly he dropped his weapon. A dark stain spread downward from his crotch.

Now that's irony. He could coolly perform an emergency tracheotomy but wet his pants in the face of a demon.

The Windago kept coming, pressing Mike farther and farther into the darkness. She reached out one long arm and grabbed for the poor man.

He screamed and backpedaled.

"Shit! Leave the poor guy alone. He's too young for you, Lilia David." I took a chance that there was still a morsel of humanity left in the creature. I had no proof that she and her mate were the reclusive author Howard Ebson and his longtime companion. But I had killed the mate last autumn and Howard hadn't shown up the next day to receive a lifetime achievement award. Lilia had accepted it for him with bad grace.

The Windago hissed and turned her attention back to me. She reached spectral hands toward me.

"Don't let her touch you. She'll freeze-dry anything she touches." I could see ice crystals forming in the air around me. I stayed firmly in the center of one circle of light.

Allie dragged Mike into another. He held his arm

awkwardly, cradling it against his body. He whimpered in pain.

Damn. I really hoped he hadn't been bit. If he had, I'd have to kill him before three days had passed and he became a Windago.

Anger shot liquid fire through my veins.

The Windago paused at the edge of the light.

I could see the fuzz around the edges of her shadows. Hair. Akin to Sasquatch.

I'd killed a dozen Sasquatch in one battle. There was only one Windago tonight.

"Come and get me, Lilia. I dare you." I swung the Celestial Blade closer to her.

She snarled. Red pinpoints of light in the region of her eyes glowed brighter.

Before she could think about risking the light, I took the last step I needed. My blade whisked across her middle, slicing through fur.

But not hide.

She retreated with the wind and disappeared behind a spindly little maple at the verge of the parking lot. *You killed my mate. Now I'll replace him with yours!* she screeched.

"Laugh's on you, Lilia. I don't have a mate anymore."

So you think now.

An unearthly silence followed her pronouncement. My gut grew cold.

That was hardly any fun at all, Scrap complained. He dropped back to his normal form, tinged only a little bit pink.

"There's beer and OJ in the car. Meet me at home and I'll feed you," I whispered.

He popped out.

"You didn't see anything, Mike. You hear me, Mike?" Allie demanded her partner's attention.

"But . . . but . . ."

"You didn't see anything. You didn't hear anything."

"But . . . but . . ."

"If you say one word, you'll be strapped to a desk

from here to eternity filling out paperwork. You got that?" She held him upright by the lapels of his jacket. He nodded, eyes wide in fear.

Fear of her, or of the Windago?

I pulled on his left arm, the one that hung limply at his side. Slashed jacket and shirt sleeve. The skin beneath looked an angry red, like a cat scratch. No trace of blood.

"You'll be okay. But watch that for traces of infection. See you tomorrow, Allie. I'll fill out your forms then." Jauntily I waved and climbed into my car for the short drive home.

►►►

Exhaustion, mental and physical pulled at my limbs and my eyelids. I wanted nothing more than to crawl under the down duvet and sleep for a week.

I really needed that vacation.

So, of course, Scrap chose that time to sit on the bedstead and lecture me for two hours about the dangers of letting the Windago get away. About letting Donovan come too close to me. About our need to call on the Sisterhood for help. About my need to do more research. About the dangers of letting Darren stay in the house too long. About his need to choose my wardrobe. About my failure to provide him with enough mold to sustain life. About the lack of beer in the fridge.

Dill added his own litany of grief. He was running out of time in limbo. His Powers That Be demanded I get rid of the imp and embrace Dill. He ran the same arguments over and over.

"Dill, you used to have a sense of humor," I reminded him. And myself. "Time was you'd belittle those Powers That Be with puns and scathing commentary on their pompous attitude and useless pronouncements.

Silence.

Could he be just a construct trying to force me to get rid of Scrap for a demonic reason?

I clenched my teeth and repeated Gollum's statement. "No one comes back from the dead."

Smelling of sulfur and brimstone, Dill vanished in a huff.

"I can't go back, Dill. I have to move forward," I whispered into the silence.

And then Scrap started to clean. He was very frustrated that he'd gone to the trouble of transforming and hadn't even gotten a taste of Windago blood.

Dust and stray socks flew through the air. The sharp smell of pine cleaner filled my head and made me sneeze. Mom is the only person who can outclean Scrap. And she prefers bleach.

On and on he went until the drone of his voice finally lulled me to sleep. I think he moved on to the kitchen then.

I did not sleep well. My dreams took me back to the Citadel. Back to a time when I still grieved for Dill so heavily I could hardly think. Back to a time when Scrap was new to me and I had yet to build enough confidence in myself to understand why *we* must be the ones to fight to preserve humanity from demon invasions.

My nightmares back then had repeated themselves often. They went on and on until I could no longer tell if I remembered a dream, or remembered reality.

Face your personal demons in your own reality and they might go away, Scrap had whispered to me in the dead of night when I dared not sleep.

He had a point.

"Sometimes they are like huge gorillas, but more human. Bigfoot?"

Sasquatch. Big, ugly, hairy, with fists like clubs and teeth like daggers.

"Yeah."

What else?

There were more. There were always more. Every time I dreamed, my fertile imagination came up with a different demon. Big ones, little ones, humanoid ones, squid ones, bug ones. I described a few.

"They come out of doorways into a big featureless room. It's all white and round and I can't see its limits unless a door opens. And all the doors are different."

That's the chat room. You can pass into any dimension from there.

"Is that like the eleventh dimension?" That wasn't the right term. I couldn't remember the details of the program I'd watched on TV about String Theory. Or was it Membrane Theory? Some scientists apparently had begun to believe in alternate universes. Ghosts could be explained as a temporary overlap of those universes.

That pushed more of my creep buttons. What if in another reality Dill had not died?

I think I cried myself to sleep both that night back at the Citadel and this night snug in my own bed on Cape Cod.

Chapter 17

J AWOKE FRIDAY morning feeling heavy and groggy. The clock told me it was pushing nine. The telephone beside my bed rang seven times. I ignored it. Too wrapped up in my own fog to bother.

It rang again. Another seven times. Its shrillness cut through the cobwebs in my brain.

"What?" I snarled on the sixth ring.

"This is James Frazier of the *Cape Gazette*. I'm looking for a Miss WindScribe."

What? How?

"Wrong number." I slammed the receiver back into its cradle.

It rang again. "Ugh," I groaned and dragged myself into the shower. The sharp sting revived me a little. Nothing really helped until I stumbled downstairs—careful not to bump my head on the overhead beam that crossed the steep flight that was little more than a broad ladder—and dove into my first cup of coffee.

Everyone in the family knew my habits and I found a stack of notes propped up on the coffeepot.

Idly I wandered back to the closed door leading to Gollum's apartment. He opened the door on my first knock looking fresh and alert. He'd traded his summer uniform of pressed khakis and polo shirt for crisp cords and turtleneck. With his glasses perched atop his head, I could see his mild blue eyes. I read concern there and something else I wasn't sure I wanted to identify.

"Mom and Darren headed for Boston, at some ungodly hour this morning. If I heard her correctly when she tried to wake me, I think they are looking for rings. She made coffee if you want some," I croaked, cradling my cup of the life-giving substance.

"Thanks, but I've already made myself a pot here. About an hour ago Allie took WindScribe down to headquarters to question her about other relatives who might take her in."

"You look ready to tackle the world."

"Which you don't. I have a meeting at the college at eleven. Then I need to head up to Boston for the lecture tonight. You coming?"

"Wish I could. But I don't quite dare leave with MoonFeather coming this afternoon. And WindScribe. I'm wondering if she has a drug problem. What are you lecturing on?"

"The Windago."

"Aren't they a Midwest phenomena?" One of them had followed me from Wisconsin anyway. That area had about the coldest north woods I could think of to harbor those nasty critters.

"Originated here in New England, then moved west with the native tribes." Gollum looked like he might settle in for a prelude to tonight's lecture.

"What got you started on that horror story? I thought European demons were your specialty." I needed more coffee if I was going to let him get started.

"I began looking for the shadow demons who freeze-dry their prey that you stumbled across last autumn in Wisconsin."

I suppressed a tremble in the back of my knees. Then I gave a brief recounting of last night's adventures.

"Damn. I knew I should have gone with you."

"What could you have done?" Somehow I just could not imagine Gollum fending off three teenage muggers or a vengeful Windago. He researched. I fought.

"I don't know that I could have done anything other than deter the muggers just by being male and you not being alone. I feel useless. I could have collected more data on the Windago so that you could be better prepared next time."

"Next time I don't think she'll come alone," I mused. But who among my acquaintances would she claim as her new mate. I didn't think Dill's ghost would satisfy her.

Something in Gollum's expression as he looked at me shocked me to my core. "Lilia will come after you next," I said quietly, not sure I wanted to face any side of that issue. "Do you have some kind of charm or ward to keep her away from you when I'm not around?"

"I think I can manage." He quirked me a lopsided grin and gestured me into his new lair and retrieved a sheaf of notes from the desk. "Windago victims are said to have their hearts frozen." He perused the papers with only half his attention. Unusual.

The other half of his attention seemed to be on me.

Way outside my comfort zone.

"Lucky I didn't let one of those things touch me," I said. Once again I saw in my mind Mike cradling his arm against his chest. "We may have a problem. I think we need to keep an eye on Allie's new partner. He may have gotten tagged."

"If he was, you know what you have to do." Gollum looked me square in the eye.

I nodded and shivered with more than just the cold drafts that plagued my house and eluded my caulk gun. The enormity of my task as a Warrior of the Celestial Blade hit me anew.

I was charged with keeping these horrors away from humanity, killing them when I could, driving them back to their own dimension when I couldn't.

Alone.

Without the support of my Sisterhood.

"Looks to me like your heart has been frozen," Dill quipped from his post by the desk. He leaned against it casually, long legs stretched out. "If you had a heart, you'd take pity on me and let us be together as we are meant to be."

I ignored him.

Just then Gandalf, Gollum's long-haired white cat darted between his legs and squeezed past me and out the door.

"Sorry," Gollum apologized as he dove for the errant beast.

Scrap swooped down the stairs and brushed past the fleeing cat. He came up with a pawful of white hairs, laughing inanely. Then he sneezed. Green slime sprayed the walls. I hoped it was invisible to everyone but me.

"You're going to clean that up," I admonished my imp.

He just laughed some more, flitting in a circle above the cat's head.

Gandalf snarled and swatted Scrap, claws fully extended. He drew blood from Scrap's butt.

This means war! Scrap yelled. He sounded decidedly stuffy.

"What's going on?" Gollum asked, scratching his scalp.

"Ongoing feud between our familiars."

"Did Gandalf hurt Scrap?"

I forgot that Gollum couldn't see either Scrap or Dill. *Yes, he did. I'm bleeding!*

"Put some iodine on it," I snapped. "And leave the cat alone."

"I'll just put him back where he belongs." Gollum scooped up the cat and threw him into the apartment, closing the door sharply behind Gandalf.

I heard the cat's smug purr of triumph through the closed door.

"I need to show you something." I led Gollum back into the kitchen. From there, I showed him the door hidden behind some pantry shelves that opened onto the cellar steps. "There's another entrance from the outside, but that's covered with snow at the moment." I led him down the freestanding wooden steps, added many years after the root cellar was dug.

"This place is really old," he said, caressing ancient beams and drinking in the dank smell of mold and laundry, counting rows of preserves.

"Mom cans every scrap of fresh fruit she can find." I picked up a jar of peach jam.

Gollum inspected it as if it held demon brains. He opened it and jerked his head away from the stench. The preserves had a thick skin of mold on the top. "She used old paraffin to seal it. You'll have to toss the whole batch."

"Nah, Scrap will love it." I put it back on the painted shelves with more chips than paint. "No dairy in peach jam to aggravate Scrap's lactose intolerance. What's important about the cellar is back here," I continued.

I ducked behind the wooden steps to a thick old door made of many two by fours. "Here's the spare key," I said as I used it to open the heavy padlock on a reinforced crossbar. Then I handed him the little piece of brass.

"What do you have to keep locked up and hidden?"

"Originally this was a place to hide from Indian attacks, then a priest hole for the few Catholics in a very Puritan neighborhood. During the Revolution it hid American spies from the British. Later it was a way station on the Underground Railroad. Now it's my armory."

The light came on automatically as the door swung open.

Gollum whistled through his teeth. He eagerly grabbed an elaborate German short sword with gold on the curved guard and etched along the slender blade. "Is this real?"

"Yeah. Seventeenth century. A collector's item. Weighs about fourteen ounces. I really liked the metalwork." Something else had drawn me to the blade when Scrap and I found it in a back alley pawnshop in Boston. I couldn't explain it. So I didn't.

I remembered clearly the store where I'd found it while Christmas shopping last December. Scrap had tugged my hair and urged me out of the crowds and the noise of holiday shoppers. Away from clanging bells, and unrelenting cheerful carols played over clashing store sound systems. I'd wandered reluctantly off the main streets into a long, dark alley filled with litter and smelling of stale beer and urine.

Scrap had pushed me urgently, not giving me enough time to think about where I was going or why.

The sword shone brightly in the dingy window display of the shop. The sword was the only thing of interest or value to me in the jumble of "collectibles."

The blade called to me. I had to have it. I couldn't go home without it. The shopkeeper had charged me a bloody fortune for it. But I knew it would cost double that on the open market.

"More important than the beautiful craftsmanship, it's a working blade, as is every piece in here." I swept my hand across the neat racks of swords, battle axes, and crossbows with quivers full of broad-tipped arrows. I could bring down a charging boar with one of those.

None of the weapons would stop a demon. But they would slow them down if Scrap needed a break in a pitched battle.

"This is absolutely gorgeous." Gollum tested the balance of the blade expertly, then snapped it through the air listening to it sing.

I wondered where he'd learned that technique, or why he should use this as a test for the temperament of the blade. I could do it, but only after months of practice with a foiled weapon. This man had as many secrets as Donovan, and was just as mute about them.

Gollum sighed and replaced the short sword. Then he reached eagerly for the most important weapon of all, hanging in pride of place dead center in the rack.

I stayed his hands. "Yes, it's an exact replica of the Celestial Blade, but made of wood."

"What kind of wood? It looks like metal."

He'd seen me wield the Celestial Blade; he knew what it looked like.

"The Sisters call it imp wood. I've never seen the trees they make them from. It holds an edge forever. I've never had to sharpen it. Want to train with me?"

"Wish I could." He looked at his watch, an elaborate hunk of metal with numerous dials and buttons. I think it could do everything but whistle "Dixie." Maybe it could do that, too.

"I've got to get to the college. Maybe later." He made to return the key to me.

"That's the spare. I want you to keep it while you are here. We don't know what we're getting into, and I want someone I trust to have access to weapons in case of emergency."

"Where's the other key?" he asked, slipping it on the same key ring as his car keys and the house key I'd given him.

"In a zipped pocket within a zipped pocket in my purse."

"Not someplace a stranger could stumble on it. Even if they stole the purse."

"Not likely. And there's another copy of it on a chain around my neck. Now go to your meeting before I decide the Windago really did touch me and I eat your arm off. Time for breakfast."

I hate cats the same way Tess hates bats. Only I know that bats are benign and cats are truly and totally evil. Gollum only thinks he locked the cat in his apartment. I know the beast turned invisible and slipped out again before the door fully closed.

So I hunt the cat. Upstairs and down. I stalk by smell and by sight. Meaning I can't smell anything when I'm near the cat, and my eyes water heavily when I get even closer. Hearing is no good because cats are totally silent unless they want to be heard; then they sound like a troop of elephants thundering across the plains.

Oh, no! He's down in the cellar, working at opening the door to the armory. I'm not sure my babe locked it properly. The padlock is in place, but the light is shining beneath the door. That only happens when something lodges between the door and the jamb.

Good thing that cat doesn't have opposable thumbs. I've got to warn Tess about this.

But first I'm going to torture that cat. Serve him right for decorating my bum with claw marks. He scratched off one of my warts. I worked hard to earn that one!

When I'm done with the cat, I must paint the scratches with iodine. War paint. Or makeup. Anyway, I'll make myself look pretty. I might even get a new wart when I win this battle.

Chapter 18

*In esoteric cosmology the sun and moon pictured
together represent the extremes of creative solar
power and undirected lunar imagination.*

WITH SCRAP BUSY stalking the cat, I decided
on a trip to a home furnishing store. I really
needed to do something about the kitchen. The only
other rooms in the house big enough for everyone to
gather was the dining room. Too formal. Or my office.
Too cluttered with my private things. No one messes with
my office and lives. Not even Scrap dares to clean it.

Bright sunlight and no wind. Safe to step outside. I
hoped.

Mom and Darren had taken the SUV to Boston. That
would cost them a small fortune in gas even though that
car got better mileage than most in its class. But Darren
could afford it. Maybe the SOB would top off the tank.
But I doubted it.

That left me with Donovan and his four-wheel-drive
station wagon. Not a heavy car but safer than mine. That
would also give us some private time on neutral territory. Maybe I could pry some personal information from
him. Like what kind of being he truly was.

I braved the cold and armored my defenses against
his seductive charm. Then with teeth gritted and eyes
half closed, I knocked on the cottage door.

Donovan greeted me with a high-pitched growl that sounded so much like an angry bat I almost went scuttling back to the house.

Steeling myself to face my fears, I knocked again.

"What!" Donovan yanked the door open.

"Sorry." I backed down the three steps and lost my footing on a gloss of slick dew.

Before I could fall flat on my butt, Donovan reached out demon-quick and grabbed my arm. In the next instant I found myself upright again, in his arms, our bodies pressed intimately close. His mouth hovered scant inches above mine.

The world disappeared. I saw only his handsome face, felt only his arms holding me tight, knew only that I wanted him. Desperately.

He felt like the other half of me.

Lilia's next target?

We clung together for endless moments.

Eventually, the cold penetrated my awareness. As sanity filtered back into my mind I noticed something else.

"Who hit you?" I traced an ugly red-and-blue bruise around his left eye. Red lines marred the white around his warm chocolate-brown eyes.

"It doesn't matter." He blushed. I didn't think a man as coolly self-possessed as Donovan Estevez could do that. The infusion of blood highlighted the sharp planes of his cheekbones and intensified the coppery tones of his skin. He looked more Native American than ever. I wondered what the Dutch and Russian ancestors in his lineage had contributed.

"But it does matter. You are a guest in my home. I'm responsible . . ."

"D doesn't care about responsibility or hospitality or anything but his own agenda."

"And what is your stepfather's agenda?"

Stone-cold silence.

"Okay." Inside, I burned with curiosity and anger at his silence. Then I put on a bright face, totally false. I had my own agenda that included a trip to the mall. "Give me a ride to the mall, and I'll buy you brunch."

"I have appointments. Work."

"Have you eaten?"

"No."

"Then let me buy you breakfast, and you can drop me off. Pick me up later."

His stomach growled. "You know I can't resist you." He flashed me his grin.

I forgot to breathe. If only he'd kiss me.

Stop that! I slapped myself mentally. "Donovan, we need to talk. Just the two of us. We need to clear the air between us before we do something stupid."

"Like fall into bed together again?" He kept grinning as he grabbed his leather jacket from the back of the nearest chair.

"Yeah. Like that."

We went to the I-Hop on the fringes of the mall parking lot. They served breakfast all day. When the waitress had our orders and I had a steaming cup of coffee in front of me—Donovan had opted for an anemic looking herb tea—I looked him square in the eye and broached the subject uppermost on my mind.

"Why did Darren hit you?"

"I tried to warn him off your mother." He ducked his head, trying to hide the hideous bruise.

"Why did you let him hit you?"

"I didn't *let* him. D is fast. But believe me, he didn't come off unscathed."

I raised an eyebrow in question.

"Let's just say I don't think he'll be thinking fondly of the wedding night for a couple of days at least. No visible bruises, though. I'm more subtle than he is."

"Wait a minute. He called you D when he arrived. You just called him D. You just want to confuse us?"

And Dill's parents had called him *and* his sister Deborah *and* his brother Dylan "D." A cold more frigid than the weather knotted in my belly.

"His people think it's hilarious to all call each other

D, so normal people don't know who they are talking to or about."

"But his 'people' aren't really people, are they?"

"Partially. Only mixed-bloods get out of their home dimensions in human form. Full-bloods can't transform anywhere but their homes."

"So they have to kidnap humans to breed Kajiri—half-bloods—who can come and go across the dimensions with impunity."

"Something like that."

"Explains the beauty and the beast legend."

"Yeah."

"So what are you if you don't have Damiri blood running in your veins?"

"I am fully human now. Mortal, too."

"And before?"

"Don't ask, Tess. I can't tell you. I want to. I want you to trust me enough to love me, to be the mother of my children. But I took vows, signed them with my blood. If I tell anyone my origins, I have to answer to the Powers That Be, probably with my death, a very long and painful death."

I digested that for a bit. He'd come close to admitting the truth of his origins. That was better than the nonanswers I'd got before.

"What are these infamous Powers That Be? Anything like God, or the Goddess Kynthia worshiped by the Warriors?"

"All of that and more. You don't want to be called before them. No human has ever survived a summons. Few other beings do either, come to think of it."

"But you did."

Again that stone-cold silence.

The waitress interrupted with our food: pecan French toast with eggs and sausage for me; cholesterol-free scrambled eggs and whole grain toast for him with a glass of OJ. Like the Damiri demons, he had to watch his weight. Another contradiction.

"Why can't Scrap come near me when you are

around?" I blurted out when the first hunger pangs had been appeased.

"How can you get away with eating all that fat and starch?" he asked in turn.

Stalemate.

Again.

"Can you see my scar?"

"I'm mortal, remember. The scars left by the imp flu aren't visible to my eyes. But I felt them with my fingers the night we made love." His eyes grew warm with memory.

Heat spread delicious languor through my veins.

"I would love another opportunity to explore . . . new heights with you, Tess."

So would I.

"Not yet, Donovan. When I know that I can trust you."

Which meant I had a lot of research and discovery to do since he couldn't and wouldn't tell me about himself.

Two and a half hours later, Donovan dropped me off at the house laden with bulky packages of curtains, cushions, and tableware to complete my kitchen. I'd gone with hunter-green prints dotted with images of mallard ducks. Totally different from the neutral blue-and-brown calico Dill and I had chosen four years ago. I'd also found a set of juice and water glasses, napkin rings, and salt and pepper shakers with the same mallards.

Scrap and I had barely set the table and I was ripping open the café curtain packages when Josh Garvin arrived with MoonFeather wrapped in blankets and pillows in the back of his sedate sedan. He carried my aunt into the sitting room with gentle ease. Only seven years older than me, he was absolutely devoted to Moon-Feather. His hands gripped her slight form with an intensity that said more than any protestations of love.

MoonFeather looked a pale shadow of herself. In twenty-four hours she seemed to have lost ten pounds she didn't have to lose, and her skin had paled to the color and texture of old parchment.

I couldn't help a muffled gasp at first sight of the ravages of pain and hospital food on her. Scrap paled to a translucent gray, about as thick as cigarette smoke.

"I'll mend quickly now that I'm out of that hospital," she said as Josh deposited her on the sleeper sofa I'd just pulled open for her. "I need clean air away from the psychic waves of pain and fear, and some decent natural cooking." She settled back against the cushion, head drooping in exhaustion.

Josh grabbed an extra pillow and stuffed it beneath her heavily bandaged leg. "Keep it elevated and force fluids," he said in his melodious tenor, handing me a printed sheet of hospital instructions. He'd had some success in the courtroom with that voice lulling juries into trusting him implicitly.

Good thing Donovan didn't have that voice.

"I'll get her crutches out of the car. But she's not supposed to be up and about, only trips to the bathroom." He looked sternly at MoonFeather.

We both knew she wouldn't obey those instructions unless we tied her down. I wouldn't have either.

I left them speaking softly, lovingly, to make some herb tea, a restorative concoction of MoonFeather's rather than the pathetic stuff sold in stores and served in restaurants. I didn't know what all my aunt put into this brew, but I smelled mint and mullein and chicory root. Maybe it had some magic in it as well. I never knew with MoonFeather. The infusion made a dark and thick liquid. Coffee addict though I am, I was almost tempted to try some.

The teakettle had just boiled when Allie drove up with WindScribe in tow. The girl looked as pale and insubstantial as dappled autumnal sunshine deep in the woods. She wore a set of my sweats and one of Allie's civilian parkas that hung to her knees. She looked about her with wide and bewildered eyes.

Clear eyes. No drugs glazing them today. With luck,

she wouldn't find any more. I'd made sure Mom's migraine meds were in the cottage. Nothing stronger than aspirin left in my house.

I opened the door and ushered them into the warmth of my kitchen. Mike remained outside, wandering the fringes of the parking area, examining the lumps under the snow that might be real garden gnomes. Then again, they might not.

I wondered what he'd do if one of them kicked back when he got a little too enthusiastic about removing snow with his boot.

WindScribe got the first cup of tea. She looked like she needed it more than my aunt. Allie settled in with a cup of coffee, strong and black.

"You going to be okay here alone?" Allie asked as she downed the last drop of scalding liquid. "We've got to get back on patrol. The snow is melting and the traffic is getting thick and dangerous."

"We'll muddle through. Mom and Darren should be back any time. You want to come to dinner? Gollum's in Boston, but I'm fixing cod sautéed in wine and lemon for the rest of us."

"Love to, but I'm going to Gollum's lecture in Boston." With a wicked smile she ducked out.

Why did I feel so empty inside?

Before I could figure that one out, WindScribe raised her head from her mug of tea and fixed me with a clear and determined gaze. "I'm going up to my room. I need some privacy for a change."

Probably to find a way to do more drugs.

So much for wispy and vague helplessness.

Chapter 19

*T*HE HOUSE GROWS quiet. MoonFeather naps under
the influence of pain meds. WindScribe shuts me out of
her room. My Tess settles before her computer, staring at a blank
screen or playing solitaire. Frustration and depression grow in her
as she accomplishes nothing. Her emotions are my emotions. I
have to do something or sink ever lower into darkness and drag
her with me.

I could help her finish those last four chapters, or write the two
short stories commissioned for anthologies. But she won't talk to
me while anyone who doesn't know about me is in the house. Secrecy is more than an oath to the Sisterhood. Secrecy is our protection from superstitious mundanes who will look upon us as
minions of the devil rather than their saviors from the depredations of demons.

MoonFeather would understand.

WindScribe is a puzzle. She still smells of tranquilizers and Tess'
clothing rather than herself. I can't sniff out her motivations.

Of course, if that damned cat weren't around, I could smell
more of everything. I alone know just how much evil oozes
out of the cat's graceful fur and wide eyes. Everyone else
thinks he's pretty. Or cute. Or that his purring will help Moon-
Feather heal.

Bah! It's all an act to cover up his plot to take over the world. Or at least this house.

Meanwhile Tess pounds her rolltop desk and stares at the fire. We really need a vacation.

An aura of menace hovers around us like a miasma of sewage. I dare not leave long enough to do some research. Fifteen garden gnomes litter the yard, ready to attack the moment we let our guard down.

The j'appel dragons are in charge of the chat room today. I could easily slip by them. But where would I go? How do I call the Windago away to another, easier prey? Or track the puzzle that is Donovan?

I think I'll search his luggage. Darren's, too. Who knows what demons pack for a week in the country.

The cat will do as fine a job of searching as I could. Now all I have to do is herd him over to the cottage.

"Tess!" Donovan called as he burst into the house unannounced.

I'd been so absorbed in a Mahjong game on the computer I hadn't heard his car.

"Tess, my love, where are you?"

"In the office. And I'm not your love." I yelled back at him. From here I could keep an eye on MoonFeather and monitor both staircases for signs of WindScribe emerging from her "privacy." Both sets of steps had unavoidable and distinctive creaks and groans. Not to mention the crossbeams waiting to conk the unwary.

I had a lot of hard questions only she could answer. Best she be in a good and gracious mood and totally clear of drugs when I tackled her with them.

"Oh, Tess, wonderful news." Donovan grabbed me out of my chair and twirled me around the cluttered room.

Dizzy and laughing, we kissed. And stilled. And kissed some more. The simmering passion between us exploded. His mobile mouth softened against mine.

I was lost in his magic.

I melted against him, too overwhelmed to care about

my reservations and lack of trust. My arms crept around his waist, pulling him tighter against me. Eagerly, I ran my hands up the lean muscles of his back, reveling in his fitness and strength.

His fingers tangled in my hair.

Our tongues met, twined, explored.

"Let's celebrate and go fencing," Donovan breathed when we finally came up for air.

"What are we celebrating?" I rested my forehead against his chest, not trusting myself to look into the warmth of his eyes.

"I just cut a deal that's going to save my computer gaming company and get me back on solid financial footing once and for all." He rained kisses on my cheeks, my chin, the corners of my eyes.

"That's good. What kind of deal?" I could manage mundane details. Thought beyond that was more than my passion-fevered brain could handle. Born of our natural chemistry or his magic? I couldn't tell and, at the moment, didn't care.

"The largest maker of arcade games in the country just bought the rights to ten of my computer games. I've already got arcade versions programmed. All I have to do is deliver the sets of CDs and collect a whopping big check and continued royalties." He kissed me again.

"And you want to celebrate by engaging in fencing?" I laughed beneath his mouth.

He swung me around again. "We could go back to the cottage and lock the door . . ."

"I shouldn't leave. My aunt . . ."

"Where is everyone?" He lifted his head finally, looking as if he sniffed the air. Maybe he just listened to the quiet. The only sounds in the room were the crackle of the fire and the rasp of our breathing.

I told him the distribution of bodies.

"D called me about a half hour ago. He and Genevieve are headed back from Boston now. They'll be here in another hour or so. Surely you can leave two adult women alone for that long."

"It's nearly rush hour. Darren and Mom will be at least three hours . . ."

"We've got cell phones. MoonFeather or WindScribe can call us. The *salle d'armes* is only ten minutes away."

"I need some exercise. Let's do it. But I'm calling Dad to come sit with MoonFeather until Josh gets off work. They can eat the damned fish." Decision made, I felt lighter, freer. And much happier.

I didn't care that Donovan hung out with demons, had worked to make a homeland for the half-bloods, and wouldn't tell me a damn thing about himself. All I cared about was the fact that he made my blood sing and we were going fencing.

Still laughing, I dashed up the old stairs to my room, careful to duck beneath the crossbeam. I reached out and patted the dragon skull on the way. The murmur of a soft voice stopped me short three steps down. The top of my head barely cleared the landing.

WindScribe sat on my bed cuddling Gandalf the cat. "You understand the need to be free, my friend," she said. "Freedom belongs to all creatures, even you. That horrible man Gollum should never have locked you up in the teeny tiny apartment, should he?"

The cat yawned and purred as he plucked at something shiny on the bedspread with his fluffy white paw.

WindScribe shuffled several other objects around, her fingers never idle. Her bare toes also fidgeted and clenched to a rhythm only she could hear.

I crept up one more step to see better. The witch had scattered the contents of my purse over the candlewick bedspread and examined every coin, every dirty tissue, and credit card with intense scrutiny. She wore my favorite mint-green wool slacks and sweater set, too.

"I've made it my mission in life to free all the captive creatures. What is so wrong with that?" she said in her wispy voice.

"What's wrong with that is that dogs and cats aren't street smart and get hit by cars. They don't know how to feed themselves, so they raid garbage cans and eat things that make them sick and kill them," I said. "What are you doing with my purse?" I climbed the last two steps and yanked my wallet and car keys out of her hands.

Anxiously, I checked to make sure all my credit cards were in place. Car and house keys: check. Key to the armory still secreted in its zippered pocket. Cash intact. Coins? Who knew. I rarely counted it except when I needed it. Was there a check missing from the book? Maybe. I might have written one and forgotten to record it.

"The lipstick you wore yesterday was so pretty, I thought you wouldn't mind if I tried it." WindScribe opened her eyes wide in innocence.

"Ask next time. Now get out of my room. I'd like some privacy while I change." I glared at her. My exuberant mood vanished, replaced by a simmering boil.

"There's no need to be so uptight. I didn't mean any harm." She slunk back to the connecting door to her attic room, gathering the cat against her chest, almost as a talisman.

"The road to hell is paved with good intentions." I grabbed the corner of the missing check that stuck out of her pocket.

"I've been to hell. And I won't go back," she announced firmly as she slammed and locked the door.

Interesting. Very interesting.

Darren is a worse slob than Tess. Clothes strewn about. Used tissues on the floor nowhere near the trash basket. Snack crumbs scattered about and crushed. He even missed when he used the toilet. And he left the seat up. Mom is going to love this. She lives to be a martyr to other people's messes.

Donovan, on the other hand, is so neat it looks as if he hasn't been in his room at all. His duffel bag is still packed, and I can't open it. His laptop is still in its case. I can't even smell him on the bar of soap in the bathroom. The only shaving tackle around the sink belongs to Darren.

If Donovan did not have a scent that I cannot identify, I would believe he doesn't exist. He leaves no taint in the air where he has been. Only where he is. Or does the reek of demon in Darren merely overwhelm the faint traces Donovan leaves behind?

I have heard nothing of his kind in all of imp lore. Imps have to know about many demons cataloged in the ghetto census. How else can we fight them when we become our true selves in the form of the Celestial Blade?

I light a cigar and blow smoke all over Darren's dirty laundry. Mom hates tobacco smoke. If she thinks Darren has a habit, maybe she'll call off the wedding.

Oops! Got to scram. Donovan comes. His aura fairly pushes me out the back window as he enters the front door. I flit around to the front and peer through the windows.

And wouldn't you know it, just when I've finished searching, the blasted cat shows up.

Donovan pushes open the door, and the cat dashes into the cottage, purring and drooling.

See! I told you that cat was evil. If Donovan and the cat cozy up, it proves they were both spawned in some dark recess of one of the hells.

Wait. What is this? The cat strops Donovan's legs, leaving long white hairs on his black pants.

Donovan curses in that curious language of his, full of pops and clicks and hisses. Definitely a demon tongue. "Why couldn't you wait until I had my *white* fencing knickers on?" Then he kicks the cat. It flies out the still open door and lands on its feet. Then it struts over to me with that smug look on its face.

I retreat to my babe's gym bag, giggling all the way.

Maybe the cat isn't *too* bad. Sometimes. I'll have to cure it of its attitude problem, though.

Achoo! But not now. I can't breathe.

Chapter 20

"*B*LADES DOWN!" I screamed as the tempered steel foil shattered in Donovan's hand. My arm grew numb from fingertip to shoulder from the force of his blow. Then I began to shake and ache.

A spot of red appeared on the right arm of my fencing jacket, just below the elbow and the extra padding of the underarm protector. Donovan's foil had shattered, and he'd continued the attack with ragged steel. My parry had diverted his touch to my forearm, away from a potentially dangerous wound to my breast, even with a plastic chest protector.

I stood staring in shock at the jagged end of his considerably shortened foil. It had torn through my jacket and left a bleeding gash. Eventually, I gulped and dropped my own blade on the floor. Basic safety precaution.

After nearly an hour of warming up with other fencers, and winning those bouts, we met on a strip with no one else to fight. I simmered with adrenaline and sexual tension.

We'd been sparring back and forth for close to the fifteen-minute limit with a score of three to three. We'd each received two points from red cards—penalties for fighting *corps á corps,* body to body. If you are close enough to kiss, you are too close to fence.

Then I parried his next attack on my sixte, the high outside line, and cut over for a solid riposte. A move he hadn't expected. His surprise and frustration at being unable to score on me must have made him lose his temper.

His counter parry was hard. Far too wide a movement with far too much force behind the blow for ordinary sport fencing with foils. Sabers maybe. But not these slender fourteen-ounce blades.

His riposte had been too fast to register the broken blade before it struck and drew blood. The fact that he'd hit off target on the arm showed how much his temper had robbed him of point control.

The clatter of wary fencers dropping their blades on the floor sounded loud in the sudden hush. Only after safely downing all weapons did they look around to find the cause of my alarm.

Just because sport fencing weapons have been foiled, or blunted, does not mean they are entirely safe. The whole reason for the padded jackets, masks, gloves, and rubber tips on the blades is safety. We wouldn't use them if we didn't need them.

Coach Peterson stomped over, shaking his head and muttering something about untamed Indians with more money than sense and not enough discipline.

In his current temper, that described Donovan perfectly. Behind my mask, I swallowed a shaky smile.

"Oh, my gosh, Tess! Are you all right?" Donovan ripped off his mask and grabbed my bleeding arm. The fierceness of his grip only made me hurt worse.

He'd struck with more than ordinary human strength. He shouldn't have been able to hurt me like that wielding only foils.

Coach continued to grumble as he picked up the broken pieces of Donovan's foil and retreated to the benches along the far wall of the *salle d'armes* where he kept a tackle box of tools and spare tips.

Donovan helped me remove my mask and escorted me to the coach's side, clearing the strip for the next pair of fencers. I still trembled with shock—both from the blow and the knowledge of just how short Donovan's temper was. I'd seen what happened to demon halflings when they lost their temper.

They transformed and ate people. Innocent people. Honorable people I liked and respected.

Donovan's computer game company was named Halfling Gaming Company, Inc. for a reason.

"Jacket off, Tess. Let's take a look at that," Coach ordered.

My hands shook too badly to manage the left side zipper. Donovan gently opened it for me and helped me shed the tight garment.

"Not too bad. Bleeding's slowing down. You'll bruise pretty bad, though," Coach said. He held my arm from wrist to elbow. Gentle. Reassuring.

"I'm so sorry, Tess. I know better than to let my temper rule me on the strip." Donovan guided me to a bench and urged me to sit.

I continued to stare at the splotch of blood, that had spread out from the jagged inch-long cut.

"Cold water, antiseptic, and a bandage will take care of that," Coach said. "Staring at it like a couple of moonstruck lovers won't. And ice for the bruising," Coach added. "Should be a disposable pack in the first aid kit in the back."

"I'll get it," Donovan hurried away and was back in seconds. He slapped the pack against the bench to send the catalyst into the slush and freeze it.

"No fixing this blade, Donovan." Coach shook his head. "After a blow like that, I wouldn't trust Tess' blade either. You've probably weakened it."

"I'm so sorry, Tess," Donovan apologized again, kneeling in front of me while he held the ice pack on my wound.

"If I were you, Tess, I'd hit up Mr. Estevez for a replacement blade. Make him get you a de Paul, or one of those new Italian blades everyone is raving about. The more expensive the better," Coach said and glared at Donovan. He carefully put the broken pieces into a long canvas bag for safe disposal.

"Hey, Gareth," he called to a lanky youth hovering nearby. "Run a broom over that area and make sure we got all the slivers."

I think I giggled. My usual reaction to shock. One that kept me from crying at the sharp pain that now invaded my entire hand and shot up to my shoulder.

"There's gauze pads in my purse," I said. "Two or three should cover this until I can get home and properly bandage it." It would probably be three quarters healed by that time. The imp flu had left me with all kinds of antibodies and extraordinary powers of recovery.

"Let me," Donovan said. His slow, sexy smile brightened as he removed the ice pack and kissed the wound. While he was at it, he licked it clean of blood. He ran his tongue along the gash, savoring the taste of me.

The whole move could have been extremely sensuous, a prelude to long, slow lovemaking.

So help me I couldn't break his magical hold over my senses.

Then last night's dinner conversation slammed into my memory. Vampire bats licking tiny cuts in their prey. Feeding off of their blood. Returning to the same victim time after time. Damiri demons becoming the source of vampiric legends. Drinking blood.

Only then did I notice that the dark bruise around Donovan's eye had almost completely healed.

Yeah. *Tell me again you aren't a demon.*

I yanked my arm away from his touch and dashed for the restroom, suddenly sick to my stomach and shaking all over. I splashed cold water on my face and neck. Then I washed the injury over and over with soap and hot water. Public restroom, antibacterial soap. Was it enough?

He'd tasted my blood. He could find me anywhere in any dimension to drink again.

"Scrap," I whispered, hoping against hope I was far enough away from Donovan for him to come to me.

Right here, dahling. Oooh, that's a nasty scratch. He hovered over the sink.

"D . . . Donovan licked it. Can you please clean it. Make sure you get rid of every molecule of him."

Don't know. He dropped to the counter, cocking his head and peering intently at the angry red gash. The skin already tried to knit closed. I pressed on either side to make it open again. Making it bleed again. I didn't want so much as an atom of Donovan's DNA inside me.

Scrap flicked out his tongue and jumped back, nearly crashing into the mirror.

"What?"

His saliva is poison to me. He spat and gacked.

I turned on the cold water. He drank and spat three times.

Then I stuck my arm under the stream. The water flowed over the wound, taking away the fresh blood. Then I soaped and rinsed it three more times.

"Does that mean he's poisoned me, too?"

Doubt it. But this gives me an idea. Mind if I duck out for a few? I need to do some research.

"If you've got an idea about what Donovan is, then go for it. But don't be gone long. I don't intend to stay close to him any longer than I have to."

Scrap popped out. I breathed deeply. Eventually I gathered enough courage to face him again with a calm visage if not a quiet gut.

Donovan had already fished the gauze pads and tape out of the zipper pocket in my purse for me. I bandaged it myself.

▶▶▶

Poison. What is poison to me besides demon toxin? Donovan carries no trace of demon in that bit of saliva I tasted. I'd know. Believe me. I'd know if he tasted of demon.

An old memory tickles my brain. I may have tasted something similar before.

I hop over to Lincoln, England, for a chat with the father of all imps, the one carved in stone inside the cathedral.

He's not inclined to chat. Turning into stone will do that to a body.

I've been in modern churches. No problem getting in or out. Same with this cathedral. Because of the imp glaring down from his perch? Does his presence get me past the gargoyles?

Just to test my theory, I scoot across the Channel to Notre Dame de Paris. This place has more than its fair share of gargoyles. Old and venerable ones with a great deal of power. I stand outside on the porch for a long time. Eventually, a human comes along and opens one of the doors. I follow nearly on his heels, walking every step. This is hard for me. My legs are bandy and short. They hardly support my weight. Imps are meant to fly.

And fly I do. Backward. The portal to this church repels me.

Above me, a particularly ugly gargoyle laughs when I land on my bum in a mud puddle.

Why? What have I done to offend a hideous gargoyle?

Disaster. My fall has stripped me of two of my warts. How *humiliating.*

I am so ashamed of my loss that I cannot bring myself to share this experience with anyone. Not even Tess.

Chapter 21

"I NEED A FAVOR," I stated as Donovan pulled his car out of the *salle* parking lot. What better time to ask than when he'd just inflicted bodily harm?

"Name it, L'akita." Worry pulled the corners of his mouth down. "Do you need to go to the ER?"

I inspected the swelling beneath the ice pack I still held against my arm. I slung my parka over my shoulders so I could keep it there along with some pressure. Hardly any redness left at all.

"No. I need backup when I confront Allie's new partner."

"Confront? Sounds ominous." An almost grin. I could tell his blood was still up. He needed a fight.

"About twenty-four hours ago, my Windago may have tagged him. If he's going to turn, he'll be showing symptoms by now."

"Got a cover story if we have to kill him?"

"He attacked and tried to rape me. I fought him off in self-defense."

"Local courts and cops going to buy that?"

"I hope so. He's new to the area. From Miami. Not well enough known to be one of the 'good ol' boys.' "

"From Miami?" Donovan's face took on a new rigidity.

"What do you know?"

"Suspicion only."

"Spill it!"

He looked away, swallowed deeply, made a big deal of using his turn signal at the next corner.

"Stop stalling and tell me."

"D's headquarters is in Miami. He has fingers in a lot of different pies. I find it too coincidental that a new cop from Miami shows up in a small town at the same time as D announces his engagement to a local woman. Then he gets tagged by a Windago? Too much."

"Yeah. If he'd come from Boston or New York, he wouldn't look so suspicious. Allie's in Boston with Gollum. This will give us a chance to talk to him without her interference."

I called police dispatch on my cell. "Hi, Millie, this is Tess." Right person on duty for this kind of call. Millie was the secretary for Mom's garden club.

"Yeah, what ya need? Allie's off duty," she said around a wad of gum. I knew from experience that she chewed and chewed on grape bubble gum for hours without blowing a single bubble. When the flavor ran out, she added more.

"I know Allie's in Boston for the evening. But I'd like to talk to her new partner, Mike Gionelli."

"Gionelli?" Donovan mouthed in surprise.

My curiosity level rose three notches. He knew the name. Too many coincidences.

"Whas up, eh?" Millie sounded relaxed, ready to settle in for a good gossip.

"We're having a party in the next few days. I wanted to invite Mike to meet the neighbors socially before he has to meet them professionally."

"Yeah, I heard about your mom, eh. When's the wedding?"

"A few weeks. But we want to have an engagement party first. Know where I can find Mike?"

"Long Wharf Café. He's got an apartment nearby and

takes most of his meals there. You tell your mom I wish her the best, eh. I can run a background check on her new beau if you need me to."

"That would be . . ." Underhanded. Sneaky. Yeah, all that and more. Necessary. "Could you do that, Millie? Legally?"

"Sure. No problem. Can't have some furrener making time with one o' our own now can we, eh?"

"Good idea. Go ahead and start the process. And report back to me, Millie. Just me."

"Even if it's bad news?"

"Especially if it's bad news." Then, as an afterthought, I asked, "Did anyone do a background check on Dill when we got married?" He was a "furrener," too.

"Just your dad. We figured he had a right to."

"Yeah, he did, I guess."

"We didn't find anythin' on him, though, eh."

"Didn't think you would." And I doubted they'd find anything on Darren Estevez either.

"Say, you ever find that raccoon what bit Moon-feather? I thought she had some kind of special connection with critters and they left her alone, eh."

"Uh. Yeah. My out-of-town friends found it, dead on the road."

"Found on road dead. Just like my old Ford, eh. Glad I finally got rid of it."

We both chuckled at her tired joke. "MoonFeather whacked him good on the head with a cast iron frying pan. Must have given it a concussion and it got confused. Someone ran over it. We had it tested. No sign of rabies."

"Good thing. I hear those shots ain't fun, eh."

Another moment of chitchat and I closed my phone.

"Must be a slow night," Donovan chuckled.

"About usual. Millie always has time to gossip."

"Even on a Friday night when the bars are hopping and the parties going strong?"

"Yeah." I told Donovan how to find the Long Wharf, three blocks behind us. He made an illegal U-turn, skidding the tires. Another driver yelled and shook his fist but didn't stop.

We found Mike in a corner booth with his back to the wall and his nose in a book. Not one of mine.

"Mind if we join you?" Before he could object, I scooted in next to him. Donovan frowned at me as he took the bench seat opposite. We blocked the guy in. He couldn't run if our conversation became uncomfortable.

I waved to the waitress, signaling a need for coffee and pie. She brought it right away along with water. She refilled Mike's ice-tea-sized glass with more ice water.

"So, Mike, where'd you come from?" I asked, in my friendliest down-home, folksy way. I'd learned a lot from Millie over the years.

"I told you. Miami." He folded down a page corner to mark his place and closed the book.

I scowled. That was no way to treat a book. So I dug one of my own bookmarks out of my purse, placed it neatly inside and smoothed out the corner. "What did this nice innocent book do to you to deserve that kind of treatment?"

"Um . . ."

Donovan just laughed. "Books are sacred to writers," he half whispered as if confiding a deep secret ritual to an initiate.

Keep it friendly. Let him relax. He'd be more likely to confide in friends.

Only he didn't relax. His slender body tensed as he drank half his water.

"Why are you here?" Mike asked, staring directly at Donovan.

"You know who I am."

"Yes."

"And you know what I am," I added, more a statement than a question.

"I've heard."

"Then you know you can't lie to us," Donovan persisted. "You can try, but you know we'll see through it."

Mike looked at the cover of his book, suddenly fascinated by the minimalist artwork and lettering of the latest thriller. My books sold well. I'd be extremely happy with a quarter of that man's numbers.

"He's not in your league for world building and emotional depth of character," Mike mumbled, still tracing the book cover with his finger.

"Thanks." Damn. Hard not to like the guy.

"I have a better question for you, Mike," Donovan stilled the man's hand with his own fierce grip.

Mike was forced to look into Donovan's eyes. He remained calm. I knew the strength in Donovan's hands and arms and winced inwardly for Mike.

"The Windago tagged you last night. Any swelling, signs of infection?"

"No. It didn't break the skin."

"Irritability? Sensitivity to light? Overwhelming desire to get lost in the woods alone?" I added my own questions.

"No."

"He's clean." I sat back and sighed with relief.

"Not entirely." Donovan maintained his hold on Mike.

I suddenly wished I had the comb. Then I could read Mike's aura clearly and know for certain who, or what, he was.

"How well do you know my father?" Donovan continued his interrogation.

Mike gulped hard. I watched his Adam's apple bob and his tanned face pale a bit. "Hardly at all. I've barely met him."

"Perhaps I should ask, how well your *family* knows Darren Estevez."

Mike yanked his hand free and sat as far back in the corner as he could squeeze his slender frame. He reached for his glass of water and downed the remainder of it in one gulp. Then he signaled the waitress to bring him more. She refilled his glass and my coffee cup then retreated a bare few feet, cleaning an already clean table.

I jerked my head toward her to make certain the two men were aware of her eavesdropping.

"So, there is a connection," I said quietly.

"A loose one," Mike admitted. "Look, I'm just an average guy trying to get by, do my job, and go home at night with a *clear conscience.*"

How should I read the emphasis of that statement? Or his body language? Or Donovan's for that matter?

"In other words, your family owes D something. He pulled strings to get you sent here as his spy as repayment," Donovan spat.

"I didn't want to do it," Mike insisted. "But I had to, or stand by and watch . . ." He shuddered and downed another glass of water.

I shoved mine toward him and he gulped that, too.

Donovan looked as if he wanted to strangle the man.

"I'm not one of his followers," Mike insisted. He drank Donovan's water and looked as if he needed more.

Our helpful waitress showed up with a pitcher. She poured water and ice ever so slowly. Watching the three of us more than the tall glass, remembering what she was doing, just before the glass overflowed.

"I know how D can manipulate things, make you feel as if his agenda is your own idea, then leave you to face the consequences alone," Donovan admitted once the waitress had retreated. "Believe me, I know. He's a master at making other people take the blame for his actions. So what are you supposed to report to him?"

"Anything I can find out about Tess and her family. But I haven't said anything yet. I haven't told him about . . . about . . ." he looked around cautiously. "About the Celestial Blade."

"And you won't," I whispered.

"Ever," Donovan emphasized.

"Ever," Mike repeated, almost mesmerized by his gaze.

"And you'll run by me anything you tell Darren before you tell him," I insisted.

"O . . . kay." He licked his lips. "Okay. I can do that, let you help me frame the words so I don't tell him anything of value while making it sound like some deep dark secret."

"Good man." I patted his shoulder. "You watch Allie's back and do as you're told, and we'll all be best friends before this is over." I slid out of the booth. "Oh, and remind Darren that I have killed before. I don't like doing it, but I can and will to protect my family and friends. I just added you to the latter list."

At least I wouldn't have to kill him forty-eight hours from now.

Mike nodded, looking relieved and grateful.

Donovan followed me. He tucked a generous tip in the waitress' pocket to buy her silence.

"What kind of demon is he?" I whispered once we were safely locked inside Donovan's car.

"Doesn't matter. He wants to be mostly human. How'd you guess?"

"If he weren't already a demon, the Windago tag would have turned him. I'm almost glad he's Kajiri. I like him."

"He's the kind of guy I'm trying to help. The trapped ones who don't belong on either side of the chat room."

Admirable. If that was *all* Donovan wanted for the halflings, I might learn to trust him.

I really wanted to. My body cried out for his touch. My mind longed for the mental intimacy of long heartfelt conversations with him.

I'd get none of that until he told me the truth. All of it.

Chapter 22

Hey diddle, diddle, the cat and the fiddle, and the cow jumped over the moon. The little dog laughed to see such sport, and the dish ran away with the spoon.

"*W*HERE'S MOM? I don't see her car," I said the moment Donovan and I entered my mostly dark house. A new nervousness felt like a lead weight in my stomach.

The light over the stove and a dying fire in the hearth showed an empty kitchen. Clean dishes in the drainer. I opened the fridge to find remnants of the cod in wine and lemon sauce. Someone had cooked and eaten dinner.

Both Dad and Bill were decent cooks. I snitched a bite. Even cold it tasted wonderful. MoonFeather must have supervised.

"D said they'd be back about an hour after he called me, and that was three hours ago," Donovan mused. He whipped out his cell phone and punched a number. After an endless ten heartbeats he shook his head and pocketed it. "Either the phone is off, or they are in an area with no service."

"I don't like this." I stalked through the house, checking for signs of invasion.

We found Dad, Bill, Josh, and MoonFeather playing Scrabble in the dining room. The four of them plus

WindScribe could have polished off the fish easily. Bill would have washed the dishes even if he hadn't eaten.

"You are supposed to be in bed," I greeted my aunt. She looked pale and drawn, but better than I expected.

She grimaced. "I'm getting bed sores from that mattress," she grumbled. At least MoonFeather had her leg propped up on a pillow on one of the extra chairs. A small concession to her injury.

"Where's WindScribe?" A bubble of panic threatened to burst in my throat. I hadn't counted the mounds of garden gnomes in the yard when we came in. They'd promised me two more days to prepare.

When I thought with my head and not my hormones, I realized I didn't totally believe Gollum when he said the Orculli trolls would honor the temporary truce until the declared day and time of battle.

"She's in there." Bill jerked his head toward the sitting room, now MoonFeather's bedroom. He looked a little disgusted.

Then I heard the faint strains of a TV show theme song. I grimaced when I recognized a slightly obscene and totally inane animated feature of a science fiction show. It had a big cult following, but I refused to watch more than the first five minutes of the first episode.

WindScribe laughed loud and long at some piece of dialogue or slapstick action.

I grimaced.

"How did the reunion go?" I asked MoonFeather. "Did she deign to recognize you?"

"Hmf," MoonFeather grunted concentrating on her letter tiles.

"WindScribe called her old and the puppet of male politicians, then turned up the volume on the TV," Dad grumbled.

MoonFeather wouldn't say anything bad about our guest, even if she deserved it.

"Any phone calls?"

"Just James Frazier of the *Gazette*. We told him wrong number," Bill said, not lifting his eyes from his tiles.

"Good. I don't want him talking to WindScribe yet."

"Actually, she refused to speak to him," Dad said. He quickly rearranged his tiles, his eyes glowing with triumph.

"Any word from Mom?"

Dad shook his head. "Haven't see or heard from them," He yawned. He didn't look overly concerned, engrossed in compiling ever more complicated words out of his tiles. A peek at the score sheet at Dad's elbow showed that Bill was winning for a change. Probably MoonFeather's pain meds and Dad's concern for his only sister were interfering with their concentration. Josh looked like he'd rather be holding MoonFeather's hand than playing a game.

"I don't like the idea of Genevieve marrying a man she just met," MoonFeather said quietly. "We know nothing about Darren Estevez. He gives off a strange aura that makes me suspect they are not compatible." The closest I'd ever heard her say anything negative about a person.

"I'll say they aren't compatible," I agreed. "Maybe I should call Allie and see if there are any accident reports . . ." Then I remembered that Allie was in Boston with Gollum. I didn't expect them until after midnight. Another three hours from now.

But I could call Mike or Millie if I really wanted to know. Could I trust them to keep my anxiety a secret. Not Millie. Maybe Mike.

"Your mother is a grown woman, and I presume her fiancé is a responsible adult as well. Let them worry about themselves," Dad said. He placed three tiles on the board. "That makes your 'vamp' my 'vampire' with the e on a triple word!" he chortled, adding up his points.

I nearly choked. I'd had too many reminders of vampires and other undead creatures in the last twenty-four hours. I edged away from Donovan. Before I knew it, I had the entire length of the dining room table between us.

A car door slammed. I gasped and started.

"That's probably them now," Dad said. He stretched his back and added up the score again. "I'm ahead by ten points."

"I think I'm done in. Can we evict the little . . . lady from my room now?" MoonFeather asked. "Even the ghosts don't like that TV show. They're hovering outside their usual places," she whispered in an aside to me.

"I'll persuade WindScribe to find another entertainment," Donovan said and retreated into the sitting room.

I left them to turn on the kitchen lights and start a new pot of coffee.

A second door slammed. Masculine and feminine chatter. I turned to face my mother, trying desperately for a smile and a welcome. Instead, a stern frown overrode my emotions. I felt like the disapproving parent with an errant daughter who'd broken curfew.

I wasn't ready for the role reversal.

Gollum and Allie wandered through the mudroom into the kitchen.

"What are you doing here?" I blurted out.

Gollum blinked behind his glasses. I couldn't read his eyes, but his posture screamed surprise. "The lecture was from six to seven," he said blandly.

"Oh," I said flatly. I sagged. All my righteous indignation flew up the chimney. "I thought you didn't go on until eight or so and didn't expect you until midnight."

"What's wrong?" Allie asked. She stepped lightly, almost warily, eyes searching the shadows.

"Mom and Darren aren't home yet. They've been gone since early morning and they aren't answering the cell phone."

Gollum's eyes opened wide, and his glasses nearly slid off his hawkish nose. "You don't think . . . no, he wouldn't . . . would he?"

"Would he what?" I snapped.

"Kidnap her. He must want something from you. Maybe he figures holding your mother for ransom will be more effective than marrying her to get to you."

I gulped. "She had her heart set on a church wedding . . . Could he be so cruel as to crush her hopes like that?"

"He's Kajiri." Gollum sounded so matter-of-fact and emotionless I almost slapped him.

This was *my* mother we were talking about.

"Scrap, can you find Mom?" I called into the ether. I had no idea where the brat hid. With Donovan occupied with WindScribe at the other end of the house, my imp should be able to come to me.

No need, dahling. Scrap appeared in front of me, hovering on his tattered wings, sporting a fair amount of iodine on his bum and streaked lavishly around his eyes in a weird makeup job. He waggled the end of his pink feather boa at me.

I had to bite my cheeks at his garish appearance. Then I had to pinch my nose as he farted and blew black cherry cheroot smoke in my face.

"You've been into some milk," I gagged.

Whatever. The cat didn't want it. At least not after I painted his nose with iodine. Scrap flashed his bum toward me and waggled his barbed tail. *Mom and Darren are driving down our street as we speak. They should be pulling into the drive about . . . now.*

Sure enough, I heard the crunch of gravel under tires.

Again, I sagged. This time in relief.

"Tess, sweetie," Mom gushed as she practically flew through the door.

"Mom?" Was this young, vivacious, attractive woman with short, highlighted hair and a new stylish suit with—gulp—*slacks* really my mother?

Mom always wore skirts and pearls and kept her hair in a tight French roll.

"Mom?" I choked out again.

"Oh, sweetie." She lapsed into the slight lisp of her French-Canadian accent. "You'll never guess. We drove to Maine and got married!"

Chapter 23

The word lunatic comes from the Latin lunaris for Moon. A lunatic exhibits the kind of insanity that waxes and wanes with the phases of the moon.

I Stinko comes into the kitchen, but he does not eject me. The presence of Darren, a true demon, overrides Donovan's power. Just like when we fought the Sasquatch last autumn.

I turn a bright vermilion. I lengthen and twist. My need to slay Darren consumes me. Only when he is gone from this life will Mom and my beloved Tess be safe.

Yet Tess does not command me to transform. If we attack Darren, he can only defend himself by becoming a giant bat. That would appall Mom. But would she believe that her new husband could actually be a demon? Would she trust her own eyes? Her faith would not allow her to believe the truth.

Then again, Darren might remain in human form and allow Tess to kill him, forever driving a wedge of unforgiveness between her and her mother. Is that his goal? Weaken Tess by separating her from her family.

Or, worse, having her condemned as a murderess.

Her wise head prevails.

Still, the need to become a weapon, to taste his tainted blood on my blade becomes a burning ache. If I do not change soon,

I will burst into flames and consume us all in the fires of the six hundred sixty-six levels of hell.

I must duck into the chat room to douse the flame within me.

►►►

"Married! How could you be so stupid?" Donovan yelled from the butler's pantry entrance.

Scrap was nowhere in sight.

"Marrying Genevieve was the smartest thing I could do." Darren smiled in a sickly-sweet sort of way that told me he didn't mean a word of it.

Mom, however, drank it in like iced sparkling water in the desert. She couldn't take her eyes off him, as if she needed his direction to breathe.

"That tears it. I'm going to a motel." Donovan plowed through the kitchen. "Let the lovebirds stay in the cottage. I'm out of here. It's been fun, Tess. *L'akita*. We'll talk tomorrow." In a flurry of cold air and slamming doors he was into the mudroom.

"Come back here, son," Darren ordered. He dropped a bundle of shopping bags and blocked the outer doorway.

"I am not your son. I was your ward. And only because you manipulated my naïveté. I do not have to obey you like that tribe of gangbangers you sired," Donovan snarled. He raised his clenched fists.

"Now, boys, there is no need to fight," Mom said. She fluttered around the inner door, looking pale, fragile, helpless, and more beautiful than I'd ever seen her.

"There is every reason to fight if this undisciplined child refuses to obey," Darren said. His eyes narrowed and he, too, brought up his fists. "You've only been mortal for fifty years, hardly enough time to learn the proper ways of the world," he said, so quietly I'm not sure anyone but me heard.

"Oh, a fight. I do so love a barroom brawl," Dill drawled from his post in the kitchen nook. " 'Bout time someone showed D what it feels like to be on the receiving end."

Did he mean Darren or Donovan?

Why had he shown up now?

My head started to hurt. Like when I'd worn the comb too long.

Or not enough.

"I'm here to help you out, of course, lovey. I don't see an imp around, and there is a fight brewing," Dill answered one of my unvoiced questions.

"I have tasted the blood of an honest warrior tonight, D. Do you still want to fight me?" Donovan squared his shoulders and took on an aura of calm authority.

Darren blanched. He dropped his hands back to his sides, but he kept his level gaze on Donovan.

Until that moment I hadn't realized how much they looked alike. Or how closely Dill resembled them.

My mind whirled in confusion.

"We will finish this later, D. For now I thank you for the offer of privacy with my bride." Darren stepped aside.

Donovan stomped past him and down the two stairs. Before his foster father could gather the bags and enter the kitchen, we all heard Donovan's car backfire and gravel spray beneath his speeding tires.

"Oh, dear, I was hoping we could all be one happy family. I do so miss having all my relatives around." Mom pouted prettily. She did it well and I often wondered if she practiced it before a mirror.

Darren took his cue and enfolded her in his arms. "There, there, *querida*." He patted her back affectionately.

"Dad and Bill are in the dining room with Moon-Feather. Don't you want to share your good news with them?" I asked.

"You can tell him. Right now I'm just going to slip upstairs and fetch my toothbrush and my nightie." Mom kissed Darren long and passionately.

I rolled my eyes upward.

Allie caught my expression and shared it with me.

Gollum looked like he wanted to take notes.

"Well, if we aren't going to open a bottle of champagne, I'm going home," Allie said.

Darren and Mom didn't look up from their lingering embrace.

"I'll call you in the morning," I said, escorting her to the door. "I had an interesting conversation with Mike tonight."

Allie raised her eyebrows in question.

I shook my head, indicating I wanted privacy for that discussion.

"And I believe I shall retire to my own rooms," Gollum added. "Gandalf will need his supper and I have some notes to record. I'd like to share them with you, Tess, when you get a minute."

"Sure. I'll be in when people are settled." Oh, for the days when I lived all alone and dreamed of going to Mexico for my vacation!

At last Mom broke the clinch worthy of a romance novel cover. "I'll just be a moment, *cheri.*" She positively skipped toward the stairs.

I made to follow her.

"Wait a moment, Tess," Darren said. He grabbed my arm, right over the healing wound. His grip would leave bruises. More bruises.

I couldn't help but wince and try to pull away. He held me firmly. Easily.

"Get your hand off me." Mom wasn't around. I had no reason to pretend politeness, or that I liked this guy.

"Let's get a few rules straight first." Darren tightened his fingers on me.

I nearly dropped to my knees in pain. Only extreme willpower kept me upright.

"Scrap?" I called. "I might need some help here."

"He won't help you, lovey," Dill said. He didn't move from his lounge against the wall by the nook. "But if you banish the imp, I'll break this guy's neck. Been wanting to do that for a decade or more." Dill's eye sockets glowed red. He loomed larger than life. But he remained across the room, as separate from Darren as Scrap was from Donovan.

That was something I needed to explore. Later.

"First off, since your mother and I are now married, I think it more appropriate that you move into the cottage and leave the house to us." Darren's dark eyes turned steely.

"Not on your life, buddy. In case Mom hasn't told you, the entire property is mine. She lives off my largesse, not the other way around." I held his gaze, promising him retribution if he didn't let go of my arm. My fingers were already turning numb.

He looked surprised. Then his eyes narrowed. "That can be changed. We will live in this house. With the ghosts and all of the other garbage you've collected. It will make a nice retreat for my people. Good thing you left the zoning for a bed and breakfast intact."

"You are welcome to the ghosts. But the house is mine. In fact, I think you should start looking for new accommodations immediately. You aren't welcome here. So make the new house big enough to host family game night. Surviving that is more challenging than fighting a Warrior of the Celestial Blade."

Darren smiled knowingly. Like he knew he'd get the last word. "And another thing. I'll take the comb."

Everything inside me froze. So this is what it was all about. The Kajiri wanted the comb and the magic it gave me.

"The comb is mine."

"Not anymore. You gave it to your mother, in front of witnesses. I am now her husband. What is hers is mine. Legally and now metaphysically."

"Over my dead body."

"That can be arranged."

"Are you forgetting who and what I am?" *Scrap, dammit, get your ass back here.*

"Never. But I have you in a bind. Hurt me, and you destroy your mother."

"She'll recover."

"Will she? Look how long it took her to recover from your father's betrayal. How much worse will it be if her beloved daughter hurts or kills her new husband. No, I think I'm safe. Safe enough to take the Kynthia brooch as well as the comb."

How did he know about *that?* Scrap had found a gold brooch in the shape of the Moon, Star, Milky Way configuration the Goddess assumed in the skies. Only after he gave it to me did I discover that the brooch signified leadership of the Sisterhood of Celestial Blade Warriors. It was mine now, not that I lead the Sisterhood, but because of some metaphysical law of finders keepers.

"The entire otherworld knows you have those two artifacts of power. If you want your mother safe, *alive,* and happy, you will turn them over to me."

"I'll kill you first."

"Tess!" Mom screamed.

Darren dropped my arm as if I'd burned him.

"Take that back," Mom raised her voice further. "You just don't want me to be happy. You want me dependent and needy so you can have control over everything you touch."

Psycho babble from Mom? What had Darren done to her? Again, she gazed soulfully at him rather than look at me.

Probably just the dim light, but I thought her eyes reflected red for a moment, like a flash in a photo. Gone the moment I thought I detected it.

"I told you that all that mucking about with fencing would come to no good." Mom stamped her foot in a most unladylike manner. "You were never a violent person until you started playing with swords. Now take that back, or I'll never speak to you again."

"Promise?" I smiled sweetly to cover my own amazement. How much had she heard? Not enough if she still defended Darren.

"I meant what I said, Darren." I left the room as fast as I could and still maintain a fragment of dignity. I nearly ran through the house and upstairs, frightened out of my wits, for myself and my mother. What could I do to separate her from Darren now that they were legally married?

Killing Darren seemed the only way.

Too late. Too late. I return to Tess, cooler, composed, ready to do her bidding and not mine.

Too late. I should never have left. Then we could have slain Darren out of hand. I would have tasted his blood and known that I had done a good thing. Mom would have seen Darren for what he truly is, a demon bat who sucks blood.

I know now that Darren must die. For Mom's sake. For Tess' safety. For my own satisfaction.

Chapter 24

*T*IME TO CHECK ON all my responsibilities. Josh tucked MoonFeather into her bed. Dad and Bill packed up the Scrabble game, kissed me good-bye and went home. That left WindScribe. I wondered why she had refused to talk to our local pest . . . er I mean reporter. She seemed the type to want to flaunt her "otherness." Why not to the press?

"We need to talk, WindScribe. Or should I call you Joyce Milner?" I said as I topped the stairs and entered my room.

"Joyce is dead," she said from her perch on my bed in front of the blaring television.

I switched off the set.

"I was watching that!" she protested and pouted as prettily as my mother.

What is it with these ditzy dames that they always look beautiful when their petty emotions should make them ugly?

"Now you and I are talking. We can't do that with that mindless stupidity intruding."

"It's not stupid. It's funny!"

I let that one pass. "WindScribe, I've promised to go

into battle for your freedom. I'm putting my life on the line to keep you here in your home dimension. I need to know something before that happens." I remained standing, in a position of authority. She didn't strike me as the kind who would open up to a friend sitting next to her.

Reticence and evasiveness are habits long learned and hard to break. I realized she needed time to formulate her story before going public to James Frazier, or even private to me. She'd had all day. What else had she been up to?

Maggie, the upstairs ghost who usually flitted from room to room, seemed entrenched in the guest room where Mom had slept last night, refusing to come near WindScribe.

"I don't know anything." She suddenly found the candlewick pattern of my bedspread fascinating.

"Then tell me about Faery. What's it like?"

She shrugged. "It's just another place." She still wouldn't look at me.

"Must be a special place if your coven put together a tricky and dangerous spell to take you all there." I let my voice go soft and a bit dreamy. "When you first stepped into this world, you said you'd been kicked out of Paradise and wanted to go back. So tell me about it."

"It's pretty there. Lots of flowers. Always warm so we didn't need the artificial confines and pretenses of clothes." Her face took on a wistful look.

"What kinds of flowers?"

"All kinds. Some from here. Some from every other dimension in the universe. Everything grows and flourishes and becomes better than they are in Faery."

"Sounds lovely. Healing. You needed healing when you went there," I said. From what Allie had said, Joyce had suffered a difficult life with an abusive mother.

"Wicca healed me," she asserted. Finally she looked me in the eye.

"MoonFeather says Wicca offers spiritual healing to any who ask." I doubted WindScribe had healed as much as she claimed. Not with her drug-induced nightmare of being locked in a closet beneath the stairs. Some nightmares we never recover from.

"I couldn't have gotten into Faery without healing."

"Did something happen in Faery that allows you to see Scrap?"

"I can't see him anymore." She looked off into space beyond my left shoulder. "The touch of Faery that allows you to see things as they truly are lingers in your perceptions. But not for long."

She's lying, Tess. She sees me now. Look at the way her pupils contract and the lines around her mouth tighten.

"Can you hear him?"

Of course she can't. We're communicating on a tight beam rather than a broadcast.

"I didn't know he talks."

Lying again. We had a talk about her choice of lace over brocaded ribbon to lengthen your blue slacks.

Traitor! I slammed back at him. *Couldn't you have talked her into asking my permission or for a loan of other clothes?*

"I never see . . . saw his mouth move."

"Sometimes Scrap talks way too much." I glared at him before turning back to WindScribe. "Who rules Faery these days?" I asked more gently.

"Some silly king. He had lots and lots of rules that were impossible to learn. And he kept changing them without telling anyone." The pout came back.

"Did you break one of his rules? Is that why he kicked you out?"

"I'm tired. I want to go to bed." She slithered off the bed and ducked around me so fast I couldn't catch her.

My protest was still forming in my mouth when she slammed the door to her attic room. The lock snicked closed like a period at the end of a paragraph.

Desperate for answers, I used my cell phone and dialed the secret phone number of the Citadel.

A phone on the other end rang once. Then the signal died, cutting me off from help.

➤➤➤

"Where is the brooch now?" Gollum asked when I'd told him about my conversation with Darren.

Talking to WindScribe wasn't doing me any good. So I decided to brainstorm with Gollum. He might not talk about himself, but he'd talk endlessly on a variety of other subjects.

"In a safety deposit box in Providence," I replied quietly, in case anyone was listening outside the apartment. Actually the repository for the sacred brooch was a jeweler in Boston who specialized in storing valuable pieces and heirlooms while providing good replicas for everyday wear. My replica was in the bank in Providence.

Paranoid? Me?

Of course. I feared retaliation from the Sisterhood who felt that the piece belonged to their elected leader more than I feared a demon would steal it. Until tonight.

"You might look for a different repository. If it gives off a magical aura, a gifted hunter could home in on it with no trouble." Gollum's eyes lit with a bit of excitement. Was he a "gifted" hunter?

"Scrap tells me there are a couple of other pieces in the vault with a stronger magical aura than mine." The jeweler's vault, that is.

"Then keep it there," Gollum replied on an equally quiet whisper. He turned up his small stereo. Opera, a light aria I couldn't identify, filled the apartment and masked our voices. "We don't know what kind of metaphysical or magical authority the piece grants. We don't want it falling into the wrong hands."

"I agree. Darren is getting nothing from me. And as soon as I can convince my mom that he is a con man through, and through, he won't even have my mother."

"Good thinking. But we have another more immediate problem."

"WindScribe and the toothy garden gnomes." I just couldn't think of those little guys as Orculli trolls. Trolls are big and hairy and live under bridges.

Gollum pulled a book from his briefcase. The fat, trade-sized volume looked well worn and had a dozen Post-it notes protruding from the pages.

I read the title. "A Field Guide To Wild Folk: Faeries, Gnomes, Pixies, and Sprites." The author's name was long, unpronounceable, and Italian.

"A year ago I would have laughed out loud that someone actually needed a field guide for critters out of fairy tales," I said on a nearly hysterical giggle.

The music shifted to something militaristic, right on cue. I paced in time to it.

"And now you know that fairy tales sometimes come true. The grim ones, not just the cleaned up versions published by the brothers Grimm. Did you know that their original manuscript was quite accurate and quite dark, but the Church ordered revisions more consistent with their worldview?" He thumbed through the yellow flags, reading a few lines on each page.

I nodded. Of course I knew that. The gesture was lost on him. His entire attention belonged to that book.

Gollum thumbed through more pages, finally stopping about two thirds of the way through. "Sit down and then look at this."

I plopped onto the cushy sofa that threatened to swallow me. Dill had picked out the furniture in the apartment. I had never had the chance to spend any time in here. Before or after he died.

We'd headed west on that final, and fatal, trip less than a week after we moved into the house.

Now I wondered at the rather feminine choices of overstuffed furniture covered in bright floral chintz. I liked it. I doubted that Dill would. Who had he chosen the furniture for?

Where was he anyway? If he haunted any part of the house, it should be here.

"I haunt you. Not the house, lovey," he reminded me from his casual slump against the computer desk that Gollum's laptop now occupied. "And I kind of resent your new boyfriend taking over my office."

I ignored him rather than retort that Gollum was not my boyfriend. Colleague; yes. Friend; yes. Lover? I didn't think so.

"What do you think of this guy?" Gollum held the book out for me.

Right there, in full color, sat an excellent watercolor print of the little king of the garden gnomes; complete with droopy red hat and golden feather. The bit of gold braid around the crown was more elaborate in the picture, more crownlike and brighter. I wondered if losing WindScribe had given his gold a bit of tarnish.

"That's our guy." I peered at the microscopic print beneath the picture. "King Scazzamurieddu, a Laúru of northern Italy."

"This is a bad translation," Gollum said. He sat down next to me, pushing his glasses on top of his head. He took the book back. "I have an original Italian version in storage. The names are all mixed up. He should actually be an Orculli of the Tyrol district. But they did get the hat right. It's his most prized possession. Some folklorists believe the hat is the secret to his magic."

"So why is he here?"

"What this book doesn't say, but a friend of mine in Boston told me, is that the Orculli were drafted to be pandimensional prison guards. Their punishment for stealing the rest of us blind is to imprison more dangerous beings. They also are accused of bringing freezing temperatures and icy roads when in a bad mood. King Scazzamurieddu is the prison warden."

"What kind of crime warrants pandimensional imprisonment?" Darren had spoken of metaphysical laws of possession. Was there really a codification of laws that applied to all races in all the many universes?

"I don't know. But apparently WindScribe committed a big crime if Scazzy is willing to cross dimensions and battle a Warrior of the Celestial Blade to get her back." He lost himself for a moment reading more about our foe.

"Somehow I don't think petty theft is involved." I remembered the contents of my purse scattered across my candlewick bedspread. "WindScribe is spacey and immature, but she doesn't strike me as a hardened criminal."

"Beware of first impressions, lovey." The music went cold and eerie like a ghostly wind in bare trees. "I caught her picking the lock on your desk. Expertly. She was looking for drugs. Lucky you flushed the lot."

"Do you feel a draft in here, Tess?" Gollum heaved himself up and inspected the windows.

I immediately thought of the Windago. My spine remained free of the typical warning flares and I heard only an occasional gust whipping through the woods, not the wail of a demon.

"It's an old house full of drafts. Feel free to build a fire in the wood stove in the bedroom. It's probably more efficient than the fireplaces in the rest of the house."

"I don't think Donovan left you a lot of wood."

I heaved a sigh and laid my head back against the very soft cushions. With my eyes closed, I could almost believe I was somewhere else, far away from the problems that had descended on me.

"Mind if I stay here a while and pretend I'm on a beach in Mexico sipping *piña coladas?*"

"Sure go ahead. I'm going to see if anyone knows how to fight King Scazzy."

"Simple: steal his hat."

"If only it were that easy."

►►►

A gentle kiss to my forehead awoke me. I left my eyes closed, drifting in a warm, safe cocoon of wool blankets and a long hard body pressed next to mine.

"Dill?" I murmured and reached to hold my husband close.

"Sorry," Gollum grumbled. "Wouldn't you be more comfortable in your own bed?"

I'd fallen asleep on Gollum's cushy sofa.

I opened my eyes a crack and groaned at the loss of my wonderful dream and having made the *faux pas* of all time.

"Yeah, I guess I'd better."

"What happened to the house rules? We sleep in beds and not on the furniture?" he quipped. A half smile tugged at his mouth.

"That rule was for you. You don't sleep in *my* armchair." I twisted to untangle my legs from the lovely blanket he'd wrapped me in. "What time is it anyway?" I couldn't get my arm free to check my watch.

"About two. The house is quiet, and all the lights seem to be out."

"Did you find out anything more about our Orculli trolls and King Scazzy?"

"Nope. All of my colleagues agree that he's the prison warden, but no one knows what kind of criminals he guards. Amazing what kind of information is available in a chat room. I met the most interesting man from Russia. I knew of his work, but had never had the opportunity to chat with him before."

"I guess we'll have to have a long heartfelt talk with WindScribe in the morning." I yawned and stretched. If we tied her to a chair and threatened her with hot coals, we might get some straight answers. I would never torture her with imprisonment in a dark box like her mother had.

That kind of abuse might explain her need to set things free and avoid constraint by a seat belt.

"Thanks for letting me nap. I feel much better than I did when I came in."

"Any time, love."

Chapter 25

*N*OW THAT IS MORE like it! In time Tess will realize that her best interests lie (or is that laid) with Gollum and not Donovan and his ilk.

Maybe if I pretty her up a little, Gollum will be more bold. That's the only thing that will penetrate her thick skull. Let's see now, a little makeup wouldn't hurt, and some nice wool slacks rather than sweats—she'll never go for a skirt unless it's one hundred degrees outside with an equal humidity, or she's going to a place that almost requires a dress. Let's see what we can find in the closet. I'll just lay it out for her, maybe help her get the hint.

What! The sapphire blouse and sky-blue pants are missing. I can smell them in the house. Where can they be?

That thieving, conniving bitch! WindScribe has stolen half of Tess' best wardrobe! And she's altering them. Taking in seams to fit her willowy figure, adding trim and lace to pant legs to lengthen them!

That look is so passé. But then the waif has been out of the loop for thirty years or so. She needs an education in fashion as well as manners.

"Tess dahling, wake up. I've got some things to tell you about your guest and the monster cat. I forget to tell you about the cat and the armory door yesterday. Sorry. I got busy. Tess, stop swatting at me. Tess, will you please wake up."

Finally. She sits up and listens. Then she glowers. Then she sets her chin.

Ooooooh, there's going to be trouble. Maybe a fight. I can't wait.

Then she plops back down and covers her head with a pillow. I don't think she heard me at all.

Much to my surprise, Mom and Darren showed up for breakfast Saturday morning just as I started fixing johnny cakes—a kind of cornmeal pancake—sausages, and eggs. I expected them to sleep in, or go out, or do just about anything to avoid me after my confrontation with Darren the night before.

A light New Age instrumental played in the background. Nothing that demanded we listen, an easy accompaniment to life. Just as Darren entered the kitchen, I noted a muted bass string underlying and adding tension to the melody.

There was a new strain about Mom's eyes and mouth, but she put on a good show of being the happy bride, sitting close to her new husband and chattering brightly and sipping coffee and orange juice. But she didn't touch him like she had the last two days. She didn't meet his silent and penetrating gaze. Even when he spoke the bastard French Mom had invented as a child. (How'd he learn it?)

And she had reverted to her dress and pearls. The only remnant of the makeover was her short hair and brighter makeup.

Maybe there was hope for an annulment yet.

Especially if Darren's fight with Donovan had made the wedding night less than expected.

My mind shied away from the intimate details that might cause this kind of tension between them when they'd only been married less than a day. I remembered my own honeymoon with Dill and sighed with regret that I'd never share that kind of closeness with him again.

"You can, lovey," Dill whispered. His voice was a near caress on my ear. "You know what you have to do."

He asked too much. Too late. If he'd started haunting me right after his death, I'd have given anything for us to be together, even my own life. But he hadn't shown up until last autumn, right after I'd had my first otherworldly fight. Right after I'd asked Scrap to transform into the Celestial Blade for the first time.

There was something fishy about the deal Dill offered and the timing, and I don't mean last night's supper of cod with lemon and wine sauce.

Gollum came in just then with a bag of fresh apples and oranges and made a second pot of coffee.

MoonFeather hobbled in on her crutches, grumbling about not spending another minute in that bed and what could she do to help. I set her to putting together a fruit plate. She sat at the island in the middle of the kitchen, out of my way yet still close enough for me to fetch things for her.

WindScribe drifted down wearing my blue outfit all tarted up with lace and braid trim from my bag of scraps for costumes. I ground my teeth together, determined to speak to her the moment we had a speck of privacy.

Manners were universal. Or they should be. If she'd borrowed some sweats, I'd have bought her some clothes at the mall today. But no, she went for my expensive clothes. I didn't feel like I owed her a thing.

We ate together at my new table with the new linens and things. I was happy with the décor. It gave us something to talk about to cover the false brightness in Mom's voice and posture. She fiddled with her pearls, and ran her hands uncertainly through her short hair.

"I hope you haven't made a mistake, Genevieve," MoonFeather whispered to Mom during one of the lulls in conversation.

Mom glared at her. I could almost hear her mental shout: *Mind your own business, witch.*

MoonFeather reared back as if slapped.

I swear no words passed between them. Only negative energy. Extremely negative energy.

"What are we all doing today?" Mom asked. She sounded brittle and fragile.

"I'm searching the Internet for a good price on a trip to Mexico," I said quietly. The clouds and wind and icy temperatures had come back. No shadows. Was that good or bad for drawing Windago out during daylight?

"I'll be setting up my office at the college," Gollum said.

Coward, I mouthed at him for deserting me with this mob.

"I guess I won't be doing anything but reading in bed," MoonFeather grumbled.

WindScribe looked a little panicked. What was she going to do with the day? With the rest of her life?

"I'd like to see a bit of Cape Cod. Never been here before," Darren finally said.

"Fine. We can find a real estate agent to take us around and look at properties." Mom didn't sound fine. She sounded angry. With him?

Hopefully.

Then they all dispersed. Except WindScribe.

"Would you help me with the dishes, please?" I asked her. I'd made quite a mess. I always did when I cooked. For the last two years Mom had done most of the cooking and all of the cleaning. I couldn't expect her to do that anymore. At least not until she got rid of Darren and life got back to normal.

Normal? What is normal? Not my life certainly. What with a grieving Windago stalking me, Orculli trolls, strangers stepping out of Faery, Mom marrying a demon, and me all hot and bothered for a different demon . . .

And then there was Dill. Could he really come back to life?

No. I wouldn't go there even in my imagination. Some things were just too creepy.

"I guess I can help. There isn't much else to do. The only TVs are in MoonFeather's room and your bedroom." WindScribe sighed as if prison shackles weighed heavily upon her soul as well as her shoulders.

"What are your plans, WindScribe?"

"What do you mean?" That panicked look was back, like a wounded bird ready to flee.

"I mean, you can't stay here forever. You need to find a job, get an education, do something with your life."

"Isn't there some kind of cosmic law that says, since you rescued me, you have to take care of me?"

"You aren't a lost puppy, WindScribe. You are a person. You have to take responsibility for yourself."

"You're just mad that I took your lipstick without asking." The limp, frightened child vanished from her countenance, replaced by a wary fox.

"I'm mad that you have so little consideration for everyone around you." I drew on every skill I had learned in my years as a teacher to maintain a calm demeanor. Anger only begat anger. "You've taken my clothes and altered them so that I can never use them again. You monopolize the television so that others are forced out of the room. You don't seem interested in communicating with me or anyone else in the house."

"I've been through a traumatic experience," she whined. "It's like . . . like battle fatigue. Or that Stockholm Syndrome or something."

"We call it posttraumatic stress syndrome now. And you need to talk about it. To me, to a social worker, to a psychiatrist. To MoonFeather. Someone."

"No one would believe me." She pouted prettily.

I was getting tired of that expression. On her. On my mother. Even Donovan looked like he'd practiced it.

"Try me. I've had some pretty weird experiences. I doubt even you could top them for strangeness."

"My coven was kidnapped to Faery. They have so many impossible rules no one could learn them in a hundred years. They threw me in prison with trolls as guards, and I escaped." She threw out the explanation as if it was a fast ball.

Was that movement outside the window? Like a face peering in, then ducking down?

I chilled, waiting for the wind to howl like a Windago. Nothing. The weather remained calm. Cold, but calm.

"I know some of what happened. Gollum and I talked about it last night. I've fought your prison guards and killed a couple of them. They wounded MoonFeather. She's my aunt and a dear friend. What I don't know is which rule you broke to send you to cosmic prison." I threw the ball right back to her. "It must have been a bad one."

"You know?"

"Yes."

"How?"

"Because I am a Warrior of the Celestial Blade. It's my business to know. And I have to fight your prison warden again for your freedom tomorrow at noon. A fight that may cost me my life, and Gollum's as well if he helps me. So you might think about giving me a damn good reason why I should take on that horde or I just might let him have you."

"You . . . you can't do that." She looked truly frightened now.

"I can and I will if you don't come up with some explanations."

"But . . . but . . ."

Before she could come up with another excuse, Donovan walked in without knocking. WindScribe took one look at his scowl (or was that the infamous pout) and fled.

We had only washed half the dishes.

"There's a reporter skulking about outside. I evicted him. Forcibly," he reported.

"Make yourself useful." I tossed Donovan the dish towel.

"Look, I . . ."

"You don't have a choice. If you stay one more moment without helping, you are out of here. Permanently." I applied my emotions to scrubbing an already clean skillet.

Donovan rolled his eyes and wiped the oversized fruit bowl that wouldn't fit in the dishwasher. We endured several moments of silence that became almost companionable.

"I like this," he said quietly while pouring soap in the dishwasher. "Domestic cooperation."

"It's nice to have help. For a change," I replied noncommittally. I tucked the last of the juice glasses into the rack. Dried tomato juice coated the sides. It looked like blood. Darren had drunk from that glass. The rest of us had OJ, including Scrap. Only the imp's glass was half beer.

Should I set the glass aside and have the crime lab test it? What if he'd tapped one of Mom's veins for it?

No. I'd poured the tomato juice myself. I was overreacting.

"Why are you here, Donovan?" I was so tired of waltzing around half statements; not saying what I knew about him; not getting answers.

"Because you are in danger and I worry about you." He draped the towel over his shoulder and grasped my arms, turning me to face him. He didn't turn on the magic mojo, but he was still a damned attractive man.

"Not good enough." I looked up into his eyes, trying to force the truth, the whole truth and nothing but the truth out of him. "I've been in danger before. Scrap and I came through it okay."

"D will suck you dry and spit you out into the garbage heap of the universes if I don't do something. He tried with me, but I escaped him." His eyes burned with an intensity that frightened me. I had no idea how deep or dangerous his anger was. I did know that, when enraged on the fencing strip, he could knock me flat, disarm me, and then laugh about it as if breaking rules and codes of honor was just a joke.

"I've already told him he can't have what he's looking for." I gave him my own version of an intense gaze. He needed to know I was serious about this.

"Which is?"

I held my tongue. I could play this game of secrets as well as he.

"I should know what he wants, why he came here. But I don't. I'm not in the loop like I was last year." He shook his head and looked away.

I'd won that staring contest at least.

"And which loop is that?"

Silence.

I wrenched myself out of his grasp and began scrubbing the now empty counters.

"Tess, I've never made any secret of how attractive I find you." He touched my shoulder gently.

"Thank you."

"I've also told you that I've never met another woman I'd be willing to settle down with, have children with. Our babies would be beautiful, filled with strength and talents way beyond that of normal humans. We aren't normal, Tess. Neither of us could be happy with a mundane human. We belong together. We owe it to the future of all the races to have children that will carry on our legacies." He dropped his head as if to kiss me.

I backed up a step, putting as much psychic distance between us as physical.

Though I wanted to kiss him. I longed to hold him close and just feel good for a change.

I held off. He'd tasted my blood. Savored it.

"That's all? You want me to be your brood mare. No ring, no marriage, no honesty. *No* communication. Just go to bed with you and push out a dozen brats for posterity! No, thank you. You've said your piece, now get out. I have work to do and a battle to prepare for."

"Tess, that's not what I meant."

"Well that's the way I interpreted your half truths. Now get out. Just get the hell out of my house and out of my life." I instantly regretted my words. A vast lonely gulf opened up in my heart. But I wouldn't take it back. I couldn't. Not until he told me everything.

Including why it was so important to create a homeland for half-blood demons that he'd mortgaged his entire financial empire for it. He'd lost everything when we destroyed his casino in order to close a rogue demon portal. Yet as far as I knew he hadn't given up on that homeland.

For the Mike Gionellis of this world, I could understand. He seemed like a good guy despite his demon heritage.

But he just wanted to fit in with humans, not separate himself in a halfling homeland.

So the great project was to create a halfway house for Donovan and Darren as much as the lumbering Sasquatch and other uncivilized beasties who couldn't just get along.

What about the Windago and whatever else was out there? What did they want besides *my* blood?

In the nook Dill silently applauded me. "He's not good enough for you, Tess. Besides, you still belong to me."

"You can get lost, too, Dillwyn Bailey Cooper."

"He's here?" Donovan's beautiful brown eyes opened wide. Panic flashed across his face before he mastered the errant emotion.

"Yeah, the ghost of my husband still haunts me. You'll have to stand in line with all the other supernatural beings who want a piece of me." Disgusted with them both as well as myself, I threw the sponge into the sink and nearly ran back to the sanctuary of my office.

I passed WindScribe at the far end of the butler's pantry. As I wound through the dining room I heard her say, "I'll have your babies, Donovan Estevez."

Chapter 26

"**S**CRAP!" TESS CALLED me.

I could tell by the tone of her voice that she was not happy.

"Cellar. Now. Work out."

Oh, boy, she is not happy. I can smell her anger even over the cat, and . . . is that jealousy oozing out of her skin? Crap. I'm in for a tough time as she flings the Celestial Blade around. She gets so erratic she has no control when she's this mad.

I follow her down the steep steps to the cellar. Her sandy-blonde corkscrew curls bounce and fly about as if attached to her head by small rubber bands. I reach out and tweak one, trying to lighten the mood.

My babe just snarls at me. Then she flings herself off the last three steps, bracing on the banister and landing neatly in a tight turn next to the armory door beneath the stairs.

Oops! I forgot to tell her when she was awake about the faulty latch and the nosey cat trying to get in there. It's not my fault. I got caught up in keeping that horrible cat in his own domain and out of mine. I have a job to do, too! Besides, I had to cover the scratches on my tail with iodine, like Tess told me to. And a little red paint here led to a little more there, and so on and so forth.

It's not my fault.

Well, mostly not.

Maybe partly.

"Babe?" I probe delicately.

She mumbles something even I can't decipher as she fumbles inside her sweatshirt for the key.

No light shows around the doorway. I breathe a big sigh of relief. The cat probably pushed the door closed while it was playing with the latch. Or the ghost did. I'm safe from a tongue-lashing at least

But not safe from the replica blade. Tess reaches into the armory and grabs it without looking. She's on me in less than a heartbeat, swinging the twin moon blades right and left, up and down, circling, twisting.

"Maybe you should try meditation," I suggest. Then I have to jump hither, thither, and yon trying to stay above her, below her, just out of reach. She can't hurt me. Much. I'm only partially in this dimension. But the blade is made from my essence. It is an exact replica of me when I transform. A part of me had to go into the crafting of that blade. I don't know what will happen if she actually connects with me on the cutting edge of one of those blades.

Too close. She snags my tail in the tines of the left-hand blade and flings me in a dizzying circle.

I pop out of this dimension and back again behind her in half a breath. I tweak one of her curls. "The Sisterhood might have some information on WindScribe and the Orculli trolls."

"I called, they didn't answer." Another vicious slash with the blade.

I jump high and cling to a ceiling beam while I take a breath. "You could try reaching out to them from a deep meditative trance. You've done it before," I say.

The blade comes back over the top of her head and nearly cleaves me in two.

Pop out and then in again, this time in front of her. My stubby little wings fight the air keeping me aloft. I'm getting tired.

But so is Tess. She has burned too much energy out of anger and not spared enough for calculation. When she fences, she *thinks*. Now she is just reacting.

I can use this. I fly right high, left low. She follows me with wild and wide swings of the blade. I flit back to the middle, then, just as she rears back for a hard blow, I dart high left and she misses. When she recovers, I'm already at the low left and tying the end of my pink boa around her knee.

She sees my decoration and begins to laugh. Hysterical, high-pitched gales of laughter. She is out of control.

I'm worried.

"Is something wrong, Tess?" Gollum asks from the bottom of the stairs. We'd been so preoccupied neither of us noticed him come in.

Bad move. We have a battle to fight tomorrow. One moment of inattention will be the death of both of us. If I die, she dies. If she dies, I die. For imps, there is no ghostly half life like Dillwyn Bailey Cooper has. No afterlife with a benign deity. Nothing. Death is the end. I do not wish that to happen.

A Sister at the Citadel—Jenny, I think—lingered in a wasting half death for nearly six months after her imp, Tulip, got tagged by a demon claw. Jenny clung to life; so did her imp. Until they were both bare shadows. I had to do something. I couldn't let their torture go on.

I gave them both mercy.

Tess was there. She knows how horrible that time was for Jenny and Tulip. She didn't argue with me. She just held Jenny's hand at the end, letting her know she wasn't alone. If that's not faith, I don't know what is.

We both mourned them.

Neither of them came back to haunt us. Tulip can't. He's dead and gone for good. Sister Jenny is at peace.

If Tess dies tomorrow, neither one of us will have peace.

►►►

I choked on my own laughter at the sight of Gollum appearing so suddenly in my cellar. How did he open the door and get down the stairs without either me or Scrap noticing?

Three deep gulps of air and I thought I had my breathing under control again. I'd worked off a goodly portion of the steaming anger that drove me. Now I had only aching shoulders and cramping fingers where I gripped the blade too tightly. White knuckles and trembling knees betrayed my weaknesses.

"What's wrong, Tess?" he asked again. "You usually fight with more . . . aplomb than brute force reaction."

"What's wrong?" I hate it when I parrot back a question to avoid answering it. Kids used to do that to me all the time in the classroom.

Remembering why I still boiled, Donovan's arrogant assumption that I'd be willing to become his brood mare without a thought for why I resisted a relationship with him sent new waves of adrenaline through my body. And this time my brain received some of it, too.

Faster than thought I whipped the blade up to his throat, spun him around, and pinned him to the door of the armory with the shaft across his throat.

"Don't suppose you want to talk about this?" he asked in a choked gargle.

"No, I don't want to talk. I want to fight. I want to kill that little bastard of an Orculli so that I can kick a dozen people out of my house and take a much needed vacation in Mexico." I pressed harder against the shaft of my weapon.

Gollum's face turned a little purple. He inched his hands up to grasp the staff and lever it away so he could breathe.

His strength and coolheadedness surprised me. I was dealing with Guilford Van der Hoyden-Smythe the nerdy scholar, wasn't I?

Wasn't I?

Something in his eyes sent frissons of alarm up my spine.

Before I could register the emotion, I found myself propelled backward and pinned to the opposite wall in the same manner I'd imprisoned him. Shelves pressed awkwardly into my spine.

Gulp.

And Scrap had the nerve to roll on the floor in a fit of giggles.

"You do more than a tai chi regimen every morning."

"I have studied a number of martial arts. You'd be surprised and horrified at what I can do." He eased up on me a little. His face went blank, telling me more than he wanted to.

He'd done something awful with his martial arts and regretted it daily.

The Gollum I knew didn't fight. He observed others fighting and took notes.

But there was the time last autumn when Marines and Homeland Security had arrested us. I was in trouble from a strange reaction to their tazer. The medic wanted to give me tranquilizers to calm my convulsions. The drugs would have killed me. My brain operates a little differently since my bout with the imp flu.

I came back to consciousness to find three Marines down and Gollum's hands on the throat of the medic.

"How'd you do that?" I choked out.

"I work out." He shrugged off my query into his abilities. As he shrugged off any questions about his past. "Mostly aikido these days."

I'd heard of that martial art but didn't know much about it. Something about using an opponent's energy against them.

"Maybe I shouldn't ask you what is wrong, Tess," he said quietly. "So I'll just tell you to talk. What happened to get your knickers in such a twist?" Steel entered his voice, like I'd never heard before. What had happened to the Casper Milquetoast I thought I knew so well?

Homeland Security had asked a lot of questions about the time he spent in Africa while in the Peace Corps. He'd just admitted to knowing martial arts. Something had to connect the two. I knew it in my gut.

Shocked into truthfulness, I blurted out my conversation with Donovan and . . . and WindScribe's infuriating response to it.

"So are you considering having children with Donovan?" he asked, blinking away the scary stranger he'd become and replacing him with the familiar quirky nerd.

"Not on your life! What's my guarantee that they'll be human? What's my guarantee that he's not some kind of black widower who will kill me—most horribly—as soon as I push out the required number of brats?"

"Good points. So do you feel the need to have children any time soon? Because if you do, we could do it together." He blinked again, and something I couldn't identify crossed his face.

"Children? The way my life is going, I have no guarantee that I'll still be alive twenty-four hours from now. I'm not about to bring a kid into this crazy life with women falling from the sky, a demon marrying my mother, pandimensional prison wardens challenging me to a duel."

"None of us have a guarantee that we'll still be alive in the morning, Tess. Life is uncertain." That blank face again. Like he needed to forget something to keep his sanity.

"So, eat dessert first."

He grinned.

We both relaxed. The terrible pressure of the shaft relaxed against my throat.

"Want to let me go?" I asked, gesturing to the Celestial Blade. "I'm calm now. I promise not to hit you."

Don't believe her, Scrap chortled.

I stuck my tongue out at the imp.

"Just remember that when you do feel your biological clock ticking, I'm available." He gently traced the scar on the right side of my face from temple to jaw with the little finger of one hand while still holding the staff in place.

I didn't yet understand how he could see the scar when no one else could. It was as otherworldly as Scrap. He couldn't see Scrap. Very little about Guildford Van der Hoyden-Smythe made sense.

Maybe the aikido had some spiritual discipline that gave him insight into the otherworldly but not full access.

So what do you say to the man's proposal? Scrap took flight, dusting himself off from the dirt on the floor and the bruises of our fray.

In my mind's eye, I could more easily picture Gollum as a father of my children than as my lover. The idea didn't suck, though.

A gentle warmth trickled through my breasts and down between my legs.

Would he be a kind and considerate lover? Or was he a slam-bam-thank-you-ma'am-think-only-of-himself lover?

That question brought memories of the one night I had spent with Donovan, before I knew of his nefarious schemes and questionable heritage. Warm and delicious memories of passion shared. We'd taken hours to explore each other's bodies, culminating in explosions of multiple orgasms. I smelled again the dry musky scent of his skin. Felt the strength of his hands as he kneaded my breasts. Tasted the saltiness of his . . .

The anger wanted to boil in me again. I didn't have any left.

I had only Gollum's mild blue eyes, magnified by his glasses, staring at me, demanding some kind of answer. Not daring to hope.

I couldn't hurt him.

I couldn't encourage him either.

"I'll think about it. When my biological clock ticks loud enough and long enough, I'll let you know and we'll make a date with a turkey baster." Ungently, I thrust the staff back at him.

He stumbled just enough for me to slip free and bound up the stairs.

I trusted Gollum to put the thing away and properly lock the door. That was more than I could say for anyone else in my life at that moment.

Chapter 27

Celtic people of Europe revered rivers, lakes, and ponds, and in particular springs. They were especially sacred to Eostre, the Goddess of the Moon, fertility, and healing. They cast votive offerings to the Goddess into water sources, a tradition held over in the wishing well.

AFTER MY ENCOUNTER with Gollum in the cellar I didn't want to be alone, where I'd have to think about our conversation. So I stopped in to see my aunt.

"I want to go home," MoonFeather stated the moment I poked my head inside her door.

"That's not such a good idea, MoonFeather." I sat on the edge of her mattress and looked deeply into her eyes.

She'd banished the fogginess of the pain pills. New creases at the corners of her mouth told me she still hurt. A lot. But didn't want the drugs to interfere with her thinking.

"I can get around my house as easily as I can here on crutches. More easily since my floors are level and I don't have to go up or down two inches every time I move from one room to the next." She crossed her arms in a huff.

"That's part of the charm of living in an old house." I tried to dismiss her concerns with a blasé gesture.

"It's a pain in the ass," she snorted. Her sense of

humor began to shine through. It still had several layers of pain and willfullness to peel away though.

"I may be able to speed the healing a little if you will trust me," I offered cautiously.

"How?"

"Scrap."

"The imp?" Her focus narrowed to my left shoulder, and I wondered, not for the first time, if she could see him.

This was getting spooky. I wondered if our lengthy stay in the world outside the Citadel thinned the layers of invisibility around Scrap.

"Yes," I said cautiously. "Scrap, can you lick Moon-Feather's wounds to negate some of the Orculli toxins?"

Don't know, babe. I can do it for you. We are bonded.

I translated for my aunt. "MoonFeather and I share common blood origins. Will that help?"

I can only try.

"Just a little to begin. How long should we wait to see if it affects her negatively?"

Not long, dahling. If I'm toxic to her, she'll feel the first drop of imp spit.

"Go for it, Scrap. Remember, just a little around the edges to begin." I lifted one corner of her bandages, exposing two stitches that closed the horrible gash. A little blood seeped around the sutures and a surgical iodine solution stained her skin a hideous orange-red.

Scrap dropped to the mattress. He cocked his head, staring at the wound for three long heartbeats. His little snubbed nose worked, separating the individual scents of blood, skin, antibiotics, painkillers, and whatever mixed in MoonFeather's blood. Then his forked tongue whipped out and in. One drop of dried blood disappeared.

Tastes weird, Scrap confessed. *It's you but not you.* He looked immensely satisfied.

I watched MoonFeather's face for any trace of change in color or texture.

"Well, what's happening?" she asked impatiently.

"I think Scrap can continue. But take it slow, buddy, in case we've missed something.

Too eagerly, he lashed the wound with flicking lick after long savoring lick.

I exposed the entire wound.

"That feels good. It needs air to heal. Doctors don't always know what's best," MoonFeather sighed and leaned back on her pillows.

I plumped them a little for her.

"So, will you take me home, or do I drag Josh out of his office and make him come get me?"

"MoonFeather, can you wait one more day? Please?"

"Why?"

I closed my eyes, gritted my teeth, and told her about the upcoming battle with King Scazzy.

"Noon on the day of the full moon. Palm Sunday. Good instincts on Gollum's part. Two forces draining energy from the prison warden."

"How did you know about him being the prison warden?"

"I have my own research tools." She pointed to a load of books Josh had brought her now scattered across her bed. "I also spent some time talking to your Gollum in the middle of the night."

"He's not *my* Gollum." Or was he? Our strange conversation in the cellar seemed a whole lot stranger now that I thought about it.

I shuddered and shivered and banished any thoughts I might harbor of taking Gollum as a lover. Or a husband. Or as the father of my children. We were friends. Why complicate and possibly endanger with sex my only normal relationship?

"So what is your strategy for fighting off this King Scazzamurieddu?" MoonFeather brought me back to reality.

"I'll fight him like I did the Sasquatch. He's a demon. Right."

"Not quite," Gollum added from the doorway. His

face reflected some dark emotions. How much was left over from our encounter in the cellar I couldn't tell.

Scrap, having finished his ministrations in short order flitted behind Gollum's left shoulder, in the place tradition assigned to death. The imp looked just as grim and subdued.

If Scrap was worried, I should be, too. My stomach cramped with anxiety.

Both MoonFeather and I looked to Gollum for an explanation.

"King Scazzamurieddu is the prison warden of the universe. He has a job to do. He's doing it in trying to retrieve WindScribe. He doesn't judge her. That's for other powers. He enforces that judgment. By thwarting him, we are going up against some mighty powerful forces, disrupting the cosmic balance."

MoonFeather blanched. "That, Tess, is something you do not want to do."

"What can I do? I'm pledged to protect the girl. In a way, I rescued her. Therefore, I'm responsible for her." WindScribe's words came back to me. Yes, there was some sort of cosmic law that made me feel as if I had to defend her. Once she was safe she had to look after herself. Until then, I had to protect her.

"You must look to your Goddess for inspiration," MoonFeather said solemnly.

"But I don't believe . . ."

"You may not believe in your Goddess, but she believes in you."

A sense of power and mystery swirled around us. Reality tipped slightly to the left. The subdued colors in the room took on more vivid hues.

"Tonight, at midnight, just before the moon sets, it will be close enough to full for our purposes," Moon-Feather whispered in that otherworldly voice that carried the wisdom of the ages.

Chills ran all over me. I sat, awestruck, listening.

"Go out to Miller's Pond where it marks the edge of your property," she continued. "There you must cast into the deepest waters that which you treasure most. Murmur a prayer, any prayer that feels right, conclude the prayer with the words 'Blessed Be.' When the moon sets, it will look as if she has eaten your votive offering."

I returned to my kitchen to find Mom fixing lunch. A rich soup filled with vegetables and chunks of chicken simmered on the stove. She sliced cheese and bread at the center island with her back to the table where Darren and Donovan glared at each other.

I flipped on the radio to the easy jazz station. I didn't like the house too quiet. When only silence surrounds me, I listen for things that are not there, like Dill's step or a Windago hovering in the wind.

"Thanks for cooking, Mom." I kissed her cheek, and took the opportunity to scrutinize her expressive face.

Like me, she wore her emotions openly. I sensed less strain in her than this morning. The tension was across the big room in the nook between her husband and his foster son. And her eyes were clear. She was happy for herself, not because Darren commanded it.

"Did you have a successful morning?" I asked her brightly.

Behind me, Gollum helped MoonFeather navigate the narrow butler's pantry with its tilted floor and then the two-inch step down into the kitchen.

I had no idea where WindScribe had taken herself. Silence above stairs, so she wasn't watching television.

Scrap, check on her for me, please.

She's rooting around the medicine cabinet in the bathroom. Won't find anything stronger than aspirin in there.

Mom's migraine meds?

In the cottage and her purse.

I sighed in relief.

"We found a darling house," Mom said. She turned the full force of a genuine smile on me.

"Damn near as big as this place," Darren added. His smile looked like a gloat. "Newer, too." Like that was a plus in a historic area where status came with the age of one's dwelling. "More efficient design, doesn't ramble like this one. Not hard to change the zoning if we decide to do that B&B thing."

"But it's not in as good a shape as this house." Mom handed me the platter of bread and cheese to put on the table. "D, will you help me with the soup pot?" The look in her eyes was as full of infatuation and admiration as it had been yesterday.

Darren had worked his mojo on her again. I wondered why he hadn't this morning? Maybe he needed time between bouts to recoup his powers. A weakness, perhaps? I'd need every advantage when it came time to fight him.

"It's the old Milner place," Darren said, lifting the big kettle from the stove and carrying it to the table as if it weighed no more than a loaf of bread.

I paused to breathe. WindScribe's name before she took a craft name had been Joyce Milner. I looked around for evidence of her presence and her reaction to that bit of news.

A flicker of movement in the dining room might have been her. Then again it could have been one of my ghosts, benign or otherwise, or even Scrap. No telling among these creaking old timbers.

"We'll need to do some remodeling, since the house has been empty for almost three years and hasn't been updated since the forties," Mom continued. "But we can get it for far below market value."

"We're going to make a cash offer this afternoon." Again Darren nearly gloated. "As soon as I call my banker."

I wondered if he used the same banker as Donovan. Vern and Myrna Abrams had demon connections but fought on the side of humanity with me last autumn. They'd also required Donovan to sign his mortgage papers in blood.

"I can have the kitchen I've always dreamed of," Mom sighed. "And I'd love to cook for all of D's family

when they come to visit. Did we tell you that he has
seven children besides Donovan? I love a big family. Always wished I had more than just you three." She nearly
floated to the table and took her place at the head—the
place where I should sit since I owned the house and
was officially hostess.

I let the slight slide. This time.

Or was that every time?

"While you take care of the financial things, darling,
I'll call on Father Sheridan and make arrangements for
us to have a church blessing of our marriage," Mom
added.

Did Darren forget to breathe?

"I can design invitations and announcements on the
computer for you," I offered. "I'll send a bunch of them
by e-mail to our relatives and friends. We should have a
reception at the church. The parish hall will host a lot
more people than we could have here." I narrowed my
eyes and watched Darren's reaction. I needed to know
what he'd do if he actually had to enter a church. I'd
even show up to watch.

Donovan hid a smirk behind his hand.

"I've already told James Frazier from the *Gazette*
about the engagement. He said he'll print an announcement tomorrow." Mom looked incredibly proud of herself.

"When did you see James?" The pest hadn't called
today . . . that I knew of.

"He was just driving by the Milner place and stopped
to chat," Mom replied.

"He asked a lot of questions about your other
guests," Darren said, watching me closely. "Like how
MoonFeather really got hurt and how you know Miss
WindScribe, where she came from, that sort of thing.
Sounded to me like he knew things he shouldn't and
wanted confirmation."

"Strange that he'd be driving past the Milner place. If
I remember the house correctly, it's on a dead end." I

smiled sweetly at Darren, letting him know I would not be drawn into his probing conversation.

"Did . . . did you say the old Milner place?" Wind-Scribe whispered from the doorway.

"Why, yes, my dear," Mom replied. She looked a little puzzled, as if she couldn't remember who WindScribe was. I'd only told her that she was a friend, temporarily homeless. "Do you know the house?"

"Yeah. Why is it empty?" The girl looked terribly young and frightened. One of those amazing shifts she did from vicious to vulnerable in an eye blink.

"Old Mr. Milner developed Alzheimer's. I believe he's in a nursing home," I told her. She didn't register the medical term. I'd forgotten that it had only entered our everyday vocabulary in the past decade or so. "Such a shame when people forget everyone around them."

Mom jumped in to fill in gaps in the story. "I heard tales that he confused his wife with his mother. He had to be put away when he began accosting every teenage girl he saw on the street, demanding to know where she'd been and why she ran away from home. He thought that every one of them was his missing daughter."

"How awful," WindScribe choked. "Wh . . . what happened to his wife?"

"No one knows. She just locked the house and walked away the day she put her husband in the nursing home." Mom shook her head in dismay. "Such a waste. Janice Milner was quite an asset to the garden club. She got a little tiddley at parties, but no one minded. She was a happy drunk."

I almost gagged on that statement. I remembered the old bitch from some of Mom's garden teas when I was in high school. Janice Milner had a tongue on her that could flay a person alive. Then she'd laugh herself silly, totally oblivious to the embarrassment she caused.

No wonder her daughter had turned to the local Wicca coven as an escape. She'd probably have chosen to stay in Faery forever just to avoid her mother. Except that she'd broken a rule and wound up in an other-worldly prison.

What had she done?

"That family's tragedy is our good fortune." Darren didn't rub his hands together in glee, but he might as well have. "The township just put the house on the market. It's going for back taxes and the residual on the mortgage."

Legal wheels grind slowly. It took three years for foreclosure and confiscation.

"But the house was badly neglected even before it was abandoned." Darren narrowed his gaze to me. "We'll have to impose on your hospitality a while longer, Tess, until we can get the roof repaired and the plumbing updated. I'll find a contractor to redo the kitchen to your specifications, *querida*." He kissed Mom's palm, pausing to lick and nibble on her fingers.

Yuck.

"In the meantime, we can plan an exquisite wedding reception," Mom sighed. She blushed prettily.

"We'll have to find the perfect dress and veil for you," I said. I tucked into my soup so I wouldn't have to engage Darren's gaze any longer. Something about his eyes unnerved me. They looked human and yet . . . there was a redness to the brown iris and a slight misshapen quality to the pupil—like it wanted to shift to the vertical from round.

Oh, yes, this man was part demon. I wondered that everyone he met didn't notice it.

But not everyone knows that demons exist. And not everyone is on the lookout for them.

I checked Donovan's eyes for any hint of otherworldliness. Nope. His pupils were perfectly round, and the iris remained that rich chocolate brown I'd almost fallen in love with. Damn, I wished he weren't so attractive.

Time to change my attention.

"A pity about the Milner daughter," Darren pushed,

shifting his attention to WindScribe. "She'll never get to go back home now."

"If she's even alive. Thirty years is a long time to go missing." Mom's gaze turned wistful and she turned an unfocused stare out the window toward the garden gnomes that had multiplied in the yard between the house and the cottage.

"Maybe she had a good reason for running away and staying away," WindScribe whispered. She kept her eyes down as she tiptoed to the table.

"From what I heard, she was running with a bad crowd, a bunch of witches intent on disrupting the town." Darren fixed WindScribe with an intent gaze. "Bad thing, witches and black magic. I think the Milner girl did something terrible, committed some crime, so that she shouldn't come home, even if she could."

I don't think I could have kept my head down and my eyes averted under such scrutiny.

MoonFeather gasped. "Have you ever heard of the threefold law, Mr. Estevez?" she asked sweetly. Too sweetly.

He blinked and shifted his attention.

"Whatever you do in life, good, bad, or indifferent comes back to you threefold," MoonFeather continued. "I believe that firmly. I make a point of never saying anything bad about someone, even if they deserve it."

Silence rang around the table at my aunt's oblique put-down. She hadn't said anything bad, yet still she'd let the man know he'd stepped over the line.

"Now, now, no fighting while we eat. It upsets the digestion. We should say grace, even if it is a bit belated." Mom held out her hands to join with Donovan and me.

I grabbed one of Mom's hands eagerly and took Gollum's in my other. He joined the circle to WindScribe. Would she, in turn, take Darren's at the end of the table? Donovan reluctantly placed one hand in Moon-Feather's. She extended hers to Darren.

I bit my lip, wondering if he dared exclude himself

from a family tradition. A family he'd joined by marriage. He was a part of us whether he liked it or not.

Whether I liked it or not.

I wondered if he'd survive family game night tomorrow. Sunday, with Uncle George, Grandma Maria, and my sister Cecilia. Maybe Dad and Bill would show up for a change.

Just when I thought Darren would push back his chair and leave us, rather than say grace, he clutched hands with MoonFeather and WindScribe and bowed his head. His lips even moved as Mom recited her favorite prayer and invoked her Christian Trinity.

Chapter 28

Highly prized among Masonic memorabilia is a jewel of black onyx with a carved head of Isis set in an ivory crescent Moon. Below that, dangling within the curve of the Moon, is a five-pointed star representing Sirius—the Dog Star.

"TESS, CAN I talk to you a moment?" Mom asked from the doorway to MoonFeather's room.

"Sure. Just a minute while I finish changing this dressing," I replied. I steeled myself to look at the angry and seeping wound. The doctor had packed it with collagen to fill in the gaping hole left by the gnome ripping a chunk out.

The skin knit cleanly beneath the stitches. Scrap's ministrations had worked miracles in just hours.

"It doesn't look too bad," Mom said, peering over my shoulder.

"It's a mess," MoonFeather grunted.

I'd done my best to keep from hurting her when I ripped off the old bandage, but I could tell from the strain around her eyes and the whiteness around her lips that all was not well yet.

"I need to go home," MoonFeather continued. "I need to poultice this with special herbs and spells to negate any . . . foreign infection."

Demon venom, in other words.

"I wouldn't worry about that," I said looking directly into her eyes. "Much of the infection is gone."

"Actually, what I have to say might be better said in front of witnesses. D is very big on witnesses to this sort of thing," Mom said, hardly pausing for breath.

That surprised me enough to look up from placing new gauze over MoonFeather's war wound. This sounded akin to the argument I'd had with Darren.

"Since I cut my hair, and I've already married D, I won't be needing your comb to hold my wedding veil. I know you treasure this and I want you to have it back." Mom thrust the antique into my suddenly shaking hand.

"Mom, I wanted you to have this for a reason." I examined her expression, posture, and her eyes for signs of what was truly going on and found only my Mom.

"I know. And I want you to have it back for a reason. Now put it away before D stashes it in a safety deposit box or finds a more obscure hiding place. You need this." Mom turned abruptly and flounced away.

"My, my, my. So my ex-sister-in-law has a spine after all," MoonFeather mused.

"Or was that a plea for help?" I asked, more worried than ever.

"I give this marriage three months max before she dumps him."

"Maybe not quite so long," I returned. "She's seeing him for what he is." I held up the comb and nodded to it.

"And that is?" MoonFeather raised her thick eyebrows at me.

"Would you believe me if I told you he's a half-blood Damiri demon?"

"From the dangerous energies that swirl around you, and the evidence of garden gnomes come to life with more teeth than a shark, I'd believe almost anything, Tess. Now why don't you sit and tell me precisely what is going on. Maybe I can help."

And so I told her the entire story. I spoke of my time

in the Citadel learning to be a Warrior of the Celestial Blade. My adventures on the high desert plateau of central Washington last autumn came out a bit more hesitantly. Then the words flooded out in a torrent. I felt lighter and freer with each revelation.

Her brows sank lower and lower as she narrowed her eyes and tensed her shoulders.

"Make certain the votive offering you give to your Goddess is something you treasure above all things. Not because of monetary value, not because the world is jealous you possess it. Give what your heart clings to. Nothing less will ensure your safety tomorrow in battle," she whispered as she clung to my hand. "The world cannot afford to lose you."

MoonFeather's advice to make a votive offering to a Goddess I didn't believe in was just too weird. Even for me.

Scrap's suggestion to seek advice from my friends at the Citadel sounded more logical. They didn't answer the phone, so I had to revert to other methods that didn't rely on technology.

But where in this very full household could I find the privacy to properly meditate?

Gollum's apartment of course. He was still at the college. I called his cell for permission to take refuge there.

"My door is never locked to you, Tess," he said quietly. "Do you need some background music. I can recommend . . ."

"Thanks, but I have my own."

"You might let Gandalf help."

"The cat? How can that pesky critter . . . ?"

"Take him into your lap and let him purr. You'd be amazed at how much easier it is to meditate with that rhythm echoing your heartbeat."

"But Scrap is allergic to cats."

"Does Scrap help you reach out through the ether beyond mortal awareness?"

"Noooo . . ."

"Then try Gandalf. If it doesn't work, lock him in the bathroom."

That sounded like a wonderful idea. So I grabbed a CD from my collection, a couple of blue candles, and a stick of incense in a scent compatible with the candles. I chose these because I liked the color, not because of any spiritual symbolism.

"Are we having a pot party?" WindScribe asked when she saw me lugging my stuff out of my office.

"No." I didn't feel like explaining myself to *her*.

"I'm bored. What am I supposed to do all by myself?"

"Read a book. I've got lots all over the house. Take your pick." Then I slammed the door to the apartment in her face.

Deep within the apartment I found some cherished peace and quiet. The sounds of life from the house and the road remained outside these insulated walls. I set up my candles and incense on the coffee table in front of a worn leather recliner. Why fight an uncomfortable posture with no support sitting in the middle of a cold floor? The idea in meditation was to relax. So I stretched out and let the chair cradle me.

The upholstery still smelled of Dill's aftershave and his unique male scent. I drank it in along with the incense. A gentle throbbing drum and wordless chant from a Midwestern tribe wafted over me from the stereo.

My body eased immediately. Some tension lingered across my shoulders and my fingers still clenched.

Starting with my forehead, I consciously tensed and relaxed each muscle group until my entire body felt more liquid, my spirit lighter. Then a series of visualizations stripped more and more tightness from my psyche.

Gandalf levitated to the arm of the chair. I reached over and ran my hand the length of his silky body. He vibrated from head to toe in a pleasing rumble. I didn't have to look at him to invite him closer. He stepped lightly into my lap, circled once, and stretched out with paws and head on my chest. That rippling purr caressed my soul.

With a sigh I let my mind drift in ever expanding circles. Gradually, I sent those circles west, across mountains and plains, jumping mighty rivers and climbing bigger mountains and plunging down to the high desert plateau of the Columbia River Basin. Mile by mile I sped across my memory of the route to the Citadel hidden in a deep ravine not far from Dry Falls.

A question mark appeared in my mind. Telepathic contact is not exact, often symbolic.

"Who?" I whispered.

An image of a bubbly blonde. Gayla, the woman I had dragged in out of a thunderstorm and nursed through the imp flu. Sister Gert had tried to refuse her entrance, the infirmary was full, resources stretched to the limit. Maybe Sister Gert sensed that this bright and bubbly personality would become a rival for the leadership of the Sisterhood. Whatever, I couldn't leave her out there to die alone. Under Sister Serena's direction I had lanced the festering wounds of the infection. Our kinship went deeper than our scars.

What followed wasn't truly a conversation, but it's easier to convey in that manner.

"I need advice," I whispered with voice and mind.

"Should I get Sister Serena or Sister Gert?"

"Let me talk to you first." I sent a flood of information about WindScribe, the Orculli trolls, the Windago. At the last second I tucked in a bit about making a votive offering.

"All other dimensional beings are evil! You must kill all you encounter." Sister Gert's voice blasted across the miles in an almost physical manifestation.

I winced at her volume and intensity.

"But the prison warden of the universe?"

"He's a troll. He's evil."

I always knew the leader of my Sisterhood was single-minded, with blinders on. Was that a redundant statement? Well, Sister Gert embodied redundancy.

"What about my leadership brooch, Teresa?" Sister Gert continued, barely stopping for breath. "When are you going to return my brooch?"

I let a long chasm of silence come between us. Scrap had given me the brooch. I wasn't about to give it to a woman I didn't like and barely respected.

"Don't worry about the right or wrong of the Orculli trolls," Gayla intervened. "Just do what you have to do."

On a more private line of communication I sensed an upcoming vote between her and Gert about leadership of that particular branch of the Sisterhood.

"Okay. I can handle a fight with the trolls, though I'd like backup. Any chance of linking me to another Citadel?"

"I'll see if there are any rogues in your area," Gayla said.

"Rogues? I thought I was the only one."

"Not anymore. Things are changing. New portals opening. A lot more traffic back and forth. We can no longer work in isolation."

"And Gert doesn't believe that," I confirmed. "The old ways have worked so long she can't envision any kind of change."

"Correct." Hesitancy, like there might be an eavesdropper.

"Good luck with the election. The Sisterhood needs you."

"They need you, too. My first change will be to open communications."

"Then make sure someone answers the telephone." I felt a lot more comfortable and less alone with Gayla in charge.

"Gotcha."

"What about the votive offering."

"You have to question that?" Gayla came through almost as strong as Sister Gert had before. "I would think that would be the obvious course of action."

"Obvious to you. I'm not sure I should bother . . ."

"Bother, Tess." Gayla's tone turned soft, confidential. A friend giving sound advice.

"If you think it will help . . ."

"I know it will."

"How do you know?"

"Because I believe."

Scrap believed in a number of Gods and Goddesses. Mom had a deep and abiding faith.

I wished I could believe in something bigger and better than just my own strength and resolve.

Chapter 29

GRADUALLY I ROSE up through layers of meditation to an awareness of reality. I felt refreshed in mind and body, as if I'd slept deeply for an entire night.

Not for long.

A crash of cast iron frying pans hitting something metallic brought me the rest of the way back with a jolt. My temples throbbed. Candlelight pierced my eyes like a laser strobe. Too fast. I'd come out of the trance too fast. I don't think my soul had a chance to catch up with my body.

I leaned forward and blew out the candles.

Another crash from the region of the kitchen, muffled by distance and thick walls.

I winced and tried to huddle back into myself.

I crawled out of the recliner, my joints just a little liquid with languor. Time to be the adult in the household.

I trudged through the house toward the kitchen, making my way by feel more than sight. I could too easily tip over from extreme relaxation to headache.

Blinking against the glare of sunset coming in through the bay window, I stood stock-still in the doorway from the butler's pantry. WindScribe stood in the middle of the kitchen with a small saucepan in her hand, ready to throw it. MoonFeather sat at the island, out of the direct path of the girl's aim.

Allie held a defensive position in front of the refrigerator, ready to duck or retreat when the next missile flew. A pile of heavy cookware lay at her feet and a big dent shadowed the fridge door behind Allie.

Damn, that would cost a mint to repair. I couldn't afford to replace it.

Mike skulked at the breakfast table, not much more than a shadow, recording everything in a notebook as well as with a small digital recorder.

"What is going on here?" I asked as mildly as I could while I wrestled the pan out of WindScribe's hands.

She whirled on me with hands extended like claws, ready to rake my face with her broken nails. For all the time she spent primping with my lipstick, she could have borrowed a nail file and used it.

"She's lying!" WindScribe screeched. At the moment she sounded akin to the Windago.

I reared back.

"She's spreading vicious lies about me."

"Want to explain that?" I asked Allie.

"Actually, I am the one guilty of speaking too frankly about the WindScribe I knew in the past," MoonFeather said. She sounded calm, but her eyes held shadows of inner pain.

"So why is she attacking Allie?"

"Because I tried to get her to speak honestly." Allie shrugged and took a cautious step toward MoonFeather at the island.

"They both lie. I never did those things. Never, never, never," WindScribe insisted. Fat tears welled up in her eyes and she . . . pouted.

That convinced me she lied. Her pout was too studied, too pretty. A mask.

"What did you accuse her of?"

"According to the old police records, the night before

the coven went missing, WindScribe broke into her neighbor's house and stole a diamond pendant and three valuable cocktail rings. Then she took a false prescription for Darvon to the pharmacy and had it filled—which she didn't pay for. When she left, she shoplifted a bunch of candles and incense."

"Lies!"

"Darvon?" I asked.

"It's rarely used now," MoonFeather said. "A powerful painkiller. Too addictive and too many abuses."

"So, thirty years in Faery didn't cure your addiction?" I cocked an eyebrow at the girl.

"I'm not addicted." She stamped her foot like a two year old. Physically, she might be eighteen, but I don't think she'd matured beyond twelve.

"Then what happened to an entire bottle of thirty tablets of tranquilizers?"

"I'm not addicted. I need help opening my mind to the wonders of the universe. Only when we break through the barriers that society imposes upon our psyches can we experience true vision. But I'm not addicted. I'm not. Only losers get addicted."

I let that one pass.

"Speaking of losers, we picked up the girl from the mugging last night, Julie Martinez," Allie said. "She really was the ringleader behind the muggings. And the boy Francis Jorgenson is recovering from his broken trachea," Allie told me. "The DA says you acted in self-defense. No charges against you. All three kids are facing trial in adult court. They're seventeen and high school seniors."

That was a relief. And a sadness. Those kids had destroyed their promise of a future. Much as WindScribe was doing, or had done.

"So, Allie provides the police record from thirty years ago, and I'm guessing you, MoonFeather, corroborated the story from personal experience. You'd seen her stoned more than once."

"I will not lie. I had witnessed WindScribe indulging

in her little ... hobby too many times. Not always in her quest for enlightenment. I'd noticed her wearing expensive jewelry and exotic perfume I did not believe she or her parents could afford. As much as I believe in the threefold law and refrain from speaking ill of anyone, I felt that Allie needed to know the truth."

"What happened to the jewelry?" I asked.

WindScribe clamped her mouth shut and shot me a mutinous glance.

"I'm guessing you used it as bribes in Faery. Maybe one of those shiny baubles got you out of King Scazzy's prison?"

"That would mean ... no, I won't believe it. I can't believe you'd actually do something so . . . dangerous." MoonFeather shook her head, grabbed her crutches, and made to leave the kitchen.

I stopped her by simply removing the crutches from her grasp. She had to remain sitting.

"You won't believe what?" I asked.

MoonFeather kept shaking her head.

WindScribe edged sideways toward the outside door. Mike shifted position, ready to grab her as she passed him.

"Let me guess," I said trying to capture Moon-Feather's gaze. "The coven planned a different spell. They wanted to invite some of the faeries here. For enlightenment. Maybe to improve Earth in some way. But WindScribe deliberately altered the ritual. They all got whisked away to Faery instead."

WindScribe gasped.

MoonFeather's silence confirmed my suspicion.

"A dangerous thing to try, WindScribe. But stealing the jewelry and stocking up on pain pills before going makes it premeditated, not an accident."

"I didn't think she was that stupid," MoonFeather whispered. "Perhaps desperate is a better word." She looked up, having found a way to avoid saying anything bad about the girl.

"Stupid is the right word," I said. The threefold law

was MoonFeather's path, not mine. I didn't believe in Gods and Goddesses and karma and destiny and such.

If I told myself that often enough, I'd believe *that*. And I wouldn't do something useless like make that votive offering tonight at moonset.

"The statute of limitations has run out on the theft," Allie said. "I can't arrest you, WindScribe. But I have to warn you that I am watching you. Anything like that happens again, and I will put you away. Our prisons are probably just as nasty as anything King Scazzy can come up with." She turned abruptly and left. Without saying good-bye.

She was pissed. Really pissed. I hadn't seen her like this since junior year in high school. She'd caught Zach Halohan—the chief constable's son—cheating on a final exam. Then she got into more trouble than he did for tattling.

"How's your arm, Mike?" I called after him as he tried to slip out the door unnoticed.

"Fine. You don't need to worry about me."

"Was he hurt?" Allie poked her head back inside from the mudroom.

"Ask him."

"I will."

"You had better clean up the mess you made, Wind-Scribe. If you want anyone to cook for you, those pans all need to be washed and put away properly." I turned on my heel and exited as well.

Maybe I could justify having Gollum pay for the repair to the fridge out of the trust fund.

"I suppose you are going to desert me, too?" Wind-Scribe sneered at MoonFeather. "Of all these losers and control freaks, I thought you would understand."

"I understand. I do not approve. I've learned a lot about freedom and the responsibility that comes with it. Running away is not the answer. Drugs are not the answer."

"Then what is!" WindScribe demanded.

"That is something you have to figure out for yourself. Me telling you won't help at all. I'd help with the washing up, but as you see, I cannot stand. Tess, will you help me back to bed?"

"Your ghosts are afraid of her," MoonFeather whispered as we negotiated the step down from the butler's pantry to the dining room. "They are all huddled in the library, as far from her as they can get."

"What can frighten a ghost? They're already dead?"

"What is dead but another transition? Ghosts have more transitions to make than most of us."

Another pan hit the floor.

The sun set. We all gathered for a dinner of stew and fresh rolls in the formal dining room—except Donovan. He seemed strangely silent and absent. WindScribe had managed to put enough stuff away to give me enough pots to cook with. But the kitchen was still a mess.

The wind came up. I jumped and started at the first rattling window.

Gollum didn't come home.

I picked at my food, listening diligently for the sound of his van wheezing across the gravel drive. No one else talked much. We watched each other and waited for someone else to make the first move into or away from politeness.

Finally, my cell phone rang. I breathed deeply for the first time in an hour at the caller ID.

"Gollum."

"Tess, I think I need your help."

"What's up?" I couldn't disguise my instant alertness from anyone. They all seemed to listen in, with different intent.

"Have you noticed the Wind?" He spoke cautiously, as if aware of listeners.

I caught the special inflection. "Yes. Where are you?"

"Just about to turn in at your street. But this van is top-heavy with a high turning radius. I'm afraid she'll tip over."

She as in the van or in Lilia David the Widowed Windago?

"On my way."

"Tess, what can possibly be more important than finishing your dinner?" Mom admonished me. She looked at Darren rather than me.

"She's an adult, Genevieve. Let her run her own life," MoonFeather came to my defense.

"A little politeness toward your mother is expected," Darren said. He smirked, as if he were my real father and not an unwanted step.

"My house. My rules," I gave him back the same sickly sweet smile. "I'm done. I cooked. Someone else can clean up." I stared meaningfully at WindScribe as I dashed for the kitchen.

Scrap turned scarlet and began stretching before I got my jacket zipped.

By the time I reached the gravel, he was fully extended and ready to taste monster blood.

The wind whipped my breath away and tangled my hair. I twirled the Celestial Blade above my head, cutting through the suddenly warmer air.

No change.

Then I spotted Gollum's van inching around the corner to the drive. The wind buffeted the big vehicle. It shook and rocked back and forth.

Mine! The wind whistled. *My new mate.*

"No," I screamed. My heart beat overtime. I couldn't run fast enough to Gollum's side. "Leave him alone, bitch." I slashed the blade at every shadow.

YiiEeeeek!

Scrap hit resistance.

I followed that particular shadow toward a bank of azaleas. Brittle branches broke beneath our feet as I forced Lilia to retreat.

He's mine, she insisted.

I had trouble seeing which shadow she might have blended with. The security light didn't penetrate this far.

Then I heard the ominous sound of Gollum opening his car door.

"Get in the house now," I ordered him. "She can't violate the sanctity of a home."

I can now. You killed one mate and now you steal another. He's mine. By cosmic law I claim him.

"Halt." King Scazzy popped between us. He held his hands up.

Suddenly my blade froze in place. I glanced up. Scrap's eyes blinked at me in bewilderment from the right-hand blade.

Lilia stilled as well. The sound of the wind roaring in my ears dropped down several notches.

"Lilia claims that man as mate," King Scazzy said in his most authoritative voice.

Deep in my gut I knew I had to respect his authority in the matter. He was the prison warden of the universe after all. He had the power to force me to keep holding my weapon in one position, high above my head.

I do.

"I can't allow that," I replied. My arms ached to move again, to lower the blade. To—Goddess forbid—drop it. But I knew if I did drop Scrap, then I forfeited my right to defend myself and Gollum.

"Do you have a prior claim?" the little king asked.

The universe stilled. My perceptions tilted a little to the right. I fought for and found a new balance. The strain in my arms and shoulders lessened.

"Do you have a prior claim?" King Scazzamurieddu repeated his question.

"Answer him, Tess," Gollum whispered behind me. "Please answer him. I think we're dealing with cosmic justice here."

"I told you to get into the house." What was I supposed to do?

I knew. Still I wavered in indecision, unwilling to make the commitment demanded by these otherworldly creatures.

"I can't retreat. The king of the Orculli has blocked my passage with some kind of force field."

I chanced a quick glance at him. His glasses drooped and I saw concern in his mild blue eyes.

My mind whirled through several scenarios and probable outcomes.

"I claim this man as my own," I said boldly. I didn't specify what I claimed him as—mate or friend.

"Very well," King Scazzy said. "My battle with you tomorrow at noon still holds precedence. Lilia David, you must wait until the outcome before pursuing your vengeance for the death of your mate."

Nooooooo, she wailed and faded into the distance, taking the wind with her. *I need a mate. I cannot hunt without a mate. I will not be denied.*

"You will wait," Scazzy commanded.

I have waited long enough! Suddenly, the wind intensified. It gained a new depth of chill that turned my sweat to frost.

"You have violated the sanctuary of this home. Do so again and I will have no choice but to invalidate your claim."

I will have justice. Next time I do not come alone. This last came as a mere whispered promise from a great distance.

I lowered my blade in relief. My arms trembled from the strain of holding it up in one place so long.

"Never thought I'd thank a troll," I said by way of backward obligation.

"Do not thank me yet. We still have a rendezvous at noon." Scazzy popped out, leaving me alone with Gollum.

Heat filled my face with a blush. What exactly had I claimed, and what did I do next?

A flash nearly blinded me.

Gollum ran with wicked speed behind the sole remaining oak guarding the entrance to my drive. He emerged a heartbeat later with James Frazier. He held the reporter by the collar of his down jacket in one hand. In the other, he carried a huge and complex camera.

James looked entirely too smug.

Chapter 30

"*D*ON'T YOU DARE publish that photo," I warned James with deadly menace. Once more I raised the Celestial Blade.

We can't do this, babe. He's human, Scrap moaned deep inside my mind.

"He may be human but he is evil."

A faint chuckle from Scrap. *Not evil enough.* The weight and balance of the blade began to fade.

I made a tossing movement, so that the reporter would think I'd dropped it instead of it disappearing into thin air.

"You can't stop me, Tess. The public has a right to know that you harbor monsters in this corner of Cape Cod."

"I don't believe your outraged indignation, James. We went to high school together. You were a sneaking tattler then, and you're a stalking, evil snake now." I shook my fist in his face.

He gulped and flailed as Gollum lifted him slightly. He had to stand on tiptoe to maintain any balance.

"I have taken a vow of nonviolence," Gollum admitted. "But you strain my willpower, Mr. Frazier."

That was new information. I filed it away to pursue later. Presuming we had a later.

"I have rights," James insisted. "Give me back my camera."

"In a moment." Gollum dropped him.

He stumbled and almost fell to his knees. His awkwardness gave Gollum time to fiddle with the camera.

"Fortunately, he's gone digital. I just deleted an entire series of photos of our little encounter." Gollum grinned hugely as he handed the camera back to James.

A safe and sane solution. But I really wanted to break the damn camera. And James' head.

"I doubt your reading public will be interested in our rehearsal for live-action role-playing games," I told him. "We're going to a con soon." As good an explanation as the truth.

"Con?" Ever the reporter, James whipped out a notebook and pencil.

"Short for convention. Science Fiction and Fantasy Convention. I attend five or six a year to promote my work and meet with other writers, editors, fans."

"And will Miss WindScribe attend with you?"

I glared at him. Gollum reached for his collar again, his other fist clenched.

"I found her high school photo. She hasn't changed in twenty-eight years. Do you have an explanation for that?"

"Her daughter," I said with finality and marched back toward the sanctuary of my house.

I heard James fumbling through the brush. Then Gollum caught up with me and slipped a supporting arm about my waist.

"You need to rest before the moon sets at midnight. I know that even a short fight takes a lot out of you."

"We need to talk about what happened."

"Later. When the rest of this is settled."

▶▶▶

Hours later, at eleven-thirty, the house was quiet. The only light spilling out the windows came from my bedroom in the loft and from the tiny light over the stove in the kitchen. Mom and Darren in the cottage had doused the lights and grown silent. I'd turned off the stereo, the better to listen for eavesdroppers and unseen watchers.

Even Scrap kept his mouth shut. He hovered somewhere nearby, but he didn't sit on my shoulder like he usually did. After two beers with OJ he had a slight orange tinge and droopy eyes, like he needed sleep. Elsewhere.

I missed the reassuring almost weight of him.

The wind retreated. Barely a breeze ruffled the upper branches of the trees. No Windago nearby at the moment. I had no doubt she watched me from a distance.

Using a penlight, I made my way carefully out the back door and over ice and slush along a faint trail in the woods behind the house. I carried the magical comb with me. A heaviness surrounded my heart and threatened to bring tears to my eyes.

"Tess, wait up," Gollum called softly.

I heard him shuffle along the path. I couldn't bear to turn and face him. I wouldn't let him see me cry over what I knew I had to do.

"You shouldn't have to do this alone," he said quietly, draping a long arm around my shoulders. "We belong together by some cosmic law I don't understand, so please, let me help you."

"Thanks." I leaned into him, just a little. His friendship as well as his body helped warm the ice crystals that threatened to shatter inside me.

Too soon, we broke clear of the patch of forest and emerged into the clearing made by Miller's Pond. Centuries ago, someone had dammed the creek that ran through here and erected a grist mill at the west end. Only a few foundation stones remained of the mill, but the dam and the pond lingered, reminders of our pioneer ancestors.

As kids, my friends and I used to sneak out on hot summer nights to gather here and tell ghost stories. We invented tales of seventeenth-century witches thrown into the depths to test their powers. If they rose to the surface and survived, they must be witches and so were taken away and burned at the stake. If they sank and drowned, then they were innocent and buried in holy ground.

But what if one of them swam away over the dam and disappeared where the creek entered the sea less than a mile away? We shivered and made up tales of the witch's curse over all who tried to profit from the pond ever afterward. Because the witch's accuser received all of her property as a bounty.

Made for a lot of false accusations. A threat to make sure women "behaved" so they wouldn't invite the lust or envy of a malicious neighbor.

I trembled with my own fears that night.

The setting moon, just a hair off full, dipped into a small gap in the trees. Its silvery light made the pond ice shimmer with an unearthly glow. A black splotch in the middle showed where the ice had begun to break up. It looked like a black hole in space—an entry to another universe.

Maybe it was.

I shivered with more than just the cold, remembering the witch's curse that none would profit from this pond again.

Making a votive offering here might be a bad idea.

Gollum looked just as uncomfortable as I felt. But he stood stalwart beside me.

"I know the water is only ten feet deep at the most. I've swum here in the summer." Dill and I had giggled together over the prospect of skinny dipping in the pond on hot summer nights. He hadn't lived long enough to share that experience with me.

I almost wished he would show himself tonight, let me know he approved of what I did.

"Do you have a prayer or invocation?" Gollum whispered.

Neither one of us seemed willing to disturb the unearthly quiet surrounding this ritual.

"Nothing special. I've always felt that if there is a God or Goddess, they'll know what's in my heart. I need help tomorrow. I'm obligated to protect WindScribe, to keep her here in her home dimension. The Orculli trolls are obligated to fulfill their destiny as the prison guards of the universe. We are both right. They are too numerous for me to count. I don't really know how to fight them, other than with the Celestial Blade. Will it be enough?"

I turned the comb over and over in my hands. Regretting the loss of its beauty as well as its powers to allow me see through a demon glamour. I also regretted losing this because Scrap had found it for me. He gave it to me out of love.

Before I could change my mind, I drew back my arm and hurled the comb toward the black depths of the pond.

I lost sight of it flying through the darkness. Then I heard it clank and skitter against the ice at the edge of the hole. It bounced and slid back toward me.

"Yeep?" I squelched a cry of surprise.

You throw like a girl! Scrap laughed. He sounded relieved as well as his usual sarcastic self.

"Oh, my," Gollum said, adjusting his slipping glasses. "I do believe your Goddess has rejected your offering." He ventured two steps upon the ice, clinging to a sapling for support. With his long arms he stretched and retrieved the comb from its landing place, practically at our feet.

"I don't understand . . . this is the most valuable thing I own."

But you don't truly treasure it, Scrap reminded me.

I repeated his comment for Gollum.

"He's right. There is something more important to you."

"I don't treasure *things*. I treasure people. My mom, my aunt. My friends. Even my nasty sister is more important to me than any of the possessions I've accumulated."

Gollum raised one eyebrow and captured my gaze. The moonlight made angles and hollows of his face. An image of his skull, frozen in horror nearly covered the face I'd come to treasure almost as much as my family.

"Okay, there is one thing. But I'd hoped . . . Goddess, don't make me do this." Crying quietly, I drew a picture frame from inside my parka.

"Tell me about it. Let me treasure the memory as much as you do," Gollum whispered.

"Dill made the frame." I traced the rough carving of the wooden edges.

And with the memory came his presence, leaning against a tree. Tension nearly vibrated from his ghostly form.

"Don't do this, Tess. Don't throw me away."

"Dill embedded special agates and arrowheads he'd found into the wood."

"Making a choice to let me die, so you can move forward, I can understand," Dill said. Then his tone turned bitter. "Throwing me away like this is cruel, Tess."

My fingers caught on a rough edge of knapped flint.

"That's a bird point from the predecessors of the Okanogan peoples," I heard him say, both in my memory and from somewhere amidst the trees.

"And the picture?" Gollum pressed.

"Our wedding photo. In Reno. We both wore jeans and western shirts and Stetsons. Mine was white. His was black." Two fat tears landed on the glass covering the photo. "It's the only picture I have of him. We were together such a short time."

"Have you made a copy of the photo?" Gollum asked gently.

"Of course. But it's not the same. Not the actual

photo of our wedding. Not in the frame he made especially for it."

"This is very important to you, Tess. I don't think I could make a votive offering to any God of such a treasure."

"And that's why I have to do it."

"Please, no, Tess," Dill pleaded. "We can be together. Let me fight the Orculli with you instead of the imp. Please, Tess, don't throw me away."

"Don't, Tess." Gollum put his big hand over mine where I held the picture and frame. "We'll find another way for you to defeat the Orculli."

"I might defeat them, but will I survive?" I whirled and shouted in the direction of Dill's ghostly presence.

Silence.

That was my answer. Dill wanted me to die, so we could move onto some other plane of existence together. Or have our spirits cease altogether. He didn't care if I lived or died. He was already dead. Why shouldn't I be as well?

This time I flung the photo and frame away like a Frisbee. It bounced against the ice, slid and slithered to the edge. There it teetered a moment.

"I can't believe you did this!" Dill protested. "I may not be able to hit you, but I know things that can!" His form flickered in and out of view.

My heart rose in my throat, almost hoping the Goddess would reject this offering as well. Had I ever truly been happy since Dill died? Would I ever be a complete person without him?

Remember the times he told you to stop writing to go rock hunting with him? Scrap whispered. *Remember how often he found other things for you to do rather than write? He didn't want you to be complete. He wanted to own and control you.*

A puff of wind caught the frame and made it sway. Back and forth it teetered on the edge of acceptance, on the brink of rejection and reality.

I think I gasped. My drying tears burned icy trails on my cheeks.

Then with an audible sigh, the wind let the frame go and it plunged into the water.

The moon sank below the horizon, gobbling up the thing I treasured most. The thing I needed to let go of most.

Chapter 31

DRAINED AND EXHAUSTED, physically and emotionally, I let Gollum lead me back toward the house. I rested my head against his shoulder. His arm enveloped me, warming me against the chills that racked my body, inside and out.

Maybe I cried.

Maybe I was beyond tears.

Scrap settled on my free shoulder, rubbing his insubstantial face against mine.

They knew what this had cost me.

I wasn't certain I did. Yet.

Dill remained anchored to the edge of the pond, staring helplessly at the black hole in the center of the ice.

As we stepped free of the woods, a little more light filled my side yard, between the house and cottage.

I straightened away from Gollum. The lawn should be in total darkness. The moon had set and a fine mist covered the stars.

The mounds that had been ugly garden gnomes were missing. Had the Goddess banished them when She accepted my votive offering?

I should have such luck.

Gollum pointed to the cottage where a dim light seeped beneath the blinds in the living room. A vague shadow stood under the window.

I must have made a noise. The shadow turned and beckoned us forward.

Senses alert, Scrap on my hand, ready to lengthen and sharpen into the Celestial Blade, I shifted my balance to an aggressive stance and stepped into the shadows.

"Listen!" WindScribe hissed with a finger to her lips.

I just barely heard her.

Gollum stayed close behind me as we pressed ourselves against the rough siding. His head remained a scant three inches beneath the window ledge.

Angry whispers drifted to my ears.

"You have to do your part, D," Darren demanded. Though of a similar mode, it was deeper and more commanding than Donovan's.

"No. You've stepped way beyond the bounds of decency on this one, D," Donovan returned. I could imagine well his tense stance with fists clenched, shoulders hunched, and head thrust forward. I'd seen him on the edge of a fight before. I'd also seen him dissipate strong emotions in a crowd ready to turn into a riot.

Why wasn't he doing that to his foster father?

Maybe he couldn't. Darren had his own talent to lull fears and calm anger. He was probably immune to the same magic in others.

"What does decency have to do with it?" Darren said casually, no trace of emotion. "We are pledged to a mission. The end is in sight."

"Not this way. Not with Tess' life in jeopardy."

"If she needs to be eliminated, like that worthless traitor Dillwyn Bailey Cooper, then she will be."

I nearly choked on my own breath.

"Tess, no," Gollum stopped me with panicked words and a fierce grip on my arms. "If you charge in there now, your mother will hear everything. Are you ready for that? Scrap may not be able to help you. He can't get near Donovan."

Rational good sense. I didn't want to hear any of it.

"He knows something about Dill's death. He suggested that he *murdered* my husband." I was shaking again. My teeth chattered.

Where was Dill at this moment of truth? He should be in on this.

I needed to *do* something.

"Hush, they're still talking," WindScribe said. That girl was starting to unnerve me. She was everywhere, sticking her nose into everyone else's business but her own.

And she never wore a coat or shoes. How much of Faery still clung to her?

I wondered if there was a lock that could hold her. I really wanted to put her away somewhere secure until this was all over.

Gollum pushed me back to our place beneath the window. I dragged my feet, looking over my shoulder to the front steps. Ten paces away. I could bolt and run.

"What about the witch, WindScribe? You going to kill her, too?" Donovan demanded.

"No need. She's so stupid and naïve she'll end up getting herself killed. King Scazzamurieddu needn't be so diligent in his duty. She'll be a lot less trouble to the universe meddling in this dimension, than bribing prison guards with sex and diamonds." Darren yawned. "She barely needed my help to escape."

My ears pricked. Darren had aided her prison break! He also sounded like he knew why my charge had been imprisoned. Donovan probably knew, too.

"I went along with you on the necessity of eliminating Cooper. He was a loose cannon, ready to spill our plans to the wrong people. I am as committed to your Great Enterprise as you. I was committed before I fell! That's why I did fall," Donovan ground out.

Fell from what? I wanted to scream. But I didn't. I needed to hear more.

"Then act like you think this is important."

"I won't let you hurt Tess. Or her mother," Donovan insisted.

"You don't have a choice. I am head of this clan. Leader in the Great Enterprise of creating . . ."

"I am not part of your clan. I never have been. I was given to you because I resembled your bat form. You manipulated the Powers That Be to see things your way without a thought for what was best for me. Nothing binds us. And I will stop you from hurting Tess."

"Not bloody likely, boy. I am stronger than you. And I have the backing of the clan."

"The clan is scattered. Your children are more interested in staying human, blending in. They're too inbred to have the intelligence to be useful."

"My children are dedicated!" Darren wailed. "They would never deny their true heritage."

Sounded like rationalization to me.

"Your children are dedicated to fast cars, skiing in the Alps, snorkeling in Fiji, and electronic toys," Donovan laughed. "Who do you think are my biggest customers for computer games? Your children."

A long silence followed. Long enough that I wondered if I should retreat while I could.

"It's just you and me here, D," Donovan said. "You don't have the clan to back you up."

"You've been spoiling for a fight for a long time, D. If I didn't find you useful upon occasion, I'd take you down right now," Darren replied.

"Name the time and place. But not here. Not where Tess and her mother could be caught in the backlash."

Darren laughed. An evil, hideous sound that echoed around the cottage and the immediate environs.

New chills ran up and down my spine. I wondered that Mom didn't hear it and cry out in alarm.

"I'll find you, when I'm ready, D. Until then, watch your mouth and watch your back." The sound of a fist hitting flesh. Someone stumbled. A lamp crashed to the floor.

What little light there was vanished.

Before I could react, Donovan stormed out of the cottage and over to his car. He raced the engine and skidded on the gravel as he turned onto the main road.

"Next time, D. Next time I'll be the one who does the hitting, and you the falling," Darren chuckled. "But then you've already fallen once." He silently closed the door.

Time for answers. I marched up to the worn wooden steps of the cottage.

Both Gollum and WindScribe caught me.

"Not now, Tess. Wait until morning when you have a clear head," Gollum insisted. "And Allie to back you up."

"I'm cold," WindScribe whined.

I could see tears in her eyes and moisture gathering around her nose. She was my responsibility—at least until noon tomorrow—even if she didn't have enough sense to get in out of the cold.

Had my mother ever felt this exasperated, frustrated, aching with grief and bewilderment when she had to deal with three fractious teenagers alone, after her divorce from Dad?

Most likely.

If she could cope, so could I.

But first thing in the morning I was going to corner Darren and demand explanations. With or without my mother present. A violent showdown was coming. Soon. I felt it in my bones.

Silently, the three of us trooped back to the house. I sent WindScribe up to my bathroom to take a hot shower and go to bed. I didn't want to follow her. I wasn't ready to close down my mind and body for the night.

"I've got a bottle of single malt," Gollum offered.

"Did it start as my bottle?"

"Nope. Bought this one all on my own. Highland Park, you usually go for the more expensive stuff."

"Tonight I'll take it. Even if it isn't as complex as Lagavulin."

"I'd call Highland Park a full and robust flavor, without the taint of iodine from exposure to the sea," Gollum said. He kept his arm around me as he guided me toward his sofa.

"But Lagavulin is the fire of the gods wrapped in velvet."

The sharp amber liquid he poured for me burst upon my tongue like something magic and wonderful, then warmed me all the way to my toes as it slid down my throat. Sipping scotch is a three-step process. First the sniff. Highland Park has a flowery touch to the nose. Then roll the sip around the inside of the mouth. Here the flavors of peat and salt and other good things come into play. Then the swallow and the whiskey explodes like fireworks against the taste buds.

"Usquebaugh!" I sighed. "The water of life."

"Whiskey. The only word in the English dictionary acknowledged to have come from the Gaelic," Gollum said. For once he didn't have his professor face on. "Although I have my own theories about the word quaff. Is it derived from quaich, a footed beer cup? The only proper beverage one quaffs is of course beer. Quaffed from a quaich." He sounded a little tiddly on only one shot. Usually he needed more. A lot more to get drunk.

"Do you ever turn it off?"

"Turn what off?"

"Your head. All the vast quantities of esoteric trivia stashed there."

"Upon occasion."

"Like when?"

"When I'm making love to a beautiful woman," he said in a rush, then blushed.

"What did you say?" I couldn't have heard him right. I didn't want to have heard him right.

"Well, uh . . . um . . ."

"Never mind." Dangerous subject. Even more dangerous the way he looked over the top of his glasses at me, then hastily looked away, afraid I might catch his gaze. And hold it.

"Well, hit me with some more trivia. Like anything you've learned about the Orculli trolls that will help me fight them. Anything you've gleaned about the Great Enterprise of the demon world. Anything you might have heard on your occult grapevine about my dead husband."

Chapter 32

A child born on the first day of the full moon is said to enjoy a long and healthy life. But those who take sick on this day are in for a lengthy and serious illness. Possibly fatal.

ONCE MORE I WOKE up on Gollum's couch. This time morning light streamed through the windows. It looked like the weather had finally broken and we might, just might, be headed for a warming spell.

Could this be the Goddess breaking the hold of the Orculli on our weather? Gollum had said that unseasonable cold was often attributed to the little trolls.

The Windago also brought unseasonable freezes.

Whatever. I welcomed the warmth and basked in comfort for just a moment.

Gollum had pulled a soft open-weave blanket over me and tucked it under my chin. I was fully dressed and he was nowhere in sight.

I breathed a sigh of relief. I may have spent the night with him, but I hadn't slept with him.

"Coffee," I sighed as the rich scent wafted in from the main house. The door was open, and I heard muted conversation.

Yawning and stretching, I wandered through the house, checking for signs of anything out of place on my way into the kitchen. Sleep still made my eyes and limbs heavy. Or was that the aftermath of too much scotch?

Gollum was making a huge pot of coffee, humming along to a CD of filk. He had a fine tenor. The first time we'd gone to a con together he'd bonded with my filking friends. He'd also pushed me to sing long before I was ready. When I finally did, at a belated wake for a dear friend, he'd been as responsible for freeing my voice as anyone.

For a moment I was glad I had claimed him in front of the Windago and the Orculli.

Mom manned the stove. The enticing scent of sizzling sausages wafted toward me. I also caught the rich doughy smell of steaming waffles. Heaven.

Gollum handed me a large glass of orange juice and a fistful of vitamins.

"Thank you. Bless you. How did you know?"

"I had more scotch than you did." His eyes twinkled behind his glasses. He looked good this morning. Freshly showered and shaved, in a forest-green silk turtleneck covered by a Nordic sweater in more shades of green and brown and his usual chocolate-colored cords.

He looked better than I did with my tousled curls and splotchy eyes.

"You look like you slept in those jeans, Tess," Mom said sharply.

Well, I had.

"Breakfast is ready. You'll have to change later." She was back in her new white pants suit with the ruby blouse. Her inevitable pearls graced her neck. Every hair was in place, and her makeup was perfect.

She had a tightness about her eyes and a tremor to her hands that told me she'd had a migraine and taken heavy drugs to combat it. The pain might have vanished, but the pills left her fragile, almost frail.

No wonder she hadn't intervened in the argument between Darren and Donovan last night. An elephant gun exploding next to her ear wouldn't rouse her from those drugs.

"You're all dressed up," I said as I slid into a kitchen

chair facing the bay windows and the cottage across the yard.

"D and I have an appointment with Father Sheridan after Mass. To arrange the blessing of our marriage." She actually preened as she set a plate before me filled with a succulent waffle. Melting butter flowed out from a fat pat in the center. Then she plunked a second plate on the table overflowing with sausages and fried tomato slices.

I reached for the maple syrup—the pure stuff from Vermont.

Gollum slid into the chair next to me and stole half the waffle.

I considered slapping his hand, then thought better of it. We'd shared a lot last night. Personal stuff, wants and desires, politics to religion to fashion to education. I knew more about him as a person but still didn't know much about his history and family. That would come. Some barriers had fallen between us.

"Is Darren going to Mass with you?" I looked at the clock on the microwave. Nine-thirty-five. They didn't have much time to get to church.

"Of course," Mom replied sharply. She stared out the window, worry creased her mouth and her eyes. "I'd better go hurry him along." She marched out the door, leaving it open and letting in the cold but not frigid air.

"Do you think Darren will actually set foot inside a church?" Gollum asked.

"That is something I'd like to see. Will he disappear in a cloud of smoke? Will he meet a force field that throws him out?" Like had happened to Scrap once when he tried entering the newly blessed refectory back at the Citadel.

That was something I'd have to ask him about. It reminded me of how he'd been blocked from entering a room with Donovan.

But Donovan wasn't blessed. If anything, he was as much a demon as Darren.

What had he said last night?

I was committed to the Great Enterprise before I fell.

"What do you suppose Donovan fell from?" I asked.

Gollum chewed in silence for a moment. Then he got up and poured more batter into the waffle maker. "From grace?" he replied.

"But that would mean he'd been in a state of grace at one time. Like an angel. He's no angel. That I'm sure of. Could a demon, even a half-blood, enter a state of grace?" The Church didn't think so. That was one reason they littered their cathedral roofs with gargoyles.

"Depends on the human half of his blood. If that ancestor had been up for sainthood, maybe the spiritual quality they imparted to their offspring . . ."

An ear-splitting screech tore the air.

"Mom!" I pelted toward the cottage.

She screamed again and again. I felt the sky might tear open from her anguish.

My heart beat overtime and climbed to my throat. I couldn't cover the one hundred yards to the cottage fast enough. The distance seemed to grow longer, my goal farther away with every step.

"Scrap? Where the hell are you? I need you now!"

Right here, babe. He flitted ahead of me on wings that beat faster than my racing pulse. He flashed between curious yellow and happy lavender.

No demons or evil lurked close by.

What was going on?

Finally, I reached the steps. Gollum overtook me and yanked open the storm door. The main door swung free.

We came to a skidding halt. Mom stood in the middle of the room, hands covering her face, eyes wide in horror.

Darren lay face up on the floor, dark blood pooled around him from a deep and long gash through his chest. Death had glazed his eyes and turned him blue with cold.

▶▶▶

The sweet smell of blood and death filled me with longing. I needed to stretch and sharpen, to taste this demon blood myself.

But there were no live demons present. I took no part in this death.

Never truly sated, I dropped down beside the corpse. My tongue lapped at the chill, stale blood. Instead of satisfying my thirst, it tasted sour. He'd been dead too long. I spat it out in disgust.

My internal combustion engine remained well below the boiling point. Nothing changed in my normal cute self, gray green with six lovely warts.

Curses. I can't earn any more beauty marks from this death.

Chapter 33

GOLLUM MUST HAVE called 911. I sure didn't.
Allie and Mike roared up the drive in a four-by-four rig, followed closely by Joe Halohan, the chief constable, in his unmarked sedan, and by a third officer in a squad car. Followed by an ambulance. Followed by the tiny compact of James Frazier, reporter for the *Cape Gazette*.

I had my hands full with Mom's hysterics. She wouldn't leave the cottage. She wouldn't stop screaming. Finally I grabbed both her arms and frog-marched her outside.

Once free of the sight of her dead husband, Mom's screams reduced to sobs that shook her entire body. I feared she'd pass out from lack of breath. Or hyperventilate.

Somehow, I got Mom into the house and plied her with a cup of tea.

WindScribe ate the waffle Gollum had started a lifetime ago, hardly noticing the noise and fuss around her.

"Take a plate to MoonFeather," I finally snapped at her.

"Oh." She looked up with wide, innocent eyes as if I'd

disturbed some deep and meaningful meditation. Her eyes were glassy. Had she found Mom's migraine meds?

For once, she obeyed without questions or whines.

Allie and Chief Constable Halohan trudged across the melting snow—completely free of gnomes—each with one hand resting on their weapons and notebooks in the other. Mike trailed behind, head twisting right and left, looking at everything and . . . and . . . was he sniffing?

First time I'd ever known a cop to use his nose with the same intensity as his eyes. I didn't think smells were admissible evidence.

He swung his arms freely, no trace of a wound from the Windago. He looked so very human I doubted demon blood in him. And Scrap didn't react to him. Must be pretty diluted demon blood.

I braced myself for the torrent of questions. Who was the victim? What was our relationship? Why was he in my cottage? How did we come to discover the body? I answered them all as simply and honestly as I could. I had nothing to hide.

Right?

"And where were you at three this morning?" Allie finally asked. Her eyes constantly shifted, searching for something or someone.

Scrap flitted about making faces at her. He knew she couldn't see him. Did she sense his passage through the air? Perhaps she was looking for one of my ghosts.

Dill had remained absent since I threw his picture into the pond at midnight.

"I was asleep at three," I replied.

"And you, Mrs. Noncoiré, I mean Estevez?" Allie turned her attention fully on Mom.

"I . . . I was . . ." Mom choked and fell into another spate of sobs. "Will someone turn off the damned music. It's giving me a migraine!"

"We might as well give up on her for a while. She's in shock. Won't get anything out of her until tomorrow at best," Halohan grumbled.

I watched Mom visibly gather the ragged pieces of her psyche together. "I . . . I had a migraine last night. I took my pills. Darren was considerate enough to sleep in the spare room so he wouldn't disturb me." That could be the truth. When Mom had one of her "spells" and took her meds, nothing could wake her for close to twelve hours.

No wonder the quiet music on the stereo grated on her fragile nerves. I always had music on the stereo. In the aftermath of the drugs was the only time she complained.

"How did you get out of the cottage without stumbling over his dead body?" Mike asked. Anger tinged his voice. He stood with his feet braced, knees locked, and his body tilted forward in an aggressive stance.

I'd seen Allie confront traffic violators and belligerent drunks before. But never with as much violence simmering beneath the surface as Mike displayed.

As if he were taking the murder personally. How close were his family ties to Darren Estevez?

Both Chief Halohan and Allie looked askance at him.

"I woke up about seven-thirty feeling quite well and refreshed," Mom explained. "The cottage was still dark and quiet, so I crept out without turning on any lights. I wanted to surprise everyone with a big breakfast before we went to Mass. Oh, my gosh, it's gotten so late. What will I tell Father Sheridan?" Mom threatened to fall back into her hysterics.

I couldn't tell if she lied or not. She'd dissembled for years, covering up for Dad's sexual preferences. I'd learned to lie with a straight face from the mistress of untruth. She was so good I think she truly believed her altered view of reality.

So many emotions crossed her face and filled her eyes with new tears I couldn't delve beyond the surface to find the truth behind her words.

"The body wasn't in the direct path from the back of the house to the front door," Halohan said, making notes.

"Still . . ." Mike persisted.

"Give it up, Mike. This thing isn't going to be settled in an hour," Allie warned.

"Isn't it?" Mike turned to me. "The victim was stabbed. Lots of blood. No weapon on the scene. We need to search both the cottage and the house." He locked his gaze on me fiercely as he kept his knees from bending.

"Mike," Halohan protested. "We know these people. We should be looking elsewhere, into Mr. Estevez's past."

"His foster son maybe?" I prompted. I'd watched Donovan leave in a huff near midnight. Who was to say he hadn't come back? Gollum and I had been at the other end of the house, in the apartment. We probably wouldn't have heard him.

Should I volunteer that information?

Never volunteer anything to the dirty rotten coppers, Scrap snarled in his best Chicago gangster voice.

"Good idea. Any idea where Donovan Estevez is?" Halohan glommed onto that tidbit eagerly.

"He said he was staying in a motel nearby," I offered. "I don't know which one."

Speaking of the devil . . . Scrap popped out as we heard the crunch of gravel under tires and a car door slam.

"Chief Halohan, do we really know anyone here?" Mike asked. His voice remained cold and unfeeling. But I sensed heat behind it, waiting to explode like Mount St. Helens.

"There have been a lot of strange reports and complaints by the neighbors the last year or so," Allie said hesitantly.

"And I find it too coincidental that both mother and daughter married someone they barely knew and then became widowed shortly thereafter. There's money involved." Mike continued.

That stopped me cold. How did he know that? Only Allie could have told him. Or Millie, chief gossip and police dispatch. But she'd only say something if Mike asked.

That was something to think about.

Rather than address that issue, I rounded on Allie.

"Allie, how could you? You're my best friend. You *know* me."

"Does she?" Mike snarled.

Allie swiveled her head looking into the empty air, a silent signal that she searched for Scrap—a big secret I'd kept from her for three years.

"Lots of nooks and crannies in these old houses," Halohan mused, scratching his chin. "Wouldn't hurt to look. The perp could have stashed the weapon close by to avoid getting caught with it."

"There is that room under the cellar stairs you keep locked," Mom volunteered. She wouldn't look directly at me. I had no idea if that statement came from her or from some lingering influence of Darren's.

My throat froze in horror. The armory. Stashed with more than a dozen very sharp and lethal weapons, new and antique.

And the Celestial Blade.

Scrap, wherever you are, get the blade out of there!

"You don't have to be so helpful," I hissed at Mom.

"I was only being honest. Which is more than I can say for you," she replied in a huff.

What had got into *her*?

A demon still influences her, Scrap whispered from somewhere else. *Look at her eyes. That's not a drug haze. It's demon glamour.*

"Let's have a look," Halohan said. He aimed for the kitchen access to the cellar. "You have a talk with the son, Allie."

"I have to get the key to the priest hole." I stalled and remained sitting at the table. If I called it the armory, they might arrest me before they even looked.

Halohan halted in his tracks. "Where?"

"In here," I sighed. Then I led him through the maze to the office and my purse inside the desk drawer. A quick search of the zipped pocket came up empty.

The copy around my neck I wanted to keep secret.

My heart raced in panic. I fumbled around inside the black hole of a purse and found only the fairy key chain with house and car keys—both my hybrid and Mom's SUV. Then a slow and methodical grope into the corners at the bottom. Still nothing.

Finally, I dumped the contents out on the desktop. As wallet, comb, sunglasses, PDA, and cell phone tumbled over the surface, I spotted the elusive key to the armory on its gargoyle chain with a mini flashlight attached. Someone had tucked them into a corner behind the computer.

Not me. Even in a hurry I'd not be so careless. I said so to Halohan.

He scrawled another note. "Who else has a key?" he asked, not looking up from his hen scratching.

"I gave a copy to Gollum."

Halohan looked blank.

"Guilford Van der Hoyden-Smythe. The gentleman who met you at the cottage."

"The nerd. Yeah. Why him?"

"I trust him."

"And not your mother?"

I just rolled my eyes. He knew Mom well. His wife belonged to the same garden club—the one that sold hideous garden gnomes to raise money.

"Yeah, I guess not. If your mother had a key, the whole garden club would, too. In fact, since she knows about the room, they probably all do, too. Not hard to have a locksmith out and make a duplicate." He took the key from me.

I noted that he'd donned latex gloves.

"Anyone else have access to *this* key?"

"You saw where I keep my purse. I don't lock it up in my own house. But I didn't think anyone else knew to look inside a zipped pocket inside another zipped pocket."

Donovan had dug through the purse in search of a bandage for my cut forearm.

"You've got a lot of people visiting. Lots of strangers wandering in and out." He made another note.

WindScribe poked her head out of MoonFeather's room. I waved her back inside. No sense involving them until we had to. MoonFeather was innocent. I knew that. She could barely hobble about on her crutches let alone get across the yard quietly in the middle of the night, stab a full grown man/demon, and hobble back quietly.

WindScribe? She'd dumped the contents of my purse onto the bed. She could have looked further. Last night I'd sent her to a hot shower and bed at midnight. I didn't think she could creep down the noisy stairs without me hearing her.

Both Gollum and I had drunk a lot of scotch. Would we have heard anything?

We trooped down the cellar stairs, collecting along the way a squarely built woman wearing a forensics team jacket and carrying a huge black case.

Cold sweat trickled down my back. I kept telling myself that I had nothing to fear. I was innocent.

But the clock kept ticking, and the number of people in various uniforms in my house and my yard kept growing.

How was I supposed to meet King Scazzy in battle in less than an hour with all these authorities hanging around?

Scrap, where are you?

Keeping away from Donovan.

Great. Just great.

Too many bodies filled my cellar. I was supposed to be the only one who came down here. Mom did to do laundry and select preserves, but that was it. Scrap and I trained down here. No one else.

No one.

Gollum and I had sparred down here once.

The forensics woman dusted the padlock with a black powder. "It's clean," she grunted.

"Wiped?" Halohan asked.

"Looks like it." She didn't clean the powder off. "Some scratches around the keyhole. Might have been picked. Can't say for sure. Could be just wear and tear."

Halohan used my key to open the lock, still wearing his gloves.

My teeth wanted to chatter. I clamped them shut.

A bellow and a slamming door stopped us all. "Tess, what the hell is going on?" Donovan pounded down the stairs.

"Donovan," I said gently, stopping him from barreling into the overcrowded cellar. He seemed to fill the room all by himself, the top of his head nearly brushing the ceiling beams. The dirt and cement block walls crowded closer using up all the air.

"It's D. All they'll tell me is that he's dead." Donovan dipped his face close to mine. The gesture was oddly intimate and conspiratorial.

I blanked my mind to the allure of his scent, his heat, his charm. Easier now. All I had to do was remember how he relished licking my blood off a wound he'd inflicted on my arm.

"Chief, I understand that I need to talk to you about viewing the body before the autopsy. There is a ritual . . ."

"Don't you worry, young man. We'll get a rabbi or priest or whatever you need to oversee the autopsy, make sure everything is done correct and respectfully." He placed a big hand on Donovan's shoulder in reassurance.

"I doubt you'll find a shaman from *his* religion," Donovan snorted in disgust. "No. I must see the body *before* the autopsy. The ritual must be performed before you cut him open."

"Can't let you alone with the body. Might destroy some clue."

"I don't need to be alone. I just need to perform a ritual," Donovan insisted.

"Donovan, your foster father was stabbed in the middle of the night. This is a criminal investigation," I tried to explain to him. All the while my mind whirled with questions. What kind of ritual? Would Donovan do something so that all vestiges of demonhood disappeared?

I really wanted to be there when he did whatever he needed to do.

"Stabbed? I don't understand." Real bewilderment clouded Donovan's eyes. "No ordinary blade . . ."

"That ain't no ordinary hunting knife," Halohan whistled as he pointed to the replica Celestial Blade. He ran a fingertip along the curved cutting edge and yelped. His finger bled through the gloves. He popped it into his mouth, glove and all and sucked on it.

"Holy shit," the forensics woman said. She took two steps into the armory and stopped dead in her tracks. Her head bounced around like the oversized bobble-head of a doll in the back window of a car.

"So that's where you keep it," Donovan whistled through his teeth. "Can I hold it? I didn't get a chance to examine it the one time I saw you use it."

I tried merging with the wall. Somehow this wasn't going to turn out pretty.

"You use these things?" Halohan looked at me with new respect and deeper suspicion.

"I collect blades. A hobby I picked up after I started fencing. You'll find my sport gear upstairs in my bedroom. I don't like displaying sharpened blades on my wall. Someone could easily slice off something important if they tried playing with them. Or steal them to commit a crime. So I store them here."

"Oh, we'll look upstairs, too. But I don't think we'll find anything more interesting than this." The forensics woman backed out of the tiny room carrying a blood-stained weapon very gingerly.

"Careful, that's a seventeenth-century German short sword. Very rare and worth a small fortune," I protested. A long thin blade with a gold etched bell guard. It weighed fifteen ounces and was perfectly balanced. It sang when I snapped it through the air. It very closely resembled a modern sport fencing foil. Except this one wasn't foiled. The point was lethally sharp. And now covered with blood for about ten inches from the point up the blade. From the foible almost to the forte.

I wanted to grab the antique away from these people who had no respect for its place in history.

"We'll take care of it, all right. What's this?" The forensics woman looked closer at the bloodstain. "Strange metal that's being eaten by the blood as if it were acid."

"More likely strange blood," Donovan muttered.

Heat flooded my face and made my knees weak. She'd found the murder weapon. And it probably had my fingerprints all over it.

Chapter 34

"YOU HAVE THE right to remain silent . . ." Allie began the ritual of arrest up in the kitchen. She looked happy about it.

"What about fingerprints, Allie?" I protested, tensing my muscles against her grabbing my wrists and pinning them behind my back with her cuffs. "Your tech said it had been wiped clean of prints."

"What's going on?" Mom asked. She looked dazed and confused. Very much herself.

I would be bewildered, too.

"Tess? Tell me what's happening." Now she chose to take her gaze out of hiding and fix me with a stern look.

I opted on my right to remain silent. Anything I said at this point might get me into deeper trouble.

"You didn't kill him, did you?" Donovan asked on a whisper.

I was sure Allie heard him. Mom, too.

"Oh, my!" Mom placed one well-manicured hand over her mouth. Her nails matched her blouse. Instead of ruby, they now looked blood red.

Allie clamped handcuffs on my wrists. I couldn't feel more awkward.

"Oh, Tess, you shouldn't have. We'd have worked out any differences you and D had," Mom added more fuel to the fire.

I almost caught a hint of a glowing ember from hell deep behind her eyes.

"Mom, don't help!"

"This is stupid," Gollum bellowed from the doorway.

At last, the voice of reason.

Everyone paused to look at him. Fury splotched his bony cheeks and made his glasses slide all the way to the end of his nose. For once, his mild blue eyes blazed with emotion.

A new fear crept through me. I'd never seen Gollum angry before. Suddenly the strength in his shoulders and the clenching of his fists alarmed me.

I had a wisp of a memory: *A Marine lieutenant and a corporal lying unconscious on the floor of an office trailer with thick bruises on their necks that looked like fingerprints. A Marine sergeant held a gun to Gollum's temple shouting at him to back off.*

But I'd been barely conscious at the time, with severe muscle spasm from an industrial-strength military-grade tazer gone astray in my wacky nervous system. I couldn't be sure if it was a memory or a dream.

Just as I could never be sure whether my nightmares of demons were real or the product of a wasting fever. Scrap said they were both. . . .

Either way I didn't want to be on the receiving end of Gollum's anger.

"Tess couldn't have killed Darren Estevez. She spent the entire night with me," Gollum stated with a straight face and a fierce look.

"Tess, you didn't!" Mom shrieked, as if sleeping with a man outside of marriage was worse than killing her husband of only thirty-six hours.

Allie inhaled sharply. Her face looked hurt. Then she hardened and yanked on my handcuffs so that my shoulders threatened to dislocate. "That tears it. You're coming down to the station, right now."

Jealousy. Allie and I had never had that between us. We'd always liked different boys in school. Always backed off when the other showed signs of interest in someone.

"Allie, it wasn't like that," I whispered desperately.

"Wasn't like what?" Halohan barged into the conversation. "You sure she didn't sneak out when you were asleep, young man?"

"We didn't sleep much." Gollum held Halohan's gaze steadily, not blinking.

"You slept with *him!*" Donovan exploded. "You slept with that bastard. Doesn't our relationship mean anything to you?"

"It's none of your damn business, Donovan. We only slept together once. Then you turned into someone I'm not sure I want to know."

"I'm still the same man you couldn't wait to fall into bed with," he ground out.

"Are you? We have no relationship, Donovan. We've made no commitments."

"I asked you to bear my children."

"And I declined. Commitment, marriage, and happily ever after weren't part of the offer. I'm free to choose any man I like as a bed partner. And I don't choose you."

He bolted out the door, knocking police people aside in his angry hurry. WindScribe appeared out of nowhere and followed him. She climbed into his car while he was backing out into the lane. Then he peeled out like a devil was after him.

"That true, Tess?" Allie asked. "You slept with Gollum?"

The hurt in her voice almost broke my heart.

"We slept the entire night together, in my apartment," Gollum insisted, daring anyone to contradict him.

"We'll sort it out down at the station." Halohan jerked his head for Allie to take me out to the squad car.

"Don't worry, Tess. I'll have a lawyer down there in minutes," Gollum called after me.

"What about my noon appointment?" I dug my heels into the slushy grass. Allie yanked again on my arms.

"Can't you see I'm trying to save your life? If you are safely locked in a jail cell, Scazzy can't kill you," Allie snarled at me. "Though why I should bother saving your traitorous hide is beyond me."

"That isn't the issue."

"It's the only issue that really matters. I'm still your friend, I guess. Sometimes, like right now, I wish I weren't." Allie looked back at Gollum standing in the doorway with longing and pain. Then she leaned her greater height and weight into propelling me forward. I had no choice but to climb into the back of her huge four-wheel-drive rig. Not a graceful maneuver with my hands cuffed behind my back.

"Does this mean we have to cancel family game night?" Mom called after me.

▶▶▶

Tess isn't going anywhere, anytime soon. I should go hold her hand, so to speak, but there are things happening that tweak my curiosity.

There are too many people in uniform at the house to sort out the emotions and the tensions. If they find anything interesting, I can discover it, too, by peeking at their reports. I'll wait to go home until the police decamp.

So I pop over to Donovan's motel room.

I have to watch from outside the window. I think I know the source of that forcefield. I've felt something similar before. Twice now. But that theory is just too outré for words. Too humiliating to admit.

He and WindScribe are going at it hot and heavy. Oh, my, he does have a beautiful body. Lovely muscles ripple beneath his smooth skin. Not a lot of body hair. I do so admire lovely men. No wonder Tess turns to pudding every time he walks into the room. The only thing more beautiful than this man naked is an imp covered in warts.

Now, WindScribe is just another female to my jaundiced eye. Too skinny with hardly any boobs. He takes his time, working with hands and tongue. He captures WindScribe's gaze with his as he slowly, ever so slowly enters her.

She squeaks in passionate wonder. Her eyes glaze and her muscles ripple all the way to her curling toes.

She is transparent to me. I can see through her skin, to all her inner workings. And young as she is, she hasn't kept fit. Too much fat under the skin. Few females can measure up to Tess for beauty and muscle tone. She doesn't think so, but she doesn't look at her own soul. I love Tess more than life. She's my warrior, and I her blade. Our lives have melded to the point that if she dies, I die. If I die, she dies. That is an intimacy far deeper than mere sex.

Speaking of which . . . where did WindScribe learn to do *that*? She isn't the innocent teenager she pretends to be. Before she went off to Faery with her coven, she'd been around. Several times. Either that, or she spent her time with the little folk servicing the king . . . and all of his minions.

Oooh, so flexible. And Donovan measures up to the task, in more ways than one. He is so virile and potent. He is like the Damiri. They breed and breed and breed. She's ripe. And eager.

They reach their peak at High Noon Exactly. How appropriate.

She's following through with her offer to bear Donovan's babies.

I don't think Tess is going to like this even though it will be weeks before anyone but me can know for sure if the pregnancy will hold.

It's over all too soon.

A cold wind blows up. I have felt this wind before. Icy, bitter. It smells of Windago.

Goose bumps appear on WindScribe's skin. She cuddles close to Donovan and burrows beneath the covers. He takes longer to notice, merely accepting her desperate seeking of warmth as the prelude to more sex.

I turn blood red without bothering with any shades of pink. My body stretches and sharpens. I need to transform. But I have no warrior nearby to handle and control me.

Without Tess, I can do nothing. I am nothing. I am useless.

I bang on the window and shout at Donovan. *Beware. Hide. Get ready to fight.*

He can't hear me.

WindScribe jumps and starts.

"It's just the wind banging a branch against the glass," he soothes her.

No, no, no! It's more than that. Danger.

Why do I bother? Donovan out of the way will make life easier for Tess. I've fulfilled my obligation to warn him.

Three swirling black forms made of air and ice catch hold of me and slap me away. I fight for control with inadequate wings and insubstantial weight. A real imp would have enough weight to work with gravity to fly into the face of these demons.

There just is not enough of me.

Three Windago. They always hunt in mated pairs. But Tess killed the mate of one of them back in Wisconsin. They'll not let go of that grudge easily. Lilia has found reinforcements for her vengeance.

If she can't get to Tess, she'll humiliate her by taking the one she has vowed to protect. They have the backing of someone, some*thing* very powerful if they are out during daylight. Are the Windago WindScribe's punishment for escaping her cosmic prison?

Before I can claw my way back to the scene of action, the Windago blow down the motel room door. Cheap plywood has no resistance.

WindScribe screams. Something heavy hits the wall. A stream of Damiri curses spew from Donovan.

Finally, I am able to cling to the window frame and watch. Only watch. I ache to transform. I thirst to taste Windago blood.

Without Tess, I can do nothing but watch.

The Windago grab WindScribe by her long blonde hair. She fights them with teeth and nails and feet and fists. Her blows strike only moving air and freezing cold.

Donovan rights himself and grabs a lamp. He turns it on and breaks the bulb. Then he jabs the nearest Windago with the weapon. Sparks fly. The demon crackles with electricity gone awry. He jerks and spasms. His semihuman form is outlined by lightning. He becomes a storm.

Thunder rumbles around and through him. Lightning strobes the room and nearly blinds me.

Then he stops and crumbles to freeze-dried coffee grounds.

Now the Windago are down another mate. They will double their efforts at revenge. They will not remate from within. They must each turn another human.

His companions flee, dragging WindScribe by her hair. Where her heels touch the ground, sparks shoot out like fireworks on the fourth of July.

Donovan drops to his knees and pounds the floor in his frustration. The boards warp from the force of his blows.

I creep away. Useless. A normal imp would retreat to Imp Haven to gain comfort and succor from his Mum. I can't. My Mum would grind me to a pulp for my failure.

So I slink back to Tess, doing my best to hide the truth from her. I would die if she rejected me.

But I am a failure.

Chapter 35

*In a 1744 hieroglyph by de Hooghe, Virgo repre-
sents ever germinating life under the dominant influence of the Moon.*

AN HOUR PASSED in my holding cell. Then
two. Noon came and went.

I hated to think what would happen if I didn't show
for my battle with the Orculli trolls.

I rattled the cell door, uselessly. I screamed to be let
out. I cajoled and offered bribes to my guards. Nothing
worked.

I couldn't see if anyone occupied adjacent cells—the
intervening walls were solid cement. I couldn't hear evidence of occupation either. Sunday midday; last night's
drunks had cleared out, and no one else was likely to
need incarceration until later.

Where was Gollum with his promised lawyer? Or my
dad, or anyone who could help me?

Where was Scrap? Probably off indulging in a feeding
frenzy of mold. He'd be fat and limp and useless from
overeating when he returned.

Even Dill had not returned since . . . since I had
thrown him away last night. I wasn't sure I truly wanted
him gone now that he was.

My heart sank. My whole life seemed one big failure.
I'd committed myself to saving WindScribe from her

fate and failed. What good was being a Warrior of the Celestial Blade if I let a little thing like arrest for murder and jail interfere with my duty?

Slumped into a corner on the low cot, I stared at my hands, worrying the calluses I'd built up on palms and fingers from training with the blade.

"Mom always did blame me for everything that went wrong, even when I was Cecilia's scapegoat," I grumbled. "Now she blames me for murdering her husband. How could my own mother think I did such a thing?"

That set me to prowling the cell again. My muscles ached with the need to *do* something. Anything.

"Maybe she is still in demon thrall." I plopped down again, too depressed to think straight. "I detected hints of red embers in her eyes when he was around.

Scrap slid down the wall and sat next to me, silently chomping on his cigar. He looked a peckish gray.

So he hadn't had an orgy of mold. What had he been up to?

The guards kept wandering through, sniffing the air for evidence of violators of the no smoking rules. I couldn't summon enough humor to laugh at them.

"We're in trouble, Scrap."

You think this is trouble? I think this is a nice quiet vacation. He leaned back against the wall, both paws behind his head and blew fanciful smoke rings around the end of his black cherry cheroot. But there was a wary edge to his voice and his posture.

"What if . . ."

Not to worry about the long term. The murderer will be found, and you'll be released. In the meantime, you get to relax and let them feed you. Nice and warm in here.

"What about WindScribe?"

Worthless bit of trash. Let the Orculli have her. She had to have done something hideous and dangerous to the entire universe or they wouldn't want her back so bad.

"No human is totally worthless. And if she is so dangerous, why won't anyone tell me what she did?"

A whoosh of air displacement announced the entrance of an otherworldly visitor. My curiosity woke up and banished some of my worry-induced depression.

King Scazzy popped into the cell just inside the door. He waddle-rolled over to the cot and jumped up beside me, a higher jump than I thought possible for a twelve-inch-tall garden gnome. Make that a semilevitation, semijump.

Then he wiggled between Scrap and me, sitting on the edge of the cot with the aura of assuming his throne.

I bunched my muscles, ready to fight the guy with teeth and nails and willpower. I didn't have anything else handy.

Except Scrap. And he didn't seem inclined to transform. He continued to lounge on the cot blowing smoke rings as if we didn't have a care in the world. Though he did darken from gray to flame orange. He needed to go vermilion in order to become the Celestial Blade.

"Greetings, Tess Noncoiré." Scazzy inclined his head graciously.

I snapped my gaping jaw closed. "Greetings, King Scazzamurieddu." I kept my head rigidly upright.

"The Orculli honor you, Warrior of the Celestial Blade."

Scrap turned his back on us. At the moment I didn't have a blade to be warrior of.

"You do?"

"Of course. We share many duties and purposes."

"Such as?"

"Keeping the demon world in check."

"Oh." Such a brilliant conversationalist! I searched my brain for something scintillating and important. All I came up with was another "Oh."

"I have come to tell you that, much to my dishonor, the one you call WindScribe, but that is not her true name, has escaped me once again."

I breathed a sigh of relief.

"Who you talking to?" The policeman in charge of guarding these cells wandered by, peering into the corners of my cell.

The place was free of shadows and hiding places. Still King Scazzy managed to fade and blend into the walls. He took on the translucent aspect of Scrap, a little fuzzy around the edges, with the wall showing through from behind him.

"I'm so bored I'm talking to myself. Can I have a magazine or a book or something to read? Please?" Before the prison warden of the universe showed up, I had been going stir crazy. In stir.

Hey, is that where the term originated? I'd have to look it up when I got out of here. If I got out of here.

"Sorry, Miss. No reading material in holding. You'll have to wait for an arraignment and more permanent accommodations." The officer wandered off, shaking his head.

King Scazzy brightened back into view.

"So WindScribe is on the loose again," I picked up the conversation where we'd left off before we were so rudely interrupted.

"Not exactly." The gnome had the grace to blush a little.

"What happened?" My heart sank once more. Scrap turned an embarrassed green and nearly disappeared.

"She ran to the fallen one, Donovan Estevez, for refuge."

Again a reference to Donovan Estevez falling. From what? I didn't have time to think about it.

"The Windago found them together," King Scazzy continued. "The demons born of the north wind hold a fierce grudge against you, Warrior, and took WindScribe in revenge. I do not know what force gave them the power to appear in daylight."

"Windago!" I bolted for the cell door, ready to storm through it by sheer force of will if necessary. "They'll freeze-dry her." I couldn't imagine a worse death. I'd faced it myself.

First, they will dance her through the forest until her feet light sparks, Scrap said, huddling into the corner, as far from Scazzy as he could get and remain on the cot.

"You have to help her." I rounded on King Scazzy, full of fury and anxiety.

"The Windago have their orders. They will return her to my custody once she is exhausted and so full of pain she cannot escape again."

"Alive or dead?"

"It makes no difference to me. Dead, she will be less trouble. Alive, I will fulfill my duty." The gnome jumped down from the cot and looked ready to disappear again.

"Just a minute." I grabbed for him.

He eluded me. All I came up with was his cheerful red hat with a bit of tarnished gold braid.

Scazzy whirled on me, covering his naked head with his hands. He had about three hairs, each the length of his body, growing out of his bald pate. I'd cover that head, too.

"My hat!" he wailed. "You have to return my hat."

These nasty little critters valued their hats above all else, even their freedom. The hat was the source of their power. Maybe it was only vanity. Maybe the hats were like Scrap's warts, earned in battle at terrible cost.

"Tell me something first." I held the hat on one finger, twirling it idly.

"Anything. Please. I'll do anything short of releasing my prisoner to retrieve my hat."

"Interesting. The hat is almost as valuable as your honor."

"My hat is my honor. My life is pledged as security to my duty as Prison Warden."

"That, too, is interesting. But what I want to know is why is WindScribe considered such a dangerous prisoner? She's a ditzy teenager with a lot of lessons to learn, and a craving for drugs, but she's basically harmless." I hoped. But I was seriously doubting that statement myself.

Even Scrap sat forward with interest now.

"Not harmless. In her misguided naïve belief that all creatures deserve freedom, she loosed some Midori, full-blooded demons, from their ghetto. Without restrictions. Without wards. Without thinking." Scazzy hung his head and shuddered.

"How is that different from Donovan and Darren working to make a homeland for demons?" I sat down again and continued to twirl the hat.

"The Damiri work for a homeland for Kajiri, *half-blood* demons." Scazzy looked at me as if I were stupid.

"Enlighten me."

"Have you ever encountered a Midori?"

Nope, Scrap added. *I'm smart enough to keep her away from them.*

"What about the Windago we met in Wisconsin last year?" I still shuddered in memory of the fear they'd put in me.

Scrap rolled his cheroot around in his mouth as if tasting the memory of that fight. *Nope, they were human turned Windago, not Windago released from their own world. Lots of human hormones and enzymes in their blood.*

"And how would you know that?"

"Your imp lacks honor in his past. Do not probe too deeply if this troubles you. The darkness in his past is perhaps why he cannot remain in the same room as Donovan Estevez," Scazzy warned.

Scrap turned so pale a gray I wondered if he would disappear.

A long moment of silence passed around the room, each of us trying to break it. But with what?

"I admit that there is severe prejudice against the Kajiri," Scazzy finally spoke. "They are dangerous, but they also can be controlled with logic and intelligence. They are capable of leading almost normal lives among the race that is their other half, if allowed. They have no real place in the universe, living in the demon ghettos, or among their other ancestors. Outcast and shunned by both."

"And full-bloods, Midori, aren't intelligent or logical?"

Both Scazzy and Scrap shook their heads with horrified expressions.

We keep them locked up in their ghettos for a reason, Scrap said.

"If Midori demons are so dangerous, how did Wind-Scribe get close enough to let them out?"

Scazzy shrugged. "I am not privy to how the crime was committed. Only that she did it, was judged guilty, and is now my responsibility to imprison. I suspect she had help but do not know who would have the audacity. Or the stupidity to foment such a plan."

"Darren Estevez, for one." I reached forward, almost willing to give him his hat back. He raised his hand to grab it from my finger.

Then I jerked it away again. Other pieces of information eluded me.

"How well did Constable Mike Gionelli know Darren Estevez before the murder?"

Scazzy clamped his mouth shut. He looked longingly at his hat.

I wadded it up and contemplated eating it. Not that I would, but he didn't know that.

"The one you know as Michael Gionelli is Kajiri," Scazzy admitted.

"Half Damiri?"

"No. He belongs to another tribe."

I moved the hat closer to my mouth.

"He's of the Okeechobee. A water demon. His home is the swamp in Florida near where Darren Estevez has his headquarters. In his natural form Mike looks rather like an alligator. He, or his tribe, probably owe Darren Estevez something. A lot of money or a debt of honor. Something big enough for Darren to call in his marker by making Mike spy upon you, Tess Noncoiré."

"Ironic that a water demon pissed his pants in fear of the Windago," I laughed.

"He does not spend much time with his demon kin. He is one of the ones who try very hard to remain human, and protect humanity from others of his kind. He is not happy to be Darren's patsy."

"If he's part demon, even just a little bit, then getting bit by a Windago would have no effect on him."

"If the one you know as Lilia David tagged him to become her mate, her venom would have no effect on him. If she sought to kill him, she could."

"Okay. One more thing. Donovan claims he's not Damiri. That he was adopted by Darren as a teenager. After he fell. Fell from what? What is he? I know he's not fully human."

"He is fully human now. Very long-lived and hard to manage, with many Damiri characteristics, but human." Scazzy dropped his hand back to his side, meek and cooperative.

The lack of his hat must be preying on his arrogance and self-righteousness.

"How long is long?"

"The one we now know as Donovan Estevez was originally created eight hundred years ago. He fell and became human a mere fifty years ago."

"Weird, he looks maybe forty human years . . ." I mused. "What was he before he fell? And what does the darkness in Scrap's past have to do with Donovan?"

"I cannot say."

"Cannot or will not?"

"Both. My life is not worth that bit of knowledge." Faster than I could react, he jumped up, grabbed his hat, and bolted into the otherworld with a pop and a foul wind that smelled of sulfur and burning sewage.

Chapter 36

JOSH AND ALLIE ARRIVED on the heels of King Scazzy's departure.

"You're free to go, Tess," he said, standing taller and more confidently than I'd ever seen him. But I'd never seen him in court. Rumor had it he was a formidable presence before a jury.

Allie unlocked my cell door, keeping her gaze on the ground. I pushed past her roughly.

"Tess?" she said quietly.

I raised my eyebrows but said nothing.

"Tess, I acted in haste in arresting you. I had my reasons." She finally looked me in the eye, defying me to unleash my anger.

"You interfered."

"I saved your life."

"You don't know that."

"You aren't invincible, Tess. And there are others, too many others, who might have been hurt in the fray."

She had me there.

"Tess, I need to get you home," Josh said anxiously.

"We'll talk later, Allie." How was this going to affect our friendship? Was twenty-three years of relying on each other enough to overcome the breach in our trust?

It had to. It just had to. I couldn't lose Allie. Not now. "I'll call you, Allie. We have to talk."

"Tomorrow night at Guiseppe's as usual? It's Monday cannoli night."

"I don't know. Depends on a lot of things. But we'll talk."

I followed Josh out of the police station, drinking in the fresh air and warm sunshine.

A wild wind blew from the south bringing rapid changes in the weather. About time. But I knew my mother hated the wind. It often triggered her migraines. Like the one she had last night.

The snow melted rapidly, leaving a slushy mess. I spotted a few crocus and snowdrops poking their shy heads into the spring brightness. The grass looked a brighter green than normal. Almost surreal. A sign of new life and hope.

A camera flash exploded in my face.

"James Frazier, do I have to break that thing to keep you out of my life?" I clenched my fists and jumped at him, ready to rip the camera to pieces. And maybe him, too.

"Tess," Josh's voice ripped through my pent-up anger like a broadsword through cotton. "Not now. He is within his rights."

"See, I told you I have rights. The public has a right to know what's really going on in our quiet little peninsula. Did you know your house is haunted, Tess?" He whipped out his notebook.

"Of course. It's a matter of public record. The ghosts were included in the earnest money agreement when I bought the house. Along with the dining table and twelve chairs, the appliances, and the curtains." I did my best to swallow my emotions and present a bland face to him.

"But did you know there's a ghost standing between the police and the closet full of weapons?"

Hmm. WindScribe wasn't around, so Godfrey was back doing his job.

"I haven't been home in several hours. How could I know?" I marched over to Josh where he stood by his car. An upscale midsized sedan.

Now I just had to face my mother. She'd be in a rare temper what with the wind and Darren's murder.

"Did Donovan get to do his ritual over Darren's body?" I asked.

"Don't know." Josh shrugged and held the car door open for me. He wouldn't meet my gaze.

"Tess, I can't continue as your lawyer," he said the moment we closed the doors and locked them against James trying to jump into the backseat, notebook and camera in hand. "I got you released because Halohan and Allie Engstrom arrested you without enough evidence to back it up. But you can't leave town, and they will be watching you closely until they find the murderer."

"Thanks. But why can't you . . . ?"

"Because I'm too close to you and your family. I can't examine evidence and testimony objectively. I've left messages with Marsha Thompson. She's the best criminal defense attorney on the Cape. You should hire her. She's expensive, but she's the best."

"I understand."

"MoonFeather took a phone message for you. She told me to tell you about it but not mention it to anyone else."

"This sounds ominous."

"I hope not. Gayla says she found you some help, but it's not close. Will come as soon as possible."

"That is good news. Even if it is a bit tardy."

"There's something else." He looked hesitant again. Not good in a lawyer. "I have to go up to Boston for a week. I've taken on a big case. An important case. This could really make my career. I've got to go. Can Moon-Feather stay with you while I'm gone? She's not as strong or as well as she likes to think. The wound isn't healing properly. I spotted signs of infection when I changed the bandage just before I came to get you. I'd take her with me, but . . ."

"Of course she can stay. You go do what you have to. And I'll call Marsha Thompson first thing in the morning."

"Thanks. I'll see if Marsha will give you a discount as a professional courtesy to me."

"Good. Now take me home. The best way I know to keep her fees from bankrupting me is to find out who really did kill Darren Estevez." I set my jaw and stared straight ahead, letting my mind whirl and spin, trying to find something out of the ordinary to settle on. Something I should know but didn't yet.

"Leave the investigating to the police, Tess."

I smiled and nodded but didn't commit.

From the quiet anxiety of the police station, I stepped into the roaring fury of my mother and aunt in a territorial dispute over my kitchen.

MoonFeather stood tall, braced on her crutches with her wounded leg tucked behind her. Mom set her much shorter, squarer body directly in front of her.

A burning branch of sage in MoonFeather's hand was the obvious source of contention.

Gollum's cat, Gandalf, sat in a puddle of sunshine watching the two women as if he waited to pounce on the victor and consume her for his dinner.

Scrap blew a smoke ring in the cat's face and dodged into a high corner. Gandalf hissed and batted at the imp with bared claws.

The cat was loose. Where was Gollum?

"I will not have you taint this house with your devil worship!" Mom screeched.

"The devil? Satan! I don't even acknowledge the existence of such a being. How can I worship him?" MoonFeather retorted with more venom than I'd ever heard in her voice. She waved the aromatic smoke in Mom's face.

Mom launched herself at MoonFeather with nails extended and teeth bared.

Josh yanked his love out of the way. I barely inserted myself between the two women in time to catch Mom's arm just shy of her target.

"Quiet!" I screamed in my best schoolteacher voice.

Quiet hummed against my ears.

"Last I knew, this was *my* house," I snarled at both women. And it would stay my house despite Darren's attempts to get it away from me.

"We need to call Father Sheridan," Mom panted, still glaring at her sister-in-law.

"Maybe I should wait to perform my cleansing ritual until after *he* leaves!" MoonFeather said, straining against Josh's strong arms.

"You need an exorcism. You and that piece of teenage trash Tess dragged home. I'm calling Father Sheridan right now," Mom's face had the pinched look of the onset of another migraine.

Rebound headaches were worse than the original. She was not well.

She's still got a bit of demon thrall coloring her aura. Scrap told me blowing another smoke ring—not directly at the cat but close enough to set it hissing. *The evil wants to cling to her, so it sets her against the cleansing.*

MoonFeather blanched. She retreated rigidly against Josh. "Don't bring that foul pervert anywhere near me," MoonFeather said, her voice deadly calm.

"Pervert?" I asked. I'd never heard my aunt say anything remotely negative about anyone before. What did she have against gentle old Father Sheridan?

Mom spun on her heel and reached for the telephone before I could grab her. "About what I'd expect from a whore of Satan."

"No." I yanked the receiver out of her hand. "This has been a strange and upsetting day for all of us. Why don't you go upstairs and lie down, Mom." I herded her toward the stairs. "Josh, put MoonFeather to bed."

"I'll not spend another minute under the same roof as that woman," MoonFeather protested. She resisted Josh's urging. He simply picked her up and carried her down one side of the butler's pantry.

"I want to sleep in the cottage." Mom dug in her heels at the foot of the new stairs in the dining room. "I won't sleep in a house with that heretic!"

"You can't, Mom. It's . . . the police haven't finished cleaning up the cottage yet." Another shove toward the back of the house.

"They . . . they wouldn't let me see Darren. I need to go to him. He can't rest peacefully until I see him." She tried to flee out the door. Tears splotched her cheeks.

I held on tight. "Mom, you aren't making sense. When you've rested and gotten rid of the headache, we'll call Father Sheridan and make funeral arrangements. He can take you down to the morgue to view the body."

"Call your father. He'll know what to do." This time Mom went meekly upstairs to my spare bedroom.

Finally, the house quieted. I took a long hot shower and settled down to some lunch, leftover breakfast actually. No one had cleaned up the kitchen, and the waffle batter looked close to fermentation. But it tasted good, along with the sausage patty and fresh coffee. Lots and lots of fresh coffee with thick cream and three sugars. I might even leave an inch or two in the bottom of the cup to grow mold for Scrap. He deserved a treat as much as I did, even if he was lactose intolerant.

Gollum returned bearing thick deli sandwiches. I ate one of those, too, just to keep him company. He'd brought in a couple days' worth of mail as well.

Such a nice man. I could get used to having him around. Would he be so kind as to take out the garbage? A brief check showed me he already had.

Definitely worth keeping around.

"Did Donovan get to do his ritual over Darren's body?" I asked around a mouthful of rye bread and pastrami.

"Don't know. Halohan did take him over to the cottage. Two officers kept me from following or peeking through the window."

"Damn. I really wanted to know what that ritual did."

"So did I. Totally esoteric and undocumented rituals. I could write an academic paper on it. A secret religion existing right here in the U.S., not in some hidden Third World country. Do you think Donovan would tell me about it?"

I glared at him. He did get carried away sometimes.

Finally, he wound down and looked a bit sheepish. He pushed his glasses up onto the bridge of his nose.

"I've got bad news," he said taking my hand across the kitchen table.

"I know about WindScribe." I left my hand in his. It felt good, natural. Undemanding. That was something Donovan would never allow to happen. He always pushed and wanted more than I was willing to give.

"How?" he asked, allowing his glasses to stay on the end of his nose so I could see the sincerity in his eyes.

"King Scazzy popped into my jail cell and told me. Something about honoring my status as a Celestial Warrior." I recounted our conversation.

"Did he tell you that the Windago took her from Donovan's motel room?" His grip on my hand grew tighter, more reassuring. "They were in bed together. Naked."

"She didn't waste much time." I drew a deep breath, wondering what I truly felt about that bit of news. Not as hurt as I expected. I was the one to reject Donovan, not the other way around. He wasn't here to work his magic on my emotions.

"Well, she returned to this world starkers, only fitting she be taken from it again the same way," I said.

"Good girl." Gollum patted my hand and returned to his sandwich.

"Do we have any chance of getting her back?" I got up to refill our coffee cups. "Is there such a thing as a cosmic lawyer who can defend her?"

"Not that I've heard," Josh said returning from MoonFeather's room with their empty plates. Gollum had brought enough sandwiches for everyone. Only Mom's remained untouched. Last I looked, she was sleeping with enough drugs in her to knock out an elephant.

"How much do you know about WindScribe?" I asked warily.

"Enough. Your aunt and I came together through a pagan circle. I believe there is a lot more to the universe than we can observe through the normal five senses."

"If we find a precedent, would you argue in her defense?" Gollum asked. His expression looked brighter than it had since we'd discovered Darren's body. "Donovan's case might give us some clues, if he'll give us some details."

"That would be the case of a lifetime." Josh's face turned wistful. "As long as it doesn't interfere with my case in Boston. I've got to get on the road. Thanks for looking after MoonFeather. Don't let her do too much. And I'd recommend you keep the priest away from her. In her current mood, there is no telling what she might do. She's looking for spells to ward the house against invasion."

"What is that all about?" I asked. "I've never heard MoonFeather say anything against anyone before. And she called Father Sheridan a pervert!" I couldn't imagine the short, slender man with a kindly twinkle in his eyes harming anyone. In his late fifties, he'd only been Mom's parish priest about ten years.

"That is not my secret to reveal." Josh looked at his shoes. "Suffice it to say that her anger is not against Father Sheridan personally. And her anger is *for* someone else."

Gollum waited until we were alone again before

speaking. "I'll do some research, call Gramps, see if there is a precedent for retrieving the girl."

"I want to talk to MoonFeather. There's more to this than just a misguided teenager trying to act out her ideals of freedom."

Chapter 37

THE DAY DRAGGED on and on. Mom slept. MoonFeather pretended to sleep rather than answer questions. Gollum holed up in his apartment with the telephone and the Internet.

Sunday quiet ruled.

Donovan stayed away. The police came and went from the cottage. They strung their bright yellow crime scene tape and they ignored me. The bugaboo of a false arrest lawsuit hung over them. One more wrong step would land all of their butts in deep trouble.

I hated that Allie would be caught in the aftermath of this. She'd only been trying to help, keeping me from my scheduled battle with King Scazzy and his minions.

She'd saved my life, but she'd probably cost Wind-Scribe hers.

I sat at my desk staring at the computer screen and the bright wedding announcement I'd created. Was it just yesterday? Or the day before? I couldn't remember. Events merged and splashed into each other in my memory.

With a flick of the mouse I deleted the invite and began a new announcement. How did I word the death of a man I barely knew, who'd been married to my mother for barely thirty-six hours before his murder? Did I need to send it to the entire list of people Mom wanted to come to the wedding?

I should be doing something. Talking to Father Sheridan, making funeral arrangements, writing an obituary, consulting Dad. Calling a lawyer.

Instead, I finally finished those last four chapters and e-mailed them. That took hardly any time at all.

Twilight lingered as long as the day, stretching into nothingness. I wandered about the house I'd so lovingly decorated together with my own husband. Our marriage had lasted longer than Mom's. An entire three months before Dill died horribly in a fire.

I'd escaped by the skin of my teeth. Dill hadn't been so lucky.

Donovan owned the hotel that had blossomed from the ashes of the place where Dill died. A much bigger and classier lodge than the original generic and cheap motel. The place had been overinsured, and he profited well. I'd heard rumors that the fire was arson. Murder.

Darren had suggested that he'd started the fire just to kill Dill.

Too many parallels in names, in physical appearance. In whirlwind romances.

In death.

"About time you started making connections between me and Darren Estevez and his clan," Dill said. I couldn't see him among the shadows of the library, one of the three rooms on the ground floor of the original house that shared a chimney.

The house suddenly seemed darker. Full night had descended outside. And in my heart.

The moon had not yet risen. Would it shine through the clouds in the sky and in my life?

Half of me sighed with relief that Dill hadn't disappeared completely from my life. The other half screamed in frustration at the questions he forced me to raise.

"Were you a half-blood Damiri demon?" I finally asked the question that had plagued me for months. I'd never had the courage to face the issue.

Never dared wonder if our love had been merely the reflection of demon magic on my emotions.

"You know I can't answer that question," he said, still not showing himself. "You aren't smart enough to deal with the truth."

"Can't or won't?" I'd had this conversation before. With King Scazzy. With Donovan.

Silence.

I slammed my fist against the mirror that hung over the fireplace. The glass tilted, swinging on its wire support. Moonlight shimmered across the silvered glass.

A full moon rose outside. Reflected in the mirror, I saw it as clearly as if I was standing by Miller's Pond.

A full moon. The time when a demon or a troll or a ghost, any otherworldly being was at his weakest. I could hear Dill, but I couldn't see him because of the timing.

Gollum had selected today for the battle with the Orculli trolls for WindScribe's body and soul because they were vulnerable near the full moon.

The Windago would be just as vulnerable. Perhaps more so, since they consisted primarily of wind and shadow.

"Gollum!" I cried running down to his apartment. "How do I find the Windago? Scrap, get your sorry ass away from stalking the cat. Time to go to work!"

I skidded to a halt in Gollum's living room. He sat in the armchair, feet on the coffee table, surrounded by a bevy of beautiful women, all draped in bedsheets, blankets, and towels and nothing else.

➤➤➤

"Nine, ten, eleven," I counted the half-naked bodies. An occasional leg or breast kept peeking out from the casual covers.

Gollum had a goofy grin on his face and for once kept his mouth shut.

"No. Oh, no. I can't take these women in. I'm not running a frigging boarding house for refugees from Faery!" I wailed. They could only be the missing coven. Why were they here? Why had they come back now?

WindScribe. It all came down to WindScribe. Somehow everything that had happened this weird weekend came down to WindScribe.

"Windago?" A tall brunette with skin the color of moonlight asked. She seemed to be the oldest of the missing coven, not more than twenty-four. Probably their priestess or whatever title a leader of a Wicca coven took. She had a classic beauty with a tall forehead, long face, and slender nose.

"Ooh, you don't want to mess with Windago. They are so mean," whispered a stout blonde in a pouting little girl voice. Her hair was as vague in color as her voice.

"What do they look like?" a third young woman asked. Her hair and eyes were a medium brown, medium height, a little pudgy. The sparkle of curiosity that lit her face and posture changed her from utterly forgettable to quite attractive.

"Dangerous is the word," the brunette added, frowning at Little Miss Curiosity.

"I have to deal with the Windago. They kidnapped WindScribe," I insisted. I didn't want to face them. Again. I wanted to hide in hot and sunny Mexico. But I couldn't. I owed it to WindScribe to bring her back.

Hell, I owed it to humanity to reset the balance of demons in this dimension.

I heard the clump, clump of MoonFeather's crutches coming down the hall from the main house. The sound stopped abruptly at the doorway.

"Oh, my," she gasped. One crutch clattered to the floor.

Gollum ducked and dashed to help her. He looked almost grateful to free himself from the press of lovely pulchritude.

As one, the coven turned to face my aunt. Some of them weren't exactly careful about keeping their drapes secure. Gollum blushed.

I was beyond being embarrassed by them.

"MoonFeather?" the tall brunette asked. "What happened to you? You look so . . . old."

"Because I am old, FireHind. You've been gone for twenty-eight years." MoonFeather made her cautious way into the little room. Gollum trailed in her wake.

"I've never known you to lie, MoonFeather," FireHind replied indignantly.

"I still don't. You've been gone for twenty-eight years. Time runs differently in Faery. Everyone knows that."

"Twenty years." FireHind sank onto the sofa, her sheet billowing around her.

"Twenty-*eight* years?" Miss Curiosity bounced. Her ample breasts, belly, and upper arms wobbled with her excitement. This one looked more solid than the other. More alive and less . . . wispy. "Have we entered into a true Age of Aquarius? The world should be at peace and plenty now." She clapped her hands and nearly dropped her beach towel. The terry cloth would have wrapped around me twice but barely covered her once.

"I'm Larch, by the way." She held out a hand to me.

I shook her hand, trying not to snort at her comment. In answer, I flicked on the TV with the remote. CNN came up automatically with their headline story of the latest terrorist bombing in Iraq followed by an in-depth report on the ongoing civil war-induced famines in Africa.

"Peace and plenty are still elusive, ladies. Politics are dirtier, drugs more pervasive, and crime more rampant than ever. You missed a lot."

Gollum grabbed the remote and turned off the blaring ugliness of our lives.

"Get rid of these chicks," I told Gollum, not bothering to lower my voice. "It's the night of the full moon. This is our one and only chance to get WindScribe back from the Windago."

"Oh, you mustn't confront the Windago," FireHind

said. She seemed to have recovered from the shock of the time difference a little faster than the others.

"They have WindScribe, one of your own!"

Silence.

"WindScribe has chosen her own path," a small voice whispered from the rear.

"No one chooses to be kidnapped by the Windago," Gollum nearly shouted. "Do you know what the Windago will do to her?" he asked peering over the tops of his glasses.

Silence again.

"They will drag her by the hair, making her dance faster and ever faster until her heels strike sparks from the Earth. They will dance her through the heavens until she literally dies of exhaustion," he explained, straining to retain something of his calm teacher demeanor and failing.

"Even so. Violent confrontation is never justified," the dark-haired leader pronounced. She sat back as if uttering an imperial edict from a jeweled throne.

"After what she did in Faery, I'm not surprised," Larch whispered.

FireHind glared at her fiercely. "Shut up, Larch."

What did she do in Faery? No time to pursue that snippet of information.

"I don't intend to confront them. I intended to kill them," I snarled.

"Violence is never the answer, dear," FireHind admonished me as if I were a child. Looking at her, and hearing her, she seemed much more the child than I.

"Nearly thirty years in Faery, and you still haven't grown up," MoonFeather huffed.

"I beg your pardon! I am an adult."

"Yeah, right."

"Yes, she is right," the blowsy blonde replied. "She is our leader and much older than the rest of us."

MoonFeather and I rolled our eyes. "She chose her name correctly. MilkweedFluff," my aunt whispered.

"If the Windago have kidnapped WindScribe, then we

must perform a ritual. We must bring balance and harmony back into their lives so that they will release her," FireHind said decisively.

This time, Larch rolled her eyes in concert with MoonFeather.

As one (Larch a little belatedly but not much), the women shifted into a lopsided circle facing inward. They raised their hands, palms out to shoulder level, keeping their elbows bent. A solemn hum wove out of their throats.

"I have learned that I can bring harmony and balance into my own life. I can teach others who *want* to learn to do the same. But no one, *no one,* can impose their beliefs or their lifestyle on another. We do not have that right, even with demons." MoonFeather thrust her right crutch at me, thus freeing her hand. Which she used to swat FireHind's hands down.

"What has happened to you, MoonFeather? You've grown hard as well as old." Tears appeared in Fire-Hind's eyes.

"I've grounded my hippy ideals in reality rather than a cloud of marijuana smoke," MoonFeather replied. "And I've learned that some things we can work to change, others we can only pray about. Knowing the difference is the true source of wisdom."

"Demons know nothing of wisdom, nothing of peace or harmony or balance," I added. "They know only how to breed and how to feed themselves. Part of their dietary needs are to torment their prey on the way to their stomachs."

Gollum nodded at that. "Kajiri demons—those of mixed blood with humans—have some reasoning ability. They have to in order to blend in with us. Midori demons—full bloods—act only on instinct." He was back into his professor mode, his comfort zone.

I had the bad feeling that the Windago who had captured WindScribe were Midori, enlisted by Lilia David. They'd respond to the instinctive need for revenge for a lost mate. Respond with violence against any target she directed them to.

I had the fight of my life ahead of me, and I was running out of time.

"Deal with them, Gollum. I'll find the Windago myself."

"You don't find them, Tess. They find you. All you have to do is step into the woods on a windy night," he said. A note of warning and worry crept into his voice.

"I'll deal with the ladies, Tess," MoonFeather said. "I'll send them back to Faery so fast, they won't have time to be missed. They have no place here anymore." With that, my beloved aunt rounded on the eleven women, a steely glint in her eyes.

What if Faery won't have them? Can I give them to the cat as toys? Scrap giggled. *Ooooo, this is getting fun.*

Chapter 38

The Inuit moon spirit, Tarqeq, a mighty hunter, has been given the difficult task of watching over human behavior. When Tarqeq sleeps during the dark of the moon, humankind can exceed their bounds of propriety and misbehave, often in disgusting ways.

COPS OUT FRONT. Cops out back. Someone watched every exit from my home. I really didn't want them following me, asking questions and seeing things they couldn't understand. Otherwordly things they must discount.

I couldn't ask Allie for help. She was in enough trouble as it was.

Backup from the Warriors of the Celestial Blade hadn't shown up yet.

I had to do this. And it looked like I would have to take on a tribe of Windago by myself. I shivered with preternatural cold even before they touched me.

"You're going to need help," Gollum said, following me from window to window.

"You volunteering?" I almost wished that he would. But I also wanted him left behind, safe. Guarding Mom and MoonFeather and the errant coven if things went terribly wrong.

"No. I was thinking you should call Donovan. He has some experience in this field. And I believe he needs a distraction. He blames himself for WindScribe being taken." Gollum closed the curtains behind me as I moved to the next window.

He picked up the walk-around phone from my office so that he could continue following me. "We need to talk," Gollum said into the telephone. If the line was tapped, we didn't want the cops to think I was doing something untoward. "Come over now."

I listened in on the kitchen extension.

Donovan grunted something.

"It involves your girlfriend."

"Which one?" Donovan still sounded disgruntled and reluctant.

"Take your pick. Just get over here."

Within five minutes, I heard his car on the main road. He walked up the long lane to the front door from the street rather than drive past the cottage and into the gravel parking area by the kitchen.

I met him at the front door—hastily unsealed for the purpose. In his black leather jacket, black jeans, and a black turtleneck, with his hair a little rumpled, the wings of silver hair at his temples glistening in the porch light, he looked good enough to eat.

I'd never know if the chemistry between us was natural or a product of his demon upbringing and sympathies. Teenagers absorb information like sponges—even when they want you to think they aren't listening. Who knew what skills he'd learned from Darren.

He accepted my plan for getting WindScribe back with a curt nod. "I want a piece of those demons. A big, lethal piece," he said.

"Take your pick of weapons," I told him as we descended to the cellar. Halohan had only taken the German short sword. (I cursed every time I thought of demon blood corroding the metal while it sat in an evidence bin somewhere.) The other weapons had all turned up free of fingerprints and signs of recent usage.

"The Celestial Blade?" he asked hopefully.

"Since I'll be using the real one, I suppose you could

take the replica. That is—if it will let you hold it." I flashed him a wicked grin. "Oh, and you have to stay ten yards away from me until we actually find the Windago, otherwise Scrap can't get close enough to me to be of any use. Once we are in the presence of demons, their essence overrides your barriers."

As I opened the armory door, a jolt of memory surfaced. Donovan making a half-statement when Halohan found the short sword with blood on it.

"If an ordinary blade couldn't kill Darren, then what did?"

"That was no ordinary blade." Donovan stood in front of the replica Celestial Blade, hands firmly clasped behind his back.

"Meaning?" Of course it wasn't ordinary. Real, not replica, seventeenth-century pieces were rare and hard to come by. I knew of only a handful of that particular model designed for dueling, in this country.

"It had an otherworldly aura about it." Donovan looked pleased that he had information and power that I did not.

"We had specially forged weapons at the Citadel. For when imps got tired or sickened. For novices who hadn't bonded with imps yet. Forged with magic. Scrap could smell it, but I couldn't."

"The short sword was akin to those. Forged with magic."

"Scrap?" I called into the ether.

As close behind you as I can get, babe. He sounded closer than usual when Donovan stood beside me.

"Did you have anything to do with me buying that particular sword last year?"

Meaning?

"Don't get evasive and noncommittal. You've given me a couple of otherworldly artifacts. The comb and the brooch. And the dragon-skull gargoyle. Did you direct me to that blade in particular?"

Maybe I sensed something down that alley. In that

pawnshop, Scrap admitted. *It is a pretty sword. I do like pretty things. Shiny.*

"Origins?"

Unknown.

"Uses?"

Obviously it can kill a demon. Something special in the forging of the metal.

Good enough explanation for me. In the seventeenth century witch hunts happened in Europe every other year or so. A lot of them in Germany. Witches got blamed for crop failures during the Little Ice Age from the fourteenth century well into the eighteenth century. Maybe someone had a reason for imbuing special qualities in that German blade. Like real witches and demons mucking with the weather.

"Anything else in here that appeals to you?" I asked Donovan. I didn't think any of the other blades were special in the same way as the short sword. I'd bought or traded for them on the open market, through usual channels.

"Just the Celestial Blade." Donovan grasped the shaft with a tentative hand. The imp wood glowed red where he grasped it. He kept his hand there.

"Is it burning you?"

"No. It tingles all the way to my feet. I think it's recognizing me." His voice shook.

Slowly he placed his other hand on the shaft. The glow expanded to engulf both hands and arms, up into his bunched neck muscles and over the top of his head. His coppery skin pulsed and darkened to a burnished sheen.

For a half a heartbeat I caught an aura of a bat surrounding him. I backed off before the revulsion could shake my resolve to work with him during this fight.

But he had to be human now, or the blade would repulse him or burn him up.

A flash of jealousy heated my face. "The imp wood never did that with me," I grumbled.

Not that you noticed anyway.

"Were you there, Scrap, even before we bonded?"

I was with you from the moment you contracted the virus, he said softly. *I was with you when you lost your way getting to the Citadel. I kept you from driving off the road into the lake at the base of Dry Falls. I directed you to the Citadel. I licked you where Sister Serena cut out the infection, to help you heal. I watched over you in the night so that you would not be alone during your time of trial.*

I gulped. Most of that terrible journey was a blur of nightmare images.

You fought your first demons during those nightmares.

"Thanks, buddy. I appreciate you being there." One of my biggest fears was to die alone, without family or friends nearby. I'd sat vigil with Sister Jenny while she and her imp Tulip died. Tulip had gotten tagged during a battle while I was still in hospital recovering from the imp flu. He could not live. She could not live if he died. They lingered for months, neither one willing to let the other die.

The Sisters left her alone with her misery. It was their way.

But not mine. I held her hand as she died.

Ever afterward, I wondered if Scrap had held Tulip's paw in those moments. Or if he'd delivered a *coup de grace* to free them both.

I had to shake off those paralyzing memories and get back to the task at hand. Still, my body chilled and my innards began to shake in fear. And in grief.

All of it triggered by Dill's death. Would I ever be free of that?

"I hope not," he said from the corner of the cellar. "When you stop grieving, I go back to . . . whatever. But while you keep me alive in your heart, I'm stuck here and we have a chance to be together again."

"I can't, Dill. I just can't," I whispered in my mind.

"Can't or won't? Is Donovan a better lover than me? If you think you've found someone else, forget it, Tess.

You and I are bound together forever, in life and in death. You are mine, and I'll never let him have you."

My blood ran cold at his words. What if he followed through with his threats out there, with the Windago, when I had my hands full and needed all of my wits?

"Will the blade glow like this with anyone?" I asked instead of dwelling on useless emotions.

I don't know. Scrap sounded chagrined.

"If you two don't get a move on, you're going to lose the moon," Gollum called from the top of the stairs. "I removed the padlock from the cellar door. No one saw me do it."

So Gollum had some covert skills. Why was I not surprised?

"This way." I led Donovan over to the shallow steps cut through the dirt and only recently made of cement. "I'll need some help."

Donovan put his back to the slanting cellar doors that lifted upward onto a shadowy corner of the yard. A tall and ancient oak sheltered us from view of any but the most probing of observers.

"Nice hidey-hole," Donovan whispered, as aware as I of potential watchers.

I shrugged. My house had a lot of history. I hoped I didn't have to add hiding place from demons on the hunt to the long list.

As an added safety precaution, I jammed the magic comb into my hair. Instantly, the shadows came alive. I probed the depths of each of them and found them empty.

Silvery moonlight dappled the lawn. Nearly twilight. Who needed flashlights on a night like this? A night made for lovers. Or hunting demons.

My blood ran hot with anticipation. And fear.

We separated as we headed for the woods. Scrap settled comfortably on my shoulder. A friend. And a weapon. My fears abated. A little.

I took the right-hand path, Donovan the left. Scrap and the magic in the comb kept my feet on the path. I barely needed the glimmers of moonlight through the canopy of new leaves popping out to guide me. The dark took on layers and shades. Nothing hid from me.

We made our way slowly around Miller's Pond. On the far side, the forest was deeper and darker. I hadn't explored this area much as a kid because it was scarier, more prone to ghostly imaginings. Now this area was beyond my property line. I had no idea who owned it.

I smelled the dank pond and the fresh green in the ground cover. And then I caught a new smell, something old and rotten and swirling around me.

Yeep! Scrap yelped and instantly glowed red. He elongated and thinned from one eye blink to the next.

I braced my feet and clasped Scrap in the middle. With a flick of my wrists I set the Celestial Blade to twirling.

Donovan leaped out of the low shrubs, his own blade twisting and turning, biting into the suddenly freezing wind.

Burning cold surrounded me and lifted my hair. Sparks flashed near the ground. My hands went numb, and I dropped the Celestial Blade. A dozen Windago reached for me with their freezing hands and souls of ice.

Chapter 39

"AT LAST, I WILL have my revenge and a new mate," Lilia snarled at me. She almost took human form within the black swirling mass of wind and smelly fur.

Each rotation of air seemed to suck more and more warmth and strength from my body. My willpower faded equally fast.

Where the hell was Scrap? I really needed him here, in my hands to give me a boost out of this mess.

"Take Donovan, for all I care. Return WindScribe to me," I said with as much strength and conviction as I could muster.

"WindScribe will be my new mate," a second form whispered from behind me. That must be the husband to the one Donovan killed in the motel.

"Isn't that shredding some cosmic law?" I asked. My knees wanted to give out. All I had left to fight with was my brains. And they wanted to melt out of my ears. "You have orders to return WindScribe to the Orculli."

"We take orders only from ourselves," Lilia hissed.

"Don't tell that to the Powers That Be."

"Fight it, Tess," Donovan called to me. Dimly, I knew

that he swung the replica blade in efficient circles, keeping the Windago at bay, yet never quite connecting with them.

Lilia tangled her paw/hand in my hair and yanked. The comb flew free. My scalp burned.

Sparks flew from my heels where they dragged on the ground.

I clawed and kicked, tried to dig in my heels.

No, babe. Don't fight, Scrap countered from off in the bushes. The barest hint of moonlight glinted off his blade ends. *Windago draw energy from your struggle. The moon nears its zenith. Wait a moment.*

I held my breath. A lessening in the cold. A moment of cessation of movement.

Another heartbeat, dahling. That's my babe, Scrap coaxed.

Sure enough the edge of the moon cleared the treetops.

Then, before I could think twice about a plan, Scrap hopped to my hand, all red and stretching, and became my blade once more.

I swung blindly behind me. The blade bit into something. A grunt.

Tension released from my scalp. Lilia screamed in pain.

I dropped to the ground. Instantly, I caught my balance, rolled to my knees, and swung the blade again—right left, up down, fore and aft.

With each swing I pushed myself back onto my feet.

Twisting right and left, whirling my head to keep everyone within sight.

Each blow caught . . . resistance.

"Yeehaw!" Donovan chortled behind me. "Finally got one."

A long, mournful moan followed his glee. I hoped he got the lonely male.

A heavier contingent of freezing shadows pressed me closer.

I flipped the blade into reverse and used the tines on

the outside of the blade to pierce and rake ahead of me. One, two. They went down.

A third got under my guard and raked my left forearm with a frigid talon.

I suppressed a moan and clung tighter to the shaft though my left arm felt numb and heavy at the same time. I'd have a scar from that one.

Not on my watch, babe, Scrap growled. For three heartbeats he took control of the blade. I could only follow his motions, keeping a fierce grip on the weapon and on my pain.

A cold shadow shifted to my side. Scrap and I followed it. Lilia. Her eyes glowed red. She reached for me with a new desperation. Part of her fur sloughed free. Her grief and aloneness twisted her face into a grotesque mask worthy of a gargoyle.

Feeling returned to my arm in sharp pinpricks that burned all the way to my spine. I used the pain to propel the blade into a wild twist and thrust.

Lilia's head tumbled to the ground. Dark blood spurted upward. Then all turned to dust, falling back to Earth in a frozen black shower.

Four down, at least eight to go. They paired off, coming at me in twos. My arms grew listless again. Sweat dripped down my back and into my eyes. My heavy sweatshirt dragged at each movement, became too warm. But the air around me dropped below freezing. My blade lost some of its luster in the moonlight. It felt dull and heavy. The balance was off.

And they kept coming at me. I lost sight of them. Freezing tendrils of air reached for me. Every place they touched, bare skin burned with frostbite. Blood dripped from the wound on my left arm.

A few inches to the left of my foot I saw the comb, moonlight giving it an amazing luster. If I could only get my hands on it, I could see the enemy. Fight them better.

They gave me no time, not a single millimeter of space to catch up my treasure.

Exhaustion and defeat dragged me down, made me clumsy.

A Windago chortled with glee and lunged for me.

In the distance a raw hum cranked louder. Gollum or MoonFeather had turned my stereo up full blast. Bright blessings on them both.

Throbbing drums, rousing pipes, a husky voice.

I didn't need to hear the words clearly. At this distance I couldn't. But I knew them.

"Axes flash, broadsword swing.
Shining armor's piercing ring
Horses run with polished shield
Fight those Bastards till they yield
Midnight mare and blood-red roan,
Fight to keep this land your own
Sound the horn and call the cry . . ."

"How many of them can we make die!" I screamed and swung the blade with renewed vigor. I lashed out. The blade brightened and sharpened.

Then I saw her. WindScribe lay huddled in a fetal ball at the base of a tree about two meters from me. She whimpered. I saw her naked back move as she breathed.

She was alive!

New desperation to save my charge flooded me with adrenaline.

Donovan crowed again as he felled a demon. I took out two more.

The enemy faded into the wilderness. The wind died. The temperature rose a few degrees. Scrap shrank back to his normal body and collapsed facedown in the leaf litter.

I dropped to my knees, nearly sick with exhaustion and blood loss. The warming air sent a heavy languor through me. All I wanted to do was fall over and sleep.

Not yet, dahling, Scrap urged. *We've work to do still.* He tugged at my aching scalp to keep me awake. His tongue stroked the bleeding wound on my arm. The burn dissipated. Some. Not much. Enough.

Half stretching, half falling, I found the comb and stuffed it back into my hair. The world brightened. No trace of a lurking Windago. Using a ragged stump as a prop, I dragged myself to my feet and limped over to where Donovan knelt at WindScribe's side. I'd lost a shoe at some point. I was so tired I didn't care.

Scrap faded and lost substance. He needed to eat and sleep as much as I did.

Without a word, Donovan lifted WindScribe into his arms and carried her. I grabbed the replica blade and followed, wincing with every step at the disrespect to a fine weapon by using it as a cane.

The two hundred yards to the house seemed three miles or more. We took it slow and cautious. I kept a wary eye out for returning Windago.

King Scazzy awaited me. He perched on the slanted cellar doors. "Congratulations. You took the Windago out in pairs, including the one you know as Lilia David and the partner of the one Donovan killed earlier. The survivors will not seek revenge." He bowed graciously.

"Well, bully for me." I was so tired I didn't care about anything but a hot shower and bed. Not necessarily in that order.

"I will take my charge now," King Scazzy said imperiously.

"Back off, twerp. She's mine. I won her fair and square." I jabbed at him with the tines of the imp wood blade. Donovan had proved it to be nearly as lethal as the real one.

Scazzy hopped higher on the cellar doors, closer to the house's foundations. "This is not over, Tess Noncoiré." He popped out of view. "We will meet again," he warned from across the ether. His disembodied voice raised the hairs on the back of my neck and sent shudders through my exhausted body and spirit.

Chapter 40

Gollum appeared out of nowhere. "You take care of that one. I'll deal with Tess." He scooped me up into his arms and carried me through the back door into the apartment.

Donovan, still carrying WindScribe, proceeded to his car. I heard them drive off and thought nothing more of them.

I let Gollum cradle me, gaining tiny morsels of warmth wherever my body came in contact with his. It felt so very good and comforting to rest my head on his shoulder, to give him control.

Safe. He made me feel safe.

His big hands made gentle work of cleaning my wounds. He whistled through his teeth at the blood still oozing from the long gash on my arm.

"The frostbite will heal clean. But this . . ." He shook his head. "This is going to scar."

"One more to add to the collection." I just shrugged and let him soothe my hurts with a foul-smelling ointment and bandages.

"You should have some antibiotics. I'll take you to the emergency room."

"Scrap will take care of it when he recovers."

"You sure?" He looked almost scared.

I nodded, eyes closed. Too heavy to keep them open.

Another long moment of silence while I dredged up enough energy to ask the next question.

"The coven?"

"MoonFeather called in some favors and found places for them to go for the night. With other Wiccans I gathered. They seemed obligated to offer hospitality, and intellectually interested in their travels to and from Faery. They will do their best to keep their presence discreet. Allie thinks the FBI will arrive in the morning with tons of questions. We'll reassess the situation in the morning. MoonFeather is quite something. I'd like to spend more time picking her brain."

The rest of his statement drifted through the cobwebs in my mind. I'm not sure how much I heard and how much I dreamed.

I slept the sleep of the just. Or the dead. Ensconced in Gollum's sofa with him watching over me from the armchair.

▶▶▶

I awoke alone. Monday morning. Gollum was probably at the college.

Scrap got me up at some ungodly hour with his demands for more beer and orange juice. I joined him in his favorite restorative. Not bad.

From the dirty glasses in the sink, I gathered that Gollum had given him the first dose last night.

The sun poked her bleary head above the horizon. Life was looking better. I peeked beneath Gollum's expert bandage on my arm. A long black scab marked the gash. No trace of red infection. The cooling ointment now smelled of mint and didn't burn the wound at all.

We survived your first battle against Midori, Scrap said quietly around a mouthful of beer. *How do you feel?*

"You should know. You've always said we are linked closer than spouses. I get drunk, you get drunk. I'm happy, you're happy. So how do *we* feel? I'm too numb to figure it out."

Exhausted. Brittle. Fragile.

"Yeah, that about covers it."

Also a bit exhilarated.

"Yeah. That, too."

He flashed his pointy teeth at me and wiggled his fat bottom so that his barbed tail coiled and circled his glass. *I got a couple of new warts.* He showed me the hideous bumps on his elbows.

"Very pretty," I admired his new beauty marks. "Mostly, I'm hungry. How about a high-fat, high-carb breakfast at the diner on the interstate?" I asked him as he slurped the last dregs of his juice through a straw.

The imp had an orange tinge beneath the gray. He'd revive soon.

Not dressed like that, dahling. Scrap surveyed my crumpled jeans and baggy sweatshirt with disdain.

I smelled of sweat and fear gone rancid.

I'd fallen asleep in my clothes again. On Gollum's sofa. Again.

This was becoming a habit I needed to break.

But did I truly want to?

"Okay, I'll shower while you pick out something for me to wear."

I was halfway up the stairs when someone knocked imperiously on the kitchen door. At the same moment, the phone rang shrilly.

"Will someone get the door?" I yelled at the top of my lungs as I grabbed the phone in my office.

No one stirred, so I carried the handset to the kitchen door.

"Hello," I responded to both parties at the same time.

"Tess," Donovan sighed over the phone.

"Tess," Dad demanded at the door.

I motioned Dad and Bill into the kitchen while I turned my attention to Donovan.

"I have to go to Florida. Today," he said without preamble.

"So?"

"I've been on the phone all night to various relatives. There's a power struggle looming within the ranks of Damiri. D's death left a terrible vacuum."

"So go. If the police will let you." I tried to pretend his absence didn't leave an aching void in my gut.

What was it with this guy? Why couldn't I cast him off and forget that he was the world's sexiest man and most incredible lover?

Not bad in a fight either. Twice now, he'd done more than his fair share of subduing a demon horde.

He was also a demon—or a demon sympathizer. Not a safe or comfortable man to love.

That thought stopped me cold. I wasn't in love with Donovan. I couldn't be. I wasn't that self-destructive.

Was I?

"I can't leave WindScribe in the motel alone. I've given her some money to buy clothes and shoes. But she's so scattered and emotionally strung out I'm uncomfortable leaving her totally alone. Can you take her back, just for a few days?"

No, I wanted to scream. The gash on my arm throbbed in mute reminder of what lengths I had gone to in order to rescue her. "If I have to. She's going to have to grow up and take responsibility for herself sooner or later, though."

"Agreed. Just not today. Fetch her please, Tess. For me. For us."

"There is no us."

"They're calling my flight. I have to go. Just go get her. Or send someone to do it. Allie or Gollum. Someone."

He rang off before I could tell him to do something anatomically impossible.

"Your mother is on her knees in the Lady Chapel at St. Mary's with her rosary," Dad blurted out.

"And that affects me how?" All I wanted was food. Lots and lots of food, but people kept dumping other problems on me.

Welcome to the world of the Warrior, Scrap chided. He blew a smoke ring at me from his high corner perch above the refrigerator. *Pour me some more OJ and beer, and you eat some crackers. We'll call it good until we can split this place,* he added in his gangster accent.

"She's been there all night. Father Sheridan is very worried. You didn't answer your phone earlier, so he called me. She won't talk to anyone, wouldn't even acknowledge I was there." I'd never seen Dad look so sad and . . . inadequate.

"And all I wanted was a week in Mexico soaking up some sun and drinking *piña coladas* before I start my next book."

"You've got to go get her, Tess. She's so vulnerable right now. You're the only one she'll listen to."

"What makes you think she'll listen to me? As usual, this whole debacle will become my fault in her mind."

"Just go to the church and talk to her. Please."

"Tess," MoonFeather said quietly as she clumped into the kitchen. "You may need an exorcist for your mother. She needs a lot of healing, from within as well as from without."

Bye, babe, Scrap squeaked. He popped out in a puff of black cherry cheroot.

▶▶▶

I grabbed a granola bar, thought twice, and threw two more into my purse. Barely enough to sustain life, but they should get me through another hour or so until I could find the time for real food.

My tires only skidded twice on leftover ice during the half-mile drive to St. Mary's. If Father Sheridan wanted one of his parishioners to *leave* their prayers on a weekday, then something terrible was eating away at Mom.

I found her in the third pew from the front, on her knees. She rapidly ran the beads of her rosary through anxious fingers, hardly having time to say one prayer before beginning the next.

Old habits die hard, or maybe I did still have some respect for the sanctity of this old church. I genuflected toward the altar and then knelt beside my mother, bowing my head.

"Can you ever forgive me, Tess?" She kept her eyes on the rosary—blue milk glass beads worn smooth on some of the facets with a Madonna Medal anchoring the prayer chain. She'd used the same one for as long as I could remember.

"He used you, Mom. He manipulated you to gain his own selfish ends. He did the same thing to Donovan and . . ." Did I dare mention Mike Gionelli? Not yet. That connection wasn't necessary at the moment.

"He only married me to get your house."

"My house?"

"There's something special about it. That's why you attract so many ghosts. He never said what. Just that he needed your house."

There was more. I could tell in the way she paused between sentences, as if having to think how *not* to say something.

"What made him think marrying you would gain him the house, Mom?"

A long pause. Then she finally looked up at the crucifix above the altar. (I tried to avoid looking at the gruesome agony of the man hanging there.)

"I . . . I let him believe that the house was mine. Mine and yours."

"Why?"

"Trying to impress him. He was so handsome, so sophisticated, and so *rich*! I could hardly believe he was interested in me at first. I have so little. You are my greatest treasure and one success in life, Tess. But I wanted him to want me. Just me. Not the mother of a famous writer. Just me."

A bunch of things clicked into place. Something special about the house. Joint ownership of the house between mother and daughter. Marry the mother, kill the daughter. Then kill the mother, too, and inherit sole ownership of the house.

I had to keep her focused, help her heal. Then I'd worry about the house and demons and ghosts and such.

"You are an attractive woman, Mom. Any beauty I have I inherited from you. There is no reason a normal man wouldn't be interested in *you*."

"But I don't attract *normal* men. First your father and his . . . well, you know your father. Then Darren. No one else has even looked at me twice."

"Um, Mom, you're half blind when it comes to men. You don't see them when they are flirting. Chief Halohan had the hots for you when his wife left him." Remember I said something about his son being a bully? Well, his mother gave up trying to reform him and convincing his dad that there was a problem. "You pushed him aside so often he gave up." Probably a good thing.

"Then there was George LaBlanc, the first owner of the antique shop. I think he sold out and moved to Maine because you broke his heart."

"Really?" A spark of interest in her eyes. Then it winked out just as rapidly. "I didn't see it. I'm blind to good men. What's wrong with me, Tess?"

"I don't know how to answer that, Mom. But you need to come home now. There's leftover chicken soup. You have a bowl of that and some bread, then take a nap. You haven't slept much since . . . since it happened."

"If I sleep, I'll dream of D. Every time I close my eyes I see the horrible wounds, his blood. So much blood. I can't ever go back to the cottage."

"Then don't. Sleep in the room next to mine. You know I'll keep you safe."

"You can't protect me from my nightmares."

"I can keep those nightmares from becoming real." I hoped.

"I . . . I just want everything the way it was. Before I went to Florida."

"We can't go back, Mom. We can only move forward." The meaning of my words slammed into my chest like a shock wave. I had to move forward, too. I had to put Dill and his death behind me once and for all.

I had to know who killed him and if I truly could have saved him. I had to know who killed Darren. I had to know what was so special about my house. Until then, I was wandering in circles and not moving forward.

With my arm around Mom's waist, and her weary head on my shoulder, we made our slow way back down the aisle. At the door to the narthex, she turned and made a deep reverence to the altar. I did, too. We needed all the help we could get. I'd take the Divine kind as well as my own powers with the Celestial Blade.

Old habits die hard.

Chapter 41

As the sun sets, the moon rises, and the little people play on every moonbeam, sprinkling their sparkling moon dust down onto humankind.

"TAKE ME TO BREAKFAST, Tess. I haven't been out of the house in days. I need to breathe different air," MoonFeather commanded, the moment I got Mom settled in bed with a bowl of soup. Dad sat beside her, worry clouding his eyes.

"Mom . . ."

"Needs to talk to your father and then be alone with her thoughts for a while."

"I'll keep an eye on her," Gollum said. "You and your aunt need to talk in private."

So we did talk. With a lumberjack omelet, hash browns, toast with a fruit cup, and more OJ for Scrap, I filled up on fat and carbohydrates and coffee. Moon-Feather settled for a vegetarian omelet and herb tea. By the time we finished eating, we had the restaurant pretty much to ourselves. This was a working class neighborhood. Most of the patrons had departed to their jobs.

"What do you need to talk to me about?" I asked, savoring the thick coffee that was strong enough to etch a spoon.

"WindScribe."

"We'll check on her on the way home."

"You need to know some things first."

"Like what really happened on Midsummer's night nearly thirty years ago?"

"Yes." My aunt gathered herself and then speared me with her gaze. "To understand what went wrong that night, and I can only give you speculation since I was not there, you have to look at who WindScribe is."

"She's more than a drug addict teenager with great passion and little focus? Isn't that enough against her?"

"Every human is much more complex than that." She breathed deeply and launched into her narrative before she lost her courage. "WindScribe did not run to Wicca so much as run away from her mother. The woman was vicious, alcoholic, with no sense of right and wrong, knowing only that what pleased her must be right."

"That explains a lot of her daughter's values. She said something about being locked in the closet beneath the stairs and being afraid of the dark."

MoonFeather glared at me, a warning not to interrupt her. "I found love and companionship and a sense of connection to the entire universe in Wicca. I found joy in my femininity as the core of my being rather than a limitation because I was not male. WindScribe rejected that and looked only for power—a power that would allow her to wreak revenge on her mother and the world at large for the pain she suffered at her mother's hands."

I'd run into a few similar cases in the science fiction convention community. Usually the kids outgrew that phase and took responsibility for themselves and their actions. Some even went back to the families and religions they sought to flee.

My morning in the church made me think of something else. "Did she have problems with her mother's religion?"

MoonFeather gasped and speared me with a glare that could have stripped paint.

"Well, did she?"

"Do you really need to rehash the church scandals that dominate the news of late?"

"That bad, huh?"

"Worse."

I gulped and made a guess. "She was sexually abused by the local priest, probably because she asked too many questions and wouldn't take 'Because I said so,' as an answer."

"I did not say so."

"You don't have to. Is there more? Like her mother blaming her for deserving the abuse because she was disobedient. Then she got more punishment at home."

"Her mother and the local priest performed an exorcism. More like torture, if you ask me."

"No wonder she stole drugs and jewelry and ran away to Faery. She was desperate to escape this world of horror."

"Only now, after years of reflection and meeting a woman who was my contemporary at the time and is now young enough to be my daughter, can I recognize how warped WindScribe had become," MoonFeather continued.

She took a long drink of her tea and stared at her empty cup, lost in her memories. Just before I thought I should break the silence, she looked up at me again.

"At the time, we of the coven were all rebellious and gloried in just how outrageous we could appear to the staid society at large. We experimented with sex and nudity. We experimented with pot and LSD and then rejected them. They do not open the mind to psychic vision. Drugs cloud true vision. We did not see Wind-Scribe as any different from ourselves."

I'd discovered the same thing in my own brief experiment with pot in college.

"So what happened that night?" I asked.

"The coven as a whole planned a ritual that we hoped would allow us to meet beings from otherworlds, hopefully from Faery. We wanted to invite them here to us, to

help make our world better, happier, more colorful . . .
different. But I had a fight with my father, and he locked
me in my room. By the time I managed to climb out the
window and walk to the meeting place, it was too late."

"Something went horribly wrong then," I mused.
"This isn't just a numbers thing. Going from thirteen to
twelve participants wouldn't change the spell. It might
make it fail, or only work partially, but not totally reverse the outcome." I'd read a lot about ceremonial
magic to include in my books. MoonFeather had
pointed me toward good texts, even invited me to observe and participate in her rituals.

"You are correct. WindScribe changed the words, re-
versed the order of the dance. We underestimated her
need to run away from reality. We didn't know she'd
stocked up on drugs and stolen jewelry."

"And she's still running. She does things that blow up
in her face—like trying to free Midori demons—and
then refuses to take responsibility for them." Maybe I
should have let the Windago have her.

But she was human. She belonged here on Earth.
She'd only begin to learn right from wrong, heal mentally from the abuse, if she stayed here and faced her
shortcomings.

"Yes. And now we must decide what to do with her.
Like it or not, she is our responsibility," MoonFeather
sighed.

"We'd better check on her." I paid the bill and hurried my aunt back to the car. I had a bad feeling in the
pit of my stomach.

►►►

Allie's cruiser and a second squad car sitting in front of
the motel told me precisely which room Donovan had
rented.

Mike Gionelli leaned casually on the second
cruiser—a pose I associated with Dill—available to
help if needed, but not truly involved.

Only Dill wasn't available to help. He made sarcastic,

and now nasty, comments and then disappeared without explanation.

"What's wrong now?" I asked Allie. We hadn't spoken since I left the police station yesterday with Josh. Anger at her still burned, but not as badly as my worry for what trouble WindScribe might have gotten into this time.

"Where's Donovan Estevez?" Allie returned my question with one of her own.

"Um . . . did you tell him not to leave town?"

"I take it he did, then?"

"This morning. He flew to Florida to straighten out some kind of family problem. What do you need him for?" Uh-oh. Did that mean suspicion had fallen on Donovan?

How did I feel about that? As much as I tried to tell myself that I was over Donovan Estevez, I knew that if he'd just come clean about his past I might commit to him.

He'd been a big help last night fighting the Windago. His bloodthirsty glee every time he killed one of them seemed all too human. On the other hand, he had the best motive of anyone to eliminate his adoptive father. How much did he have to gain? I'd really like to look at Darren's will.

"Any idea when—or if—he's coming back?" Allie's eyes drooped, masking her emotions.

I couldn't tell what she was thinking or feeling. And I didn't like it. We'd always been open and honest with each other.

Well, except about Scrap and the Celestial Blade thing. But I had come clean as soon as she needed to know.

"He didn't say. If it's a problem, he might have had to leave his return open-ended. He might have given WindScribe some better idea of what's going on."

"She won't talk to us." Allie hitched her utility belt and shifted her feet uneasily. "Apparently, the FBI called her and tried to interview her over the phone.

She hung up on them. They called me to finish their job. Coincides with my need to talk to Mr. Estevez."

"Did you ask to talk to her nicely?"

"Of course I did," Allie sneered. "Don't I always?"

"No. Not always." I stepped up to the door and knocked briskly.

"Go away!" WindScribe cried. She sounded desperate. Or unhappy. Or both.

"WindScribe, it's me, Tess. Are you okay? Did you get some breakfast?"

"Are the police still there?" Her voice sounded closer to the door.

"Yes. Allie is still here. She just wants to talk to you about Donovan. Can we come in please?"

"I don't have to talk to the police. I know my rights."

"No, you don't have to talk to Allie. But it would help us find Darren's murderer if you did."

"I'm confused. I don't know what to do."

"Then let us come in and talk to you," MoonFeather called with the authority of a high priestess to a new convert. She'd hobbled out of the car on her own, limping but relying on the crutches a lot less. "We can't help you if you won't talk to us."

"I don't know . . ."

"WindScribe, you must be hungry. How about if MoonFeather and I take you over to the coffee shop across the street. Allie could join us in a few minutes when you feel better." Food was always my solution to problems. Good thing I didn't seem capable of gaining weight since I had the imp flu and Scrap joined me.

"No Mike," I whispered to Allie. "Can't take a chance he'll scare her away."

"Why would he . . ."

"He's a man."

"I'll come with you only if your imp comes, too. I want him to protect me."

That was a new one. I still hadn't figured out how she could see Scrap. But she claimed she'd lost the ability to see him after she left Faery. Had her perceptions changed again? No one else around me could see him or my scar. No normal person, that is. Another Warrior of the Celestial Blade could.

Was my supposed help hanging around? Neither Scrap nor I had seen hide nor hair of another Warrior.

"Sure. Scrap needs some more beer and OJ after last night. He'll be happy to join us."

You sure about that, babe? He popped into view right in front of me. Allie and MoonFeather didn't seem to notice the slight air displacement of his arrival.

Maybe WindScribe's time in Faery had sensitized her nose to Mike's demon smell. Scrap didn't turn red around him. He hadn't reacted to Vern and Myrna Abrams either. I had to presume Mike was one of the good guys.

The door opened a crack, the security chain still on. I could see one of WindScribe's eyes peering out at us. It didn't look bloodshot or swollen. If she'd been crying, it was a long time ago.

"Just the three of us," I soothed her, waving Allie to stand behind MoonFeather and out of sight.

"Okay. I'll come." She closed the door enough to re-lease the chain and stepped out.

"For heaven's sake, child, put some shoes on. I know Donovan bought you some," MoonFeather admonished. "And get a coat. I'll not be responsible for you catching pneumonia.

Even after a huge helping of strawberry waffles with whipped cream and three hot chocolates, also with whipped cream, WindScribe told us nothing we didn't know. Donovan had mentioned that Darren's family wanted to contest the will.

"What's in the will?" I asked.

Allie shrugged. "The investigators found one among his papers, but they aren't telling me anything."

"Your mother might know something," MoonFeather suggested.

I refrained from snorting. Mom avoided knowing anything about official stuff like investments and insurance policies. She left it all to me and Dad. We made sure there was enough in her checking account to cover her expenditures—which weren't much—and that was all she cared about. Dad invested part of her alimony each month so that she'd have a cushion if anything happened to him. She claimed she didn't understand things like that.

"I'd really like to get a look at that will. It might point us toward Darren's murderer," I said.

"Even if it points toward your mother?" Allie asked.

"Mom couldn't . . ."

MoonFeather cocked an eyebrow at me. "Do you really know that your mother isn't capable of violence given what we know about Darren Estevez?"

Mom wasn't the same woman who had left for Florida three weeks ago. This morning's confrontation proved that. And Saturday morning, right after her wedding night, her relationship with Darren was very strained.

If she knew that Darren threatened me, her daughter, would she resort to violence to defend her "greatest treasure and one success?"

"If we follow the money, Mom stands to lose a lot more by Darren's death. He didn't have time to change his will after the marriage. Her alimony from Dad stopped when she remarried," I defended her.

"Do we know that Darren didn't change his will?" Allie asked. "They went to Maine to get married. A *lawyer* can perform marriages there. A savvy lawyer might draw up new wills for both of them at the same time and sock them for double fees."

Hey, babe, keep an eye on the witchlet. I think she's going to bolt! Scrap warned me. He'd downed yet another glass each of beer and OJ and had regained much of his color and perkiness.

While we talked money, WindScribe had grown more and more silent. She seemed to fade into the wallpaper.

"What's wrong?" I asked, grabbing hold of her sleeve. My sleeve, actually. She had on another one of my outfits, this one in amethyst.

"It's all just too confusing. Nothing is where it should be. I'm not where I should be. It's all so *different*." She sniffed and rubbed her eyes, making them red. But no tears leaked out. She just looked as if they had.

"A lot happens in the real world in twenty-eight years." MoonFeather shrugged.

"But I've only been gone like a month! I know because I only bled once while I was gone."

"Time runs different in Faery. Everyone knows that," I said.

"I . . . I just want everything to be the way it was the day I left," WindScribe sobbed.

And I knew in that instant that she lied. I didn't even have to wear the comb to figure that out.

She's got secrets upon secrets upon secrets, Scrap said.

She had to know that Scrap would see that. Deep down, she wanted to tell someone the truth about that night twenty-eight years ago—two months before I was born. One month after Allie entered the world.

But did she know the truth or only the bits and pieces of it as she saw reality through her very warped perspective?

"This isn't getting me any closer to Donovan or to his father's death," Allie sighed. "I've got to get back to the station. The boss will probably put out an APB and a warrant on him. Fleeing the state moves Estevez up to the top of the suspect list."

"I don't think he did it," I said when she had left.

"What makes you think that?" WindScribe asked. She sounded wary and uncertain again.

"Because Donovan Estevez has deep control over his actions. If he planned it, he'd make it look like suicide or an accident, and he'd cover it up so well no one would need to ask questions. We might never have found the body. If he acted in the heat of anger, it would have been on the spur of the moment—and he has a hot temper. Believe me, I know." I rubbed the almost completely healed gash on my forearm. "If Donovan allowed the heat of anger to drive him, when he had the fight with Darren, that would have been about three hours before Darren died. Stealing the short sword took planning."

"If he didn't do it, then who did?" WindScribe turned wide and innocent eyes on me.

There's only one way to find out. Scrap departed so fast the vacuum he created robbed me of breath.

Chapter 42

Though rare, moon images are found in feminine form. Usually she is lovely, graceful, with classic facial features and hair perfectly coiffed under a stunning hat.

"SCRAP, GET YOUR SORRY ass back here!"
No answer.

"He has to return to you, doesn't he?" MoonFeather asked, searching the air with nose and eyes for a trace of my imp. Could she "sense" his presence even if she couldn't see him? If she did, that might explain why she felt the need to cleanse my house with ritual and burning sage.

"Eventually," I grumbled. "He's never far away, in case I need him, but he can stay out of sight for days if he wants." I threw money on the table for my second breakfast and stomped back to my car.

"What about me?" WindScribe wailed.

"What about you?" I snarled.

"I mean you . . . you can't just desert me. What will I do?"

"You should have thought of that before you set the Midori demons free." I eyed her narrowly as she tripped lightly in my wake. "How many faeries died because of that little stunt?"

"I don't know what you mean." She opened her eyes wide again feigning innocence.

I didn't believe her act for a second.

"Enough to get you sent to the cosmic prison for life," I finished for her.

"It was only three faeries! And they'd been mean to me!"

"Somehow, I don't think that's the end of the story."

"You're just as mean as they were." She ran back to the motel, oblivious to the traffic on the 6A.

Horns honked and brakes screeched. She didn't even look at them before slamming the door to her room so hard the frame quivered.

"Not the entire story by a long shot," MoonFeather added. "Let's go home. Scrap will return there more readily, I think."

"I can't leave the b—witch running around loose. She comes with us, if I have to drag her by the hair."

After some more conversation and a few threats, as well as cajoling and promises to call Donovan, Wind-Scribe joined us. She didn't even fight the seat belt.

I wondered how much she feared being alone.

Gollum raised his eyebrows and made copious notes on his laptop when I told him the story. I should expect something different from him?

I curled up in my office with a short story that was due while I waited for Scrap to return. I waited a long time.

Darkness fell. Dad stayed with Mom. They talked and cried a lot. The red glint of demon thrall left her eyes. WindScribe hovered in the library where she could peek out to find me in the office, or dash over to Moon-Feather's room at the smallest sound. Old houses creak and groan at the best of times. She spent a lot of time running back and forth, then returning to her corner with a humph and "I didn't really do that" attitude.

I fixed spaghetti for dinner. We each took a plate back to our respective corners.

I was on my third glass of wine—Gollum was on his fifth judging by the few drops left in the bottle—when I sensed a tiny draft and a miniscule weight on my shoulder.

"Ready to talk about it, Scrap?"

It's dangerous.

"What in life isn't?"

This is really, really dangerous. I'm just a scrap of an imp and I don't know if I can control the energies involved.

"We've got to find out who murdered Darren, Scrap."

Even if it was your mother?

That was the first time he didn't call her "Mom." My dinner and the wine turned to ice in my belly.

"Yeah, even if it was her. I *have* to know."

First thing in the morning. I need daylight. Bring Gollum. I can't let you do this alone.

"Meaning that, if you fuck up, we all die together."

Better than dying alone.

Much better than dying alone.

Scrap disappeared again. To think. To rest. To study the energies. I finally had time for my own agenda.

"What's so special about the house, Dill?" I whispered when I finally had the kitchen to myself. He seemed to hang out here more than anyplace else in the house. But then, everyone hung out here more than anywhere else.

I hadn't really been working on the short story. I'd been re-creating conversations, making lists, drawing lines and connecting dots.

Silence.

"Dill, I know you're here. I can tell because the other ghosts are all in the cellar."

Was that a faint shimmer in the air leaning against the center island?

I couldn't tell for sure under the fluorescent light. So I went about gathering the ingredients for chocolate chip cookies. His favorite, my favorite, and Scrap's favorite, for that matter.

"I liked oatmeal and raisin almost as well as chocolate chip," he said almost petulantly.

"Too bad you're dead and can't eat them anymore."

"If you'd just get rid of the imp . . ."

"I'm tired of that line, Dill. Now tell me about the house. You were the one who insisted we spend more than we'd budgeted on it. I said it was too big and would cost a fortune to heat. But you insisted and filled my head full of dreams of a dozen children." I looked longingly at the new table and chairs in the nook. I'd burned the symbol, the promise of those children along with the round table Thursday. Now it was Monday night. Only four days. It seemed a lifetime ago.

"I didn't really want those kids. I just knew they'd happen. My family always has lots of children. Can't seem to stop it from happening." Dill looked over at the nook, too. He frowned at the new decor. Not his choice. Not his table. Not much left of the real Dill in this house.

"What's so special about this house that you chose it over newer places that required less maintenance and cost less to heat, with just as much floor space and land? Why is it the ghosts are content to stay here and not move on? Why was Darren willing to kill again to get his hands on this house?" I stood facing Dill, hands on hips, feet *en garde*.

"Can't you feel it, Tess?" he asked, eyes wide in innocence. "You're pretty dumb and insensitive if you can't. Just an ordinary bitch when I thought you a Celestial Warrior."

"Typical. When you don't want to answer, you sidestep the issue and accuse someone else of being inadequate."

"Well, you are," he sneered. "If the Powers That Be hadn't promised me a new life, I'd be outta here in a flash rather than be tied to a sniveling wimp like you."

I raised my right hand, clutching a huge wooden spoon, ready to clobber him. Only I couldn't. He was dead. And I was alive.

And I didn't have to put up with him much longer.

"Tess? Who are you talking to?" Gollum asked. His glasses stayed firmly on the bridge of his nose as he looked around the kitchen. Jaw dropping in amazement, his gaze lingered on the shimmer in the center.

"Guilford Van der Hoyden-Smythe, meet my ex, Dillwyn Bailey Cooper." I turned my back on them both and started blending flour and baking soda in a measuring cup.

"Uh . . . Tess . . . that isn't the ghost of Dillwyn Bailey Cooper," Gollum stammered.

I sensed him moving closer to me, standing between me and Dill.

"What do you mean it's not Dill?" I whirled to face them both.

The equinoctial moon, only one night off of full, chose that moment to peek through some light clouds and flood through the big bay windows of the nook.

I could still see Dill as a small, semisolid core within layers and layers of wavering black energy.

I wasn't wearing the comb. This was more than aura. More like a pure essence of darkness.

As I watched, a taller, darker being coalesced out of that miasma. Long fangs dripped red blood; pasty white skin stood head and shoulders above my tall husband. It had a human shape, but a blur where the face should be. Except for those fangs. It wore an old-fashioned black suit and opera cape.

My mouth went dry and my eyes froze open.

At the moment of recognition, the demon snapped out of this dimension in a rancid puff of black smoke.

My knees trembled. Gollum wilted.

We held each other up for a long moment, clinging together in disbelief.

"Was that Dill's true form?" I whispered, afraid I'd call it back into being.

"I don't think so," Gollum said on a gulp. "You said several times it acted out of character for Dill. What if it was a shape-changer?"

"Some*thing* that wanted me to believe it was Dill."

"An envoy of the Powers That Be. Something sent to trap you, make you willingly give up your status as a Warrior of the Celestial Blade."

"Not Dill." I blinked back hot, stinging tears. "Now that I've recognized it for what it is, it can't come back. Were any of my ghostly visitations my Dill?" A vast emptiness opened in me. Now I truly would never see Dill again.

"I don't know. I believe you must renounce Scrap and your Sisterhood voluntarily before it could kill you."

"Someone is so desperate to get rid of me, they sent *that?* So desperate they conned Darren into marrying my mother just to get the house. So desperate they told Darren how to free WindScribe from cosmic prison. I think I'm scared, Gollum."

"I think we need more information."

"Before they try again."

Chapter 43

WE SPENT THE NIGHT together again, drinking my scotch and eating chocolate chip cookies until we fell asleep, me on the sofa, him in the armchair. We kept the nasties at bay and drew comfort from not being alone should they come again.

Tuesday morning Dad and Bill took Mom and Wind-Scribe to do some necessary shopping right after breakfast. I think my parents had more meaningful conversation and did more healing yesterday than they had in twenty years. Though still fragile, Mom appeared to have found a bit of acceptance of the weekend's events.

Gollum, MoonFeather, and I gathered for a council of war in the kitchen.

"Time travel has often been theorized. I don't recall anyone successfully completing it," Gollum mused when Scrap had outlined his plan.

Time is just another dimension, Scrap said importantly. I think he warmed to the notion as we progressed.

"We only have to go back about forty hours," I said. "That can't be too dangerous. And we don't have to shift locations. We can go stand in the cottage. The police removed the crime scene tape yesterday afternoon."

If I manage the timing right, we won't be gone more than a few minutes, Scrap said solemnly. His tail twitched nervously.

"Let's do this before I lose my nerve." I dragged Gollum out of the house to the cottage.

"You need a watcher," MoonFeather called after us. "And a ritual circle." She tossed one crutch away and clumped forward. She carried a small cloth drawstring bag with a pentacle embossed on it.

"She's probably right," Gollum admitted. He slowed to allow my aunt to catch up to him.

As I unlocked the cottage door, the smell of death rushed out to greet and smother me. I stepped back too quickly. Gollum caught me as I teetered on the top step. I let him hold me a moment until I regained my balance. It felt good. Like we were a team.

After a moment we crept inside. MoonFeather swept open the curtains, letting sunlight flood the small living room that ran the width of the building.

"Shouldn't we wait until midnight or something?" I asked. Something felt wrong, but I couldn't put my finger on it.

"Midnight rituals are really only to hide from prejudiced outsiders," MoonFeather said self-righteously. "Or if we needed a particular moon configuration."

I want the bright light of day to lead me back, Scrap said. He sounded uncertain. Maybe I was picking up his mood.

The chalk outline of the body stared up at me from the nubby green carpet. The dark stain from Darren's blood spread out beyond it. He had fallen below the window to my right. I hugged the built-in glass-fronted bookcases to my left.

Gollum walked around the outline, examining the position. "Was he faceup or facedown?"

"Faceup, I think." I didn't want to look at the outline. Memory of the sight of his lifeless eyes staring into the distance and his blood pooling beneath him set my breakfast of pancakes and bacon with grilled tomatoes to churning.

They tasted vile the second time around. Especially the strawberry jam I'd put on the pancakes. Too sweet.

"Over here, I think," MoonFeather mused, standing next to me. "You'll be in the shadows, and even a demon shouldn't detect your ghostly presence." She dug into her little bag and withdrew chalk. "Help me to sit on the floor, Tess."

I offered her my arm to lean on as she levered her way to a kneeling position. She settled back on her heels with a sigh. "Much better."

Gollum stood beside me. Scrap perched on my shoulder, wrapping his tail around my neck in a near choke hold. Except he didn't have enough substance to affect my breathing.

Deftly, MoonFeather drew a circle around Gollum and me. She looked like she'd had a lot of practice. Then she set stubby red candles at the four cardinal points of the compass. With a few muttered prayers and scatters of herbs she lit each candle in sequence, north, east, south, and west.

"Blessed be," she breathed at last. "Do your work, Scrap. You are protected from outside interference." She sat back on her heels and closed her eyes.

No matter what happens, do not speak, do not step outside the circle. In no way may you change the events you watch.

The light twisted and tilted, coruscating across my vision. Sparkles drifted around us. My sense of balance wavered. I clung to Gollum's hand.

As abruptly as it had shifted, the world righted. The darkness of the hours between midnight and dawn crowded my sight. Movement by the window caught my attention. The lamp by the armchair was on. The one closer to the sofa still lay broken on the carpet where it had fallen when Donovan and his foster father fought earlier—while WindScribe, Gollum, and I listened outside the window. Darren stood half turned toward me in the circle of light, fists clenched, jaw tight, shoulders hunched. When he turned his head, the light made his eyes look red.

At his feet stood King Scazzamurieddu, equally angry, equally menacing. Except that his cap was missing.

Darren held it crumpled in one of his fists.

I let my gaze wander around the room, drinking in details that I might have missed back in real time. The chalk circle blazed an otherworldly blue white. The red candles and their flames appeared ghostly, mere suggestions of their place. Scrap, however, looked solid and nearly a third larger than I remembered. His weight dragged at my shoulder, so I shoved him atop my head where he proceeded to anchor himself by pulling on my hair.

Gollum and I looked mostly solid, and yet there was a subtle difference, an aftershadow of light every time we shifted or moved a hand.

"If I thought the bitch had a snowball's chance in hell of succeeding with her demon rebellion against the Powers That Be, I'd give her the lock codes to three black market weapons warehouses," Darren nearly shouted.

"But then you'd have to kill her." King Scazzy smiled. He looked so much like a harmless garden gnome the hairs on my nape stood at attention in alarm. He was his most dangerous when he appeared most innocent. "Like you killed Dillwyn when he tried to reveal to the archivist your plans to build a homeland for the Kajiri."

What? I nearly shouted. When? How? I needed to know more.

Gollum held me back from leaving the circle. Scrap took on an ominous shade of red.

"Damn straight I will kill her if I have to. When my people finally get their homeland, they are going to look to me as their leader, not some flighty teenager spaced out on faery mushrooms. I cut her loose from your prison for a reason, and that wasn't it."

Scazzy chuckled. "Don't underestimate that vacant look in her eyes. She's cunning and smart."

"Idiots are cunning. And she's an idiot, and an addict, incapable of stringing two coherent thoughts together. She's fulfilled her purpose." Darren shifted so that his back was fully to me.

"What do you plan to do with the Sanctuary, Estevez?" Scazzy asked.

Sanctuary? He'd referred to my house as a sanctuary once before.

"Would you believe me if I said I merely want to stay out of sight of the Powers That Be for a while? This land is neutral, has been since time out of mind."

"Which is why it is dangerous in the hands of an active Warrior of the Celestial Blade. She is not neutral." Scazzy pasted a fake smile on his face.

"So neutral that it seems only natural a new portal will open here eventually."

"With a little help from you, the legal owner, once you maneuver your name onto the deed."

That wasn't about to happen, even if he murdered me. The house went to charity, along with my royalties if I died.

I desperately wanted Darren to turn around so I could see his eyes, know what he was really thinking. Face the murderer of my husband. The man who had used my mother so mercilessly.

"WindScribe gets an idea in her head and she can't think any further." Darren heaved a sigh. "Passionate and single-minded. She uses sex as a drug and as a weapon. Very dangerous combinations. I need her to start a rebellion when and where I dictate. Won't help me much if she does it in a place so far away from *my* portal we can't use it."

"Then you'll give her back to me for safekeeping when you are done with her." Scazzy's gaze peered into every shadow in the dark room. I got the feeling he saw in the dark as well as in the light. Maybe better, considering Gollum wanted me to fight him at noon.

"You can have the brat now as far as I'm concerned. You just have to convince my new stepdaughter to let her go."

"If I take WindScribe before the honorably scheduled battle, will you back me with the Powers That Be?"

Darren paused. His neck and jaw muscles tensed.

"If you are fully committed to me in this. We eliminate the Powers That Be, and you are free of your job as prison warden. I want WindScribe out of the way, so I can get on with my own plans for Tess. Killing her at the moment would raise too many questions and bring too much official attention to me and my plans."

"You don't think I can take Tess Noncoiré out?" Scazzy cocked one bushy eyebrow.

Darren snorted in derision. "I've heard what she did to an entire clan of Sasquatch. I'm placing my bets on Tess. But I'll hand over the girl after Tess has it out with you. You can still honor your promise," he snorted in derision.

"I'd watch my back if I were you," King Scazzy said quietly. His gaze fixed on the door to the kitchenette.

I swung my head in that direction, deathly afraid I'd see my mother there. Afraid that she'd heard this entire bizarre conversation.

The doorway was empty. But I heard a scratching sound, like someone moving from the back door in the kitchenette through the narrow passage.

I needed to break free of the circle, go see who approached, and if it was my mother; stop her from murdering her husband.

"Don't pull that trick on me, Your Majesty," Darren sneered. "You won't slip away from me so easily. I wasn't born yesterday." Darren kept his gaze fixed on the Orculli troll rather than heed his warning.

"I mean it, D. Look behind you." King Scazzy looked oh so smug. He knew what was about to happen and wasn't going to do more than the minimum to prevent it.

He had his own agenda. From the half grin on his

face, I surmised that he was on an information-gathering mission rather than agreeing with Darren Estevez and his grand schemes.

"Why should I look? So you can run away from my summons the moment I take my eyes off of you?"

King Scazzy heaved a sigh.

WindScribe, wearing one of my pink flannel nightgowns, slipped silently into the room on bare feet. She held the German short sword in front of her in a classic *en garde,* as if she knew exactly how to wield the weapon.

I think I squeaked.

King Scazzy peered directly at me with a puzzled frown. Then he turned back to Darren. "Honor compels me to warn you once more to turn around and watch your back, D."

Darren finally looked over his shoulder. His eyes narrowed in suspicion as he turned to fully face Wind-Scribe. "Put that down, little girl. Before you hurt yourself."

Silent, determined, and lethal, WindScribe advanced upon Darren.

He batted at the blade with his hand. It had no edge, but a wicked point. She performed a perfect circular parry and riposted beneath his guard. She thrust the sword into his gut, pushed upward and twisted in an assassin's expert move.

I almost heard his heart burst as the sword tip penetrated.

A gush of bloody air escaped his mouth. Then he just . . . crumpled.

Scazzy grabbed his red cap from the dying hand and popped out.

WindScribe smiled. "That will teach you to cross me, Darren Estevez. I will be queen of the otherworlds. I will create and control the new portal. No one will ever hurt me again." She left by the front door, closing it quietly behind her, the sword still dripping.

I gasped. Hot bile climbed up my throat.

Gollum pulled me against his side, burying his face in my hair.

Before I could react, Scrap whisked us away.

The world tilted again. Air rushed around us. I felt a chill. I had a vague impression of a vast open space. And something large, blue, and menacing advancing toward us.

Just passing through, guys, Scrap called.

Then with a thump and a give in my knees I was back in my cottage staring at the chalk outline of where Darren had died the day before.

A death I had just witnessed.

Chapter 44

"**I**T DIDN'T WORK," MoonFeather sighed, opening her eyes.

Gollum expertly brushed an opening in the chalk circle with his toe. "Oh, but it did," he said, stepping free of the dubious magical protection.

"But . . ."

I knew I could do it! Scrap chortled and preened. He glowed bright green with satisfaction. An undertone of pink on his skin told me we'd come close to a demon in the chat room between now and then.

"You never left!" MoonFeather protested.

Between one eye blink and the next. Scrap sounded surprised at his expertise in a precise takeoff and landing. He flitted about the cottage living room, hesitating over the places where King Scazzy, Darren, and WindScribe had stood.

"Someone moved the body," I breathed. The outline was slightly to the left of where I'd watched Darren crumple. "He landed on his side. We found him on his back."

"Are you certain?" Gollum asked. He planted his big feet within the chalk outline. "King Scazzamurieddu stood just there." He pointed to the spot beneath the window. "So Darren must have been here."

"Turn on the chair lamp," I instructed. I couldn't bring myself to step outside the protection of Moon-Feather's magic circle. Something menacing still lingered in the room. Maybe it was just my imagination, but I couldn't seem to banish the image of Darren's bleeding body on the floor; the wet slurp of the sword piercing his heart; WindScribe's cold smile.

Maybe it was knowing that I was now a target for the Powers That Be because of my house.

What had Gollum said last night? I needed to voluntarily renounce Scrap and the Sisterhood, become a neutral person again.

Maybe it was Scazzy's accusation that Darren had killed my husband.

Dill, my heart screamed. *You didn't have to die!*

I turned cold and trembled from deep in my gut.

Gollum leaned over and flicked on the lamp. The sunshine flooding through the window masked the effect I sought.

"If you look closely, you can see the circle of light cast by the lamp. Darren stood inside that circle," I said, not looking at Gollum. Not daring to see the pain in his eyes.

Gollum peered closely at the carpet and took one long step to his right. "Good observation. But who moved the body?"

I grew colder still. "Mom. When she discovered the body. She turned him over to see why he didn't move. Maybe to see if he was still breathing."

"Judging from the amount of blood, he stayed alive for quite a while. You stop bleeding when the heart stops pumping," Gollum said. He had on his professor face, delivering facts in a lecture. No emotion. No horror.

"How? She stabbed him in the heart. I heard it!" No wonder Mom had come unhinged. I had when Dill died in my arms.

You didn't have to die, my heart kept screaming.

"She who?" MoonFeather asked. She wore a resigned look, as if she knew, but didn't want to admit it.

"Darren was part demon. Maybe his heart had an extra chamber or something," Gollum posited, ignoring my aunt.

"Would the autopsy show that?" I asked.

"She who?" MoonFeather demanded.

"WindScribe," I said quietly. "She came in the back door through the kitchen and killed him in cold blood."

MoonFeather sighed in relief.

"You didn't think that Mom . . ."

"I'm afraid I did, my dear." She straightened her slumping spine and settled her shoulders. "So how do we prove it?"

"I'm not sure. But I've got to call Allie." I finally gathered my courage and stepped outside the circle. I looked briefly at the telephone on the lamp table. No, I wanted out of this charnel house and back into the comfort of my own home. I also needed some time alone to think about WindScribe's final statement.

I will be queen of the otherworlds. Worlds. Plural. A new portal here at the house. And Darren had said something about providing her with the lock codes to black market weapons warehouses. I had to stop the bitch before she led an army of fully armed Midori demons across all the dimensions right through my parlor.

And then I needed a long talk with Scrap about Dill.

"Witnesses," I muttered as I prowled my office. The black screen of the powered-down computer stared at me accusingly. If I wasn't going to write, I should be on vacation in Mexico soaking up sun and color and inspiration, not obsessing about the murder of my mother's husband.

The marriage only lasted thirty-six hours. Or less, for Goddess' sake!

Since my brain wasn't working at the moment, I took care of a little bookkeeping. Paying the bill for the storage of the Kynthia brooch gave me pause. On a whim I called the jewelry store in Boston. I needed to know the thing was still there.

"Thank you for returning my call," the head honcho said when we finally connected.

"Huh?"

"I left a message with a young woman yesterday afternoon."

WindScribe. Just like the flakey brat to forget an important message.

"Is everything all right? No one has stolen my . . . er . . . jewelry?"

"Of course not, Ms. Noncoiré. We have never had a single misplaced item."

I breathed a sigh of relief.

"I called because a registered package arrived in yesterday's mail for you in care of us. We took the liberty of opening it. A small, exquisitely cut black diamond, exceedingly rare, beautifully cut, with only a small flaw, arrived by post in an unmarked jeweler's pouch. The note simply said, 'For the brooch.' "

"For the brooch?" I gulped. Who? What? My mind spun with endless questions.

"I checked, personally. The stone will fit precisely into one, and only one of the empty settings on the brooch. Would you like us to set it for you? The cost is quite modest since you provided the stone."

"I did? I mean, yes. Please do."

"I presume the stone carries a significant symbolism for you. Congratulations on the occasion."

I rang off. A black diamond. What significance?

Of course, Scrap gave me the brooch in honor of defeating the Sasquatch in pitched battle. Could the black diamond be for my battle against the Windago?

If so, what would happen when I'd completed twelve battles and the anonymous donor had filled all the empty spaces on the brooch?

I should live so long.

Back to my current problem. I'd let the metaphysical

stuff sort itself out on its own. It seemed to do that with or without my interference.

What was the easiest way to bring reliable witnesses into the situation and not alert WindScribe what I was up to?

"Hello, Cecilia. Mom wants to resume game night tonight," I told my sister on the phone. "She wants life to get back to normal. And she needs to have the family gathered close around her." The *only* way to get the family together without starting a war among us was to put a Trivial Pursuit game on the dining room table between us.

"I'll call Uncle George and Grandma Maria," Cecilia volunteered. She didn't even protest that it was Tuesday night instead of Sunday.

Then I called Dad and insisted he bring Bill, too. With the family lined up, I decided to add a few outsiders. Gollum was a given. He'd be there whether I wanted him or not. And I wanted him. Outsiders who represented the law came next, Allie and her boss Joe Halohan. Mike Gionelli?

No. I didn't think so. I'd deal with him when I had to. Not before.

That left one more player in the drama. My new stepbrother, now ex-stepbrother. Donovan Estevez.

"What?" he growled into his cell phone.

"How fast can you get back here?" I didn't bother introducing myself. He'd either recognized my number on caller ID or he'd know my voice. I'd never forget his.

"I can't leave. The family is tearing itself apart over D's will." He sounded frustrated, and a little scared. No matter how much he, or I, disdained our families, they were . . . family. Important to our emotional well-being, an anchor to who we were and where we came from.

"What is in the will?"

"You sure you want to know?"

"Yes."

"The police didn't tell you?"

"They've told me squat. But I'm about to reveal to

them the real murderer. It would look better if you were here, since you are currently their prime suspect."

"Shit!"

"What's in the will?"

"He and your mom signed mutual wills at the time of their marriage. You do know that in Maine, any officer of the court, including lawyer, can perform a marriage?"

"Yeah. A couple in my senior high school class eloped. Their folks tried to have it annulled using that as their argument. The marriage wasn't legal because it hadn't been performed by a judge. What's in the will?"

"The lawyer who performed the marriage drew up a simple but ironclad will for each of them. They left all of their worldly goods to each other. Your mom is now a very wealthy woman. But D's kids and extended family are all set to contest it."

A long whistling breath escaped me. "I'm surprised Halohan didn't zero in on Mom as suspect number one."

"You say I'm their prime suspect now?"

"As of this morning. Your leaving town didn't help."

"Who did it?"

"I don't want to say on an open line." I might be on my cell phone—free long distance, minutes didn't even count when I called Donovan or Gollum since we all had the same carrier—but I suspected eavesdroppers within the house.

"If I leave now, all hell will break loose."

"You can go back tomorrow. But I need you back here by nine tonight. Ten at the latest."

"I'll do my best," he grumbled and muttered something more. A loud crash and shouting in the background, and he disconnected without further explanation.

"Wow!" Gollum said when I related the conversation. "Does she know?"

"I don't think so. She hasn't said anything to me. Or asked any questions about handling the money." I settled back onto his sofa. It felt like an old familiar friend after sleeping on it so many nights running. A big yawn threatened to take me to la la land once more.

"That family of half-blood Damiri could be your next battle." He settled in the armchair across from me and planted his feet on the coffee table. We'd done this before, here and in a couple of hotel rooms as we plotted the next move.

"I'll let the lawyers handle it. Right now, I need your help." I got up and grabbed a couple of beers from his fridge. We each took a long gulp before he spoke again.

"Help with what?"

"Making some new question cards for family game night. Then you can teach me how to stack the deck. You do know how, don't you?"

"What makes you think that?"

"Because you know or can find out anything."

Chapter 45

Moon symbolism has been present in religion since the beginning of recorded history. The crescent moon and star closely identified with Islam probably came originally from Byzantium, and may have been borrowed from ancient Persia before that.

I SERVED COFFEE AND tea and some bakery cookies. Gollum and I had eaten all the homemade ones. Grandma Maria, my mother's mother, complained a bit about the disruption of her "schedule," meaning a series of sitcom repeats on TV on Tuesday nights. Uncle George, my father's brother, demanded a drink before he'd cleared the doorway. Dad and Bill sort of slid in unnoticed by anyone but me. I was the one counting bodies.

Cecilia blew in wearing her red PTA power suit. She glowed with triumph and eagerness. Then she blew out again, in her yellow power pickup, more interested in pushing her agenda on some new playground equipment at the school than her agenda in controlling the family. "By the way, James Frazier is outside with his camera and a man in a black suit and sunglasses," she said offhandedly at the doorway, and was gone before I could question her further.

Allie and Joe Halohan came last, uniforms made casual looking by removal of ties and tool belts. I didn't doubt that they each had guns hidden on their persons somewhere.

Mike Gionelli followed in their wake. I hadn't invited him, but Allie insisted.

"You okay with him, Scrap?" I whispered while alone in the kitchen.

For now. He's got a lot more human in his bloodstream than demon. I can't smell any evil in him. Scrap perched on the mantel blowing smoke rings at all who passed by him.

"FBI and a reporter outside," Mike whispered as he passed me, confirming Cecilia's observation.

"We'll have something for them later," I returned, equally quietly.

Donovan would come when he could get here. A message on my cell phone had informed me he was hoping to get on a flight that would land in Providence at seven. An hour's drive from here. At eight, I hadn't heard from him.

His presence wasn't essential to the proceedings, but I hoped he'd arrive in time to be fully exonerated. Why, I don't know. Donovan in prison as an accessory to murder would make my life a whole lot simpler.

Gollum escorted WindScribe over from the bottom of the new stairs.

Twelve people gathered around the massive table, filling all of the high-backed chairs. Any more and I'd have to drag in extras from the kitchen. I bumped Uncle George from the armchair at the head of the table nearest the fireplace. This was my house, after all. He mumbled and grumbled about preferring his poker night with his drinking buddies at McTs. But he settled his ample butt next to Grandma Maria. Gollum took the place to my right, Allie to my left. Mom sat next to Allie, looking small and frail. This couldn't be easy for her. But she needed to confront the murderer of her husband.

I needed to do the same.

Somehow we all maneuvered things so that Wind-

Scribe sat opposite me at the other end of the table. Bill and Dad flanked her. She couldn't avoid my direct gaze.

We began in the normal fashion working our way through the normal deck of question cards. Moon-Feather and Dad took on the job of moving game pieces around the board for those of us who couldn't reach.

With this many people, it took a while to work around the table. Gollum made sure that WindScribe's first four questions came from her own time period, Vietnam era politics, Nixon, the Bicentennial celebration, even sports. Her confidence and relief at answering each one correctly showed clearly in her expression and posture.

The rest of us got normal questions about more current events and scientific breakthroughs.

I watched a puzzled frown deepen on WindScribe's face between her turns as each round progressed. She seemed to shrink in her chair, trying to hide from the probability of getting a question she couldn't answer because she'd been stuck in Faery for twenty-eight years. With each move on the board, she became more and more aware of just how much she had missed and how hard she'd find it to fit in to modern life.

The theme from *Star Wars* on my cell phone stopped the action just before WindScribe's fifth question. Donovan's number flashed on the screen.

"I'm turning into your driveway now," he barked. He sounded tired.

"Just in time," I answered smoothly and hung up. "Go ahead with the game."

Gollum drew a card from the top of the pile. I watched him palm it and produce a forgery. No one commented on his sleight of hand. Either they didn't see it, or my family accepted cheating as normal. I was betting on the latter. We get cutthroat sometimes on game night.

"Name the scientist responsible for mapping the human genome," Gollum read in his professorial voice. He speared WindScribe with a look that would have set students quaking in their leather sandals.

I heard the crunch of gravel and the banging of a car door.

"Oh, who could that be?" WindScribe sprang to her feet and made a mad dash for the kitchen. "Donovan, you're back!" she squealed.

We all waited in silence. Answering a question or admitting you didn't know the answer was a nearly sacred ritual among us.

WindScribe appeared a moment later with Donovan's arm wrapped around her waist. She clung to him like a lifeline.

Scrap popped out of the room. Not far, I sensed.

"I guess we have to end the game now," she said brightly.

"Answer the question," Uncle George growled.

"We don't end the game until someone wins," Grandma Maria added.

"I . . . um . . . we can't continue and leave Donovan out. It wouldn't be polite." Near panic crossed Wind-Scribe's features. Then her eyes narrowed, and she settled into a fiercely defiant posture.

I could well imagine an automatic weapon in her hand. Or an eighteenth-century German short sword.

"Answer the question," Halohan added. He'd become as deeply involved as the rest of us.

"Or take the penalty," Allie said.

"You're all being mean to me," WindScribe pouted prettily.

"Not at all, my dear," MoonFeather admonished. "We are simply playing a game. "Now abide by the rules." Her face took on a look of sternness that had sent me running for a place to hide in the woods when I was a child. "Rules are important."

"Donovan, make them stop," she pleaded.

"Far be it from me to break the rules." He shrugged and disengaged himself from her embrace. He moved to my end of the table and placed his hand on my shoulder as he dropped a kiss on top of my hair.

I almost leaned into his warmth and strength. His

hand felt quite natural in the place where Scrap usually sat, as if we belonged together.

Gollum's look of sad resignation kept me upright and determined to proceed. Donovan and I didn't belong together. At least not in this lifetime.

"Glad to see you came back voluntarily," Joe Halohan said.

"I need to go back to Florida tomorrow, Chief, but I wanted you to know that I'm available should you need me in the investigation. I'm not guilty. I just have a volatile family that needs attending to."

Halohan grunted his acceptance of the explanation.

"Still not an excuse to skip town without notice," Mike said. He kept his eyes on his hands rather than meet Donovan's gaze.

Tension there. Something to deal with later. Wind-Scribe was looking anxious and ready to flee.

"Perhaps you'd accept a different question, Wind-Scribe?" Gollum said. He pretended to draw another card. "Who is the King of the Orculli trolls?" He read it as if it were just another normal question from the pile.

"That's not a real question!" WindScribe nearly screamed.

"Oh, but it is," Gollum said. He held up the forged card for inspection. Amazing what you can accomplish with a scanner and a good graphics program.

"Answer the question, girl," Grandma Maria demanded. "I know the answer. Surely you should."

My mouth fell open at that.

"Well, anyone who's read one of the field guides to wild folk knows that," my grandmother retorted. I had to get my omnivorous reading habits from somewhere. Why not from her?

"You're ganging up on me. I won't stand for it." Wind-Scribe stamped her foot. She tried for that innocent little girl look and failed miserably.

"We're trying to get you to take responsibility for your commitment to the game," I said sternly. "But you aren't good at taking responsibility. Your mother was

right. You aren't good at anything. You'll never be pretty enough or smart enough to do anything but fail."
I echoed some of the things MoonFeather had told me about Mrs. Milner's abuse of her daughter.

"Do you suppose we should just throw her out?" MoonFeather asked. "She doesn't seem interested in following the rules."

"And the next question is where were you going to get the weapons to lead an armed rebellion?" I added.

My family looked more than a little bewildered, but good sports, one and all, they played along with our charade.

"She couldn't follow through with that either," Donovan said on a yawn.

"I will!" WindScribe said. "I will lead the demon tribes to victory. I'll be queen of the otherworlds. And this one, too!"

"The wild imaginings of a drug addict," I said.

"Stop it! It's real. And I am not an addict." WindScribe shouted. She looked ready to tear her hair.

"If she's not an addict, why did she try to steal my migraine medication?" Mom asked. No coaching there. Mom had really caught the girl up to no good.

"Shut up. You're nothing but a demented, shriveled-up old woman. I don't know what D saw in you. You couldn't help him. But I could. I'm the one who killed the king of Faery and got access to the demons. I'm the one who planned everything."

"Is that why the ATF sent me down here, to stop your little war before it got started?" Mike asked.

That surprised everyone, including WindScribe.

She pulled an automatic weapon from the back of her waistband, beneath her sloppy blouse. My blouse that fit her sloppily, that is. She aimed it between my eyes. At this distance she could hardly miss.

Chapter 46

*M*y skin turns bright vermilion. I stretch and twist as far as I can. But no command comes from Tess to transform. I can't get any closer to her than the doorway to the butler's pantry, right behind WindScribe.

She is the source of evil that compels me to become a weapon of good. Her lack of demon blood keeps me from overcoming the force field that surrounds Donovan. Even Mike's traces of demonhood is not enough to overcome Donovan.

His mojo is so powerful I don't want to ever get in a fight *against* him.

If I can't get closer to Tess, then Tess must come to me. Without Donovan.

I need a distraction.

Hmmm.

"Boo!" I shout in WindScribe's ear.

She remains impassive, as if I'm not truly here.

Damn. Why is it she can see me sometimes but not now when I need her to?

"I think you want to put that away," Halohan said sternly. His hand shifted to his hip. He hadn't worn a holster when he came in.

Allie's hand went to her boot top. She must have a gun hidden there.

I couldn't relax. The gaping maw of the gun muzzle stared right at me, followed me when I shoved my chair back and to the left, closer to Donovan.

Was she desperate enough to risk shooting her lover?

Gollum slouched in his chair, almost disappearing beneath the table. Great. Now he turns coward.

"Really, now, it's only a game!" Grandma Maria snorted.

"No, it's not. It's a bunch of silly rules that no one can understand," WindScribe insisted. Her eyes looked wild and unfocused, bright hair tangled as she combed it with the fingers of her left hand.

Halohan eyed her suspiciously.

"Well, I've had it with other people's rules. I'm in charge now." Suddenly she lost the druggie scatter-brained demeanor. She assumed a new air of confidence and serious menace. Lines radiating from her eyes made her look considerably older. Hard experience gave her those lines, not accumulated years.

"As long as you've got the gun, lady. Didn't know we were playing 'Clue,'" Uncle George muttered. He fiddled with his game piece.

Why couldn't he be his usually clumsy self and spill his beer or something, anything to get WindScribe's attention away from me and the trigger of her big honking gun.

"Is that what you did in Faery?" MoonFeather asked. "Take control of the rules, make your own?"

"Of course. But that silly little king kept getting in the way. He should have thanked me for opening the door between our two worlds. But no. He insisted I was violating some long tradition. He talks of hospitality and fair treatment, but he keeps the Cthulu demons locked up in cages. He *attacked* me when I let the poor beasts free."

"Poor beasts?" Donovan quirked one eyebrow up. "Last I heard, the Cthlulu eat everything and anything in their path, growing larger with each meal until one of them will fill an entire ocean. The magic of Faery that keeps every being the same size is the only way to contain them. They aren't even allowed to guard the chat room." He spoke softly.

No one but me was listening anyway.

Again I wondered why those things were allowed to survive. Balance be damned. I didn't want Cthlulus or Damiri, or Sasquatch, or any of the monsters loose in my universe. In any universe.

Gollum seemed to have melted into the floor. So much for his help.

"All creatures deserve to be free!" WindScribe screamed. Then calm descended on her like a cold mask. "So I snapped the Faery king's neck with a twist of my hands, easier than killing a chicken."

A whistle escaped through my teeth. "You killed the king of Faery?"

WindScribe shrugged. "So what?"

"And then you armed a band of demons and tried to take over," MoonFeather finished.

"Get off your high horse, old lady. You'd have done the same. I marched beside you in peace demonstrations. The place was ripe for revolution," WindScribe sneered.

"No, I wouldn't," MoonFeather sighed. "There is a difference between protest marches or organizing voter registration to right a wrong and . . . and arming thugs."

"Thugs with a taste for human blood," Donovan added.

"What in the hell are they talking about?" Dad asked.

"The girl's crazy. Clinically insane, if you ask me," Halohan replied. "And the rest of you are walking a fine line between vivid imagination and downright delusion."

"You got that right," I said. WindScribe might be crazy, but she remained incredibly focused with that gun.

Suddenly Mom's eyes cleared. I could almost see a

light switch turning on in her brain. "Why did you kill my husband, Joyce Milner?" she asked. She fixed a gaze on WindScribe that would have made me squirm.

"My name is WindScribe!" she shouted. "I'm not Joyce. I will never be Joyce again." She waved the gun in a wild arc taking in the entire room.

All of us slouched a little lower in our chairs. Gollum actually disappeared beneath the table. Coward or practical?

"So why did you stab my husband and frame my daughter, *WindScribe*?" Mom pressed her. "What did I ever do to you? I used to babysit you."

"Nothing against you, Genny. You just happened to be in the middle," WindScribe dismissed her.

"I'd be interested in the why of it," Halohan said. He edged his chair back a little, making room to lunge for WindScribe. Allie did the same.

"He threatened you, WindScribe," Donovan said. He hadn't budged an inch, not even to cower away from that wicked little gun. Would the bullets penetrate his demon skin? "And he imposed rules on you. Rules that didn't make sense to you."

"Of course. He was all about rules," WindScribe replied. "He couldn't do this or that because it might expose him for a demon. I couldn't say this or that because it might alert his enemies to what he was doing and he was cheating everyone he met. Including you, Genny."

Mom paled. "The wills," she whispered.

"Yeah, the wills," I muttered. "His was a blind, a way of easing your mind so you'd bequeath everything to him, bypassing your children and your ex. He'd wait to kill you until he killed me and you'd inherited everything I own, including this house. You wouldn't have lasted long enough to grieve."

"You, Tess?" Donovan asked. "You were the real target?"

"Of course." Take out a Warrior of the Celestial Blade and take over the house. A very special house on neutral ground where he could build and control a new portal.

One look at Mike squirming in his chair under my scrutiny and I knew I'd guessed right.

"Sacred ground," he whispered. "Neutral ground to all races and tribes. Blessed by seven shamans thousands of years ago."

I might have been the only one to hear him.

"Only Darren hadn't counted on my will, which leaves everything to charity," I continued the primary conversation.

A dozen pairs of eyes riveted on me. "Why you?" Dad asked the question on everyone's lips.

I couldn't tell him. He'd never understand that I was a Warrior of the Celestial Blade living outside a Citadel. That I was a free radical who threatened Darren's plans to set up a home world for Kajiri demons.

"He wanted the house. He also wanted the research I'd stumbled on that would expose his scams and cheats," I said instead. "He may have been wealthy, but a lot of his money came from confidence games and semiorganized crime." That was close enough to the truth.

"It's not nice to speak ill of the dead," Mom remonstrated.

"But it's true!" WindScribe chortled. "That and much, much more. I had to kill him before he killed me. It was all too easy, hardly a challenge at all. Now the king of Faery required some planning. I made it look like an accident, but it was really me. I'm not stupid. And he found me beautiful. So does Donovan. I'm not a failure."

I rolled my eyes in dismissal.

"I'm not a failure!" WindScribe insisted. "And it's my turn to make the rules. None of you will dare break them. Because I'll shoot you dead. Now everyone lay down on the floor with your hands behind your necks."

We looked at each other rather than at her. Who was willing to take a bullet while the rest of us rushed her. An automatic. How fast could she fire? Would the recoil destroy her aim?

What did I know about guns? A blade I could judge.

Guns? I didn't want to take a chance on her taking out my entire family.

Allie nodded ever so slightly to Halohan.

"No." I grabbed her wrist. "I won't let you do it."

"You don't have a choice," she said quietly. "I owe you one, Tess. It's my job to protect and to serve."

"No. You don't owe me anything. This is my house. My responsibility." *My job.*

"Quit stalling. Get on the floor," WindScribe ordered.

"I don't think so," Grandma Maria huffed. "My arthritis." She turned a glare on WindScribe that made Mom's look weak.

"Me either. I need another drink," Uncle George leaned back and looked through the butler's pantry as if he could levitate a beer from the fridge.

"You're breaking the rules!" WindScribe looked near panic. "Hey, where's the tall guy?"

"New rule," Gollum said from right behind her. "Never, ever point a gun at someone unless you intend to shoot. And you'd better shoot quick or the rule maker will take the gun away from you."

He reached over her shoulder and pressed a nerve in her wrist. Her hand opened and the gun fell to the floor.

Allie scrambled to retrieve it.

WindScribe collapsed in upon herself, falling over the arm Gollum thrust in front of her.

I heaved a sigh of relief. Gollum was no coward. He outsmarted us all by sneaking under the table to get behind WindScribe. My estimation of him rose several notches.

Halohan was on his cell phone in seconds. Sirens sounded in the distance a heartbeat later.

Donovan tried to gather me in his arms. I resisted his allure, giving my smile to Gollum instead.

"I guess she forfeited her turn. Can we continue with the game now?" Grandma Maria whined.

>>>

"Half of D's wealth goes into a blind trust, administered by me, to continue the family enterprise," Donovan told my mother over a brandy and cookies in the kitchen some hours later.

Halohan had taken WindScribe off to the mental ward of the hospital in an ambulance, with James and the FBI hot on their heels. Allie had left instructions for everyone to stop by the station tomorrow to give depositions on the evening's happenings. Bill took Uncle George and Grandma Maria home. Moon-Feather had retired to her room with her cell phone to call Josh.

The house felt empty, even though it was still full.

Maybe because Gollum had retired to his apartment to leave the family discussion to the family.

"The other half of the estate, D left to you, Genevieve, naming me executor of the will," Donovan continued. "I'll do my best to see you get as much of it as possible, but he has legitimate sons and daughters who will contest the will in court."

"I . . . I didn't expect much. I knew he had money, but I didn't think he was *wealthy*," Mom replied. She seemed fascinated with the amber swirl of brandy in her glass.

I watched her closely for signs of the grief-madness or demon thrall that had possessed her earlier. For the moment she seemed lucid. She'd recovered faster than I did when widowed dramatically by murder.

"Is there enough in the estate for a compromise?" Dad asked. He had his calculator and a legal pad in front of him. He piled up numbers on the pad at an alarming rate. "Give half to the Estevez children from Genevieve's portion?"

"More than enough. I was going to suggest such a compromise to keep the lawyers from eating up a huge chunk of it. Even giving away half, there's enough for you to live comfortably for the rest of your life, Genevieve." Donovan patted her hand possessively.

I guess he did have a claim on her now. But she was *my* mother. I should be the one taking care of her.

"I don't think I want to buy the Milner place now. It's too big for just me."

"You're welcome to continue here," I offered. Somehow I couldn't imagine living here without her. "Will you want to go back to the cottage?" I asked tentatively. Or would Darren's ghost haunt her there?

Mom shook her head, her short hair bouncing against her cheeks, mingling with her slow tears. "I couldn't."

"Then I'll ask Gollum if he'd be comfortable there and you can have the apartment."

Mom raised hopeful eyes to me. "Th . . . thank you, Tess. I'll pay rent once Donovan clears the estate."

"You just keep cooking for me and we'll call it even."

"Thank you," Dad mouthed on a deep sigh.

A couple of problems under control. But I still had the misplaced coven to deal with. And I had some big questions for Scrap about Dill's death.

Mexico seemed farther away than ever.

Chapter 47

Women who live together in close quarters will often find their monthly cycles coinciding, usually at the dark of the moon, becoming most fertile two weeks later at the full moon.

"WE'RE HOLDING A MEMORIAL for D here on Wednesday morning. Tomorrow," Donovan said when he sought me out in the library a few minutes later. "Just your mom and your family, probably. Then I'll ship his body home to Florida for a funeral and burial on Thursday."

"What's in it for you, Donovan?" I asked quietly.

"It's just a funeral," he replied. He didn't look as confused as he tried to make his voice sound. The flickering light from the fireplace brought out the copper tones in his skin and revealed depths to his eyes I hadn't noticed before. They looked as deep and forbidding as the lake at the base of Dry Falls in Washington State, near his home.

"I meant the will. Why are you working so hard to help my mom and deprive Darren's children of their inheritance?" I held his gaze steadily, doing my best not to succumb to his allure and let my concerns all slide away.

"You aren't going to trust me on this one, are you?" He had the grace to look chagrined.

I knew in that moment that he had something to hide. Something more than usual.

"I don't trust you at all."

"You trusted me to watch your back in battle the night before last."

Was it only two nights ago? It seemed a lifetime had passed since then.

"I thank you for that. But you had something to prove. Watching my back in battle against full-blooded Windago was secondary." We glared at each other for many long moments.

The fire popped, sending an ember onto the hearth. We both jumped and did not relax afterward. I sensed Scrap hovering in the other room, anxious that he could not get close to me.

We both knew that we were too emotionally drained to engage in a fight again even if he could summon the strength to transform.

"What do you have to gain?" I asked again when the silence between us had stretched too long.

"The trust."

Control of half a large estate. He'd been close to bankruptcy last autumn when we destroyed his half-built casino rather than let the Sasquatch use it as a rogue portal into this world. A portal that bypassed the chat room where most dimensional passages took place. Did he need the money that badly to recoup his own fortune?

What about the big gaming deal he closed last Friday?

"What do you intend to do with the trust? I figure it has to be in the millions."

"Maybe buy an island in Polynesia and turn it into a resort where my people can go on vacation and let themselves be who they truly are without prejudice or restrictions." He settled into a wooden rocker across from me.

"And who are your people?"

"You know I can't tell you that."

"These Powers That Be sound like a cop-out to me.

Something gets uncomfortable to talk about, and you blame your silence on them."

"That's not fair, Tess. You've never had to face them." He looked at the floor, studying the broad wooden planks intently.

"I've faced Sasquatch, Windago, and Orculli trolls. I've witnessed the Goddess of the Celestial Warriors in the sky. Maybe I should face these mysterious Powers That Be and get some questions answered."

"If you think getting me to answer a question is hard, the Powers That Be make me look like a tattletale with diarrhea of the mouth."

"Then spill some information."

He replied with another lengthy silence.

"Okay, back to something you will talk about. The will. Why you? I heard you and Darren fighting. You worked hard to keep him from marrying my mother. Why did he trust you with that kind of money and responsibility?"

"Because he knew I'd do something with the money and not fritter it away on cars and drugs and unsound investments."

"Why didn't he do something with the money? Seems like he was just sitting on it for a long time."

"His dreams were too large. He wasn't willing to start small and build. He wanted it all at once or not at all. His kids are too inbred to dream at all."

"But you aren't inbred." I wasn't satisfied with that explanation. Not by a long shot, but I'd take what I could get. And this was more information than I'd been able to pry out of him yet.

"I'm one of a kind." He flashed me one of his disarming grins.

I ignored it, fingering the magic comb in my pocket.

"You are human. King Scazzy said as much. Extremely long-lived but human. How long is extremely long-lived?" Scazzy had told me. I wanted to hear it from Donovan himself.

"You don't want to know."

"Try me."

"I came to life at the same time as the Citadel near Dry Falls was first built to guard the demon portal."

Came to life, not became human. Came to life as what?

He looked too smug for that to be the entire explanation.

Then something else he had said hit me between the eyes just as powerfully. "When you said that Darren's kids would waste their money on cars, drugs, and fly-by-night investments, what kind of drugs do demon spawn use?"

He stood and turned his back to me, peering out the high, small windows into darkness.

"Do they consider blood a drug?"

He nodded.

"Human blood?" I felt suddenly dizzy and nauseous.

"When they can get it."

"And you *sympathize* with these beings? You work to give them a homeland!" I stood in my rage, fists knotted. I wanted to slay him as I had slain the Windago and the Sasquatch before them. But something about this man kept my imp at bay.

What? What? What?

"I watched the Kajiri struggle against prejudice and poverty too long. I know their intelligence, the contributions they can make to both cultures, human and demon. Some injustices cannot be measured." He rounded on me, fists as knotted as my own. "They are akin to former slaves in this country for many, many generations. Think about the prejudice African Americans have overcome and how long it took them; how much prejudice they still face. Then multiply that by one hundred."

"Scrap said that demons are locked up in ghettos for a reason. Like they *eat* other sentient beings. African Americans are human with human sensibilities. If I had my way, I'd slay every last demon that crosses into this dimension."

"And upset the cosmic balance no end." He tried to lull me with another smile. "Ever wonder why you humans don't have a balancing demon? It's because you are your own demons. The only race that murders each other with glee. By the thousands in war and individually."

You humans. He'd said *you humans.* Like he wasn't one of us.

My anger boiled so close to the surface his charm had no effect upon me.

"You are no better than WindScribe. One way or another I'll find evidence to get you locked up for a long, long time. In prison or a mental ward. Any way I can get you off the streets. To save humanity from your depredations and those of your . . . *people.*"

"Ah, Tess. Don't be that way. We were good together." He reached to trace my cheek with a gentle finger.

I ducked away from his touch.

"Remember, L'akita. Remember the night you spent in my arms, loving me time and again, hour after hour, never tiring of me?" His voice grew soft and persuasive.

Goddess help me, I did remember and longed for his touch with every breath.

"Get out of my house and out of my life. Now." I pointed toward the door.

"L'akita."

"Don't." I closed my eyes lest the sight of his awesome beauty make me forget what he truly was. Black of heart and soul.

And, oh, so achingly beautiful.

"Our lives are already entwined, L'akita. You can't banish me so easily."

"I can try. You know the way to the door." I turned my back on him, hugging myself against the need to reach out and hold him close.

"Honor obligates me to warn you. If your mother has not already passed through menopause—completely— there is a good chance she is pregnant. The Damiri are incredibly fertile."

I heard the menace of warning in his voice. My eyes

flew open in horror. I was lucky I'd made him use con-
doms the one night we had spent together.

"Thank you for the warning. I'll keep an eye on her."
He had no way of knowing Mom had had a hysterec-
tomy right after I was born. Something had gone terribly wrong. I was six weeks premature. But he didn't
know that, and I wasn't about to enlighten him. Let him
worry.

"L'akita . . ."

"Scrap says that WindScribe is pregnant," I threw at
him. Jealousy screamed through my body. Unreasonable,
unthinkable, miserable, aching jealousy. I had no right to
the emotion but it was there, like a cancer inside me.

"How?" His mouth flapped open and closed like a
fish drowning in air.

"You know how it happens."

"I mean . . ." he swallowed deeply and flushed a charming shade of mahogany. "I mean, how can Scrap tell? It's
only been a couple of days."

"He says he can smell it on her. As long as the cat isn't
around clogging his sinuses."

"I have some plans to make. I'll petition the courts for
custody, of course. I wish the baby was ours. He can be.
We can raise him together." He reached to brush a curl
off my brow.

I ducked away from his touch, too fragile to risk
breaking if we made contact.

"Go. Just go."

►►►

"You going to sleep in your own bed tonight?" Gollum
asked as I wandered toward the stairs yawning. He had
a goofy grin on his face I couldn't interpret.

"How many nights have I slept on your sofa?" I
stopped short, one foot on the first step.

He shrugged. "It felt right every time it happened."

"Yeah." Part of me yearned for the safety and security
he gave me. But I couldn't allow myself to depend upon
him. "But not tonight."

I was too fragile after banishing Donovan. I needed to learn to be alone again.

"Whatever. Holler if you need me to hold your hand after a nightmare." He turned away toward his apartment.

I almost called him back to fill the cold emptiness that yawned inside me.

"I don't have nightmares."

Scrap snorted at that.

I ignored him and made my weary way up to bed.

Mom had already tucked herself in and lay softly weeping. A hard knot in my gut reminded me how I had felt when Dill died. How close to insanity I'd strayed. I'd loved him deeply. I still did. But I also had accepted his death—finally—and knew I couldn't go back; couldn't bring him back.

We all had to move forward somehow. I was still wandering in circles.

"I need to find out one way or another if Darren Estevez murdered you, Dill. And why," I whispered to my memories of my husband, not the apparition I'd seen in the kitchen.

Softly, I pulled up a chair beside Mom's single bed and sat. She lay on her side with one hand outside the covers. I took it in mine and just held it.

And prayed that this midnight vigil would end more happily than the last one I'd sat. With Sister Jenny at the Citadel.

A tiny smile flickered through Mom's tears. "He wasn't truly human," she whispered.

"I know, Mom. I know."

I wondered what he had done to her that had nearly broken her mind. The aura of tension between them Saturday morning had disappeared. Had he used his demon whammy to abate her fears? Had he used the same unnatural charm to win her in the first place?

Undoubtedly. Donovan was capable of the same kind of unnatural influence. I'd seen it in action. That didn't make me any less lonely for banishing him from my life.

I was cold and cramped when I awoke several hours later. Mom's hand still lay in mine, slack with sleep. Her tears had dried and she breathed evenly. I crept away on tiptoe, leaving the door between our rooms open.

►►►

"Scrap," I called softly into the shadows of the cellar. "Where are you?"

No answer. I could sense him nearby, but he wasn't willing to show himself on demand. He must know what I was up to.

"I've got mold, Scrap." I held up a jar of peach jam half full of the spoiled remains. Nearly a half inch of fuzzy green and white crusted the top. I'd been saving it for emergencies. This seemed like an emergency.

Bribery will get you anything your sweet heart desires, dahling. Scrap popped into view right in front of me. He stuck his nose into the jar, wings beating overtime in his excitement over the culinary treat I held. He lifted his head on a deep inhale, as if savoring the scent of fine wine or perfume.

I pulled the jar back just enough to make it awkward for him to reach.

Faery giver! Scrap pouted.

"It's all yours, friend. If you do something special for me." I pushed the jar out just a little, just enough for him to get another whiff of the putrid stuff.

What? He backed off suspiciously, crossing his pudgy arms above his rotund tummy.

"I want to go back."

Back where? He didn't relax his guard at all.

"To the night Dill was murdered."

It was a fire. An accident.

"It was arson. That makes it murder. You heard Darren claim to have been behind it." I extended the jam a little further. "There's no dairy in this. It won't upset your tummy."

Scrap sniffed appreciatively. He turned pink, then

purple. Then virulent yellow. His hunger warred with his conscience.

Don't make me do it, Tess.

I was in trouble if he called me by name. No softening to "babe" or a drawled "dahling."

"Please, Scrap. I have to know what happened." Another proffering of the treat. I waved it beneath his nose. He crept a little closer, salivating.

You were there. You should know what happened.

"I was asleep until Dill woke me and the room was full of smoke and heat. Everything was dark, misshapen by the flickering flames. You know I won't rest until I know for certain if Darren Estevez murdered my husband." And who helped him.

No. It's too dangerous.

"More dangerous than giving in to Dill's demands and replacing you with him?"

Scrap panicked. He flashed green, red, yellow, red, purple, red, blue, and back to red again in rapid succession.

You're dead either path. You die: I die, Scrap gibbered. *Sorry.* And he popped out, leaving me holding the smelly jar of mold and shattered hopes of closure.

No Fair! No Fair! No Fair!

I can't do it.

I won't do it. It's too dangerous. The time separation is three years. *Three years,* I tell you. And the distance. Three thousand miles back to Half Moon Lake. She doesn't know what she asks.

I can't do it. I'm not skilled enough with dimensional manipulation. The Barrister demons are guarding the chat room. They'll never let me through on such a mission. *Never.*

But Tess is my Warrior. How can I deny her what she truly needs?

I sense that she does need to do this. She'll never be able to truly move on and send Dillwyn Bailey Cooper back where he belongs unless she does this.

Oh, what to do? What to do?

Chapter 48

"WE WANT TO GO back," the plump woman from the coven announced shortly after dawn Wednesday morning. She and her companions descended upon us *en masse,* and the words came out before I'd fully opened the kitchen door to them.

I had a funeral to go to at noon, then plans for afterward.

"Dragonfly, you know we can't go back. The new rulers of Faery don't like us very much," FireHind reprimanded her. "None of the candidates voted to keep us there."

I noted that they were all clad in various forms of jeans and sweatshirts, and barefoot. What was it with these women that they disdained shoes? The temperatures had warmed to the low fifties, but the air and land were still soggy with melting snow.

"I should think the new rulers of Faery would fear you after what WindScribe did," I said as they trooped into my kitchen and settled around the table and on the counters. "Killing the king of Faery couldn't have been easy."

Scrap flitted about, tweaking curls and blowing

smoke in their faces. Our previous argument was ignored but not forgotten by either of us. He punctuated his displeasure with me with an occasional fart that reeked of his lactose intolerance.

Some of the younger members of the coven kept fanning the air in front of their faces and looking about bewildered, the curious and outspoken Larch among them. The rest were oblivious to my imp's tricks.

"She snapped his neck like it was a twig she wanted to use for kindling," Dragonfly grumbled. "Then she threw him against an oak tree. No remorse, no second thoughts. He got in her way and she just did it."

"Hush," FireHind reprimanded. "We do not speak of it. We agreed."

"Under threat of death and dismemberment," Larch muttered. "But we aren't in Faery anymore. They can't touch us here in our home dimension."

>>>

Now that is something I need to find out. Can the faeries pursue these women like the Orculli pursued WindScribe?

I'm in luck. J'appel dragons are on duty. Tiny things, hardly bigger than I am. They can flame me, but they have to smell me first, and they are constant victims of sinus infections—from the sulfur fumes they burn. And their eyesight is notoriously weak until someone calls them by their true name and they grow and grow and grow to fill the chat room with angry, reptilian, winged-beasties.

So I use my small size and the stealth I learned in order to survive my siblings (not all of them survived me, however) and hop over to the leather curtain that covers the doorway I want. Beyond the curtain a clear force field in front of Faery is wavering like ripples on a smooth pond. The colors of grass and flowers are dim, the chuckling creek has become a raging muddy torrent. Uh-oh. Trouble in Paradise.

Changing air pressure makes my ears pop as I fly into Faery. No matter how big or small you are, when you come to Faery, you are the same size as the faeries. That's the magic this place holds. Sort of defines equal opportunity.

Don't know if I grew or shrank. That's also part of the magic. And how faeries defend themselves. With deception and mystery. No one knows much about them other than that they are incredibly beautiful. Even without warts.

"You have violated our fundamental laws of hospitality!" a feminine voice screeches.

I creep closer to the knot of winged creatures gathering about the sacred oak tree in the center of Faery. Half male, half female. All wearing flowing draperies in lovely jewel tones sprinkled tastefully with diamonds and emeralds and rubies and sapphires and freshwater pearls. They all sparkle in the watery sunlight without ostentation. It is too easy to go overboard with precious gems when they are plentiful, or you are incredibly rich. Not these guys. They know when to quit. Makes them even more elegant. Even their delicate wings glisten with just a hint of sparkly Faery dust.

"I had no choice. Those women violated every cosmic law of hospitality, good manners, and trust," a male in ruby trews and tunic replied. He wears a princely circlet.

"That is for others to judge. Now we are accused of criminal behavior," the female in white and diamonds says with her delicate, long-fingered hands bunched onto her slender hips. Her circlet is platinum and set with diamonds. She outranks him.

The bunches of lesser faeries shift and form up, taking sides.

"I stand by my ruling. The human women are exiled," Prince insists. His folks nod their heads in agreement. So do some of Queenie's faeries.

"You aren't king yet," Queenie says. Her eyes narrow as she calculates her next move. "You have done nothing about the predators kidnapping our citizens. You aren't a decent prince, how can you expect to be an adequate king?"

"Thinking about seizing the crown yourself?" Prince flits one pace forward.

Have I mentioned that faeries rarely let their feet touch the ground? Well, they don't. Like insects, their wings are in constant motion, wafting a gentle perfumed breeze throughout Faery. If you ever catch a whiff of flowers out of season or climate, a faery probably just flew by.

"I will make a better ruler than you," Queenie says. "I'm older, more experienced. More concerned about my people. Wiser than you by a long shot."

This time she commands the nodding heads.

I might also take the opportunity to let you know that most faeries don't have the longest attention span. Nor are they great at making decisions. That's why they rely so heavily on their king— or queen—to think for them.

"You carry not any royal blood. You only married it," Prince snarls.

"Considering how you have mucked up," Queenie points to the raging, muddy torrent behind her. "Royal blood doesn't guarantee a gift for ruling."

"The disruption is only temporary. As soon as I state my case to the Powers That Be . . ."

"We have never had to state our case to them." Queenie almost spat. She looked angry enough to strangle her opponent on the spot. "Now we are out of balance. Our doors are open to thieves, criminals, and predators."

Uh-oh. Faeries don't fight. They live in peace and plenty. They are truly the paradise of the universes.

"Hey!" I shout at them. "Time to step back and think."

They all turn their heads to me. Questions and haughty disdain shine in their eyes.

"This all goes back to WindScribe and her coven, doesn't it?"

They continue staring at me in silence.

"Well, doesn't it? Who else could violate enough cosmic rules to get thrown out of paradise and into an Orculli prison? Now, if you tell me what they did and how they did it, maybe I can help set things right. Before you resort to violence and upset the balance even further."

Things must be really out of whack if I'm advocating peace and compromise. I'm an imp. I am the Celestial Blade of Tess Noncoiré. I thrive on blood and battle. How else do you think I survived the wars with my siblings? They didn't all come through unscathed. Some didn't come through at all. But that's the nature of imps.

Sometimes.

Okay, maybe we don't all kill our own siblings in battles over

Mum's love and her lovely home. But we do fight each other for supremacy and the right to be claimed by the next Warrior of the Celestial Blade.

I'm wondering if I should regret some of my actions.

Nah, that's just Faery. Peace and justice permeate the air and seep into you through your pores. Whether you want it or not.

WindScribe is really screwed up if she managed to violate that peace.

They turn on me *en masse* and blast me with negative psychic energy. I could have withstood it. Imps are pretty good at setting up mind blocks. But I decide to retreat. If they don't want my help, it's their loss. Let 'em live with chaos for a bit. Then they'll welcome my advice.

Time to check back with Tess. I should be able to return about one heartbeat after I left. She'll never know I was gone.

The coven really can't come back to Faery.

I called Gollum and MoonFeather in to help sort this out.

"Still running away from reality?" MoonFeather asked mildly. She had forsaken her crutches and leaned on one of my long staffs. This one had a brass dragon as a finial. One of my favorites. It suited her better than me.

"That isn't fair, MoonFeather," FireHind defended herself. "You have had decades to adjust to all these changes gradually. We have to face and accept them all at once. It's too much."

"What about WindScribe?" I asked. "She seemed to be adapting. She's criminally insane in my opinion, but she accepted that life does not stagnate, nor do people."

According to Allie's phone call this morning—at an even more ungodly hour than this invasion—the district attorney was willing to forgo the expense and trouble of a trial if the state would take the raving lunatic off his hands. WindScribe's story of being kidnapped into Faery for nearly thirty years, and then releasing demons into the world for an armed rebellion had convinced everyone, including the FBI, that she was not competent to stand trial, nor was she the woman who had disappeared twenty-eight years ago. She showed no remorse over killing Darren. In the eyes of the legal authorities that made her a sociopath.

No easy solution to that cold case.

Apparently, the FBI hadn't yet heard about the other eleven escapees.

"WindScribe is no longer one of us," Dragonfly said, almost proudly. "We banished her."

"Evicting a member from the coven is a serious matter," MoonFeather said. She assumed the captain's chair at the head of the table.

For once FireHind acceded the place of authority to her maturity, and (I hoped) wisdom.

"WindScribe acted in complete opposition to our goals, our ideals, our *faith*," FireHind said. Her voice was quiet, neutral, stating facts. Still, there was a crack in her posture, a shadow in her eyes that shouted how deeply WindScribe had wounded her personally and the coven as a whole by her violence and betrayal.

"Granted." MoonFeather nodded her head once.

"I want to go back," Dragonfly sobbed. "It's always warm there, the flowers bloom, the land never pricks our bare feet. We can be ourselves there."

That's what she thinks! Scrap chortled. *Lots of chaos and political power struggles in Faery. There's power leaking out into the chat room. Upsetting the balance.*

"Civilization does have rules of conformity to keep things running smoothly for the majority," I admitted. "Free spirits have trouble fitting in." I had experienced that as much as anyone. But I still tried to make my life look normal on the outside. I liked my life just the way it was.

Most of the time. In retrospect, now that I knew I had lived through it, I even liked the adrenaline rush of this never ending crisis-weekend-going-on-week.

"Can you send us back, MoonFeather?" FireHind asked, eyes open wide and trusting.

"What about the new king of Faery?" I asked. "Didn't I hear that he wasn't too pleased with you ladies?"

All eleven ladies shuddered.

"Didn't he kick you out as accomplices?"

"We didn't help her," Dragonfly protested. "We just didn't tell anyone what she was up to."

"Complicity in my book," I mumbled.

"Now that WindScribe has been locked up in a mental ward, we hope that the faeries will take us back. We made friends there quite easily until WindScribe . . . until she abused their hospitality in her misguided need to free all captive people," FireHind said. She, like MoonFeather, seemed deeply motivated to speak only positively about people. We were all having trouble finding positive things to say about WindScribe.

"I don't know," MoonFeather mused. She rubbed her chin with one hand and drummed the table with the fingers of the other hand. "The moon is in the wrong quarter. The season is wrong."

I could do it easily if it were All Hallows Eve, Scrap chimed in.

I ignored him for the moment. Halloween was still seven months away.

"What are we going to do?" FireHind asked, almost wailed.

"I need some time to think about this, do some research. Gollum, do you have any books that might help?" MoonFeather looked brightly at the scholar in our midst.

"Most of them are in storage in Seattle," he admitted glumly. "I can ask around, see if some of my colleagues have copies or better texts. The trouble is we have no documented cases of anyone actually succeeding in this type of dimensional travel. Only hearsay. Our best chance would be to try to re-create the original ritual and adjust it to the season and the moon. Or wait for Halloween."

Eleven frowns met that statement.

Scrap hooted with laughter and whipped around the room. *Told you so!* he chortled. I noticed how far away from me he stayed. He wasn't willing to risk having to say no to me again.

"There is an alternative," King Scazzy popped into view on the counter that separated the breakfast nook from the kitchen proper.

As one, the coven ducked and made a curious warding gesture, crossed wrists and flapping hands. Moon-Feather grabbed the staff and took a defensive position.

Scrap turned bright scarlet and landed on my hand; resident evil more powerful than a little tiff with me.

Gollum reached for his PDA and began taking notes.

Chapter 49

"*E*ASY, LADIES," the prison warden of the universe said. He held up both of his stubby hands, palms out. His nose and chin almost met as he frowned. "I come in peace, and I come alone."

Scrap and I relaxed a bit, though he remained red and stretched taller than normal. The coven all pressed themselves against walls, as far from the little man as possible.

Gollum kept taking notes.

"What do you want, King Scazzamurieddu?" I asked.

"I may be of service to your friends," he nodded his head a fraction toward me. "I can escort all eleven ladies with safe passage back to the land of Faery, with a letter of introduction to the new queen."

Oh-ho! Queenie prevailed over the young princeling. I knew she would. That lady has tougher balls than all the rest of Faery combined. If I liked women, I could go for her. Scrap bounced on my hand in his glee. *Did she get the stream running clear and soft again?*

"Partly. There are still disgruntled factions in Faery. Power leaking," Scazzy nodded at Scrap. "The portal gapes."

The coven all looked bewildered and uncertain, not being privy to the exchange.

Gollum kept taking notes.

"You'll take these women back to Faery in return for what?" The fine hairs on my nape rose straight up. I'd read enough folklore to know that fair trade across the dimensions was elusive. Bartering of favors was common, but getting the better end of the deal was tricky. Coming out of the bargain with your soul and your life intact were rare.

That's why Scrap had called me a Faery giver when I snatched the moldy jam away from him.

"I do this in exchange for your word as a Warrior of the Celestial Blade that WindScribe will never again leave the custody of your state mental hospital. And that someone honorable, like Madame MoonFeather will raise the baby she carries. We don't want the father to have full undivided influence over it."

"I can't promise that. She's not my responsibility anymore." I had an uneasy feeling in my gut. This was too easy.

"Security in that facility seems more rigorous than what I could provide in my own prison," King Scazzy chuckled. "The employees are less subject to bribes of shiny baubles. She has less chance of escape from there."

"So? Why my promise? I can't guarantee she'll stay there, or that the courts will give her baby to Moon-Feather."

"You are the Warrior of the Celestial Blade. Should she ever leave her current prison, you must slay her. Should the child go to the Fallen One, you must get her back."

Oh-ho! The baby was a girl. Not the boy Donovan presumed.

"No. I don't kill humans. Even if they are homicidal maniacs. All I can promise is that if she is ever released, or escapes, I will notify you. Then she becomes your problem. If the authorities don't recapture her first. As for the baby? I can do my best to persuade Donovan to drop his custody suit. That's it."

"Granted." Scazzy bowed his head again. The gilded feather in his red cap bobbed with him, the only overt sign that he was a king and in absolute authority over his realm.

How far did his boundaries stretch into this dimension?

"And you will really take us back?" FireHind asked anxiously. She held her arms tight against her sides and her shoulders hunched, not quite daring to hope.

"You have my word."

"Give me your cap and repeat that," Gollum demanded, coming out of his intense record keeping.

I suspected he had his cell phone camera running and audio recording as well.

"I beg your pardon," King Scazzy replied, seriously affronted.

"Among the Orculli, an oath is not binding unless the opposite party holds your cap," Gollum returned. He fixed a fierce gaze upon Scazzy over the tops of his glasses.

A staring contest ensued.

The coven got restless, wiggling in their chairs or shifting from foot to foot where they stood. Their murmurs of discontent became an insistent hum.

"Enough!" MoonFeather finally broke the tension. "Do it, Your Majesty, or we'll be here all day. We have other obligations."

"A king does not remove his cap in the presence of lower life-forms." Scazzy levitated from the counter to the table to stand in front of her.

"Oh, yeah?" My aunt snatched the cap and held it above her head where he could not reach. "Now swear to safe passage for my friends, and Tess will swear to inform you if WindScribe ever escapes from the loony bin. And I swear that if I can legally gain custody of WindScribe's daughter, I will raise her with honor."

"Blood oath," Scazzy snarled. "Only way to make humans keep their word."

I shivered and looked to Gollum for confirmation.

"An oath signed in your blood will burst into flames if you break your oath. The flames will ignite the blood in your veins as well," he said as if reciting from a text.

I had a vision of Donovan signing numerous documents to refinance his casino in Half Moon Lake after it imploded. His bankers had dubious connections to the otherworlds and the ink looked thick and dark with reddish undertones like blood. No wonder he was so excited to make the big gaming software deal and take control of Darren's trust fund. If he paid off the note, then his blood no longer bound the deal.

An honest and aboveboard approach to business must have rankled his nerves no end.

And what about that other oath? The one not to reveal his origins.

I almost forgave him his silence. Almost. He was tricky enough to get around that oath if he really wanted my respect and trust. There are always ways around a bargain in Faery.

"The oath is simple enough. I agree," I sighed. "I'll sign a promise to contact you the moment I am informed if WindScribe escapes or is released."

"Or transferred to another facility," Scazzy added. "Someplace else might prove less secure."

"I agree to sign my portion of the bargain," Moon-Feather said with less hesitation. Honor was so ingrained in her, I doubted Scazzy even needed her oath.

"Okay." That came out on a long breath. Why did I feel like there was some trick here that I couldn't see? I checked with Gollum.

He shrugged and nodded.

Scazzy snapped his fingers and a piece of parchment appeared on the table in front of me, along with an ostentatious quill pen made from a peacock-blue ostrich feather—I wondered if it were dyed or came from some bird I'd never seen in another dimension. Beside the quill lay a small penknife. A wickedly sharp penknife for pricking my finger.

Or would he demand I slit my wrist and use arterial blood?

"But I don't want to go back," whispered a tiny voice from the corner behind me.

We all turned to stare at the young woman with reddish glints in her blonde hair. She had wide blue eyes that almost matched the quill in color.

"Larch, we all agreed," FireHind reprimanded her.

"I didn't. You all overrode my objection as if I didn't count. But I do count. I don't want to go back. I want to stay here and learn and grow like MoonFeather did."

"It's all of you or none of you, ladies," Scazzy said.

"Then it will be none, because I refuse to go," Larch insisted.

►►►

OOooooh, this Larch person is someone to watch closely. She has brains and a truckload of steel in her spine. If she plays her cards right, she might become another Warrior of the Celestial Blade. We need more of them outside the Citadel.

Hmmmm, I wonder which of my siblings has a dose of imp flu to spare.

Later. Tess doesn't have time to nurse her through it or train her.

Not too much later. We need another warrior to guard this neutral sanctuary from demons like Darren or the Powers That Be.

Until then, my bets are on Larch either taking control of the coven or breaking it entirely.

►►►

"*Brava,* Larch," MoonFeather said. She beamed as if one of her own children had made the honor roll.

Plump and mousy-looking Larch returned the glow, suddenly becoming pretty in a quiet way.

"So now what?" I asked the obvious. I was really getting tired of having everyone else's problems dumped in my kitchen.

"You all go back to your hosts and ask hard questions. Like 'what am I going to do with the rest of my life.' And if the FBI asks, you are all your own daughters. The women who disappeared twenty-eight years ago are alive and well and living elsewhere," Moon-Feather said. She held each woman's gaze a moment, like any good teacher allowing her students to form opinions and make decisions.

She'd raised two children, often alone, on a teacher's salary. She still substituted in her semiretirement. Josh supported her so that she could have the time and ease to pursue her other interests, like becoming a master recycler and a master gardener and passing on her knowledge to community groups.

"It's too hard," Dragonfly wailed. She appeared to be the youngest of the group. Probably only eighteen in physical years.

"Life is hard. Life isn't fair. We all have to learn to cope," I said, hoping my quiet words would insert themselves into a few receptive minds. "WindScribe refused to accept that, and look what happened to her."

The ladies remained silent, staring at each other and into the ether.

"I'm out of here, then," King Scazzy said. "May I have my cap back, since you don't need my oath or my services."

MoonFeather examined the cap a moment, then glared at him.

"Please," he gulped.

She extended the bit of red cloth and gilded feather on one finger. He snatched it along with the parchment and penknife and popped out before she could change her mind or make other demands.

"Larch, I would appreciate it if you would come home with me. I have need of assistance for a while. My injury is healing well, but my leg is still weak." Moon-Feather rose gracefully, using the staff as a brace.

I thought she leaned a little too heavily on it, making a point rather than truly needing it.

"I . . . I'd like that, MoonFeather." Larch stood straight and as tall as her five-foot-nothing frame allowed. "Will you teach me about your herb garden? And how to use a computer?"

"I'll do better than that. I'll enroll you in the community college. Tuition, room, and board in exchange for housework and help in the garden until the end of summer. Then we will reevaluate. Now I have some packing to do, and Tess, we'd appreciate a ride back to my house."

"I'll take you in the van," Gollum offered. "And I can give Larch a preliminary lesson on your home computer. She won't get far at school if she doesn't know a few of the basics." He rose from his chair and pocketed his PDA and cell phone.

"What about us? Why aren't you helping us?" Fire-Hind asked. A gloss of anger marred her classic features. I could see a harpy just beneath the surface of her personality. She wouldn't age gracefully.

"Larch showed some initiative and backbone. The rest of you were more interested in running away from reality than coping. In my mind, she has more potential than the entire lot of you." MoonFeather stalked back to her room without looking back. Larch joined her, a quirky bounce in her step.

"I'm going for a run." I stretched and yawned. "I expect to find my house empty and back to normal by the time I get back. Scrap, where are my running shoes?"

Chapter 50

*N*OW I'M IN FOR it. Without the distraction of the coven and Donovan and Mom, my babe will be after me to go time traveling again. I know her. When she gets an idea in her head, she doesn't let go.

I wonder if I'd be safer taking a quick jaunt home to my own Mum? Maybe I can find a trinket in the Garbage Dump of the Universe to appease my babe for a while.

But that would make me little better than the coven, running away when life gets a bit sticky.

Scrap could run, but he couldn't hide. Not for long at least. He was tied to me with mystical bonds I didn't fully understand. He'd come back.

So while I waited, I stretched my muscles and let the adrenaline flow, eating up a few miles. I hadn't exercised since . . . well, since that fencing bout with Donovan a couple of days ago. And the fight against the Windago. Neither one of those sessions allowed my mind to go blank while my body drank in fresh air and worked stress toxins out in my sweat.

I didn't even mind stomping through puddles in the

light drizzle. The gray skies were brightening. Life was beginning to look good. I might even get a few days in sunny Mexico after all.

Except for the questions that nagged at my soul.

In the last year I'd learned that coincidences happen for a reason. Darren Estevez and WindScribe fell into my life to teach me something, or reveal something.

I knew how valuable my house was now.

I also knew my husband had been murdered. He didn't have to die. I couldn't prevent that from happening. But maybe I could put his soul, and my conscience, to rest if I found out what happened.

I veered down to the beach. My feet pounded the water-soaked sand until my thighs began to burn and ache. Still I ran. Wondering. Forming and tossing out plan after plan.

One way or another I had to go back to Half Moon Lake, Washington, Donovan's hometown. I had to find out what happened that awful night three years ago.

With Scrap or without him. I had to go.

You also need to find out if Dillwyn Bailey Cooper was a half-blood Damiri demon, Scrap whispered to me from afar. *Isn't that more important, babe, than witnessing a murder you know happened at the hands of Darren Estevez?*

"I'll do that later, Scrap. Darren had reasons to kill Dill that I can only discover by going back to that time and place."

The time and distance are too great, dahling. I don't know if I can keep you safe.

"I'm willing to risk it."

And if you die, who will take our place?

"Gollum will find someone to become the next Warrior of the Celestial Blade. Larch is looking like a good candidate."

Only your Goddess can select a Warrior of the Celestial Blade.

That didn't sound like the entire truth, but I'd accept it for now.

"Well, then, if I die, the Goddess will have to prod one of my Sisterhood to leave the Citadel and take my place. You're the one who keeps telling me there is a cosmic plan and to believe in some higher power."

The rain came down in earnest, soaking me more thoroughly. I ignored the chill, pushing myself to keep a steady pace as I turned back toward home.

Then a memory came to me. "Scrap, when we were in Half Moon Lake last autumn, the ghosts of the ancient guardians took us back twelve thousand years to witness the Sasquatch stealing the blanket of life. We survived that."

They are guardians. They have different skills and purposes in their existence. They didn't have the distance problem.

"Four years and three thousand miles doesn't add up to twelve thousand years in distance. I have faith in you, buddy. Why can't you have faith in yourself?"

Scrap didn't answer for almost a quarter mile.

It's the distance. It's more difficult than the time.

"How about if we get Mom through the memorial service at noon, then we fly to Half Moon Lake? I think there's a con in Seattle this weekend. We can go play there for a few days when we're done." Not as good as Mexico. More convenient. And cons had filk. I needed to sing again, blow out more mental toxins than running could accomplish.

So be it, Tess. But not alone. We need Gollum to watch our backs. We will go together. We live or die together.

I liked that idea. Gollum watching my back.

The path took me around Miller's Pond. I kept to the western edge of the water, away from the scene of my battle with the Windago. A familiar path. I knew every twist and imperfection on the trail.

Still I stumbled. I'll never know what tripped me up. But as I caught my balance against a conveniently placed oak (brimming with mistletoe in the upper branches), something square and regular in shape caught my eye.

This jarred me enough to stop me in my tracks. As far as I knew, Mother Nature didn't create much with right-angle corners.

I reached out and picked up the object at the base of the tree very gingerly with my fingernails.

Then I had to sit. Rapidly. With a thump of my butt on the squishy, waterlogged ground beside the beaten path.

I held the hand-carved frame set with agates and arrowheads that Dill had made for our wedding picture. The picture itself was an unrecognizable sodden mess. But the frame was intact, if a little dirty.

Gollum and I had stood ten yards south of where I sat now when I cast my votive offering into the pond. I'd seen it skid across the ice and plop into the water at the center.

A tear dripped down my cheek.

The Goddess had returned the precious gift to me. She approved of something I did. I hoped it was my proposed trip back in time. I hoped she smiled on the endeavor and would help bring me back alive.

▶▶▶

"Before we go, I need to show you something," Gollum said quietly as I guided Mom through the ritual of dressing and eating before a memorial service. She looked and acted numb.

I'd put on a similar show for Dill's funeral; too filled with grief to know how to let it out. I hurt so much I was afraid, if I let one tear escape, I'd shatter into a million pieces and never be able to find them all again. I wasn't sure I wanted to at the time.

Gollum opened his laptop and awakened the thing. The scrambled symbols of a saved e-mail littered the screen.

"What am I looking at?" I asked scrolling down to find the body of the text.

A line caught my eye. An address that started db.cooper@ . . . My eyes blurred before I could read the rest.

"Dill?" Too shocked to ask the next question, I continued hitting the down button.

"He contacted me three years ago. Three days before the fire," Gollum said quietly.

I couldn't read Gollum's posture or gaze. Didn't care about that at the moment. I needed to read the message.

"You have a reputation as a demon hunter. I heard about you in Africa. We need to meet. I have information that will interest you. Use this e-mail. It's private and secure."

"That's it?" I breathed. I found my hand trembling where it hovered over the damn computer buttons. "Why?"

"I don't know. That's all I have. I e-mailed him back with questions and a suggested meeting time and place. He never showed. I know now that he couldn't come because he was dying in your arms at the time. I still have a lot of questions."

"Like how he knew what you were up to in Africa?" I had a few questions about that myself.

Easier to wonder about a living Gollum than dredge up old hurts and grief with questions about my husband.

"More than that. How he found a way to contact me on an address known to a very select few who also have reputations as demon hunters. But I'm not a hunter. I'm an archivist, duty bound to serve a Celestial Warrior who escapes a Citadel. There aren't many of you. Maybe one in each generation. Sometimes not that often."

"Gayla says there are more Warriors outside now. Too many new portals cropping up to park Citadels atop each." Speaking of which, where was the supposed help she promised me now that it was too late to help?

"I have already contacted my grandfather about that. He is searching for more archivists."

"So Dill knew about demons." My whole body shivered now. From the inside out.

"I think your husband knew about the 'Great Enterprise' of creating a homeland for half-blood demons. I think Dillwyn Bailey Cooper was going to betray Darren Estevez to me. And that's why Estevez killed him."

"How did he find out about it?"

Gollum answered me with a raised eyebrow.

"You think he was one of them?" I nearly gagged on my words. I suspected the same thing but was afraid to find out.

"I do believe that. I also know that as dangerous as your proposed time travel is, it will not bring you true closure. You have to go to Cooper's parents and find out for yourself if they are half-blood Damiri."

"Next lifetime. I can't deal with this now."

But you will have to deal with it eventually, babe.

Chapter 51

The word moon is probably connected with the Sanskrit root me-, to measure, because time was measured by the moon. It is common to all Teutonic languages and is almost always masculine.

MOM MADE A GOOD show of quiet dignity as I escorted her down the aisle of St. Mary's for the memorial of Darren Estevez. Watery sunshine brightened the interior of the old brick building. Tall stained-glass windows sent it sparkling onto the altar. Dust motes looked like Faery dust. The altar guild had recently replaced the egalitarian enclosed box pews with more accessible open benches. Mom had made two of the one hundred new needlepoint kneelers.

If she leaned a little heavily on my arm to steady her steps, I was the only one who knew. She wore a new wool black jersey dress with a crossover bodice and a skirt that draped on the bias. It made her look twenty pounds lighter and ten years younger. Her hat had a jaunty brim and a eyebrow-length veil that looked like Chantilly lace. The real thing, not some cheap machine-made imitation. The black set off her pale blondeness perfectly for the occasion.

I looked horrible in black and wore it rarely. It made my skin look sallow and my sandy-blonde hair more like dishwater than ever. Since I was not the widow at this occasion, I relieved my basic midnight-blue dress with a sapphire print scarf draped and pinned to the jewel neckline. Scrap had done the honors and made me look quite presentable.

Donovan showed up, of course. This was more his ritual than Mom's as the adopted son, executor, and custodian of the family trust. He looked magnificent in his black suit, blindingly white shirt and a blood-red tie. I'd never seen him in formal clothes.

My knees nearly melted at the sight of him. I think I needed better knees.

A vast emptiness opened in my heart that I had to reject him, banish him from my life. With a deep breath and firm resolve I looked away.

Gollum flashed me a grim smile from the second pew, directly behind where I would sit. Watching my back as always. He looked quite distinguished in a charcoal suit with a pale blue shirt and subdued striped tie. I breathed a sigh of relief as Mom and I took our seats.

We recited the familiar prayers, sang the usual hymns, knelt and stood at the appropriate times. The service was mercifully short. After all, Donovan was the only person present who had known Darren for any length of time. No one had much to say on behalf of the deceased, including Donovan. Father Sheridan spoke briefly of the tragedy of cutting a life short and how those Darren left behind must move on and make the most of their lives. And that was it.

An hour later I put Mom and Donovan and Darren in his casket on board a plane to Florida. When we separated at security, I pulled Donovan aside.

"If anything happens to my mother, anything at all, I will come after you, with every weapon at my disposal," I whispered to him.

"Don't worry. I need her alive and well as much as you do," he replied with wounded dignity.

"Remember that!"

I turned and faced a shadowy figure beside a massive support pillar. The moment Donovan and Mom stepped past into the secured concourse, I approached the figure with a humped stance and a shock of longish gray hair. He might be fifty or seventy, I couldn't tell. Only that he was of middling height and stood straight and strong.

A huge and ancient imp sat on the man's shoulder.

"You're a bit late, whoever you are."

"Am I?" He gave me a smile that made the few lines around his eyes deepen. But the smile never sent a twinkle in his deep brown eyes.

Scrap preened and flashed the warts on his bum at the new imp. Must be a male and Scrap was interested.

The dignified being tasted the air with a forked tongue, snorted, and turned his head away. He had a vast array of beauty spots along his spine. Much more senior than Scrap and not interested.

"I no longer have need of your assistance," I said, standing firm.

"Don't you?"

"You're as bad as Donovan at answering questions. Time to go back to whatever hidey-hole you crawled out of."

"Breven Sancroix, at your service, Tess Noncoiré." He bowed slightly. "I have a farm in western Pennsylvania and I've been watching you for a few days. You have more problems than you want to acknowledge." He jerked his chin in the direction of the security lines.

"I have banished Donovan Estevez from my life."

"If you want to believe that, and that he is your only problem, then you need more help than I can give." He bowed again and backed up. "We will meet later. If you need me, you have only to reach out through your meditation to find me." With that he faded into the crowd as if he'd never been there.

▶▶▶

MoonFeather, Larch, and Gollum had followed us to the airport in Providence along with our luggage. My aunt and her protégée weren't about to be left behind on the next phase of our adventure.

Gollum had performed miracles in getting us the

right connections to Seattle and then a shuttle to Moses Lake. We arrived late, cranky, and feeling grubby. But Larch rallied and took the wheel of our rental car, a nice sedan with lots of trunk space and leg room. She navigated us the hour north to Half Moon Lake and the Mowath Lodge.

The flat concrete slab that was all that remained of the run-down motel where Dill had died in the fire lay just across the parking lot from the new lodge.

Not for an instant did I forget that Donovan owned the hotel made up of fourplex log cabins, two suites up and two down. Each building was constructed of massive logs. Each interior was unique, decorated in more thick slabs of wood around a theme, location, or celebrity.

From the hotel office building Donovan ran Halfling Gaming Company, Inc. and the spa under construction.

We took over one large suite for one night—the John Wayne room with memorabilia from his life and movies and western-styled furniture. MoonFeather and Larch slept comfortably in the king-sized bed in the loft. I tossed and turned on the single bed tucked under the stairs. Gollum collapsed familiarly into the armchair with his feet on the coffee table and his computer in his lap. I could never tell if he slept or not. But I was comforted that he didn't change his habits from the last time we had stayed here.

MoonFeather roused us in the desert predawn for a light breakfast at the nearby café. I couldn't eat, so I took a run around the lake. My feet crunched through a crust of minerals that smelled of fish oil and salt.

I allowed my memory to drift to the time Dill and I had come here. I cherished the vision of him exclaiming excitedly over a special rock specimen. The warm glow of triumph I had felt when I found a fossilized leaf settled on me anew. Then the ecstasy of making love on that last night . . .

Good memories. A wonderful, if brief, time together. Briefly, I considered trying to find the Citadel hidden in a deep ravine some twenty miles north of here. Would they acknowledge me if I pounded on their gates?

Doubtful.

I reminded myself that I didn't need them. They had never truly accepted me. Scrap and I were better off without them.

I'd welcome a little advice and support, though.

My stomach churned with trepidation. I could die in the next hour.

The Goddess had smiled on me.

As much as my mind rejected belief in a deity, my heart longed to believe in something. The picture frame could have been thrown back out of the ice by frost heave.

Yeah, right.

Eventually I had to return to the lodge. Best to get this journey over with. We had to check out by noon.

►►►

Once more, we gather around a magic circle, Tess, Gollum, MoonFeather, and myself. With Larch looking on as an apprentice.

MoonFeather draws a big circle on the floor with her colored chalk. Gollum sets out the colored candles, red at north, green at east, blue at south, and yellow at west. Larch sprinkles herbs in a circle around the candles.

Tess sits cross-legged in the center, palms resting upward on her knees. She closes her eyes and breathes deeply, evenly. She is open and receptive, going into a deep meditative trance.

I fear she will lose concentration. She's never been very good at meditation. Too restless, too eager to get on with the busyness of life, too curious to sit and let life come to her. She has to go and find trouble instead. That is why the Sisterhood rejected her and forced her out of the Citadel.

Life on the outside is not what I had planned when I attached myself to my Warrior. Life on the outside is not easy. Nor is it dull.

I like our life. I've killed more demons in the last six months than most imps do in a lifetime when locked up in a Citadel that guards a demon portal. And I've got the beautiful warts to prove it. Six new ones from the fight with the Windago. Midori count for more than Kajiri.

So I must be extra careful and bring my babe back home safe and sound.

MoonFeather is doing what she can to cast a circle of protection. But the onus of this journey is on me. I shiver in fear. And excitement. Not many can perform this feat.

I gather my energies.

MoonFeather lights the candles. She uses matches; no one carries a lighter anymore. She recites an invocation at each candle and drops a different herb into each flame.

I feel the energy building inside the circle. The scent of incense fills my head with new perceptions. Colors twist. The world tilts. Threads of life swirl through the air in impossible hues, blindingly bright. I grab hold of a promising tendril, the same color of pale blue as Tess' eyes, and whisk my Warrior away.

Through the chat room so fast no one notices us.

Back.

Back farther.

Back in time and space to a dimension I'd just as soon forget. Violence begets violence begets trauma and barriers in the mind. Those barriers have had three years to thicken and solidify. I'm not sure I have the cunning and intuition to break through them. But I do have a blackness in my soul and violence in my heart. They must serve me well for this journey.

Gravity shifted. The light became vertiginous. My balance adjusted. Wind swirled around me like a tiny tornado, tossing me here and there. I came to rest with a thump and opened my eyes.

I expected to view the shabby motel room from a distance, through a gray mist, like I did when I witnessed Darren's murder.

Instead, I found myself in my own body, the plump and unfit body of three years ago with my tight curls in a tangled mess reaching halfway down my back. Sleep crusted my eyes and left groggy cobwebs in my mind. I lay in bed next to Dill. Warm and gentle, beloved Dill. I wanted to reach out and touch him, hold him close once more, cherish his strength and his love.

Drowsiness left me enervated and incapable of moving.

Only your other self from the future is truly awake, Tess. Your body responds only as it did in this past time. You cannot change anything even if you try, Scrap whispered to me.

I couldn't see him or sense him. Only hear him.

A shadow passed across the curtained window of our ground-floor room. The shadow of a very large bat.

Panic closed my throat and choked my brain.

The sharp scent of smoke roused Dill.

Fear sent my heart to racing and my thoughts spinning in circles.

Chapter 52

*A new moon teaches gradualness and delibera-
tion and how one gives birth to oneself slowly. Pa-
tience with small details makes perfect a large
work, like the universe.*

—*Rumi*

"TESS, TESS, WAKE UP. We have to get out of
here!" Dill shook me roughly.

Damn straight we did. That was *we*, not just me.

I threw my arms around him as he guided me into the
bathroom. Somehow, I managed to kick the door shut behind us. I hadn't done that the last time I lived this scene.

Dill helped me climb into the shower tub. Together
we pushed up the tiny window above the tile.

"You go first, lovey. I'm right behind you." He boosted
me up until I lay half in and half out the window.

"No, Dill. You have to go first. You have to save yourself!" I cried.

He shoved me through the window with a sharp slap
to my wide bottom.

I landed on the frosted grass with a jolt that nearly
dislocated my shoulder. The cold kissed my skin but did
not penetrate to the bone through my soft frilly nightie.
I'd given up my favored less-than-sexy flannel when I
married Dill. His body heat next to me in bed kept me
warmer than cloth ever could.

Then I noticed the still healing gash on my arm from
a Windago talon. It glowed and pulsed an ugly red.

I hadn't had the scar three years ago. Not everything was the same.

"Dill!" I screamed. Ignoring the pain that ran from the base of my skull all the way to my fingertips, I jumped up and grabbed the windowsill about a foot above my head. "Dill!"

Thick smoke roiled under the closed door to fill the bathroom.

"Dill!" Where was he?

Then I heard him coughing. With a supreme effort I pulled myself upward. The demon scar ached and drove sharp burns all the way through my arm and shoulder. The me of the future with the scar had the strength to climb back through the window. The me of three years ago wouldn't have dared try.

I looked down. Dill stood doubled over in the tub, trying desperately to clear his lungs of smoke. "Coming, lovey," he gasped. "I'm not going to leave you alone."

"Take my hand, Dill. You've got to get out. Now."

He reached upward. I clasped his hand firmly. My shoulders trembled with the strain of holding myself against the windowsill. As I prepared to yank and drop, dragging Dill through the window with me, the bathroom door banged inward. Two shadowy forms lunged and tackled Dill, dragging his hand from mine.

"We can't let you escape, Cooper. You've betrayed me for the last time," Darren Estevez croaked through the smoke.

He lifted his head and stared at me. Darren Estevez.

The other man kept his head down. I knew his figure was male, nothing more. He wore a dark watch cap and darker clothing. Broad shoulders. A heavy jacket masked weight and stature. No clues to identity.

"Dill!" I propped my knee on the little ledge, ready to dive back into the fray to free my husband.

Don't! Scrap yanked at my mind so hard I slid back down to the ground.

I scrambled back and jumped for the ledge.

No. Think, Tess. Think about who you are. Think about what you would become if Dill lived.

I tried to blot out the mental probe that pierced my mind like a migraine behind the eyes.

The demon scar throbbed, adding yet more pain to Scrap's admonitions.

You can only move forward, not back. You aren't really here. And you may not, cannot, change anything.

"Dill," I sobbed. "Don't die on me again."

Think, Tess. Would Dill have let you become the strong independent woman you are with a successful career? Would he? Or would he have pushed you to give up your writing to cater to his career and push out a new baby every other year? Would he have given you the freedom to grow? Would he have let you sing filk songs at conventions when you have a better voice than he?

I paused long enough to breathe.

Sirens wailed around the corner. Men shouted and dragged hoses. They smashed open doors with axes.

And I knew in my mind that Scrap was right.

But that didn't ease the pain in my heart.

I'm sorry, babe, Scrap whispered. *You loved him and he loved you. But you cannot change the past, only observe it.*

Two bats flew out the window over my head. Bats! The one creature I fear most. Bats of my nightmares. Big bats that sucked blood.

My phobia overcame my love of Dill.

I huddled on the ground in absolute panic, covering my head with my hands, gibbering nonsense. One of them grabbed a lock of my hair and yanked it out of my scalp with its vicious claws and a squeak of glee.

Once more, firemen found me cowering on the ground in a fetal position and took me out front to the ambulance where they tried to give me oxygen. Once more, men in heavy coats with fluorescent yellow bands dragged Dill's burned body free of the carnage of the flames. Once more, I held him in my arms.

I wept softly, smoothing his sizzled hair away from his face, not minding the way it crumbled to ash in my hands.

He opened pain-racked eyes in a ravaged face. Muscle, blood, and bone shone through the cracked and blackened skin.

"I love you, Tess."

And then he heaved one last rattling breath and released the pain and agony of living.

I collapsed over him, too filled with grief to cry. Too choked to object when gentle hands dragged me away from the love of my life.

Chapter 53

*T*HE WORLD SWIRLED about me in pain and the reek of rancid, waterlogged smoke. I didn't care.

Dill was dead. I had failed to save him.

Twice.

"Welcome back," Gollum said quietly.

He crouched beside me on the floor. The chalk circle around me looked smudged where he'd trod on the markings. Gently, he brushed a tangled curl off my forehead with a single finger.

I was back in the new Mowath Lodge with massive logs forming the walls. Bright woods and clean upholstery decorated the large and luxurious room. A far cry from the shabby, generic motel that had stood on these grounds three years ago.

The only trace of old smoke that lingered was in my memory.

Outside, I could hear MoonFeather and Larch arguing about packing the rental car with luggage for four for a long weekend in Seattle.

"Want to talk about it?" he asked me.

"Oh, Gollum." My throat closed upon my tears.

He wrapped his arms around me and lifted me onto his lap. There he held me for countless moments, my face pressed against his shoulders, his hands comforting, secure. Safe.

I cried. My shoulders heaved. My gut ached. And still I cried.

All the tears I had held back for three years came forth in a tangled river of grief and pain and loneliness.

And still I cried.

Not a word passed between us. He just held me. He let me have the time to cry and cry some more until there was nothing left inside me but a gaping hole where Dill had dwelled.

And still I cried.

And still he held me. Undemanding. Keeping me safe while I was vulnerable.

Eventually, the storm of grief and tears passed. I don't know how long we sat there with me in his lap like a small child. When there was nothing left but the shudders, he continued to hold me.

At last, as limp as a wet dish rag, I roused enough to feel the strength in his arms, to cherish the calm and quiet in his heart beating beneath my ear.

"Thank you," I said and kissed his cheek. "Let's go to a con and sing silly filk songs. Then I'm going back to work. Vacations are too trying."

"Good-bye, lovey," Dill whispered. His ghostly hand might have ruffled my curls.

Then he was gone. Nothing left of him but my memories.

Gollum gave me a quick squeeze of reassurance. We untangled ourselves and joined the rest of the world hand in hand.

Just then Larch started the car. The CD picked up where it had left off.

Heather Alexander singing quietly in a pain-racked alto.

> *"I looked across the battlefield*
> *Blood seeping from my wounds—*

My comrades they did never yield,
    For courage knows no bounds—
And yet, I thought as I stood there,
    Of all that it had cost—
For what we gained, it seemed not fair
    For all that we had lost—

They spoke of honor, faith, and pride,
    Defending for our home—
Through honor all my friends have died,
    Their faith left me alone—
We fought for greed, we fought for fame,
    We killed too much to tell—
The devil and God were both the same,
    We worshiped only hell—

We fought, it seemed, for a thousand years,
    A million nights and days—
Sharing one laugh with a hundred tears,
    Seeing clearly through a haze—
Then came that day I know not when,
    Beneath a blood-red sun,
    Atop a pile of dying men,
    They said that we had won—

    Another tract of land is all
        The territory gained—
    Will that ever pay for all
    The lives here lost or maimed?
    Bodies lying all around,
        Blood bathing them in red,
    Their white eyes staring at the sun,
        These the countless dead?

    I looked across the battlefield
        Blood seeping from my wounds—
    My comrades, they did never yield,
        For courage knows no bounds—

P.R. Frost

The Tess Noncoiré Adventures

"Frost's fantasy debut series introduces a charming protagonist, both strong and vulnerable, and her cheeky companion. An intriguing plot and a well-developed warrior sisterhood make this a good choice for fans of the urban fantasy of Tanya Huff, Jim Butcher, and Charles deLint."
—*Library Journal*

New in Paperback!
HOUNDING THE MOON
0-7564-0425-3

Now Available in Hardcover
MOON IN THE MIRROR
0-7564-0424-6

To Order Call: 1-800-788-6262
www.dawboks.com